SHY

BY

NOELLE MARIE

TABLE OF CONTENTS

CHAPTER ONE

As the icy winter gave way to spring and the mountains of snow began to melt, all lingering feelings of wariness Katherine felt towards Bastian began to fade. Like the violet wildflowers speckled across the newly green forest floor, something stronger than affection began to bloom in Katherine's chest whenever she thought of the impossibly handsome man.

He'd told her he loved her.

It had taken Katherine being mauled by the corrupt Cain and falling seriously ill for the words to spill forth from Bastian's mouth, but he'd said them all the same. And to Katherine's surprise, he had continued to say them to her even after the fierce emotional storm that her near death had brought upon the pack – and especially its alpha – had dissipated.

In fact, the small brunette was fairly certain that the man hadn't let a day since the incident pass without uttering the words to her at least once.

This, of course, only served to put Katherine in an incredibly uncomfortable position. Because, except for stuttering a shaky response the first time Bastian had declared his love ("I think I love you too."), she had been incredibly tight-lipped about her own feelings. It'd been five whole months since Cain had attacked her, and Katherine had yet to let the "l-word" escape her lips again.

She didn't know what caused the word to stick to the roof of her mouth. Maybe it was her naturally reserved nature. Or perhaps more likely, it was the insecurity that enveloped her at the thought of being emotionally vulnerable to another person. But whatever the reason, the few times she'd attempted to return Bastian's sentiments, she'd only served to embarrass herself.

"I love you, Katherine."

"I...you...I care about you too."

"I love you, Katherine."

"That makes me so happy."

"I love you, Katherine."

"I...yes...that is, my feelings for you are strong as well."

She'd taken to merely staying silent in response to such utterances, hoping that despite the right words getting trapped somewhere between the back of her throat and her rose colored lips, Bastian knew. He *had* to know. She loved him too.

Which only made it all the more upsetting that in exception to pressing chaste lips to her mouth or peppering innocent kisses across her brow, cheeks, and occasionally her nose, he steadfastly refused to touch her.

It was quite the feat considering the fact they'd been sharing a bed since Katherine had recovered from her bout of pneumonia. She didn't quite know what to think, and the one time she'd attempted to rectify the situation – to be physically close to Bastian – she'd been soundly rejected.

Katherine lay in bed, idly counting the broad brushstrokes that covered the ceiling of what she had come to think of as her room. The satin sheets lay pooled at the foot of the massive mattress, having been kicked there by the restless feet of the overwhelmingly bored girl.

It'd been nearly two weeks since she'd woken from her trauma induced slumber, and she was completely healed, having kicked the pneumonia that had orchestrated a sneak attack on her lungs days ago. Her breathing was no longer labored or accompanied by a high-pitched, whistle-like noise. She'd finally coughed out the last of the thick, disgusting phlegm that'd been stuck to the inner walls of her throat.

Her health was no longer a problem. Convincing Bastian of that, however... well, that was a problem.

The man had spent the past fortnight alternately hovering over her like an overprotective mother hen and managing the alpha council. They'd taken the news of Cain's betrayal and subsequent death better than either of them could have hoped. Most members were appropriately outraged by the man's actions and supportive of Bastian's decision to take up the role of head alpha. Some, however, were skeptical of his ability to lead. Thankfully, only one dared to make his lack of faith so obviously known.

Rogue.

According to Markus, who Bastian had taken to dragging to most meetings, the man enjoyed challenging Bastian's authority at every turn. Apparently, he'd even used Katherine and her unfortunate habit of attracting trouble against Bastian, arguing that surely his attention-seeking mate needed the majority of his focus. He couldn't possibly have enough energy to run the council, and by proxy, the entirety of Haven Falls, if he was constantly worrying over her and the shenanigans she somehow always managed to get herself entangled in.

Markus took great glee in informing Katherine that Bastian had decked the man. "Knocked his dumb ass straight to the floor," he'd relayed to her with a grin.

Bastian, of course, hadn't mentioned the incident at all.

Probably because he seemed to spend every waking minute he wasn't dealing with the council preoccupied with Katherine's health and general wellbeing. He was terribly bossy and it was as irritating as it was endearing.

Katherine would yawn. "You sound tired. Why don't you try to sleep? Here, let me get you another pillow."

Katherine would wince while trying to sit up in bed. "Did you hurt yourself? Lie back down and let me check your back."

God forbid that her stomach would growl. "You're hungry? Why didn't you say something? Caleb, go make Katherine a sandwich. Ham. No, roast beef. At least four slices."

As sweet as Katherine suspected his intentions were, she couldn't help but become exasperated with the man. She was perfectly capable of realizing when she was tired or hurt. And she could make herself a sandwich if she wanted one, thank you very much.

Her relief was palpable when Bastian finally declared her well enough to be up and out of bed the day before.

Apparently, though, she wasn't well enough to shift into her wolf form and go on a hunt with the rest of the pack – sans Caleb, who'd stayed behind to keep an eye on her, of course. After all, imagine the stress it would cause her if she had to decide between having some of the leftover beef stew and frying herself up a hamburger for supper all on her own?

Note the sarcasm.

It really wasn't fair. She was eager to see how much effort she'd have to exert to transform now that she'd accomplished the task without the full moon's help for the first time. Bastian wouldn't hear of it, though, and Katherine had been forced to stay behind.

And so she ended up in bed again, the place where she'd been stuck the eleven days previous – in exception of the night of the full moon, of course – glaring petulantly up at the ceiling.

She was trying to stay up until the others returned – attempting to use her simmering anger as an anchor to awareness, but as the sun began to set, sleep tugged at her tired eyelids, and Katherine soon surrendered to sleep.

She was awakened an undeterminable amount of time later by a slight dipping of the mattress. Only on the edge of consciousness, sleep threatened to pull her under again when she felt strong fingers sweep some wayward bangs from her face before running through the remainder of her long tresses. A chaste kiss was placed on the side of her forehead – the side where her newly acquired scar lay. "I love you."

Katherine forced herself to open bleary eyes. The room was dark, but the moonlight shining through the gaps of the window blinds allowed her to see as she turned to face her bedmate – her alpha. Her Bastian.

Even only half-awake, she managed to glare at the man. But sleep had stolen most of her anger. Plus, it was hard to be angry when Bastian was half-naked. He lay on his side atop the covers, a muscled arm supporting his head as he stared unabashedly back at her. She wondered if it was the bird's nest atop her head or the pillow creases that undoubtedly graced her cheek that made him look at her with such tender eyes.

It was hard to stare into Bastian's eyes for long, though, with the moonlight splayed so attractively across his bare chest. The golden glow highlighted every ripple of muscle, from his impressive pectorals all the way down to the enticing "V" that led to the elastic waist of his sleep pants.

Katherine profusely hoped that the dark at least hid her nearly painful blush.

"I'm mad at you," she managed to forced out between suddenly dry lips. But even she knew she didn't sound mad. She sounded breathless.

The corner of Bastian's mouth quirked up. "I know," he admitted. "What can I do to make it up to you?" His free hand began to play with the ends of her unruly hair.

Unconsciously, Katherine leaned into the touch. "There is something," she confessed in a whisper.

She was close enough to see his Adam's apple bob when she moved in closer still.

"Yeah?" Bastian's rough timbre sent a shiver down her spine.

When his blue eyes fixated on her lips, she found the courage to answer him. "Yes," she confirmed before closing the remaining gap between them.

Her lips brushed tentatively against his at first, but she was emboldened when a calloused hand gripped the back of her neck, fingers threading through the little hairs there, and the kiss quickly deepened.

Nearly consumed by the need to touch Bastian, Katherine pressed her slender frame flush against his body. He groaned into her mouth.

Encouraged by his response, Katherine managed to wedge a hand between them, ghosting her fingers over one dusky nipple – Bastian inhaled jerkily, his lips freezing over hers – before allowing them to travel further down, exploring defined muscle.

A feeling – a kind of warmth – that Katherine had never felt be-

fore began pooling in her lower belly. She was so lost to the sensation that she failed to realize Bastian had stopped kissing her.

She was quickly thrust back into reality, however, when her hand brushed over a jutting hipbone. Before she could blink, the fingers that had been wrapped in her hair were suddenly grasping her wrist, non-too-gently shoving her apparently offensive appendage away.

Katherine gaped, momentarily stunned. But her surprise was quickly followed by an intense, nearly overwhelming sense of humiliation. "What-"

What had she done wrong?

"I'm tired," Bastian forced out between gritted teeth. "I'm sorry for waking you. Feel free to go back to sleep." And before Katherine could even begin to formulate a response, the suddenly taciturn man flipped over, turning his back on her.

For a long minute, the embarrassed brunette could only lie there, staring at Bastian's stupidly attractive back. She was truly flabbergasted. And in a moment of weakness, she allowed insecurity to reign.

Was her touch really that repulsive? Was her technique that off base? Katherine would be the first to admit that she wasn't exactly experienced when it came to, well... romantic entanglements.

Maybe Bastian just wasn't attracted to her the same way she was attracted to him?

Katherine quickly squashed that thought, not willing to let such a hurtful notion take root in her mind. Instead, she allowed a much more useful emotion to swell within her.

Righteous indignation.

Who exactly did Bastian Prince think he was? He'd been kissing her back! What right did he have to end their kiss so abruptly – so callously – without even a hint of an explanation?

He was tired? Ha!

Suddenly furious, Katherine shot out of bed, stomping to the bathroom, jerking open its door, and slamming it shut behind her. For nearly an hour, she sat on the edge of the closed toilet seat, debating whether or not she wanted to go back out there and demand a better explanation than "I'm tired" from Bastian – insert eye roll here – or simply beat the crap out of the man with the plunger.

In the end, she decided on neither. Truthfully, Katherine was too – hurt? embarrassed? angry? some combination thereof? – to even go back out to the bedroom and face Bastian at all. So still stinging from his rejection, she fell asleep, curled up on the cold, hard porcelain floor of the bathroom's tub.

She'd woke up the next morning buried under the covers of the bed, and neither she nor Bastian dared to bring up the incident afterwards. But due to the confusing rejection, Katherine hadn't attempted to initiate anything remotely sexual with the man again.

"What's your pretty little head thinking so hard about?"

Katherine was startled out of her morose thoughts by Zane's amused tenor. She glared at the man as he swiped the chocolate chip muffin she was absentmindedly holding straight out of her hands. Caleb had made a couple dozen of the delicious morsels earlier that morning. Gooey chocolate smeared Zane's lips as he took a large bite of the still warm confection.

"Well?" he asked again around a mouthful of muffin. "What are you thinking about that caused *that particular* expression to cross your face?"

Katherine wasn't sure what expression Zane was referring to, but she couldn't control the hot flush from creeping up her neck when she realized she'd managed to spend the past half an hour silently pouting over the fact that Bastian was refusing to touch her.

Catching sight of her quickly reddening cheeks, Zane offered her a playful smirk. "Maybe I don't want to know."

Before she could dispute his undoubtedly perverse thoughts – even if there was a smidgeon of truth to them – the front double doors were thrown open, matching slabs of heavy wood crashing against adjacent walls with two resounding, nearly simultaneous *bangs*.

Katherine jumped at the sudden noise, disregarding Zane as he choked on her stolen muffin in favor of watching Bastian storm into the house. She frowned when the man ignored her – not even sparing her a glance – as he made a beeline for the bedroom they shared, opening and slamming shut that door with the same amount of force as he had the front ones.

Markus followed him inside at a much more sedate pace.

"I take it the council meeting didn't go well?" Zane asked the question they were both wondering.

"I suppose you could say that," Markus deadpanned as he strolled into the kitchen and grabbed two muffins for himself.

When the beta didn't elaborate, Katherine huffed and pushed herself up out of her chair to go confront Bastian herself.

"I wouldn't go in there if I were you, princess," Markus warned when she took a step in the direction of the bedroom Bastian had disappeared into.

"Good thing you're not me then," she called over her shoulder before doing exactly that.

In the room, Bastian was sitting on the edge of the mattress. His tense body was hunched over on itself as he dug the palms of his hands deep into the sockets of his eyes.

"Are you okay?" Katherine asked quietly closing the door behind her and warily approaching the man. She placed a hesitant hand on his shoulder. The muscles she could feel under his shirt were coiled so tightly he was trembling.

"Fine," he forced out between clenched teeth.

"Really?" Katherine demanded, folding her arms across her chest and letting a bit of the frustration she was feeling leak out into her voice. "You flew in here like a bat out of hell and are wound tighter than a spring, but you're *fine*?"

"What do you want me to say?" He still wouldn't look at her.

"I want you to tell me what's wrong!" Katherine exclaimed. "What happened at the meeting to make you like this?" She gestured vaguely at his tension-filled form.

Bastian finally dropped his hands from his eyes and looked up at her, pinning her into place with his intense azure gaze. "*You*. Don't you realize by now that *you* are the only person who can affect me so strongly?"

"Me?" Katherine demanded derisively. "What did I do? I wasn't even at the meeting!"

Bastian shot out of bed, towering over her with his much larger frame. "Maybe not in body, but apparently you're on everyone's god-damn minds! Rogue," he spit out the name like a curse, "is demanding that you participate in the Recruiting Rites next week."

Katherine frowned.

The Recruiting Rites was the name of a special ceremony that was due to take place on the next full moon. She and the rest of the graduating class – those who were werewolves anyway – were meant to compete in a tournament-like competition designed to test their abilities and give them the opportunity to flaunt their assets to alphas in hopes of receiving invitations to join their packs. Katherine, of course, already had a pack – a pack she loved – but she still planned on participating.

"Why wouldn't I participate?" *Everyone did.*

Bastian's eyes narrowed. "Why would you?"

"Everyone does!" Katherine replied, giving voice to her earlier thought.

"You already have a pack."

"So does most everyone else," Katherine pointed out. Only turned wolves – she was the exception – didn't have one. "It's a chance to showcase my skills, however unpolished they may be. I want to compete."

Didn't he realize that she needed this opportunity? She had to prove to the community, to those who doubted Bastian's ability to lead because of his relations with her, that she was a worthy mate to such a powerful man – to such a fierce werewolf.

She needed to prove it to herself.

Bastian, of course, didn't see it that way. "No," he practically growled. "You're mine."

Katherine glared, choosing to ignore the rush of *something* that washed over her at Bastian's declaration, and focused instead on the irritation that it also caused. "I didn't ask you."

Bastian's hands reached out towards her, his fingers wrapping carefully but firmly around her miniscule biceps. "Katherine, I love you. I don't want to lose you."

She and Bastian were true mates – destined mates, even. Didn't the infuriating man realize that she would never leave him? That she couldn't even truly contemplate the idea of it?

And there he was, throwing the "l-word" around again. Katherine wasn't quite feeling reckless enough to say it back, but she was feeling brave enough to try something else. Her eyes flickered to Bastian's lips before slowly rising up to meet his intense gaze head on. "Prove it," she dared.

No sooner had the whispered words left her mouth did Bastian's lips crash into hers. So different from the last tentative – almost lazy – kiss they'd shared, this one was positively electrifying. Katherine's lips were barely able to keep up the frenzied pace Bastian's set when she felt his probing tongue pushing against them, demanding entrance into her mouth. Without a second thought, Katherine wrapped her arms around Bastian's neck and let him in.

As he ravaged her mouth, Bastian's hands slid down her arms, finding their way to just under the hem of her shirt and possessively gripping her bare hips.

In a lustful daze, Katherine was hardly aware of being picked up and set on Bastian's lap as he maneuvered them onto the bed. Goosebumps erupted across her flesh as the man moved his attention to her neck, nipping and licking at the sensitive skin there before catching the lobe of her left ear between sharp teeth and giving it a delicate tug.

"B-Bastian..." Katherine would have probably been embarrassed by the half-whimper, half-moan that escaped her mouth if she had the chance to think about it, but it was hard to do any thinking at all when two calloused thumbs began stroking her belly from where Bastian still gripped her hips. She gasped as one brushed over her belly button.

Desperate to touch the man – to make his body respond to her in the same way hers was responding to him – Katherine allowed her hands to creep up under Bastian's shirt, lightly dragging her nails over heated skin as she explored the expanse of his back.

Bastian groaned into her neck. He shifted beneath her and Katherine's heart fluttered nervously – *excitedly?* – when she suddenly realized she could feel the hard evidence of Bastian's very apparent desire for her trapped between their stomachs.

Blindly following her instincts, she molded herself against him, lifting her hips and pressing the part of her that most ached to be touched against his blatant hardness.

It was as if she'd dumped a bucket of ice water over Bastian's head.

He shot up out of bed so quickly that Katherine lost her balance and fell gracelessly to the floor, landing painfully on her butt. She blinked, momentarily stunned.

Seemingly shocked himself, Bastian stared at where she now sat on the floor. Breaking free of his stupor, he quickly reached for her, grabbing Katherine under her armpits and hauling her back onto her feet. "I'm sorry."

Embarrassed tears pooling in her eyes, Katherine pushed the man away from her. She knew the pathetic shove wouldn't have budged him unless he was willing to move, but he obligingly took a step back. "You're sorry?" she demanded angrily. "For what? Knocking me to the floor? Or finding my touch so repulsive that you felt the need to do so?"

Bastian's eyebrows drew together and the man had the nerve to look hurt. "*Katherine.* You know that's not true."

"No. I don't know that. Bastian, this is the first time we've kissed properly in months – as in like *five* of them." Katherine gathered every last speck of her courage and looked him straight in the eye. "Don't you want me?"

Bastian looked so genuinely bewildered that just the tiniest bit of her anger began to fade. "Of course I want you. I want you more than I've ever wanted anyone or anything in my life. As goddamn ridiculous as it sounds, I want you more than I want to take my next breath."

What remained of Katherine's anger deflated. But despite the soothing balm his sweet words had spread over her hurting heart, she couldn't shake her confusion or nagging insecurity quite so easily. "Then kiss me."

Bastian's stance stiffened, and he looked away from her, refusing to meet her eyes.

And just like that the hurt and anger returned. "Bastian, please."

Tense silence filled the room for a long, uncomfortable moment. When Bastian finally opened his mouth, it wasn't to say what Katherine wanted to hear. "I've got to go."

He brushed past her without a second glance.

Face sporting an angry, blotchy flush, Katherine watched in disbelief as the door swung shut behind his retreating form. Desperately trying to hang on to what remained of her tattered dignity, she just barely managed to refrain from grabbing the bed side lamp and chucking it at the mockingly closed door.

CHAPTER TWO

While the lamp had survived Katherine's encounter with Bastian intact, her self-esteem had not. As much as she hated to admit it, she was hurt. Embarrassed. Angry. And mostly, very confused.

Bastian claimed to want her. His body certainly seemed to attest to that fact if what she'd felt when she was on his lap was any indication. Yet twice he'd rebuffed her when she'd attempted to be intimate with him. He was refusing to even kiss her after the most recent attempt.

Honestly, his actions – or lack thereof – were beginning to make Katherine feel like some sort of deviant. A sexual predator of sorts. Which, considering her distinct lack of experience, was ridiculous. Laughable, even.

Except Katherine wasn't laughing. How could she when a swirling whirlwind of anxiety and hurt-induced anger swelled within her whenever she thought of the man?

She took to avoiding him. Which probably would have been more satisfying if he didn't appear to be avoiding her as well. *How could she properly give Bastian the cold shoulder if he wasn't around to give the cold shoulder to?* It was infuriating.

He wasn't even sleeping in the massive bed they usually shared together. Katherine didn't know where he'd been the last few nights, but it hadn't been with her. Unfortunately, she hadn't realized how much she'd grown to depend on the reassuring warmth of his body next to hers until it was gone.

Her sleep without him was fitful at best. Her restless legs kicked the covers here and there, equally agitated arms adjusting the pillows over and over again. She continually woke up feeling more tired than she'd been when she'd gone to bed.

A white as a sheet pallor and red rimmed eyes were the result. As was an incredibly short temper.

So when Markus threw her down flat on her butt for the fifth time in so many minutes, Katherine had had enough.

Since Bastian had been missing in action, she'd convinced his second in command to be her sparring partner. She wanted to improve her admittedly abysmal fighting skills as much as possible before the Recruiting Rites, which was set to take place on the next full moon – precisely two nights away.

Markus had been surprisingly agreeable when she'd asked for him to practice with her. Probably because he enjoyed laying her out, sadistic bastard that he was.

They'd agreed to practice in the backyard, quickly transformed into their wolf forms, and her lesson in humiliation had begun.

It didn't help matters that the rest of the pack – sans Bastian, of course – had followed them outside to watch the lop-sided fight, offering her what she was sure they thought were helpful suggestions as she was slammed to the ground again and again.

"You're too small to directly attack him like that! Wait for him to spring at you and use his momentum against him." Zane.

"Baloney! Katherine, honey, you're fast enough to take him by surprise and get a couple of swipes in before he retaliates." Sophie.

"But he will retaliate! And then she'll have lost her position! And for what? For the sake of giving Markus a few measly scratches?" Zane again.

"Uh, guys, I think we might be distracting her." Caleb – at least *one* of them had some sense.

What made it even more embarrassing was the fact that Markus was so clearly going easy on her. She'd have more than just a sore behind if that wasn't the case.

In fact, his hazel eyes, peering out of his wolfish face, were *laughing* at her.

Something in Katherine snapped.

Not waiting for the go signal from Zane, she lunged at Markus, her sharp teeth bared as she went for an unprotected shoulder. Before her canines could tear into flesh, however, Markus quickly countered her unexpected attack. Lowering his shoulder, he did what Zane had suggested *she* do and used her momentum against her, flipping her body over his with ease.

Katherine landed on her back with a painful *thud.*

Before she could even process what had happened, a naked Markus was standing over her, eyes still blazing, but no longer with good humor. “What the hell, girlie?”

Knowing that her anger was misplaced didn’t stop it from burning brightly in her chest. Concentrating on that anger, Katherine forced her body to change back into its human form, the bizarre sensation of shifting bones and flesh still so foreign to her. Quickly grabbing the t-shirt she’d shed on the grass before she’d transformed for the fighting lesson, she attempted to preserve her modesty by palming it to her bare chest. “I don’t even know why I bothered asking for your help,” she spit out at Markus, groping the ground with her free hand in an attempt to find her pants.

“Me neither,” he snorted. “You’re not even attempting to learn anything.”

“It’s not exactly easy to concentrate with an unending stream of unsolicited advice being spewed out at you.” She shifted her glare onto the other members of her pack, who were watching their confrontation with concern.

“We’re trying to *help* you. Don’t take the fact that you wouldn’t even be able to protect yourself from a goddamn squirrel out on us.”

Katherine’s cheeks flashed red hot. “Screw you, Markus.”

The man continued like he hadn’t heard her. “And don’t take the fact that you’re quarreling with lover boy out on us either.”

Katherine froze.

“Markus!” Sophie scolded, instantly making her way over to them.

“No,” he scowled over his shoulder at the incoming blonde. “I’m sick and tired of walking on eggshells around these two idiots.” He turned his attention back on the girl prone at his feet. "Look, I don't know what you guys are fighting about, but Bastian's been pissy as hell and you've been moping around the house like a petulant child. It's driving us crazy, so whatever happened between you two, suck it up and make up with him already. Got it?"

Afraid of what would come out if she opened her mouth, Katherine pressed her lips together as tightly as she could. When she was sure nothing as embarrassing as a cry would be released, she allowed a few words to escape. "Go to hell."

Unfortunately, she still hadn't managed to find her pants. So with as much dignity as she could possibly muster under the circumstances, Katherine stood up and stomped back to the house, only caring a little that she was giving them a perfect view of a full moon that they didn't regularly howl to.

As soon as the back door slammed shut behind her, however, she scuttled to her bedroom, throwing clothes haphazardly out of the closet as she searched for some scrap of fabric to cover her exposed bottom. A sheen of tears blurring her vision, she didn't even realize she'd grabbed a hideous pair of fuchsia leggings – something Sophie had probably bought for her at some point – until they were halfway up her thighs.

As unreasonable as it was to get angry at a pair of pants, Katherine felt her temper spike. More tears gathered in her eyes, and she roughly wiped the green orbs before pressing the palms of her hands as hard as she could into the sockets, willing the traitorous tears to go away.

It was positively stupid. Crying over a pair of pants. Over Markus being his usual abrasive self. She didn't know which made her more pathetic.

What was wrong with her?

Knock. Knock.

Before she could berate herself further, soft knocking on the bedroom door broke her out of her funk. Eying the slab of mahogany, Katherine was tempted to ignore whoever was on the other side.

Knock. Knock. "Katherine?"

Recognizing the hesitant voice as Sophie's commanding soprano, she sighed before quickly finishing tugging up the hideous pants that'd nearly caused another melt down and yanking open the door. Sophie eyed her carefully, the corners of her mouth dipping into a frown when she caught sight of her undoubtedly puffy eyes.

Katherine crossed her arms over her chest, resisting the urge to fidget. "What?"

Sophie sighed. "Can I come in?"

Katherine shrugged, pulling her shoulder to her ear in uncertainty. "Sure, I guess."

Needing no further invitation, the blonde slipped past her and settled herself on the unkempt bed in the middle of the room. She patted on the wrinkled sheets to her right, gesturing for Katherine to join her.

Shutting the door, Katherine obeyed and plopped down beside her. "Well?" she demanded.

Sophie pursed her lips. "Markus is a first class asshat. We both know that."

Katherine resisted the urge to snort. *Amen to that.*

"That being said," Sophie hesitated a moment, "he's not exactly wrong."

Katherine could physically feel the tension gathering in her shoulders. "What's that supposed to mean?" she asked defensively.

"It means," Sophie stressed, "that something clearly happened between you and Bastian. And believe me, I love the man, but I know how frustrating he can be sometimes... so, what do you say? Do you want to talk about it, whatever *it* is?"

Katherine sighed, nervous energy causing her to run her hands through her hair. "It's kind of hard to explain."

She watched as Sophie braced herself before asking another question. "He... he didn't *do* anything to you, did he? Something sexual that you're not comfortable with?"

It took Katherine a minute to register exactly what Sophie was asking, and as understanding dawned, she struggled to control the hysterical laughter that threatened to bubble up her throat. "No!" she choked, immediately assuring the other girl. "*No.* I... it's actually the complete opposite of the problem."

Sophie frowned, confused wrinkles appearing on her brow. "What do you mean?"

"He won't touch me. Like, at all. *Anywhere.*" There. She'd said it.

Sophie's eyebrows rose incredulously. "That's crazy," she pointed out. "Bastian loves you. You two are destined mates, for God's sake."

Nervous about the fact that she was about to air her inner insecurities out for Sophie to hear, Katherine sunk her teeth into her bottom lip. "I know he loves me. Or at least it seems that way. But maybe our bond feels more platonic in nature to him. Like I'm his sister or something. I don't know. Maybe... maybe he doesn't feel *that* way about me – the way I feel about him."

Now it looked like Sophie was the one who wanted to laugh. "That's absurd. I *am* Bastian's sister and believe me, the way he feels about me isn't at all similar to the way he feels about you. Quite frankly, it doesn't hold a candle to it. That man *adores* you."

"He doesn't even kiss me anymore," Katherine pointed out in a whisper.

Sophie sighed. "Listen, sweetie, I can't even attempt to understand the way my brother thinks, but if there is something I know beyond any doubt whatsoever, it is that he doesn't just love you, he *wants* you. Badly. Do you realize how uncomfortable it is for me, his *actual* sister, to watch him practically undress you with his eyes every time he sees you? For God's sake, I think the sexual tension between you two even makes Markus uncomfortable and that, my dear, is quite the feat."

Katherine acknowledged the comforting words with a nod, but she couldn't quite get them to take root in her heart.

Sophie seemed to sense her struggle. "Bastian's a man that requires an absurd amount of patience. Just promise me you won't give up on him, okay?"

Katherine sighed, willing with all her might for the stiffness in her shoulders to dissipate. "Okay," she agreed. "I promise."

* * *

Katherine's promise was sorely tested not even a handful of hours later at supper. Bastian had actually shown up for the meal for the first time since their "argument", for lack of a better word, and the unresolved tension between Katherine and the brooding man made it an uncomfortable affair for everyone.

Perhaps except for Marcus.

"Pass the gravy over here, will you, *sweet cheeks*?"

An embarrassed blush crept up Katherine's neck, reddening her entire face. A quick glance over the table piled high with food – three pork loafs and two overflowing bowls of steamed potatoes along with a platter of buttered bread – confirmed what she already knew.

"There is no gravy, Markus," she replied between gritted teeth.

"Oh," he shrugged in faux innocence, "my mistake."

Katherine wanted to throttle him.

And it didn't look like she was the only one. Bastian's dark eyes glowered in disapproval, the corner of his upper lip rising in a near silent snarl.

Markus had the good sense to shut his trap after that, and the remainder of the meal was spent in a tense silence broken only by the sound of metal forks scraping against ceramic plates.

As Bastian finished eating and rose to take his leave, which signaled to the others that they may be excused from the table as well, he finally broke his vow of silence and called out to her. "Katherine?"

Her shoulders hunched into each other defensively as she forced her eyes to meet the blue ones they'd been attempting to avoid all throughout dinner. She could feel the others watching her. "Yes?" she answered as dully as she could manage.

Bastian's eyes narrowed. "I need to speak with you."

Katherine's arm shot out in a grand, sweeping – and terribly mocking –motion before she could stop it. "Lead the way."

She tried not to let the disappointment show on her face when he made his way towards the den instead of the bedroom they shared together – or had *used* to share together at any rate.

She wasn't able to stop a surprised gasp from escaping, however, when as soon as the door closed shut behind them and he turned to face her, Bastian grabbed her by the waist – his large hands nearly spanning the entirety of its circumference – and deposited her gently on the top of the desk in the center of the room.

Once she recovered from the shock, she quickly grasped his thick wrists and pried his hands off from where they'd continued to rest on her hips. "Don't," she snapped at him.

It wasn't right how his touch made her heart race – how it set her skin aflame.

His nostrils flared, but Bastian allowed her to push him away. His eyes, though, remained glued to hers.

"What?" she demanded, crossing her arms defensively over her chest. "You said you wanted to talk, so talk."

Bastian's brow puckered together in a frown, but he obliged. "I've decided to let you participate in the Recruiting Rites."

Katherine positively bristled at the man's chosen wording. "*Let* me? I hate to break it to you, Bastian, but I was planning on participating whether you decided to *let* me or not."

His frown deepened. "I know. And it's only because you have a stubborn streak a mile wide that I've decided to go along with it." He took a step towards her, his fingers reaching out and grasping the edge of the desk on either side of her. He leaned into her space until mere inches separated their noses.

It gave Katherine a prime view of the days old scruff covering his powerful jaw and she tried not to swallow her tongue.

"But let me tell you something." Bastian's forceful words demanded Katherine's attention, and she jerked her eyes away from his stupidly attractive – incredibly lickable – chin. As she gazed into dangerous, blue irises her wayward thoughts shriveled away. "If you get hurt attempting to compete with your peers, if you acquire even the smallest of scratches, I will rip whoever is responsible for the injury to shreds. I will clamp my goddamn teeth into fur and blood and bone and spit mangled chunks of flesh out at your feet. Now… you wouldn't want to be responsible for something like that, would you?"

Katherine thought her heart might burst from her chest it was pounding so hard.

"So if you find yourself pitted against a bigger and better opponent – and believe me, you will – you bare your goddamn neck and lay on the ground, got it?"

She was squeezing her hands so tightly into fists that she knew her nails were bound to leave deep indentations on the skin of her palms.

"Katherine, do you get me?"

Struggling to gather her thoughts, she hopped off his desk, absolutely fuming.

"Yeah, I got you," she spit the words out like bullets. "You don't have any confidence in me whatsoever."

Bastian grabbed her by the upper arm when she tried to make her escape. "Katherine, *please* try to understand. I'm just trying to protect you. I love you."

She scoffed, wrenching her arm away from him. "You have a funny way of showing it," she scoffed, slamming the door shut behind her.

CHAPTER THREE

The problem with Bastian's threat was that Katherine believed it. She longed to be able to convince herself otherwise – that his promise to maim anyone who dared to lay a hand on her during the Recruiting Rites was merely a bluff – but she knew irrevocably that is was not.

And it put her in an unfortunate positon. Because the manipulative jackass was *right*. She didn't want to be responsible for anyone getting hurt.

What the man had underestimated, however, was the overwhelming urge Katherine had to prove herself. She couldn't shake off the feeling that the council – at least a few key members of it – thought her inadequate. Like she wasn't worthy to be in the pack, let alone the mate, of the head alpha. She wanted to show them – show everyone, especially *herself* – that she was a force to be reckoned with. If she didn't compete, she'd only validate the thought that she was a weak, submissive werewolf.

She couldn't let that happened. She *wouldn't* – even if it meant that someone got hurt.

Which was precisely why Katherine found herself squeezed between her friends Mack and Agnes on the cool evening of the moon gathering instead of with her pack. The entire graduating class – or recruits, she supposed they were considered now – stood huddled together a half mile from the other wolves at the gathering. A good chunk away from the massive dirt pit that would serve as the arena they'd be battling in.

Only Luther, the lone wolf in charge of rearing most underage bitten wolves, was with them. It was his duty to lead them to the pit as soon as the full moon reached its peak and they all changed into their superior physical forms.

Like her peers, Katherine was scarcely dressed. There was no need to waste good clothing when they were forced to change, after all. A ratty, off-white tank top and a pair of non-descript, black shorts were all that shielded her from the elements, and despite her enhanced body temperature, a chill traveled down her spine when a particularly cold gust of wind blew in from the north.

Another gust caused her hair to dance and she struggled to push the unruly mess out of her face. She nearly jumped out of her skin when Mack tucked a particularly wild strand behind her ear for her.

"Thanks," she offered, but her gracious smile slipped into a frown when she noticed the subtle tremors in his hand as he brought the appendage back down to his waist.

"Hey, are you okay?"

"I'm fine," he immediately quipped, refusing to meet her gaze.

Katherine's frown deepened. "Are you sure?" She lowered her voice to a near whisper. "Your hands are shaking."

Mack swiped one of said hands through his hair. "I'm just nervous," he admitted in a hushed tone.

Not hushed enough for Agnes's clever ears though. "And why wouldn't you be?" the girl asked. "We *all* are. This may be the single most important night of our lives. It's a chance to showcase our talents and prove our worth to the leaders of our community. How we perform tonight directly correlates with how our futures will play out. To not feel at least some nerves would be the definition of foolhardy."

Well, *that* little speech certainly caused the tiny butterflies flapping their wings in Katherine's stomach to multiply.

"It's not the same for you Agnes," Mack argued quietly. "Or even you, Katherine. Sure, you undoubtedly want to do well tonight, but you have packs that will gladly take you in regardless of how you perform. I... I don't have anyone like that. Either does Jon," he gestured at the boy talking excitedly with – well, more like *at* – Leander a few feet away. "If I'm rejected tonight, if either of us are, we could be without a pack forever. I'm not an alpha. I'd be scorned. We both would be," Mack spared Katherine a glance, "permanent outsiders like Bastian made Melanie."

Agnes look away uncomfortably, clearly not knowing what to say to that. And truthfully, neither did Katherine. In fact, her friend's heartfelt words made her feel more than a tad guilty for taking her pack and their nearly immediate acceptance of her presence in their lives for granted. She ignored Mack's mention of the girl who used to be their friend entirely, not completely sorry for the fate that Bastian had bestowed upon her.

Spying the soft glow of the moon beginning to stretch out over the trees, the brunette quickly reached for Mack's hand, folding as much of it into her much smaller one as she could.

"Any alpha would be a fool not to immediately snatch you up, Mack. You're a fierce werewolf and an even more amazing friend." Before she could say anything else, the light of the full moon beckoned her, and its pull had her body warping into that of a wolf's.

Still not completely used to the change, it took Katherine a few moments to regain her bearings afterwards. The earthy scent of evergreen trees and freshly upturned dirt assaulted her nose, and she batted down the urge to run free through the forest as her baser instincts attempted to take over her more human inhibitions and sense of... well, *sense*. When she felt in control of herself, she opened her eyes. Mack and Agnes, now in their canine forms, were still on either side of her.

As soon as she felt steady on her feet – or paws rather – the recruits as a whole began to move, Luther leading them to their destination. Mack prodded her with his long snout when for a moment her legs refused to work. She quickly regained her composure, however, and let her wolf's more animalistic side take over, effectively masking the very human trepidation she was feeling with the anticipation her wolf was basking in.

Still, she couldn't rid herself of the nagging apprehension entirely, and fear tickled the back of her mind, attempting to penetrate her wolfish shield when they arrived at the pit a short few minutes later.

Although Katherine called the arena a pit in her mind, it was really just a natural crevasse in the ground in which grass didn't quite grow properly. It was an area reserved for fighting and the exact same spot where Bastian had fought Rogue in an alpha challenge not so long ago. Sometime before the change, someone had sprayed a white chalk outline around the crevasse's perimeter and the fifty by fifty foot area was where the Recruiting Rites – both the tournament and the offers that occurred afterwards – were to take place.

It was positively swarming with wolves, many of them yipping and howling excitedly in anticipation of the Rites. Katherine and her peers were corralled into a small area off to the side of the pit specially reserved for recruits.

Katherine spotted Bastian right away. She didn't know how anyone could possibly miss him. He was the large, majestic wolf – his black fur somehow darker than the night itself – standing slightly apart from the other alphas who'd gathered to watch them.

His presence soothed her fear somewhat, but nervousness still caused a nauseous feeling to roll through her belly.

A large part of her anxiety stemmed from the fact that she didn't know who she'd be fighting. Names had been drawn anonymously by Luther to determine who would be facing who in the first round of the Rites. She wouldn't know who she'd been pitted up against until she was called into the arena.

She waited with bated breath to see who'd be first. Her stomach tightened uncomfortably when Luther stalked her way, but relaxed when he nudged another wolf – Katherine was fairly certainly the large, sinewy creature with dark brown fur was Vincent Vale, one of the more physically impressive werewolves her age – into the pit along with another large wolf—this one tawny with the lips of his mouth already pulled back into a snarl – whom of Katherine wasn't sure his name.

Luther left the pit once both wolves reached the center. Katherine watched – equally parts horrified and fascinated – as Bastian, who as head alpha was the ultimate authority of Haven Falls, released a piercing howl into the air, and the wolves clashed together.

The fight was on.

Claws and teeth sunk into fur and flesh, neither wolf giving an inch as their bodies continuously collided. It was a battle of sheer strength, and a winner could only be decided when one of the competitors was either forced out of the arena or submitted, giving up and baring his neck to his opponent.

The loud noise from the crowd only seemed to energize both wolves as the back and forth exchange of blows between them carried on. Eventually, the tawny wolf tired and the dark one took advantage by snapping his jaw around one of his hind legs. The tawny wolf howled in agony as the dark wolf tugged on the injured leg, pulling him towards the edge of the arena. It was hard to watch as the injured wolf dug his claws into the earth, fighting with all his might to stay in the match. But his strength had diminished greatly since the start of the fight and the dark wolf – Vincent – was able to drag his struggling form out of the arena with ease.

And with that, the first match of the Rites was over.

Two more matches were fought before Agnes was called into the pit along with an auburn-colored wolf Katherine knew to be Priscilla Wright. She didn't even try to suppress a gleeful howl when her friend easily defeated the snobby girl.

Mack was pulled in next, and Katherine was elated when, despite his apparent nerves, he wiped the floor with his opponent in record time, using his superior speed and intellect to send who Katherine was fairly sure was Tommy Phelps – one of Rip Brigg's sidekicks – stumbling out of bounds.

Jon was the next to enter the pit, and while he put on an impressive show, he ultimately lost to his opponent. Leander, too, swiftly lost to the much stronger competitor he was pitted against.

It wasn't until Leander was limping out of the arena that a horrible realization struck Katherine.

She was the only one who had yet to fight.

Fifteen recruits. That meant the first tier of the tournament consisted of seven matches between fourteen wolves with one automatic pass to be given to lucky wolf number fifteen.

She was number fifteen.

Somehow Katherine knew that luck had nothing to do with it.

Blood pounded in her ears as her sudden fury sent it pumping through her body at an alarming speed.

That interfering jackass.

The odds of the pass having been awarded to her through true happenstance were minimal. The odds of Bastian demanding it to be so were much higher.

She absolutely refused to look his way.

Didn't he realize how giving her this special treatment made her look? How it made her out to be some sniveling coward hiding behind her alpha?

Vomit threatened to crawl up her throat at the idea that anyone could truly think that about her.

The tournament only held half of her attention as the first match of the second round of the Rites began. Despite the fact that she had yet to compete, she was forced to watch that match and *another* match from the sidelines as well. Unfortunately, Agnes lost to her opponent in the second one.

It was then that Luther finally – *finally!* – approached her. Not quite looking her in the eye, he hesitated just briefly before gesturing for her to step forward into the arena.

It was about time.

The long wait, however, had done nothing to soothe her nerves and somehow, as her padded feet pressed into the dirt of the pit, the wolfish jeers of the crowd became even louder, echoing obnoxiously in her ears as she waited anxiously to see who her opponent would be.

The excited howls faded into the background, though, when *he* stepped forward. Her anger at Bastian, powerful as it was, nearly dwindled to nothing as she took in the wolfish form of her adversary.

Rip Briggs.

She couldn't have stopped her hackles from rising if she'd tried. *This* was who she had to fight? The behemoth of a boy who'd assaulted her a half a dozen months ago? If Katherine was a bit more self-involved, she'd almost be compelled to believe that the universe was conspiring against her.

Fear sparked within her as Rip prowled closer and she got a good look at his eyes. They positively shone with malice.

Voices of her pack rushed through her head as she desperately tried to think of a plan of attack.

"You're too small to blatantly take him on head-to-head. You're going to have to go on the defensive and devise some sort of strategy." Zane.

"Your quickness may be the only advantage you have in this match up. Use it to implement a sneak attack." Sophie.

"Look for a weakness and use it against him. Don't be afraid to go for the throat. Play dirty if you have to." Markus.

"Please be careful, Katherine." Sweet, sweet Caleb.

She was so occupied with the voices that she almost didn't realize that it was taking an unusually long amount of time for the match to begin. Glancing surreptitiously at Bastian, Katherine startled at the monstrous expression that had overtaken her alpha's features. His ears were pressed flat against his head as his mouth and nose formed a truly frightening snarl. His eyes, normally a stunning blue color, were nearly completely black as they swirled with potent animosity – animosity directed solely at Rip.

For a very long moment, Katherine was afraid that not only would Bastian pull her from the Rites, but that he'd tear Rip to shreds right in front of her as well – though she certainly wouldn't mourn the loss.

Then he met her eyes. She pleaded with him as much as she could with her emerald orbs. And slowly, almost like it physically pained him to do so, Bastian pointed his snout high into the air and, still refusing to remove his gaze from her, he howled.

Katherine didn't have time to think of Bastian after that.

Immediately, Rip was upon her. She dodged as the larger wolf attempted crash into her. He kept coming at her again and again, and she continued to evade him, her mind spinning as she desperately tried to think of a strategy. She knew that attempting to tire Rip out would be a useless endeavor – his endurance was certainly better than hers – but she hoped that she could find some sort of weakness in her opponent so that as her inner Markus had suggested, she could use it against him.

But Rip's finesse was impressive and there were no weaknesses to be found, at least not to Katherine's untrained eyes. And she was tiring quickly. She dodged and rolled, continuing to avoid him until, finally, she was just a bit too slow.

Rip pounced on her, his teeth piercing the back of her neck directly behind her left ear as he brought her down. Despite the immediate pain that blossomed, Katherine attempted to buck him off. But the other wolf was too big, easily using his superior weight to stay on top of her, pressing her into the ground until her belly was flush against it.

She couldn't move.

Fury rushed through her veins as Rip had the audacity to release the hold his teeth had on her neck, his long tongue coming out to lick the wound he'd caused before he growled threateningly in her ear, clearly expecting her to roll over onto her back and assume a submissive pose.

Not in this lifetime.

As Katherine had been forced to endure the rough lick from Rip's disgusting tongue – *Bastian was going to kill the stupid prick if she didn't move fast* – she had spied his large paws on either side of her head. And abruptly realized that his right paw hadn't seemed to have completely healed from whatever Bastian had done to it months ago. In fact, it still looked fairly mangled – the skin and fur of it puckering together unnaturally and its outer most digit half missing.

A plan quickly forming in her mind, she whimpered softly, hoping Rip would take it as a sign that she was ready to submit to him. He did, lifting just enough of his weight from her so that she could turn around to face him.

Katherine moved fast, turning her head sideways at lightning speed. Blood immediately pooled into her mouth when she sank her incisors into the soft pads of Rip's already injured paw.

Rip's responding howl was practically obscene, but Katherine refused to release her grip on him even when he tried to violently shake her off. Knowing that it would probably be her only chance to best him, Katherine tugged him forward. Lost to the pain, he hardly resisted, and with two more hard yanks, Katherine had somehow – *miraculously* – thrown him out of the arena.

And just like that, she'd won.

It took a moment for it to sink in, and as the adrenaline that had flooded her body slowly dissipated, the impressed howling of the crowd began to infiltrate her conscience. Numbly, she realized that many of the wolfish onlookers looked as shocked by the outcome of the match as she felt. As if pulled by some invisible force, her eyes looked up in search of Bastian's.

She spotted him immediately, snarling ferociously at the crumpled form of Rip, but like he felt the weight of her gaze upon him, Bastian's eyes shifted to meet hers. His face softened immediately, his vicious snarl melting into a more relaxed expression as the wrath that had darkened his eyes fled.

Katherine was tempted to say that he looked down right proud of her.

Elation filled her at the thought. In fact, her wolf felt almost heady with pleasure. Before she could dwell on the feeling too much, however, Luther was there, escorting her from the arena and into the small group of competitors who still remained in the competition.

Katherine's attention was essentially shot after that. Still, she managed to yip with sincere excitement when Mack come out the winner of the next match. With his victory, there were only four recruits left competing in the Rites. And she and Mack were two of them.

A sense of dread caused her stomach to spasm, however, when Luther urged the other two wolves to move into the pit for the first match of the third round, and she was left standing alone with Mack.

It meant that when the first match was over, she'd have to fight him.

Glancing covertly in his direction, Katherine could see that her friend was tense, his face furrowed in what seemed to be a frown. He was undoubtedly as uncomfortable as she was at the prospect of genuinely fighting a friend, no holds barred.

It was in that moment that Katherine knew what she had to do.

The battle before theirs was an intense one, ending with both wolves limping from the arena with blood dribbling from their mouths – Vincent leaving as the victor once again. As soon as the arena was cleared, Mack and Katherine were urged forward.

Katherine quickly stepped into the arena, but Mack's body language practically reeked of reluctance as he dragged himself to the pit's center. He glanced at her apologetically before, with much less hesitance than at the beginning of her last fight, Bastian howled.

Neither she nor Mack immediately attacked the other, circling each other carefully instead. Knowing instinctively that Mack wouldn't make the first move, Katherine pounced, springing forward at him in a half-hearted attempt to push him backwards.

He easily avoided her, but the attack hadn't goaded him into taking the offensive as she'd hoped. Realizing she'd have to do more than shove him to goad him into attacking her, Katherine came at him again, this time with her claws bared. She didn't hold back as she slashed at him, digging into an unprotected shoulder and drawing blood.

That did the trick.

Mack pounced at her, using his superior strength to knock her to the forest floor. She got up, determined to give the crowd a good show despite her ultimate intention of losing.

She put up a proper fight as he knocked her around, shoving her to the ground more than a few times. Despite his aggressive wallops, however, Mack refrained from using his teeth, and Katherine was grateful for the fact. One particularly brutal push, though, sent her tumbling backwards, and her side connected with a large, jagged rock half buried in the ground when she lost her balance and fell. It knocked the wind out of her, and as she struggled to catch her breath, Mack stood over her indecisively.

Katherine knew it was time, and rolling over onto her back, she bared her neck for him.

The audience of wolves who'd been intently watching their fight began to howl excitedly, and Katherine nuzzled her snout into Mack's in a silent show of affection when he immediately helped her up.

Katherine trotted out of the arena, the pain in her side already fading as she joined Agnes, Jon, Leander and the other disqualified contestants. Despite having lost, she was incredibly pleased with herself.

Her pleasure only grew when Mack beat the only other werewolf left in the competition – Vincent Vale – after another intense, blood-drawing brawl. Her friend had won the entire tournament, and she'd like to think that her excited howling for him was the loudest.

Before she knew it, Luther was gathering all the recruits together for the second part of the Recruiting Rites – the actual ceremony.

She'd learned in school exactly what would happen. They'd be called into the arena one by one. Any alpha who wished to claim the recruit in the arena as his or her pack mate would enter soon after. From there, it was the recruit's choice. A recruit could choose one of the alphas querying for him or her or even approach an alpha who hadn't stepped into the pit.

If no alpha came forward for a recruit, then he or she could still pick an alpha to approach, but the alpha could outright reject the recruit. If an alpha was unsure about an approaching recruit, he or she also had the option to request the recruit complete some sort of task to prove his or her worth to the alpha before a decision was made.

Unlike the rest of her peers, Katherine had little reason to feel nervous for this part of the Rites. She didn't have to worry about whether or not any alphas would step forward for her – Bastian had made it perfectly clear that he would. She also didn't have to choose between the pack she'd grown up in and a pack she perhaps felt she better fit in with either.

She knew without a single doubt where she belonged.

She watched as recruits were pulled forward into the arena one by one in the order in which they placed in the tournament, with the tawny wolf who'd lost at the beginning of the Rites going first. He received a surprisingly large amount of offers as four alphas stepped into the ring, undoubtedly impressed by his fortitude despite his loss.

A handful more of her classmates chose their packs before Jon stepped into the arena. Her heart ached for him when no alpha followed. She breathed a sigh of relief, however, when the alpha he approached – the alpha of Leander's pack – immediately accepted him. That alpha claimed Leander as well. Agnes received two offers when she stepped into the arena a few minutes later, but it didn't take her more than a second to choose to stay with her original pack and its alpha, Gabriela Atkins.

Many wolves, it seemed, gravitated towards the packs they were raised in, including Rip Briggs and Tommy Phelps, who both chose to remain in the pack commanded by Rip's father. Priscilla Wright, one of the few who'd actually chosen to change packs, had joined the Briggs pack as well, presumably to be with her boyfriend. Katherine tried not to roll her eyes at the idiotic decision.

Then, before she knew it, Katherine was being urged forward by Luther.

Firmly stomping down the last second nerves that threatened to rise, she stepped forward into the arena. They disappeared entirely a millisecond later when Bastian immediately stalked in after her, planting his powerful form directly in front of her. Before she could take a step towards him, however, Katherine was shocked when not one, but two more alpha wolves stepped into the ring.

Katherine's eyes widened and she watched fretfully as Bastian's ears twitched. He'd obviously heard the others step forward and his long, sinewy muscles visibly tensed. She realized it probably wasn't the smartest idea in the world to drop her gaze from his rapidly darkening one, but she couldn't help but sate her curiosity.

It'd killed the cat, after all, not the wolf. Pun completely intended.

Glancing at the two wolves in her peripheral vision, she recognized them immediately. To Bastian's right, Gabriela Atkins had stepped forward, and Katherine was reluctantly flattered. To Bastian's left, however, stood a much more nefarious wolf.

Rogue.

What was he playing at trying to recruit Katherine? Did his jealousy of Bastian truly run so deep that he'd attempt to lure whoever the man wanted in his pack to his side?

What in the hell made him think she'd consider joining him for a minute?

It occurred to Katherine immediately that he *didn't* think that, and her muscles stiffened enough to rival Bastian's when she realized that most likely he was trying to spur Bastian into an unsavory outburst. Because if the head alpha acted out when no rules were being broken – over some girl, no less – he would undoubtedly lose some of the trust that the community had bestowed upon him. His reputable control would be questioned.

And judging by Bastian's shaking form, Rogue's scheme was going to work.

Katherine could never allow that to happen.

She leapt forward immediately, burrowing her snout into the crook of Bastian's neck in an attempt to calm the war she knew was waging in his head. To Katherine's relief, that singular action seemed to be enough, and she could feel the tension in the wolf's stiff shoulders slowly drain as he leaned into her and returned her affectionate nuzzle. He inhaled deeply as he rubbed his nose into her soft fur and she knew he was taking in her unique scent and using it to ground himself.

Not even bothering to spare another glance at the snarling Rogue, they left the arena side by side.

Katherine's pack mates swarmed her, Sophie tenderly nipping her ear while the boys – even Markus—bumped noses with her in congratulations. Bastian allowed the excited touches, but was prodding her back to his side moments later, and practically curling himself around her, he refused to let her leave him the remainder of the night. Nestled against his strong, warm body, Katherine could hardly bring herself to mind.

She watched contently as the last remaining recruits chose their packs. Pride nearly burst in her chest when Mack received more offers than anyone; a record seven alphas stepped forward to offer him a place amongst their packs. Truthfully, Katherine was secretly hoping Bastian might make a move to snatch him up, but she knew in her heart that the man didn't care to expand his pack while he still adjusting to his duties as head alpha. Even if he wasn't busy with said duties, the man wasn't much of a people person.

Mack ultimately chose to join the same pack that had taken in Jon and Leander. Katherine was ecstatic for her friends – glad that three of them would be together in the same pack. She knew that Agnes was happy with where she ended up as well.

As for her, well, truth be told Katherine had chosen her pack a long time ago.

CHAPTER FOUR

In the not so distant past, birthdays had meant very little to Katherine Mayes.

Her own hadn't meant much anyway.

It was just the day that marked her another year older, nothing more and nothing less. And as ridiculous as it may sound, if it were up to her now, she simply wouldn't have a birthday.

Because birthdays meant underdone chocolate cake loaded with runny frosting made with love – the other ingredients were sketchy at best – by her dad. It meant a pile of presents pristinely wrapped in shiny paper and decorated with perfect, bouncy ringlets of ribbon by her mother. It meant a sincere hug from her usually distant older sister.

It meant family.

And her family – at least *that* family – no longer existed. Two were dead. And although her sister Samantha still lived, Katherine was unlikely to ever seen her again.

She didn't like the way such dark thoughts made her feel. It was almost like a lead weight settled over her lungs when she thought about them, preventing her lungs from expanding the way they were meant to and refusing them the oxygen they desperately needed to function.

And so she tried to avoid thinking of her deceased family altogether.

Her birthday, unfortunately, was a stark reminder of them.

It'd been nearly seven months since she'd been forced from her home in Middletown – seven months since her parents and her classmate, Brad, had been murdered – and still she skirted around the mere thought of them. As selfish as it was, most days she liked to pretend her life had started on the night of her first transformation and everything that had happened before that point in time was simply an odd sort of dream.

It was easier than one might think to live this way as very little of what occurred in Haven Falls had any correlation to the life Katherine had led before she'd been bitten. She no longer had parental figures she had to explain herself to, only Bastian. And while her pack mates were like siblings to her, they had very little in common with the girl she was truly related to by blood. Her days were filled with a flurry of activity as she went to school, bonded with her pack mates, and attempted to learn as much as she could about the small community of wolves she had found herself a member of.

With the completion of the Recruiting Rites – and with it, school – however, she was having a difficult time finding a significant distraction from the day that was slowly creeping nearer.

If only birthdays didn't exist at all.

But they did.

And when Katherine cracked open her eyes in the morning hours of the third of May – a mere three days after the Recruiting Rites had taken place – she was officially seventeen.

Instead of remaining buried under the covers and letting grief envelop her, however, Katherine forced herself to move. She dragged herself out of bed, quickly washing her face in the bathroom and throwing her hair into a sloppy bun at the base of her skull before heading to the kitchen in search of a distraction substantial enough to make her forget what day it was.

Her prayers were answered when she came upon Caleb digging through the cupboards, seemingly pulling out every spice or bit of seasoning they had stocked in the spacious cabinets.

"What are you doing?"

Pulling his head out of the cupboard it was immersed in, Caleb smiled at the small brunette. "Katherine! I was just going to come get you. Zane took down a massive moose last night and is butchering it as we speak, but I don't have enough salt and other spices to properly freeze the meat. I was hoping you'd be willing to walk into town with me and help me carry back some supplies."

She didn't have to be asked twice. "Yeah, of course." She glanced down at the over-sized, frayed pajama shirt she was still wearing. "Just let me change first."

"No problem. Take your time. I'll fry you up some eggs for breakfast."

"Thanks," Katherine called over her shoulder, hightailing it back to her bedroom and shucking the shirt off over her head. She quickly replaced it with a ruffled blouse. The leggings she'd slept in were fine, so only a minute had passed before she was heading back into the kitchen.

Her mouth watered as she watched Caleb expertly flip two fried eggs onto a plate he'd prepared for her. Toast popped out of the toaster. "Let me," she quickly asserted, grabbing the butter dish from him before he could do that for her as well.

As much as he seemed to enjoy it, Katherine was often uncomfortable at the way Caleb – as a passive omega – was always ready to serve her and the rest of the pack.

She was perfectly capable of buttering her own toast, after all.

Digging into her eggs, she watched silently as Caleb began writing what she assumed to be a list of groceries they were in need of. She was just dipping the last of her toast into a pool of yellow yolk when he'd finished.

"Ready?" he asked.

Nodding her assertion, Katherine put her dish in the sink before slipping on her shoes and following Caleb out the door.

As they traveled the dirt path into town, Katherine belatedly realized that Caleb was the only member of the pack she'd seen that morning. She knew he'd said that Zane was butchering the moose he'd downed, but where were the others?

Katherine voiced her question. "Where's Bastian this morning? And Markus and Sophie? I didn't see them at the house."

Caleb shrugged, not quite meeting her eyes as his hand came up to rub the back of his neck in what Katherine knew to be a nervous gesture of his. "Markus is helping Zane with the moose. I'm not sure where Bastian went, but I think Sophie's sleeping in." He paused before hurriedly adding, "She likes to do that on occasion, you know."

Oo-kay. They were all valid excuses, Katherine supposed, but she couldn't help but find the quick – almost defensive – way in which Caleb had answered her question to be a bit bizarre.

And it was even stranger that Bastian had just up and left that morning without trying to wake her. He'd hardly let her out of his sight since the Rites. They still hadn't made up exactly, but they'd been a lot more civil to each other since the ceremony, and he'd taken to sleeping with her in their bed again.

Katherine narrowed her eyes at her companion. *Something was up.*

Before she could question him further, however, they'd arrived at the miniscule town of Haven Falls and Caleb was quickly dragging her to the string of shops and the farmers' market that were located in the very center of it.

"Here, take this," he said, handing over a wad of cash. As he perused a stand of homemade herbs and spices, he sent her over to the fruit vendors to pick out a few of her favorites.

Katherine took her time, going through a whole barrel of apples as she search for a half dozen of the specimens that were both devoid of bruises and had a perfect red sheen. Maybe Caleb would teach her how to bake a pie with them if she asked.

Katherine also filled a small bag with strawberries and plucked up a ripe cantaloupe. She and Caleb were really the only members of the pack who cared for fruit, and the latter wasn't picky, so she knew no one would mind her selections.

After paying for the fruit, Katherine quickly stopped to pick up a sack of potatoes before assisting Caleb in filling three more bags with essentials like flour, sugar, and butter. Before she knew it, the noon sun was beating down on them, and they decided they would purchase the perishable food, like milk and cheese, after breaking for lunch at The Bistro.

It was a mistake.

Or, at least, ordering the Swedish meatballs was.

Caleb poked one of the huge, meaty masses on his plate with a fork. "They're not so bad. The gravy has some nice flavor."

Katherine fought back a laugh. It was like he was trying to talk himself into eating the brown lumps of what at one point might have been actual meat.

She'd given up on consuming her own plate of meatballs after the first one she'd bitten into had contained something that had *crunched* inside of her mouth. "They're disgusting," Katherine pointed out matter-of-factly.

Caleb looked positively scandalized. "Katherine," he protested, dropping his fork and looking over his shoulder as if the head chef of the small restaurant could have somehow heard the blatant insult.

"What? It's true," Katherine insisted. She let a small grin pull at her lips. "Nothing is as good as the food you make anyway."

"I'm hardly an expert in the kitchen," Caleb immediately argued, the tiniest tinge of pink coloring his face.

"Sure you are," she persisted, pressing on before the humble blond could deny it. "The food here is usually okay, but your stuff is eons out of its league. It's better than anything I've ever tasted."

"And that's the problem with you Princes, isn't it?"

Katherine nearly jumped out of her skin when two large hands landed with a *thump* on the edge of their table. "You think you're so much better than everyone else."

Rogue.

Katherine recovered sooner than her companion, who looked like he wanted nothing more than to grab her and bolt from the restaurant.

So not happening.

"What do *you* want?" she demanded, inserting as much distaste into her tone as possible, as she eyed the man suddenly looming over their table.

Rogue grinned, white teeth peeking out between red lips. "I'm so glad you asked. Because, you see, lately I've been wanting all kinds of things." He leaned in closer to her, his eyes gleaming with a twisted sort of amusement as she backed away from him as much as the booth she was sitting in allowed. "Nothing, though, would make me gladder than seeing your Bastian give up his place as head alpha. Be a dear and make it happen, will you? Go get yourself entangled in another mess. Something that will upset him enough that he's forced to step down. Maybe… pick a fight with a bear? Or… try to drown yourself in the falls? Either of those should do the trick."

Katherine's face was flushed a furious scarlet in response to the man's heinous suggestions, her hands shaking with suppressed rage in her lap.

Caleb, too, looked the maddest she'd ever seen the usually calm man. "Go away, Rogue," he hissed, locking an ankle around one of Katherine's in what she assumed was a show of support and an attempt at comfort.

The man seemed more amused by the demand than anything. "Or what? Are you going to make me?"

Caleb bristled. "Bastian will-"

Rogue had the nerve to laugh in Caleb's face. "Bastian will what? *Hmm?*" His dark eyes swung from Caleb's to hers. "You going to hide behind your alpha like a scared little bitch too, Katherine?"

And just like that, her temper exploded. She wasn't even truly aware of what she was going to do until she'd gone and done it. In a flash, her hand was wrapped around the salt shaker in the middle of their table and with a quick flick of the wrist, she'd pulled off the thing's lid and unhesitatingly threw the pile of salt that was inside straight into Rogue's eyes.

His responding howl of agony echoed throughout the restaurant. "You *bitch*!" the man hollered, groping blindly for her with one hand as the other desperately tried to rub the salt out of his surely burning eyes.

Caleb shoved the half-blind man away before he could lay a finger on her. Luckily, Rogue's shouts had caught the attention of The Bistro's servers, and two hustled over to restrain him. Before either could ask them any questions, however, Caleb quickly threw down some money, hoisted up their bags, and grabbing her hand, dashed out the door. He pulled her along for an entire block before finally releasing her behind the corner of a wooden building.

"What were you thinking?" the blond demanded between huffs as he attempted to catch his breath. "Bastian would have killed me if that brute had hurt you."

Katherine sucked in a lungful of air. "I was thinking that that jerkface needed to be taught a lesson. Namely, that we aren't going to just sit there and take his abuse anymore. Bastian isn't the only force to be reckoned with in our pack. Rogue deserved what he got, and I don't regret doing it at all. Not even one little bit."

Caleb stared at her for a long moment, seemingly at a loss for words before a disbelieving smile finally broke out across his face. "You, Katherine, are something else."

Katherine couldn't have stopped the blush from blossoming across her cheeks if she'd tried. "Thanks, Caleb. You are too."

Noticing that their shadows had grown quite a bit taller since they'd entered the The Bistro around noon, Katherine glanced up at the bright, cloudless sky. "What time is it? I think we should get the rest of the groceries and head home."

Caleb examined his watch. "It's a little past two. That's perfect! We should be able to get back to the house right around three o'clock." He started dragging her towards the market.

Katherine frowned. "What's at three?"

Caleb stumbled over thin air at her inquiry. His eyes flickered to her face before quickly shifting away. "O-oh," he stuttered. "W-w-well, nothing I suppose. Just seems like a good time to get back is all."

Oo-kay. There Caleb was, acting all weird again.

As he begin to fill the suddenly awkward silence between them with nervous chatter, however, Katherine didn't quite have the heart to call him out on it.

They quickly finished the rest of their shopping and arms laden with groceries, began heading home.

Caleb's smile was practically radiant as they approached the house. It must have been three o'clock on the dot if his sunny demeanor was anything to do by. Cracking open the door, he hurriedly ushered her inside.

"Surprise!"

"Happy birthday, Katherine!"

"Seventeen years old! Can you believe it?"

"Welcome to adulthood, princess!"

Katherine stood stock-still in the doorway, taken completely off guard by what appeared to be a surprise birthday party. For her.

How had they known? Was she even shocked that they did?

Unsurprisingly, the answer was a resounding *no*.

But she could hardly appreciate their thoughtfulness when she'd been doing her best to completely forget that today was her birthday at all. Now she had no choice but to acknowledge it.

There was no burnt on the outside, yet gooey on the inside chocolate cake on the dining room table, but rather a decadent, three-layer vanilla masterpiece covered in fancy, frosting roses, which had undoubtedly been prepared by Caleb. Instead of a stack of pristinely wrapped gifts, a small pile of presents haphazardly packed in paper bags and newspaper sat beside the cake.

And most noticeably of all, there was no Mom and no Dad. They would never be with her for another birthday again.

"Katherine?" *Bastian.* She knew that he and the others were waiting for her reaction to what was supposed to be a thoughtful surprise.

Panic overtook her, though, when she felt a lump of pure emotion wedge itself in her throat, and heart beating madly in her chest, Katherine did what she did best. Tears blurring her vision, she dropped the bags of groceries she was holding in her arms to the ground – through her daze, she heard the gallon of milk one of the bags had contained break open on the floor with a loud *splat* – and bolted from the room.

She didn't think about where she was going – didn't have any destination in mind really – she just allowed her feet to take her where they wanted to go. Which was apparently as far away from the Prince house as possible. She sprinted into the forest surrounding the brick building, paying no heed to Bastian as he shouted after her.

She pushed low hanging branches out of her way as she ran, ignoring the way some of the sharper ones cut up the soft palms of her hands. She pushed forward, continuing to run until one of her shoes caught on an upturned root hidden in the forest's long grass, and she fell to the ground in an ungraceful heap, barely reaching her hands out in time to catch herself before she face planted.

Once she was down, she didn't bother to get back up.

The tears came unbidden, leaking from her eyes as she was finally able to push past the lump in her throat and let out a strangled cry. Pressing her hands to her face and curling up her knees to her chest, she allowed herself to become undone.

Once she started the ugly wailing, she couldn't stop. Gagging on the tears welling up her in throat, she nearly vomited.

Bastian was upon her in seconds, but she was hardly aware of him even as his strong arms came around her and cradled her to his chest. "Shh, you're okay," he whispered in her ear. "I've got you, you're okay. Just breathe."

He didn't ask her what was wrong, but she knew how inexplicably strange her behavior appeared, and through her harsh sobs, she tried to explain. "They," *hiccup*, "They'll never," *sob*, "They'll never be here for," *hiccup*, "another birthday again."

He didn't have to ask her who "they" were. He clutched her even more tightly to his chest. "I'm sorry, Katherine, I'm sorry."

She'd long ago accepted that the death of her parents wasn't Bastian's fault. And it wasn't her fault either. But that didn't make acknowledging that they were gone any easier. She cried for a long time. Bastian sat with her, whispering words of support and crooning softly in her ear.

"Neither will *have* another birthday again." Her voice was so hoarse by the time she was able to speak that she almost didn't recognize it. The words scratched her sore throat as she forced them out, the physical pain of saying them somehow making it easier to speak them out loud.

It was an awful truth, but admitting it grounded her and soon thereafter, the seemingly endless river of tears trickled to a stop, leaving behind in their wake red, swollen eyes. Sniffling, Katherine uncouthly wiped the snot leaking from her nose with the back of her hand. Bastian didn't comment, merely tucking a strand of hair that had loosened from her bun behind her ear.

"Okay," Katherine whispered, pushing herself away from her alpha and standing on shaky legs. "Let's go back."

Bastian frowned, his blue eyes troubled, but he stood with her. "Are you sure?"

Swallowing around the lump still present in her throat, Katherine nodded. "Yeah."

She stopped him when he stepped forward and made a move to lift her up into his arms. "I can walk," she protested, forcing her tone to be firm.

Bastian looked like he wanted to argue, but smartly kept his mouth shut. Still, he assessed her carefully as he led the way back to the house. Katherine ignored his watchful gaze, focusing instead on trying to smooth out the wrinkles from her blouse.

It was a lost cause, but she didn't much care. It would match her bedraggled appearance anyway.

When they reached the house and stepped onto the porch, Bastian pivoted in front of her, gently resting his hands on her shoulders. "Wait here. I'll make sure everything is put away."

"No," Katherine immediately protested, voice hitching as she latched onto one of Bastian's thick wrists. "No," she said again more calmly, releasing him. "It was really nice of you guys to go through all this trouble for me. Pretending that today isn't my birthday – that the day doesn't exist – is stupid. My p-parents," she stumbled over the word, "would want me to be happy." She took a deep breath. "So let's celebrate."

Bastian looked torn between giving her what she said she wanted and refusing her request in an effort to protect her. After a moment of searching her eyes, though, he seemed to set his reservations aside. "Okay," he agreed, "but if it starts to become overwhelming, you'll let me know right away."

"Alright," Katherine agreed, knowing he wouldn't have budged otherwise.

She steeled herself as he opened the door.

Four pairs of eyes immediately zeroed in on them as they entered the kitchen. Hushed chatter quickly turned into a tense, oppressive silence. She could see the questions in their eyes as they took in her slovenly appearance.

"What's the matter, birthday girl? Have your heart set on chocolate cake?"

Markus broke the quiet in his usual bad mannered way, and while Katherine could have hugged him for it, Bastian looked about two seconds away from smashing in his face with his fists.

She quickly cleared her throat. "Uh, no. Vanilla is fine. I mean, the cake looks wonderful." She eyed the sloppily wrapped presents beside the confection. "It all looks wonderful, actually. Thank you guys, so much. I – I just didn't realize you knew it was my birthday."

It was a flimsy excuse for her break down at best – a blatant lie at worst – but Caleb, bless him, graciously went along with it. "We wanted it to be a surprise. We're sorry for startling you."

"No, don't be." She rubbed her chest uncomfortably, the heart inside of it still aching. "It was very kind of you to think of me. But how *did* you guys know it was my birthday?"

Zane snorted. "I know we live in the middle of a forest, but we're not complete Neanderthals. We know how to use the Internet when the occasion calls for it. We looked you up well before we snatched you last fall."

Katherine supposed that she shouldn't have been surprised. "Oh."

Sophie stood up, throwing a friendly arm around Katherine's tense shoulders. "We thought it would be a fun idea to surprise you when you failed to mention that your birthday was coming up. Of course, we never would've if we'd known you'd react so poorly, but I hope you'll still celebrate with us." She lowered her voice, a mischievous smile briefly gracing her face. "After all, it's not every day that you get to celebrate the birthday of a certified badass." The blonde winked. "Rogue will definitely think twice before messing with you again."

Katherine recognized immediately that Sophie was changing the subject in an effort to make her more comfortable, and she very much appreciated it. Even if it meant telling Bastian that she and Rogue had had a confrontation of sorts.

Still, she groaned, burying her face in her hands. "Caleb told you?"

"Oh yeah," Markus confirmed, "and let me just say that I, for one, am impressed."

Peeking between her fingers, Katherine saw Bastian frowning at her, his eyebrows puckering together as worry lines formed on his forehead. "What are they talking about?"

Sophie rolled her eyes. "Calm down, big guy. I'm sure Katherine will tell you the story over some cake." The blonde's gaze pivoted to the girl still firmly planted under her arm. "What do you say, Katherine? You hungry?"

Eying the layered cake that was almost too pretty to eat, she gave her assertion. "Yeah, let's eat."

Caleb, though, refused to let them cut into his masterpiece until he'd poked in a massive candle at the very top. Lighting its wick, he ordered Katherine to make a wish.

Squeezing her eyes tightly shut, Katherine thought of her parents. Although only seven months had passed since she'd last seen them, she found that time had taken a toll on her memory. The details of their faces were fuzzy. Was her dad's chin as angular as she remembered it? Was her mom's nose as regal as she recalled? She couldn't be sure.

The realization that the memories of her parents were following them to their graves – that even they were leaving her – nearly caused a fresh onslaught of tears.

But Katherine held it together, and as she blew out her birthday candle, she wished with all her might that wherever her parents had gone when they'd passed – she desperately wanted to believe in heaven – they were happy.

Opening her eyes, Katherine watched as a small bit of smoke from the freshly blown out candle swirled higher and higher into the air until it disappeared entirely. As it dissipated, she made a vow to leave morose thoughts of her family behind her for the rest of the evening, determined to at least try to achieve the same happiness she wished for them.

As Caleb dished up the cake – "Birthday girl, first!" – Bastian demanded to know what had happened between her and Rogue.

Not quite looking at him, Katherine poked at the spongey, white fluff on her plate. It was covered neatly with an even layer of frosting and looked delicious, but she didn't quite have the heart to eat it despite its clear culinary superiority over anything her father had ever made for her.

"It's no big deal," she finally answered. "I'm not hurt, and you'll just overreact."

Understatement of the century.

She had had to employ the strength of both Markus and Zane to physically restrain the man from going after Rip Briggs and breaking his undamaged hand the morning after the Recruiting Rites. All because the idiot had thought it'd be a smart idea to lick her.

She gazed at him under her lashes. "Can you just forget about it for now? It *is* my birthday."

She wasn't ignorant of the irony in using the fact that it was her birthday – something she'd desperately wanted to forget about just that morning – against the man. Still, she could hardly bring herself to feel guilty. Especially when it worked.

"Okay," Bastian agreed begrudgingly, clearly unwilling to push the issue and risk upsetting her even more than she already had been that day. It brought the first real smile to Katherine's lips since she'd been so unfortunately surprised hours earlier.

Katherine continued to play with her food as the others shoveled cake into their mouths. After everyone who'd wanted some received seconds, she found herself bombarded with presents as Sophie thrust the medium sized package she'd apparently purchased for her into her lap. "Here, open mine first."

Carefully lifting the lid from the plainly wrapped box, Katherine flushed and hastily shoved it back down when she saw what was inside.

Pressing her hands to her burning face, she squawked at the girl she considered a sister. "Sophie!"

"What?" she asked with an easy grin. "You're a woman now and I thought that *some* people around here could use a reminder."

If possible, her face grew even hotter.

"Let me see." Still slightly shocked by Sophie's blunt words, Katherine didn't quite react quickly enough when Zane pulled the box from her hands. Opening and reaching into the box without even really looking at what was inside of it, Zane pulled out a pair of lacey, aqua panties.

"Oh my God," Katherine muttered, hiding her face behind her hands.

He dropped the panties faster than a hot coal when he realized exactly what it was he was holding. She didn't know which of them was more mortified.

"Crap, sorry, *so* sorry, I shouldn't have-"

"It's okay," Katherine quickly cut off his rambling, snatching the box when he sheepishly handed it back to her. Sneaking a glance at Bastian, she noticed his nostrils were flared as he glared across the table at Zane.

Katherine tried to comfort herself with the fact that the man at least hadn't pulled out the sheer top that Sophie had paired with the panties or God forbid, the crimson scrap of fabric she knew to be a thong and its matching push-up bra. She'd seen both sets of underwear before she'd had the good sense to close the box earlier.

Clearly wanting to make up for his faux pas, Zane ignored Markus's snickering at what had just transpired and hurriedly handed over his own gift. She opened it to reveal a stack of bestselling mystery novels. Apparently Zane had traveled all the way to Fort Saskatchewan to buy them when he'd heard her mention in passing that they were her preferred reading material.

After offering the man a quiet "thanks", Katherine opened the gifts from her remaining pack mates in quick succession. She received a small sparring knife from Markus – he reminded her that she was "still utter crap" at fighting in her human form and promised he'd teach her how to use it – and a small box stuffed to the brim with homemade candies and sweets from Caleb.

Bastian quietly informed her that she'd receive his gift later. She tried not to think too hard about what that might imply.

Katherine and the pack whittled away the rest of the evening, staying up well past midnight playing a ruthless game of Monopoly, of which after many hours, Katherine was finally declared the winner.

Of course, Markus, who'd claimed second, insisted that he had only let her win because it was her birthday.

Katherine had just finished brushing her teeth and was in the process of pulling back the covers of their bed so that she could go to sleep when Bastian took her hand and gently reminded her that he'd yet to give her his gift.

"Sit with me," he insisted, tugging her onto his lap with one hand as the other pulled a small jewelry box out of the top drawer of the night stand.

Katherine's heart thumped painfully – *nervously* – against her ribs when she saw it. "Bastian-"

Cutting her off by simply meeting her trepid gaze with an intense stare of his own, the man began to speak. "I didn't want to make you uncomfortable by giving this to you in front of the others, and it doesn't have to mean anything if you don't want it to, but there's a ring in here." He stopped, his Adam's apple bobbing as he swallowed. "I love you. I've known that I love you for a long time now – longer than you probably think– and my hope is that by giving this to you, any doubts you may have about that – about me loving you – will disappear. This ring has been in my family for generations and every time you see it, I want you to be reminded of the simple fact that my love for you is eternal."

Nearly trembling from the stark proclamation of his love for her – and relief that he wasn't doing anything crazy like proposing marriage – Katherine delicately took the closed box from his hand, opening it with her small fingers.

She gaped at the ring inside as it was revealed to her. Golden loops encrusted with tiny jewels twisted around each other in a complicated pattern, held together at its center by an inordinately detailed face of a wolf. The wolf, made of pure gold, had sapphires for eyes and clasped within its teeth was a circular diamond as large as Katherine's fingernail.

Katherine was literally speechless.

Bastian's arm tightened around her waist. "Do you like it? It's been in the Prince family for as long as anyone can remember. My grandmother used to wear it when she was still alive."

It was too much. It was *way* too much. And yet, taking in Bastian's hopeful expression, Katherine knew she could never reject the gift – *any* gift – from the man. "It's beautiful," she answered honestly. "Of course, I like it. I… I love it."

I love you.

But that part remained unsaid.

Bastian gingerly took the ring out of its box, revealing that it had been looped through a golden necklace chain. She allowed him to slip it over her head. "I thought you might prefer to wear it around your neck. That way you never have to take it off – not even when you transform."

It was a thoughtful gesture as a ring worn around her finger would immediately break if she shifted into her wolf form with it on.

"Thank you," she murmured softly, still entranced by how much the small piece of jewelry sparkled, but she forced herself to drag her eyes away from it to meet Bastian's expectant gaze. Somehow, his blue eyes were shining even brighter than the sapphires encrusted in the ring.

"You're welcome," he replied just as quietly, running his large hands up and down her bare arms before allowing one of them to reach up and carefully cup the back of her neck. Eying her lips, he leaned forward, stopping only a hair's breath away from connecting his mouth with hers. "I know how… *tense* things have been between us lately, but may I kiss you?"

Ignoring the way a heated blush crept up her cheeks, Katherine answered him. "You can always kiss me."

A small grin tugged at the corners of his mouth at *that* response, and his lips lingers over hers for only a moment longer before he pressed them firmly to her eager mouth. Lips and tongues sensually explored each other for a long while before he finally pulled away. Mouth tingling, Katherine was satisfied to let the kiss be simply that – a kiss.

And despite how much she'd dreaded the arrival of this day – her birthday – and the painful memories that it had forced her to acknowledge, when she went to bed that night encased in Bastian's strong arms, she felt like the most loved and cherished girl in the world.

Unfortunately, that feeling would not last for long.

CHAPTER FIVE

"Is it true?"

Somehow Katherine was able to force the words out in a steady voice, which was quite the feat considering the fact that her hands were trembling. She'd attempted to stop the slight movement by clasping them together in front of her as tightly as she could, but even that had not totally suppressed the tremors.

Her very insides were quivering.

The shaking had started and hadn't stopped since she'd been awakened in the middle of the night not a handful of hours earlier by the sound of muted voices arguing angrily in the hallway outside of her room.

"You have to tell her."

"I don't have to do a damn thing."

Since then, the words she'd overheard had been repeating themselves in an endless loop inside of her head.

Katherine sleepily became aware of the sound of hushed voices floating in and out of her consciousness. Cracking her tired eyes open, she quickly became cognizant of the fact that while Bastian's side of the bed was still warm, the man's natural scent still potent in the air, it was mysteriously absent of the man himself.

Her curiosity was immediately piqued.

Cloaked in darkness, she crept noiselessly to the closed bedroom door, pressing her ear to the smooth wood and shamelessly eavesdropping on the muted voices she could hear on the other side of it.

"She deserves to know."

"Do I need to remind you who the alpha of this pack is? Because I'd be all too happy to do so."

She recognized immediately the owners of the two voices – Markus and Bastian – though judging by their tones, neither sounded particularly pleased with the other. She didn't know who the "she" they were speaking of was, but that, too, quickly became clear.

"Go ahead if it'll make you feel better, but we both know that no amount of smashing your fist into my face will erase the memory of Katherine's tear stained one from your head."

The "she" they were talking about was her.

Markus spared Katherine a glance between bicep curls. He didn't seem particularly perturbed that she'd burst into his room with nary a knock and he hadn't bothered to put the metal bar that had massive circular weights attached to either end down.

"Is what true?"

He grunted, lifting the bar to his stumbled covered chin once more. "You're going to have to be a bit more specific, princess. Mind reading isn't exactly my forte. Fighting, hell yeah. Handling knives, sure. But mind reading? Not even I'm that good."

"It's for her own good."

"Maybe right away it was. But now I think we both know that only one person benefits from keeping her in the dark... and it sure as hell isn't her."

The resounding boom of a body being slammed into the wall had Katherine quickly backing away from the door. After the brief sound of a scuffle, however, silence reigned – broken only by the sound of both men's heavy breathing – and she felt safe to once again creep closer.

After a lengthy pause, Bastian finally spoke, and Katherine's ears had to strain to hear his words as they materialized. "She'll hate me."

Katherine frowned, confident that that could never be true. She eyed the door handle, debating on whether she should reveal herself and assure the man of just that. Her curiosity had only grown as she'd listened in on their conversation, however, and Katherine's hands ultimately remained at her sides.

"Maybe, maybe not. But I know for damn sure you'll hate yourself if you never tell her. Just think about it, that's all I'm saying."

A lengthy pause ensued before Bastian finally responded. "Alright."

That seemed to satisfy Markus, and she heard the sound of heavy footsteps fading into softer ones as he walked away. Katherine scurried back to bed, determined not to be caught eavesdropping. She dove under the heavy covers, willing her galloping heart to slow.

Katherine focused on keeping her breathing steady as she heard Bastian enter the room and approach the bed before the mattress dipped with his weight. She feigned sleep as she felt his strong arms wrap around her waist. The tip of his nose poked into the back of her head as he buried his face into her hair.

It took longer than she might have expected for his tense muscles to relax, but she knew he was on the edge of consciousness when he pressed a soft kiss to the back of her neck and whispered the words near her ear. The words that would change everything.

"Forgive me, Katherine. They're alive. Your parents… they're alive."

"Are my parents alive?"

That caught Markus's attention. He fumbled with the heavy weight in his hands, nearly dropping the bar when the question shot out of her mouth. "Damn it," he swore, continuing to mutter obscenities to himself as he struggled to place the weighted bar back where it belonged. Once he managed it, he whipped around to face her. "Where did you hear that?"

It wasn't a denial.

She swallowed down the bile that threatened to rise up her throat. "I asked you if it was true."

It'd taken Katherine the rest of the night and half of the morning to work up the nerve to confront Markus. She'd stayed in bed for nearly a half hour after Bastian's whispered confession, incapable of moving her frozen limbs as the shock of hearing those words had rendered her brain basically useless.

Eventually she'd managed to slip out of the man's warm embrace and sneak silently into the bathroom. She'd stayed locked in there for hours, alternately staring at her pale as a sheet pallor in the huge mirror above the sink and kneeling over the toilet as the urge to vomit surfaced over and over again. Despite her gagging, however, nothing ever came up.

As the shock wore off, bursts of other emotions threatened to overwhelm her fragile mental state. She was terrified that she'd misheard Bastian and almost equally fearful that she hadn't. Unbridled joy fought with stinging betrayal. Katherine wasn't sure if her heart had shattered or was being put back together again.

How could Bastian have kept this from her?

Her body couldn't handle the intense cocktail of volatile emotions clashing together within her and as a result, she shook. Her entire being trembled from the inside out.

As the hours passed and the sun began to rise in the sky, Bastian had knocked on the bathroom door, calling her name. "Katherine?"

Not even close to being ready to face the man, she'd ignored him, quickly reaching for the tub's faucet and wrenching on the water. Just as she'd hoped, Bastian had assumed that she was preparing a bath for herself and hadn't heard him over the running water. So he'd left.

Waiting another hour after that to ensure that he was truly gone – at least nowhere near the bathroom – Katherine had finally managed to gather up what remained of her courage and hurriedly left the bathroom and bedroom said bathroom was attached to. She'd rushed up the stairs to Markus's room, intent on confronting the man who, presently, was refusing to look at her.

"Well?" she demanded as firmly as she could when he didn't respond to her question.

Sighing loudly in overdone exasperation, he ran both of his agitated hands through his hair. Finally, his hazel eyes found her green ones. "Yes, okay," he blurted. "It's true. Your parents are alive. But listen to me..."

But she wasn't. Listening, that is. The words, once again spoken out loud, burned themselves into her brain. *Your parents are alive.*

She bolted from the room.

"Katherine!" Markus shouted after her, jumping to his feet and taking chase. He followed her down the stairs, catching her at the bottom by roughly grabbing her upper arm and yanking her down the last step. "What the hell do you think you're doing? Look, I can imagine how this looks to you, but you can't just run away without giving Bastian a chance to explain."

With her free hand, she smacked him on the arm he was using to restrain her. "Let me go! I don't need to listen to a damn word you have to say, and if *he* even dares to try and justify this, I'll pop him one straight in his dirty, lying mouth!"

"Jesus, calm down, would you?" Markus hissed as he marched her to her room. Katherine purposely dragged her feet, attempting to yank herself free as he forcefully hauled her down the hallway. He deposited her into what she'd come to think of as her room, but had just been revealed to be more of a gilded cage than anything.

"Stay here," he ordered, slamming the door shut behind him.

Katherine knew instinctively that he was going to get Bastian.

She didn't waste any time. As soon as the door had closed, she raced towards it. Jiggling its handle, however, quickly proved to be useless. Although the door didn't have a lock, it was obvious that Markus had hastily pressed something – probably a chair – up under the knob to keep her from escaping.

But that wasn't about to stop Katherine. Nothing could now that she knew the truth.

Your parents are alive.

Abandoning her attempts at opening the door, Katherine turned her attention to the large bay window on the opposite side of the room. When she tried to lift the glass window open, however, it immediately became clear that it was jammed.

Katherine thought fast and throwing caution to the wind, she yanked free one of the small wooden drawers of the night stand. Lifting it high above her head, she threw it at the reflective glass with all her might.

Crash.

The window immediately shattered.

Having known the loud noise would swiftly gain the attention of anyone still in the house before she'd even broken it, Katherine rapidly punched out the large, jagged pieces of glass that stuck stubbornly to the bottom of the window's frame, and then, ignoring the slight sting the remaining shards caused as they bit into her palms, she pulled herself up over the window's ledge and leapt to her freedom.

She'd like to have said she landed gracefully on the grass – it was only a four foot drop, after all – but adrenaline caused her to stumble as her feet met the hard, uneven ground. Picking herself up, she raced to the SUV parked in front of the house. Saying a quick prayer that the keys were inside of it, Katherine wrenched open the driver's side door.

Her prayers were answered.

Spotting the glinting keys in the ignition, Katherine gave the situation no further thought and leaping in the SUV, brought the vehicle to life. She shifted it into drive, gunned the gas, and, ignoring the tiny prickle of guilt buried beneath the heaps of fury ruling her actions, Katherine drove away.

* * *

SUV parked haphazardly along the side of the highway several miles outside of Duluth, Minnesota, Katherine had long ago come to the realization that she'd made a mistake.

She should have thought her actions through much more thoroughly.

Because while she didn't regret leaving Haven Falls even the slightest bit, she *did* regret how recklessly she'd done it. Without any kind of money whatsoever to fill the mammoth vehicle's gas tank.

It hadn't taken long for her to realize that she'd left not only without any money to fund her sudden trip, but also without the fake passport that Bastian had had made for her months earlier. Through sheer luck, she'd somehow managed to remember how to navigate the private, gravel road that went straight through a bit of unpatrolled border between Canada and the United States and so hadn't needed the ID, but the lack of monetary funds was a different matter entirely.

She'd managed to dig out a dozen dull quarters buried beneath the pile of expired car insurance cards and maps in the glove compartment, and she'd used them to buy a cheap pair of flip-flops for her bare feet and a slice of pizza for her growling stomach at a convenience store a couple of hours earlier.

While the shoes were fine, the pizza had been a poor decision. It'd tasted more like greased cardboard with a bit of cheese on top than actual food.

Unfortunately, those twelve quarters had been the extent of her funds. And so she had zero dollars. Zero dollars to buy more food. Zero dollars to get herself something to drink. Zero dollars to fill up the SUV with gas.

She was fortunate that she'd gotten as far as she had, really. The tank had been full when she'd left Haven Falls, and according to the revolving numbers above the gas gage, she'd managed to drive a total of 376 miles before the vehicle had finally broken down – no more gas left in its tank to make it run.

And so stuck on the side of the road inside a vehicle that couldn't go anywhere, Katherine rested her head against the leather steering wheel and desperately tried to think of a way out of the mess she'd found herself in.

Only one solution occurred to her, and she didn't think she could get around it.

She was going to have to hitch hike.

Bastian would kill her.

The traitorous thought snuck up on her unexpectedly and, unsurprisingly, only strengthened her resolve to do it. "Screw you," she muttered to a man who was – *hopefully* – hundreds of miles away before jabbing the unlock button with her forefinger and pushing open the door.

The sun was setting but it still provided enough light for Katherine to feel relatively certain she wouldn't be run over as she trudged through the overgrown weeds that grew wildly on the side of the road. She hesitantly threw her arm out and stuck her thumb in the air when she heard the first car approaching.

It zoomed right passed her.

Same with the second.

And third.

Katherine had lost track of how many vehicles had ignored her, the sky growing steadily darker, when she became desperate enough to try to flag down a semi-truck. To her surprise, the big rig slowed to a stop. She eyed the eighteen wheeler warily, second guessing her decision, when the passenger side door was thrown open by a petite woman.

Katherine thanked whatever deity was watching over her.

As stereotypical as it was, she'd pictured an obese man sporting an overgrown beard and grease-stained clothes driving a monster like this. Not the short, bright eyed woman behind the wheel who was waving for her to come closer.

Even *she* was taller than the forty-something year old broad and Katherine was fairly certain she could take her in a fight if the woman proved to be violent. Confident that both her life and virtue would remain intact if she took a ride from the woman, she ventured forward, quickly scrambling up the set of stairs and taking the only other seat available in the front of the semi-truck. "Thanks so much," she offered immediately. "You're the first person who stopped."

The woman shook her head, shifting the massive engine of the truck into gear. "And thank God I was, little missy. I'd have hated to see your pretty face splattered across my television the next time I'd turned on the news. Missing girl's body found in the ditch along Highway 69."

Katherine's face heated at the blatant scolding. "My car broke down," she muttered in explanation. Not *exactly* true, but close enough.

The woman sighed. "Sorry, honey, I don't mean to sound so harsh. It just isn't safe for a young woman like yourself to be hitch hiking. Asking random strangers for a ride is dangerous. The name's Trixie, by the way. What's yours?"

Her blush cooled at the woman's – Trixie's – apology. "Um… it's Katherine."

"Alrighty, Katherine. Where were you headed before your car broke down?"

The small brunette fidgeted in her seat. "Uh… Iowa, actually. I live," *used to live,* "in Middletown. It's a tiny speck of a town a bit south of Des Moines."

"Iowa, huh?" Trixie's eyebrows disappeared into her poufy bangs. "You're a long way from home. You aren't in some sort of trouble, are you?"

Katherine immediately shook her head, half afraid the woman would throw her out if she thought that was the case. "No, no, nothing like that." *Not unless one counted being on the run from a pack of werewolves led by one undoubtedly enraged alpha as trouble.*

Trixie nodded to herself, seemingly coming to some sort of decision in her head. "Well, if that's true then I suppose I wouldn't mind making a pit stop in this Middletown. Des Moines is a bit out of the way of where I'm headed, but I wouldn't feel right leaving you out here to fend for yourself."

Genuine gratitude swelled within her. "That'd be great. Are you sure? I don't want to be too much trouble."

"Sure, sure," Trixie waved off her concern. "Think nothing of it. You remind me of my daughter."

Katherine allowed Trixie to entertain her with tales of said daughter – apparently the girl had recently moved out, leaving Trixie with a case of empty nest syndrome – as they continued to drive down the highway. Grateful for the distraction from her previously frenzied thoughts, she was disappointed when they hadn't driven for much longer than an hour before Trixie was pulling into a truck stop.

"Sorry, dear, but I've been on the road since dawn. If I don't get some shut eye soon, I'm liable to drive us into a ditch."

"That's okay," Katherine assured her, but tried to stop Trixie from dragging her out of the big rig to get a bite to eat at the small diner that shared a lot with the truck stop. "I don't have any money," she protested.

Trixie rolled her eyes. "I'm paying. Now move your hiney, girl."

Katherine reluctantly acquiesced, muttering "thank you" a million or so times as she dove into the thick cheeseburger she'd ended up ordering for herself inside. Despite the burger being well done, the protein was still a godsend for her growling belly. As they were walking back to the semi- truck, where Trixie was planning on pulling out a couple of the monstrous vehicle's make-shift bunks, she asked Katherine a question that had her stopping in her tracks.

"Do you need to call anyone to let them know you had car trouble and are going to be a little late getting home?"

She dug out a small, compact cell phone from one of her jean's pockets.

A cell phone.

It'd been seven months since Katherine had seen one of those. And while the one Trixie owned was an older, blockier version of the one she used to have before... well *before*, it was still an almost surreal experience to see it.

Why the hell hadn't she thought of asking for one until now?

Simply put, the existence of them had slipped her mind.

"Well," Trixie prompted when Katherine had suddenly gone quiet, "do you need to call anyone?"

Katherine didn't need to be asked a third time, quickly snatching the phone from the woman's hand before she could change her mind. "Yes, thank you, that'd be great, wonderful even."

Trixie frowned at her disproportional enthusiasm, but shrugged. "No problem. I'll give you some privacy," she announced before trudging back up the steps of the truck.

Katherine's hands were shaking so badly the first two times she attempted to dial the number that'd been drilled into her head since childhood that twice she'd mixed up the digits and called the wrong number. The third time, though, she finally got it right, and as she listened to her home phone ring for the first time in months, her entire body trembled in anticipation.

Brrr-ing. Brrr-ing. Brrr-ing.

On the third ring, someone finally answered. "Hello?"

She wasn't sure if she was relieved or disappointed when the voice on the other end of the phone didn't belong to either of her parents. It took her a moment to respond. "S-Samantha? Is that you?"

A pause. "This is she. May I ask who is calling?"

Katherine nearly choked on her spit. Didn't her sister recognize her voice? "Sam? Oh my god, Sam, it's Katherine."

An even longer pause. "Katherine?"

Something was wrong. Sam didn't sound like someone who'd just been contacted by her sister who'd been missing for over half a year. She sounded… *furious.*

When she spoke again, her voice was ice. "Do you think this is funny?"

Katherine's stomach churned. "I – what? Why would I think this is funny? Sam? Can I talk to Mom or Dad? Please, this is important."

Her sister huffed into the phone. "Look, I don't know what kind of deranged pervert gets off on exasperating the pain of two people who've lost their daughter, but we've heard enough lies to last a lifetime. Don't call here again."

Katherine could feel the bile rising in her throat as panic gripped her. "What are you talking about? Sam, please!"

"I mean it. If you call here again, I'm contacting the police."

"What? No-"

The dial tone rang hollowly in Katherine's ears. Sam had hung up the phone.

Katherine gracelessly vomited onto the gravel, barely missing her cheap sandals. *Had people been calling pretending to be her?* She was tempted to get sick all over again and bent over at the waist, dry heaving.

"You okay, Katherine?" Trixie was half hanging out of the big rig, frowning in concern.

Hands still shaking, Katherine blithely wiped her mouth with the back of one of them. "Yeah, fine." *Not fine. At all.* "Must have been the burger."

She hardly slept the remainder of the night, tortured by the picture her sister had painted. She'd known, of course, that her parents would have been worried about her all these months, especially with the events that had led up to her disappearance, but she wasn't quite ready to face the reality of the pain that they'd surely been in. Pain undoubtedly similar to what she had endured when she'd thought she had lost them. Pain that could have been soothed, worry eased, by Bastian if he wasn't such an incorrigible liar. Burying her face into the lumpy pillow that Trixie had borrowed her, Katherine screamed.

She was a spacey mess the following morning, half-heartily participating in conversation that Trixie forced her to engage in. Katherine knew she should have been making more of an effort to be friendly – the woman was doing her an enormous favor, after all – but she could hardly help herself as the phone call she'd made the night before played on repeat inside her head. She grew more and more nervous – her tremors increasing – as they got closer and closer to their destination. She'd nearly gotten sick again when they'd passed a *Welcome to Iowa* sign, going as far to ask Trixie to pull over on the side of the road. While she hadn't vomited, she had yanked off the necklace she'd suddenly remembered was still around her neck and nearly threw the stupidly pretty thing into a cornfield. She couldn't quite bring herself to do it, though, and shoved it roughly into a pocket instead.

Unbelievably understanding, Trixie had let her rest under a light blanket in blessed silence the rest of the way to Middletown.

It was late in the evening when they finally arrived, and Trixie graciously let her out in front of her parents' house. It looked like the woman was waiting to make sure Katherine got safely inside, so she hesitantly approached what she used to think of as her home. It looked exactly the same as she remembered it. She stared at the door, debating on whether or not knocking would be appropriate.

In the end, she couldn't quite bring herself to walk in unannounced, and so, raising her hand, she gently rapped on the wooden slab behind which her unsuspecting family awaited.

Knock. Knock.

CHAPTER SIX

It was Katherine's father who answered the door.

Her breath was sucked from her body – she could physically feel her lungs deflating in her chest – as her eyes took in Benjamin Mayes.

He wasn't looking at her, his neck straining as he twisted his head and hollered into the area of the house Katherine knew to be the kitchen. "Yes, dear, green olives sound fine."

Even from his profile, however, she could see that the man she proudly called her father had changed in the seven months she'd been gone. His dark hair, which used to have only a gentle sprinkling of gray, was now almost completely covered in the washed out color. New worry lines had taken residence on his forehead and around the corners of his mouth as well.

"Extra pepperoni?" Over the loud palpitations of her heart, she dazedly recognized her mother's voice as the soft tenor reached her ears from where its owner resided, apparently somewhere in the kitchen.

Benjamin's head turned, his mouth already open to either answer his wife or greet whomever he thought it was at the door, when their eyes finally connected. A meeting of dark hazel and bright green.

It was almost comical the way his black pupils dilated, nearly completely covering his colorful irises as they were blown wide in shock.

Almost being the key word. Katherine's stomach, which was already twisted in all sorts of knots, somehow tightened further.

"K-Kit?"

Katherine forced herself to gulp in some much needed oxygen, blinking back tears at the nickname she hadn't heard in far too long. She tensed when one of her father's hands came up and slowly – ever so carefully – brushed a lock of disheveled hair out of her face. He rested his palm against her cheek. "Is it really you?"

She nodded jerkily. "Yes, it's me. D-dad-" she choked on the word, but it hardly mattered because she wasn't allowed to get out any more than that before her whole being was swept up into a hug so familiar and comforting that she could do little but melt into it.

She sniffled as her father pressed frenzied kisses into the crown of her hair. Words flew from his mouth so quickly that she was unable to catch them all, but they were some variation of "you're okay, you're okay," and "thank God" and "I love you."

She had missed her dad so much.

After a long moment, he pulled back, but didn't remove his hands from where they had come to rest on her shoulders. "Elaine," he muttered as he stared into Katherine's eyes. "Elaine!"

And then her mother was there.

Elaine Mayes popped into the room, concern puckering her brow. She had undoubtedly heard the same tremor in her husband's voice as Katherine had. When she saw why his voice had been shaking – when she saw Katherine – she stopped in her tracks, dropping the phone she'd been holding in her hand in the process. It landed with a dull *thud* on the carpet.

Katherine greedily took in the sight of her mother. Much like her father, she'd aged considerably in the time Katherine had been missing. While Elaine had always been thin, her cheeks were now alarmingly hollow, and dark bags pulled at the sagging skin under her eyes. Her blonde hair was pulled back tightly from her face, making the unhealthy changes even more prominent.

Irrational guilt churned Katherine's stomach.

Before she could submerge herself too deeply in the horrible feeling, however, her mother was in front of her, two bony hands grasping either side of her face as she stared, disbelieving eyes shining in amazement as they took Katherine in.

Then she was crushed into a hug even fiercer than the one her father had pulled her into.

Too soon, her mother pulled back. Mirroring her father's earlier actions, however, her hands refused to leave Katherine's shoulders. It was like her parents feared she'd disappear into thin air if they let her go. Her heart throbbed painfully inside her chest as the realization that *that* was exactly what they were afraid of dawned.

"Katherine," her mother spoke, her gravelly voice a dead give-away of the fact that tears were trapped in her throat. "Oh my God, sweetheart, we've been out of our minds with worry." Her hands fluttered around Katherine helplessly. "Are you okay?" She shook her head violently. "What am I saying? Of course you're not okay! You've been missing for months! What I mean is, are you hurt?" Her mom didn't even wait for an answer before ordering her dad to start the car. "We're taking you to the hospital."

Alarmed, Katherine caught and held onto her mother's restless hands. "I'm fine," she told her, injecting as much confidence as she could into the declaration.

Her mother's responding stare contained a hefty dose of skepticism.

"Truly," Katherine tried again, looking directly into her mother's eyes, both of which were sporting a thick sheen of tears. She hoped her mom could somehow sense the truth in her words as she said them. "I'm not hurt. I don't need to see a doctor."

Elaine took a deep breath, clearly fighting the urge to grab Katherine and drag her to the nearest hospital, whether her daughter thought she needed to go or not. "Okay," she finally acquiesced. "Okay. The hospital can wait."

Katherine cringed at the implication that she would indeed be forced to see a doctor at some point. *There was no way they'd be able to tell that she wasn't exactly human anymore... right?*

She comforted herself with the fact that her parents had taken her to Hayfield Medical the night she'd been bitten by Bastian, and the doctor she'd seen then hadn't noticed anything odd about her.

Not that she had noticed anything odd at that point either. She certainly hadn't known she was a werewolf.

"But, honey," Elaine spoke, and Katherine shook the memory off, focusing instead on her mother. The woman had maneuvered her hands so that they were now the ones holding onto her daughter's. "Where in the world have you been?"

"Oh. Um, well..." Katherine's lips were suddenly very, *very* dry, and her tongue felt ridiculously large in her mouth. So wrapped up in the turbulent emotions that the news of her parents' survival had evoked, it hadn't even occurred to her to come up with a cover story.

What was she going to tell them?

The truth? *Not likely.* She was liable to end up tucked away in an asylum by the end of the night if she spouted off that she was a werewolf.

"Elaine," Benjamin spoke up, unknowingly rescuing his daughter from having to answer the loaded question right then, "I'm sure Katherine will tell us everything, but look at her. She's dead on her feet. Let her rest, maybe take a shower. When Sam and Chad get here with the pizza, Katherine will tell us what she can remember, and we'll figure out what to do from there, okay?"

So it was Sam her mom had been on the phone with. She was more than a little nervous about the idea of reuniting with her sister after their blotched telephone conversation the night before.

Elaine reluctantly nodded in allowance of her husband's suggestion. "I suppose that makes sense."

"Okay with you, Katherine?"

Latching onto the opportunity to gather herself and think of a believable story, she immediately agreed as well. "A shower sounds wonderful."

Her mother allowed her to slip her hands free from where she'd been continuing to clutch at them, but swallowed Katherine up into another hug before she had even managed to take a single step from the crowded entryway. Her father, too, wrapped his arms around her once more.

"We're so glad you're home. We love you so much," Elaine whispered into her hair, choking on the words as she forced them out.

Katherine tightened the grip she had on both of her parents and returned the sentiment with equal feeling. “I love you too.”

A weight was lifted off her chest as she said the words – words she never thought she’d have another opportunity to say to her mom and dad. When her parents finally released her from their dual embrace, Katherine hid the tears that had gathered in her eyes by hurriedly turning and dashing up the stairs.

When she arrived at and opened her bedroom door – or at least what *used* to be her bedroom door – Katherine was hit with an overwhelming wave of déjà vu.

Her parents had kept her room exactly the same.

In fact, it looked as if it hadn’t been touched at all the entire half year that she’d been gone. Not a single one of her possessions had been moved. Nothing was out of place. Even the sleep shirt she could vaguely recall having worn the night before she’d been attacked by those hunters remained where she’d thrown it – a crumpled ball of fabric peeking out from under the bed.

The fact that her parents had ensured that her room went untouched, regardless of the knowledge that she’d likely never return home to see it, caused a fresh onslaught of tears to wet her eyes.

Unwilling to look at the beige walls or purple bedspread a moment longer, Katherine quickly grabbed the first clean outfit she could get her hands on – a faded pair of jeans and fitted red V-neck t-shirt – and rushed into the adjoining bathroom.

Ignoring the chill that swept through her as she undressed and her bare feet touched cold tile, Katherine forced herself to think. *What was she going to tell her parents?*

She allowed the hot water that jetted out of the ancient showerhead to drench her until it began to run cold. By the time she’d dried her hair and slipped on the clothes she’d haphazardly picked out, Katherine was fairly certain she’d thought of an idea that could work.

Practicing the story in her head as she exited her bedroom and hesitantly descended the stairs, she’d failed right away to notice the raised voices coming from the kitchen. As she got closer to the room, however, the loud arguing swiftly caught her attention.

"What do you mean, are we sure?" It was her mother, and Katherine didn't know if she'd ever heard the woman sound so upset. Or incredulous. "Do you think we're so desperate to get Katherine back that we'd mistake someone else for our own daughter? For your sister?"

Oh... Samantha. So her sister *had* arrived home with the pizza while she was in the shower.

"Of course not, Mom, that's not what I'm saying at all! I'm just concerned. You've been scammed before. I told you and dad how many times that offering that reward money was just asking for some scumbag to take advantage of you. How many calls have you gotten from lowlifes claiming to have information about her, or some girl or another claiming to actually *be* her? For God's sake, one such girl just called here yesterday."

For a moment, tense silence reigned.

It was her father who broke it, his voice deceptively calm. "Sam… why didn't you tell us this before?"

She heard her sister sigh, the exasperation in the loud huff all too obvious. "I'm sorry I didn't say anything, okay? I'm just sick of seeing you guys get your hopes up only to have them crushed over and over again. I can't just sit here and watch you two self-destruct anymore. Mom, Dad, Katherine… she's gone."

"Sam, Katherine isn't gone. She's upstairs taking a shower. And it was probably her who called here yesterday." Her dad sounded heartbroken.

Sam scoffed – actually scoffed. "What, that girl who just happened to show up while Chad and I were out? The one who you let roam around the house unsupervised? Sure, no one's actually had the audacity to appear at your doorstep before, but I wouldn't put it past the right wackjob. Fifty thousand dollars is certainly enough initiative for that."

Surprise finally caused Katherine to reveal herself, and she hesitantly stepped into the kitchen where her parents, Samantha, and her sister's husband, Chad, were gathered around the center island.

"Fifty thousand dollars?"

Her sister had her back towards her, but Katherine could still see the way her shoulders stiffened as she undoubtedly recognized her voice from the phone call they'd shared the night before. After a long, tension-filled moment, Sam turned to face her.

Whatever barb she had readied to deliver, however, must have gotten lost on her tongue when their eyes connected. Sam's gray orbs widened in recognition, her jaw slackening and yammering up and down in astonishment. But not a single word escaped her.

"Hi, Sam."

That was all it took to snap her out of her shocked stupor. Her sister shakily approached, hesitating for only a second before wrapping her arms around Katherine's rigid shoulders. "Katherine, I... I'm so sorry. I didn't know."

"It's okay." She didn't know if it *really* was, but was grateful, at least, that her sister seemed to have been looking out for their parents while she'd been gone.

Sam pulled away, a glossy sheen of tears in her eyes as she took Katherine in. Judging by her own blurred vision, Katherine's orbs were sporting the same revealing shine. "Your hair is longer than I remember," Sam said after a while. "It looks... nice."

Katherine offered a watery smile. "Your hair is shorter." It was. Her sister, who'd worn her hair long for as long as Katherine could remember, had cut it into a short bob that curled attractively around her ears. "It looks great."

Sam nodded. When she spoke again, her voice was softer and, well... *nicer* than Katherine could recall it being in a long time. "I've missed you."

Katherine swallowed. "I've missed you too."

It was true. She and Sam had a complicated relationship – too different in too many ways to always *like* each other. But they did without a doubt love each other, and that was all that really mattered.

Katherine allowed her sister to pull her into another uncharacteristically warm embrace. When the blonde released her, however, she was slightly dismayed to find Chad waiting for a hug as well. She wasn't particularly fond of her sister's husband and since she wasn't related to him by blood, felt no obligation to pretend to be.

There wasn't anything outwardly wrong with him. Chad was classically handsome, Katherine supposed, with light brown hair arranged in a purposeful mess and green eyes a few shades darker than her own emerald orbs. And while he wasn't exactly tall, he wasn't short either.

Ultimately, he was pleasant-looking enough, but with an altogether forgettable appearance.

But what Katherine didn't find forgettable – or forgivable, for that matter – was the way he'd cornered her in the hallway at his own wedding reception, drunkenly propositioning her for a kiss.

"Don't you want to properly welcome your new brother-in-law to the family?"

She could still remember word for word what he'd said to her as he'd leaned in with an all too eager grin.

Of course, she'd blatantly refused him. And when she'd threatened to tell Sam what he'd said, Chad had insisted he was teasing and that Katherine would only make herself out to be a dippy little girl who couldn't take a joke if she told anyone.

In the end, she *had* kept quiet about the incident. Partially because she was afraid that he was right – that it *was* a joke and she was being silly – but mostly because she knew it *wasn't* one, and that it'd hurt Sam if she ever found out about it.

"Come here," Chad insisted, and Katherine didn't have a chance to object before he was forcefully wrapping his own arms around her. Katherine endured the uncomfortable embrace for only a moment – painstakingly aware of how close his hands were to her bottom – before jerking away from her brother-in-law and returning her attention to Sam and her parents, intent on forgetting that he was even in the room at all.

"Mom, Dad, is what Sam said true? You were offering a fifty

thousand dollar reward for anyone with information about me?" She could scarcely believe it, having no idea where her parents had come up with that kind of money.

"Katherine, we would have paid anyone *anything* if we'd thought it would help get you home safely." Her mother ran her fingers through Katherine's damp hair, clearly still amazed that she *was* home.

"It's not that I didn't want you home and safe, too," Sam protested. "I just didn't think that offering a reward for any information that led to your whereabouts was very practical. And I was right, too – all it did was bring homeless miscreants and drug addicts desperate for cash out of the woodwork."

Katherine internally cringed at the way Sam referred to those who were less fortunate that her.

"Anyway, my objections notwithstanding, Chad decided to borrow the money to them, which I can admit that despite my very *valid* reservations, was actually really generous of him." She glanced at her husband, the slightest hint of approval in the smile on her lips.

Katherine tried not to retch.

Chad worked for his father's accounting firm – she didn't think she could remember the pretentious name of it if her life depended on it – but from what Katherine understood, he was a manager of some sort – at least in name. She wasn't sure if he actually *did* anything.

"Anything for you, sweetheart," Chad said, pressing a kiss into Samantha's hair and throwing Katherine a wink at the same time.

Creep.

Elaine practically pushed Katherine into one of the chairs surrounding the kitchen island. Grabbing a plate from the cupboard, she loaded it with pizza covered in what used to be her favorite toppings – green olives and pepperoni – and set it down in front of her. "Eat, honey," she ordered firmly.

Katherine tried not to gag at the smell of the olives and forced down a bite to appease her mother – even if it did remind her of the cheap slice of cardboard she'd bought at that run down gas station just yesterday. Her mom cleared her throat after Katherine had somehow managed to cram down an entire slice, not even pretending to eat the one she'd dished up for herself. "Honey, please, will you tell us what happened? Where have you been all this time?"

Katherine glanced around the tiny table at the imploring faces that demanded answers, and for a second the story she'd concocted deserted her.

"The last time anyone saw you," her father interjected, "the last time *I* saw you," he corrected himself, closing his eyes, "was when our home was being invaded by those depraved burglars. One of them was discovered dead near the stairway by paramedics, but the other man was never found by the police. We hoped, God knows how we've hoped, but Katherine, we were almost certain that he'd taken you, and that… and that we'd lost you forever." He pressed the palms of his hands into his eyes in a valiant effort to hold back tears.

Katherine's bottom lip trembled as she watched her dad fight to control his emotions. "He didn't get me. I'm fine, dad, I promise. I'm right here and I'm fine."

"But if you weren't with that man, then where were you?" her mother asked.

About this, she'd decided she could tell the truth. "In Canada."

Her parents were utterly bewildered. "Canada? *What?* Katherine, how did you end up there?"

Katherine took a deep breath, preparing herself for the lie that was about to come tumbling out of her mouth. "I don't know."

"What do you mean you don't know? How can that be?"

"I'm so sorry, Mom, Dad, Sam," she said, taking the time to look them each in the face, "but I haven't come home all this time because until yesterday I'd completely forgotten that I had one."

"What are you saying, Katherine?"

"Amnesia, Mom. I've had amnesia."

CHAPTER SEVEN

She was *so* full of crap.

But in many ways, it was the perfect excuse.

By claiming to have had amnesia, Katherine was allowing herself to tell her family at least pieces of the truth.

She began spinning her tale, mixing truth and fiction to the best of her ability, blurring them together in what she hoped was a believable story. She stuck to the truth as much as possible. It *was* true that she'd been living in Canada. That she'd been found by a man named Bastian and his group of friends who'd collectively decided to take her in. That she'd been taken care of and treated very well by them.

She simply omitted the fact that Bastian, Sophie, Markus, Zane, and Caleb were all werewolves – that *she* was a werewolf now, too. And, of course, she didn't mention that it was Bastian who'd bitten her and turned her into one the first place – that, really, *he* was the one ultimately responsible for her disappearance.

Her father already hadn't taken too kindly to the fact that a man – a mere eighteen-year-old at the time, even, as she'd explained to her captive audience – had had the audacity to take in a young girl he'd founding wandering the streets of Fort Saskatchewan.

It'd been an outright lie, of course.

But what was she supposed to tell them? That Bastian had, in actuality, kidnapped her because he'd turned her into what they undoubtedly believed to be an imaginary creature?

No, thank you.

"What in the hell was this guy thinking?" her dad asked incredulously as she finished her story. "He finds a teenage girl stumbling around, clearly lost and confused, and instead of taking her straight to the nearest police station, he brings her home with him?" Splotchy patches of red exploded across his face. "He didn't," he paused, looking pained for a moment, "he didn't coerce you into doing anything you didn't want to do, did he? Anything that made you uncomfortable?"

It was Katherine's turn to grow as red as a freshly ripe tomato. Her dad had basically just asked if Bastian had molested her, after all. "What? *No!* No, Dad, I swear, nothing like that happened. Bastian is actually really nice." To her, at least. Or she'd thought he had been before she'd found out what an unconscionable liar he was.

"As nice as you claim this Bastian character to be," Elaine's tone couldn't have made her doubt of that any more obvious, "why *didn't* he take you to the police station when he found you?"

Katherine chewed nervously on the soft flesh of her bottom lip. "That was my fault. I begged him not to. At the time I had no idea who I was or what had happened to me. All I could remember was my name."

That answer, blatant lie as it was, resulted in more questions.

"What do you mean, what had happened to you?" Benjamin immediately demanded.

"Katherine, I thought you said you hadn't been hurt!" Elaine exclaimed at the same time.

Crap.

"I had a head wound," she quickly explained.

Katherine actually believed that to be true. On the night she'd fled from her house, she could vividly recall that the hunter who'd given chase had smashed her head into her car before she'd evaded his clutches. She'd felt dizzy and nauseous afterwards and had ended up vomiting and passing out at the gas station that Bastian had later met up with her at. She probably *had* been concussed. The concussion just hadn't resulted in any memory loss.

"I'm not sure how I got it," she lied, "but it was probably what caused the temporary amnesia. Anyway, it had crossed my mind that I was a runaway or in some sort of trouble with the law, so I convinced Bastian to take me home with him instead of contacting the police." So very, *very* untrue. Bastian had dragged her protesting, mopey behind all the way to Haven Falls.

Her parents continued to fire questions at her.

"And how exactly did an eighteen year old come to own a house?" her mother asked, clearly having been perturbed by that part of her story. "And why was he sharing it with these friends of his?"

Katherine licked her bottom lip, tracing the tiny, sensitive injury her nervous chewing had left there. "His parents died a few years ago and left it to him and his sister, along with a pretty hefty bank account." *True.* "They share it with their friends because it's close to the college that they all attend." *Complete bullshit.*

Her mom seemed accepting of the answer though. Before the woman could ask anything else, however, her sister finally shot out an inquiry of her own. "How'd you get that scar on your face?"

It was the only question anyone had asked that had truly taken her by surprise thus far. Katherine had almost completely forgotten about the pink scar that ran the length of the left side of her face from temple to chin. Its appearance had very much faded since she'd first acquired it months ago, but she supposed it was pretty noticeable to her family, who had never seen it fresh.

"A freak animal attack," she finally managed to force out when Sam raised her eyebrows expectantly. "It happened in the woods outside Bastian's house." At her family's aghast expressions, she quickly added, "Don't worry, he killed the animal responsible."

That was a version of the truth, Katherine supposed.

As her parents continued to question her, Katherine quickly realized she'd have to revert to the go-to answer she'd readily supplied herself with when she'd claimed to have had amnesia. She just hoped that her supposed ignorance was believable.

"Do you have any idea at all how you ended up in Canada?"

"I'm sorry, but I really don't know. There are still a lot of blank spots in my memory. The last thing I clearly remember before waking up in Fort Saskatchewan is you, Dad." Looking down and refusing to meet his beckoning gaze, Katherine began playing with a loose thread on the fringe of her shirt. "You were bleeding out on the floor, telling me to run."

She was pulled into the reassuring arms of her father for a third time that night, and Katherine reveled in the simplicity of being able to bury her face into his shirt and seek comfort in his strong embrace – it was a sensation that just two days ago she never thought she'd get to experience again.

"Do you remember anything about what happened at the house? The men who attacked us?" he asked gently. She could hear him hesitate for a moment before adding, "They were asking after you – demanding to know where you were. Do you know why?"

Katherine clutched her father's shirt even more tightly in her fists. B*ecause they were hunters. And she was a werewolf.* "No, I have no idea."

She felt him nod, a large hand coming up to soothingly rub her back. "Okay. It's okay."

Her dad allowed her to pull away from him after a few more minutes of mutually drawing comfort from each other. Before she could settle back into her chair, however, Sam asked a follow up question that had Katherine's already coiled muscles tensing further. "One of the men who broke into the house was found dead near the bottom of the stairs. According to the coroner's report, he'd literally been ripped to pieces. Obviously you aren't nearly strong – or vicious – enough to pull off something like that, but do you have any idea how it happened? Did his partner kill him? How did he do it?"

Both of her parents shot Sam disapproving looks, clearly afraid that the question would distress Katherine, but her sister shrugged unapologetically. "I'm just curious," she defended herself.

Katherine already knew, of course, that Bastian had killed the deceased hunter, but until that moment, she'd never heard how. Considering the fact that the hunter he'd killed had had a hand in murdering his parents and had nearly succeeded in offing hers as well, however, Katherine could hardly bring herself to be upset by the revelation. "No, I'm sorry. I don't know anything about it."

They all seemed to readily accept that answer, and as they reached the end of their interrogation – Katherine could think of no other word that appropriately described the barrage of questions her family had just thrown at her – she took the opportunity to glean a little knowledge of her own.

After all, what had happened after she'd been chased away from her home on that fateful night had been haunting her for months.

"So," she began hesitantly, "what happened after you told me to run, Dad? How badly hurt were you and Mom? How did you end up getting help in time?"

But it wasn't her father who answered. It was her mother.

Elaine frowned, her eyebrows puckering together in confusion. "I was never injured, honey. I wasn't home when those horrid men broke in. I had just finished making supper – beef stew, I remember – when I realized we were out of dinner rolls, so I told your father to keep an eye on the food for me while I ran to the grocery store uptown. I bumped into Ester Johnson while I was there, and you know that old bird, she insisted on unloading all the neighborhood gossip she'd collected over the week onto me." Her mom allowed an ironic smile to briefly grace her face. "Oddly enough, she was talking to me about you. She told me she'd seen you talking to some strange man outside of her house," her mom shook her head, "or some nonsense like that."

Katherine blanched and hoped her parents didn't notice her suddenly pale complexion. She vividly recalled running into Bastian in front of Mrs. Johnson's house all those months ago. Of course, back then, she'd had no idea who he was – *what* he was.

Thankfully, neither of them seemed to take note of her sudden pastiness. In fact, her mother's eyes glazed over as she became an unwilling prisoner to her memories. "When I got home, the first thing I saw was that the garage door had been destroyed," she relayed softly. "Minutes later, I found your dad unconscious in the dining room, covered in blood. Our belongings were in shambles. Your friend Brad was buried under what used to be our table. I called 9-1-1 and they were both rushed to the hospital in Hayfield." She paused and audibly swallowed. "I hadn't even realized that you'd been home, too, until your dad woke up from emergency surgery – the doctors had to remove his spleen – and told me." She sniffled and Katherine's heart ached for her mother. It obviously pained her to relive the memory. "I kept calling your phone. I remember being so angry with you for not answering," she admitted. "I left nearly a dozen furious voicemails for you before I realized that you… that you were *gone*. God, I felt like an awful mother."

Katherine reached out to her mom, wrapping her arms around the distressed woman's neck in what she hoped was a comforting embrace. "It's okay, Mom. You didn't know."

Elaine immediately huddled her daughter closer. "We reported you missing right away, of course. As soon as your father woke up and told me that you'd been in the house too. Due to the circumstances of your disappearance, the police suspected you'd been kidnapped." She took a deep breath. "Your car was found nearly a hundred miles away at some remote gas station called Gary's Rest Stop, but there wasn't any other sign that you had been there. With no further clues, your trail quickly turned cold, so your father and I came up with the idea of offering a monetary reward to anyone with information that led to us finding you. I swear we never stopped looking, honey."

"I know, Mom, I know," she assured her clearly distraught mother. After a moment, Elaine allowed Katherine to slowly extricate herself from where she sat, practically in her lap.

"Sam and Chad have been so helpful," Elaine added, wiping away the tears that streaked her face in an embarrassed manner. "They moved in right away when they heard what had happened and that you were missing."

Katherine glanced her sister's way, hoping Sam could somehow sense the immense gratitude that swelled within her at the revelation. "Thank you," Katherine mouthed to the blonde.

Sam nodded.

Katherine's green eyes shifted to once again meet her mother's teary gaze. "And what about Brad? You said that he was taken to the hospital with Dad. Is... Is he okay?"

Please let the answer be yes.

"He's alive," Elaine answered meekly after a fleeting silence.

The corners of Katherine's mouth dipped into a frown. She was relieved, of course, that her classmate had survived the savage attack that the hunters had waged on her home, but was highly suspicious of the solemn way her mother had announced his survival.

Before she could query her mother further, however, her father surprised her with a question of his own. "So where is this Bastian person that took you in? Did he drive you here? If... if what you said is true, I'd like to thank him personally for keeping my daughter safe all this time."

The request had the contents of her stomach suddenly churning with something that felt ridiculously similar to guilt. She was taken off guard by the intense emotion. And positively furious when she recognized it for what it was.

Regret.

Because she certainly didn't regret lying to her parents the way she had. She didn't feel the least bit of remorse about leaving them in the dark about her newly acquired creature status and untimely introduction to the supernatural world.

No. She felt guilty for leaving Haven Falls the way she had. She regretted abandoning Bastian without giving the man a chance to explain himself.

And she was furious because she knew logically that she *shouldn't* feel that way at all. Katherine gripped the underside of the wooden island countertop as tightly as she could in an effort to suppress both of the unpleasant emotions.

Her father cleared his throat, and Katherine abruptly realized that she had yet to answer his questions. "Uh, no, he didn't drive me. He's still in Canada as far as I know. My memory came back to me so suddenly that in my shock, I took off without telling him or anyone else what had happened. I actually hitchhiked here."

"What?!"

"Katherine, do you know how dangerous that is?"

Just as she had suspected it would, that admission earned her an immediate lecture. But Katherine tuned out her parents' voices, only able to truly focus on the absolutely *absurd* regret that was gnawing away at her insides.

She had every reason in the world to be infuriated with Bastian – every reason in the world to run from him.

The man had outright lied to her.

But a small part of her still couldn't believe that he'd actually done it. It insisted that he had to have had a good reason, at least. But try as Katherine might to think of even the flimsiest of excuses for his behavior, she came up empty. Nothing she could think of could justify what he had done.

He'd told her that her parents were dead.

He knew firsthand the pain of losing one's mother and father and yet he'd still done it. He knew how awful she felt about what had happened to them – knew how much her heart ached for them – and yet he'd continued to deceive her for *months*. For God's sake, he'd held her in the forest only two nights ago as she broke down about having to celebrate her birthday without them and *still*, he hadn't told her that they were alive.

In fact, all evidence seemed to point towards the conclusion that he'd been prepared to let her believe the godawful lie he'd told her until she herself was dead in the ground.

The betrayal stung something fierce. And yet her double crossing heart still had the nerve to feel regret.

As if what Bastian had done didn't make her want to vomit.

Forcefully jerking herself out of her spiraling thoughts, Katherine spoke out, thoughtlessly interrupting her mother as she continued to scold her about the dangers of hitchhiking. "I'm tired," she blurted, roughly rubbing her closed eyes with the palms of her hands. "Is it okay if I go to bed now?"

Benjamin sighed and Elaine's stern expression softened. Her father wrapped a comforting arm around her shoulders. "Of course, kiddo. We'll talk more about all of this tomorrow, okay?"

Katherine nodded. "Alright."

"And," her mother quickly interjected as Katherine moved to stand up from her chair, "we're going to get you thoroughly checked out by a doctor first thing in the morning. No objections."

Katherine cringed. "Okay," she agreed, knowing she didn't really have a choice in the matter.

With that, she fled the kitchen.

She hadn't been lying when she'd told her parents she was tired. As she huddled under the covers of what used to be her bed, however, her chaotic thoughts refused to let her drift off. It didn't help that despite the heaviness of her eyelids and the aching in her limbs, her bed didn't feel like it belonged to her any longer. The mattress was too small and too soft. The comforter was too heavy, the pillows too lumpy. No matter what way she positioned herself, she couldn't get comfortable.

What made it all even worse was that every time the Sandman nearly had her under his spell, the door to her bedroom would noisily creak open. Her parents weren't exactly subtle about checking in on her. She could hardly blame them, though, even as night gave way to morning and she'd yet to get any semblance of sleep.

It was as the pink and orange hues of the sunrise began to stream through her window's blinds that she was finally able to doze off.

What felt like mere minutes later, she was awakened by her mother's thin fingers softly stroking her hair. "Rise and shine, Katherine. This morning is going to be a long one."

Somehow she managed to drag herself out of bed and change into some clean clothes.

After her mom fixed her breakfast – a couple of sausage patties jammed between two buttermilk biscuits – Katherine was ushered into her parents' car, where they preceded to drive her to Hayfield Medical for the dreaded hospital visit that they'd promised the night before.

Apparently they'd called ahead, and Katherine was immediately whisked into a private room the moment they stepped foot into the pristine building. It was on the tip of her tongue to object when she realized that the room was located in the pediatrics unit, but she supposed at only seventeen she *was* still considered a kid in most people's eyes.

Even if after everything she'd been through she felt like anything but.

A smiling nurse donning pink scrubs quickly recorded her height – 5'3" as always – and weight – a whopping 117 pounds – before running a thermometer over her forehead in one smooth swipe before it even occurred to Katherine to object.

Both the nurse's eyebrows shot up as she jotted down the results onto an official looking chart. "102.7 degrees. Are you feeling alright, dear?"

Crap.

Katherine's teeth clamped down on the flesh of her inner cheek. She'd completely forgotten that her body's base temperature had risen dramatically since being changed into a werewolf. Thankfully, the nurse didn't seem to expect a response to her question as she busied herself attaching Katherine's arm to a blood pressure machine.

The machine tightened around her bicep before it beeped and began to relax its grip on her arm. The nurse frowned. "Your blood pressure is a bit low," she explained to Katherine as she wrote down those results as well. "That can be due to a number of things, the mostly likely culprit being exhaustion." She pointedly eyed the dark shadows Katherine knew to be present under her eyes. "It's still in the normal range," she assured her. "Just a bit concerning when taking your fever into consideration."

The woman handed her a papery, pale green hospital gown to change into. "Why don't you slip this on? I'll give you some privacy and go fetch the doctor."

As the door clicked closed behind the nurse, Katherine reluctantly stripped and poked her arms through the holes of the oversized gown, looping the attached strings behind her back before tying them in front of her waist. The gown was intended to be backless, but was large enough for Katherine to cover herself completely. She was thankful as she didn't exactly fancy her rear end hanging out for all to see.

Even if the only ones around to see it *were* medical professionals.

A sharp knock on the door signaled the arrival of the doctor.

"Come in," Katherine called, taking a seat on the exam table in the corner of the room.

A tall woman with her hair pulled back into a severe bun, who Katherine assumed to be the doctor, entered the room, followed by the nurse who'd taken her vitals. The doctor wasn't dressed in typical hospital garb, but rather a flattering, crème pant suit. Her greeting smile was friendly enough, but also detached – clinical. "Hello there, Katherine, I'm Dr. Morgan and I'll be performing your health examination today."

Dr. Morgan quickly flipped through the chart the nurse handed her before offering Katherine a hand to shake. The small brunette hesitantly did so.

"Do you have any aches and pains in addition to your fever?" she asked once Katherine had resettled herself.

Katherine furrowed her brows. "No," she admitted cautiously.

"Hmm. How about any allergies?"

She shook her head. "None that I know of."

"In that case, I'm going to recommend alternating Ibuprofen and Acetaminophen every four hours until your fever goes down, alright?"

As soon as Katherine nodded her head in acceptance of the recommendation, Dr. Morgan disentangled her stethoscope from around her neck. "I'm going to start my examination by listening to your heart and lungs," she explained bluntly. "Is it alright if I move your gown around a little?"

Katherine nodded her permission, wincing as the cold, metal device touched her bare skin. She inhaled, exhaled, and held her breath as the doctor instructed.

"Perfect," Dr. Morgan praised, before moving on to check her eyes, ears, and nose. Those too were given her stamp of approval.

Katherine's face heated slightly when the doctor asked to examine her breasts next, but she obligingly slipped off enough of the hospital gown so that it was hanging from her waist before lying back on the exam table.

When Dr. Morgan was finished, she quickly pulled back on the top portion of her gown. She was surprised, though, when instead of performing a pelvic exam next, the doctor allowed her to sit back up.

"Alright, Katherine, before I assess you any further, I have a sensitive question to ask."

Katherine folded her arms across her chest, not even an inkling of an idea of what that question could be. "Okay?"

"When your mother called and made this appointment for you, she mentioned that you've been being housed by an unknown male for the past several months. Is that information correct?"

Katherine frowned. "I suppose to her he's," she used her fingers to emphasis the implied quotation marks around the words, "an unknown male. But *I* know him."

Dr. Morgan pursed her lips. "Yes, well be that as it may, she's concerned that you may have been forced into having nonconsensual intercourse with this man."

...What?

Katherine could literally feel the blood rushing to her head as the words "nonconsensual intercourse" echoed in her ears – the sensation causing an unexpected surge of dizziness to pass through her.

Aware that an angry flush had exploded across her cheeks and was slowly spreading to the rest of her face, Katherine tried without to success to compose herself. "What?" she deadpanned.

"I'm asking your permission to perform a rape kit," the doctor clarified. "It's a fairly invasive procedure, but the evidence garnered from it is often essential in successfully convicting sex offenders."

Katherine's brain had stopped functioning after the "r-word" had escaped the doctor's mouth.

Rape. Her mother had essentially accused Bastian of rape when she'd spoken to Dr. Morgan.

For a moment, hysterical laughter threatened to bubble up her throat. For God's sake, Katherine had been practically begging the abstentious man to touch her for months.

At least she had been before she'd discovered what a heinous liar he was.

And just like that the urge to laugh vanished.

But the anger was still there, brewing deep in the pit of her belly.

"Get my mom," she forced out between gritted teeth when it became apparent that the doctor was still waiting for a response from her. "Please get her right *now*."

The pink-clad nurse who'd been silently observing the exam thus far immediately obliged, exiting the room and returning with Katherine's mother in seconds.

Pure concern radiated from Elaine as she took in Katherine's blotchy, red face. "What's wrong?"

Still perched atop the uncomfortable exam table, she jerked her hand away when her mother attempted to give it a comforting squeeze. She used it to gesture choppily at the doctor, who looked on benignly. "Did you tell this woman that it was okay to perform a rape kit on me?" she demanded.

Her mother wilted under her obvious ire. "It was only a suggestion, Katherine," she answered softly, "and only to be done with your permission."

"Why even *suggest* it when I told you that Bastian didn't touch me?"

Elaine frowned. "I was just concerned, honey. I didn't mean to embarrass you."

"Embarrass me?" Katherine was *livid.* "I'm pissed that you could accuse the man who took care of me the past half a year of something so vile." As much as she despised the lies Bastian had told her, she couldn't fight the innate urge to defend him. "I promise, Mom, I'm just as much a virgin now as the day I disappeared, okay?"

Elaine raised her hands in the universal sign of surrender. "Alright, alright. I believe you. I'm sorry. It's just that I'm your mom; it's my job to worry about you." Her eyes were suspiciously wet.

Katherine sighed, her anger deflating at the sight. Tension fled her stiff shoulders like air escaping a punctured balloon. "I know, Mom. It's okay." She glanced at the doctor. "No rape kit," she reiterated.

What did they think it would accomplish anyway? Even if she had been raped at some point, which she definitely *hadn't*, evidence of the act would have certainly been gone by now.

Dr. Morgan nodded agreeably to the order and Elaine hesitantly took her leave from the room.

After *that,* the pelvic exam was a piece of cake.

The blood draws and MRI scan Dr. Morgan ordered for her head – she was understandably concerned that Katherine was supposedly experiencing memory blanks from a concussion that had also triggered temporary amnesia seven months earlier – were completed without fuss as well.

They were told they'd receive the results of several tests they planned to run on the MRI images within a few weeks.

Unfortunately, the trip to the county courthouse that her parents insisted they take after the hospital visit didn't go nearly as smoothly.

The sheriff's office was located in the courthouse, and as soon as they arrived at the building, they were ushered into said office, a middle aged man with an impressive handlebar mustache greeting them as they crammed themselves into the cramped space. According to the metal plaque on the desk, the man was Sheriff Jamison Sanders.

He confirmed this as he introduced himself and handed her parents a small bundle of paper work they needed to fill out in order to withdraw the missing person's report they had filed back in October. After they'd finished with that, he invited all three of them to follow him into a more private room in the back of the building.

"I just need to ask Katherine a few questions," he said when her father asked why.

Dread caused Katherine's stomach to churn.

He led them to what was essentially an interrogation room. It was only slightly larger than the man's office, a small metal table and a handful of matching chairs surrounding it the only pieces of furniture – if they could even be considered that – filling the space. Katherine immediately spotted the blinking camera in the corner of the room.

Sheriff Sanders invited them to sit.

"Okay, Ms. Mayes, your mom and dad explained to me that you're suffering from some memory loss when they called to let me know you were coming in this morning. Nevertheless, I'm going to need you to tell me everything you can remember from the night you disappeared. Any detail, no matter how insignificant it may seem to you, could be helpful in tracking down the man who wounded your father and classmate."

Katherine took a deep breath and slowly let it out, preparing herself to lie. "Well, the last thing I can clearly recall is getting home from school that evening – cheerleading practice ran late, I remember – and finding my dad lying in a pool of blood on our dining room floor. He told me to run."

"And what's your next conscious memory?"

"Waking up on the streets of Fort Saskatchewan and meeting the man who has looked after me the last seven months."

The sheriff frowned, the heavy wrinkles of his brow becoming even more pronounced. "And what is this man's name?"

Katherine hesitated, but she'd already told her parents his name and couldn't very well withhold it now. "Bastian."

The sheriff glanced up from the small notepad that he was dutifully squiggling on. "And does this Bastian have a last name?"

Katherine licked her lips. Of course he had a last name – Prince. "Smith."

She hadn't even been aware she intended to lie until she'd gone and done it.

"Smith?" Sheriff Sanders asked incredulously.

She didn't blame him. The alias she'd blurted out *had* been terribly unimaginative.

"That's what she said," her dad answered immediately, and Katherine's lips quirked into a small, grateful smile.

The questions continued, the sheriff requesting far more details from her than either of her parents had. She did her best to repeat the same story she's told to them to the no-nonsense man.

He didn't seem particularly pleased with her, however, when she claimed to not remember the address of the house she'd been staying at all this time. "Canada" wasn't nearly specific enough for him. He also seemed doubtful of the fact that Bastian and his group of friends didn't have cell phones.

Still, it wasn't until she refused to sit down with a sketch artist that Sherriff Sanders began to lose his patience.

"Why won't you allow a drawing of this man to be made? Does this Bastian *Smith* even exist?"

"Are you calling my daughter a liar?" Her father was out of his seat before she could blink.

"Of course not," the man immediately denied, "but I do find it awfully suspicious that she's left us no possible way to find or even make contact this man to collaborate her story. With all due respect, Mr. Mayes, for all we know, this could be the man who was behind the attack on your home in October."

Even the very tips of Katherine's ears turned fire engine red at the insinuation. "Bastian is *not* a criminal and that is precisely why I don't want to sit down with a sketch artist. He doesn't deserve to have his face plastered all over the news, reporters connecting it to a crime that he did *not* commit."

Her mother wrapped a comforting arm around Katherine's shoulders. "Sheriff Sanders is just trying to help, honey."

Katherine snorted derisively.

Benjamin, at least, recognized the stubborn set of his daughter's jaw and knew she was done talking.

"Katherine said no," he reiterated to the sheriff. "Now, do you have any other questions for us or can we go home? It's been a long morning."

Sherriff Sanders sighed in defeat, shaking his head. "No, I suppose that's it then." His eyes met Katherine's briefly before he pulled himself out of his chair. "I'm really glad to see you home safe, Ms. Mayes."

The man seemed sincere enough so Katherine let go of just a bit of the resentment that she'd allowed to fill her when he'd suggested that Bastian was some sort of dangerous criminal. "Thanks," she muttered, allowing her dad to pull her out of her own seat.

Katherine spent the ride home mulling over her cover story. She could tell that Sheriff Sanders didn't believe her tale, and though his skepticism worried her a bit, she was also relieved that it seemed as if he was willing to leave well enough alone.

In was well after noon by the time her father pulled the vehicle into their driveway. Katherine made a beeline for the kitchen, impatiently peeling back the cover of the leftover chicken and rice dish that her mother had informed her was in the refrigerator before heating it up in the microwave.

She was busy scarfing the meal down when her sister strolled into the room. "Slow down, Katherine," she scolded. "You're not an animal."

Katherine fought the urge to roll her eyes. *Little did Sam know.*

"And wipe off your face when you're done. I'm taking you to the salon – my treat."

Katherine nearly choked on a piece of chicken. "What? Why?"

Sam shrugged. "Think of it as a belated birthday present."

Katherine frowned. "Don't I get a say in this?" she protested.

A trip to the salon wasn't exactly her idea of a good time.

Sam raised an expertly groomed eyebrow, pointedly eyeing the hair that she'd slung into a sloppy bun earlier that morning. "I like your hair long, but it's still in desperate need of a trim. We won't even talk about the condition of your fingernails."

Katherine couldn't resist the urge to glance down at them, but she couldn't say what it was her sister found wrong with them. They weren't perfectly manicured like Sam's were, but when had they ever been?

"Mom, Dad, can I take Katherine to the salon?"

"I don't know," her mother hesitated. It was clear that she was reluctant to let Katherine out of her sight.

Sam huffed. "We're just going to go get our hair done. The salon is literally ten minutes away. Katherine will be perfectly safe."

"I suppose that's fine," her mother relented under the weight of Sam's admittedly sound logic. "Just be back by supper."

And that was how Katherine found herself being unwillingly dragged into Samantha's shiny Cadillac sedan. It was a showy red color, perfectly showcasing the excess of money Sam had access to as Chad's wife.

"So," Samantha began as she smoothly pulled out of the garage, "I have to admit to having an ulterior motive for getting you out of the house. Tell me the truth. I know you didn't want to admit it in front of Mom and Dad, but is there something going on between you and this Bastian character? Something more than friendship?"

Katherine was so taken off guard that she didn't immediately deny it, and a smirk pulled at Samantha's lips. "There is, isn't there? I knew it."

Katherine sighed. "It's complicated," she hedged, crossing her arms in front of her chest defensively as she watched the blurred landscape pass by out of the passenger's side window.

"Well, do you love him?"

Despite everything, her entire being irrefutably knew the answer to her sister's question. It was *yes*. She did love him.

But that wasn't what she said. "I don't know."

Sam glanced slyly at her out of the corner of her eye before turning her attention back to the road. "Have you had sex?"

"What?" Katherine sputtered, glaring at her sister and futilely attempting to hide her rapidly reddening cheeks with her hands. "Of course not!"

Sam laughed outright at her response before surprising Katherine by nodding her head approvingly. "Good. You shouldn't have sex with anyone unless you're sure that you love him and he loves you."

Katherine raised an eyebrow at the surprisingly thoughtful bit of sisterly advice. "That's true," she agreed quietly.

When Sam spoke again, Katherine couldn't even begin to hope

to hide her shock. "Chad and I are getting a divorce."

What?

Despite the unease Katherine frequently experienced around her sister's husband, Sam and Chad had always appeared to be the perfect, loving couple when they were together – the couple other twosomes could only aspire to someday be.

"Don't tell anyone," she quickly added before Katherine could respond to the news. "I haven't had a chance to tell Mom and Dad yet. Chad and I were planning on doing it this weekend actually, but then... well, you came home."

Katherine felt remarkably like she was being scolded for ruining her sister's plans and a small frown pulled at her lips.

"It's been coming for a while," Sam continued, seemingly ignorant of Katherine's discomfort. "When we moved to Middletown to help out Mom and Dad after you'd disappeared, the distance between us only grew. It was the final nail in the coffin, really."

Katherine cringed. "Sorry," she said softly, sensing the hidden blame in the words.

"Don't be silly," her sister dismissed her with a wave of her hand. She didn't say that it wasn't her fault though, and Katherine couldn't help but to feel hurt.

Before she could dwell on it too much, however, they'd arrived at the salon, and Samantha pulled her car in front of the small building that declared itself Main Street All-in-One Beauty Parlor in glittery letters above the wooden slab that served as its front door.

A bell above the door made a resounding *ding* as they entered.

They were immediately greeted by a cheery, robust woman who introduced herself as Tamara. She helped Katherine into a salon chair at the same time a much quieter woman assisted Sam into another one.

The next hour passed in a whirlwind as Tamara cut and styled her hair. Her sister tried to talk her into getting her dark brown tresses highlighted as well, but watching as Samantha's head was slowly covered in strips of tin foil as she got her already blonde hair colored even lighter, convinced her that it wasn't something she wanted for herself.

She did, however, sit obediently while Tamara gave her a facial and carefully plucked her eyebrows.

She drew the line, however, when Samantha suggested she get a bikini wax as well.

"I can take care of myself down there on my own, thank you very much," she replied with a painful blush covering her face.

When Tamara was finished with her eyebrows, she finally spun Katherine around so she could look in the mirror and see the results of her hard work. "What do you think?"

The small brunette eyed her reflection carefully. She'd never thought herself ugly, not even living in Canada's vast wilderness where she was surrounded by more trees than people, but she'd never considered herself to be a great beauty either. Looking in the mirror at that moment, however, Katherine could truthfully say that she felt... *pretty*.

She'd only gotten a few inches cut off her hair and it still easily fell past her mid-back, but somehow Tamara had managed to tame the wild strands with the straight iron she had wielded for a solid half hour. It was styled to frame her face attractively, and as Katherine ran her hands through the smooth tresses, she smiled. "It looks great," she admitted.

Smiling widely, Tamara helped Katherine out of her chair and ushered her to the other side of the salon where she was directed to sit and soak her feet in a small tub that had been prepared with steaming water and some sort of soap.

What followed was a sensational pedicure that had Katherine practically melting into her chair. The tough scrub Tamara used felt amazing as it attacked the rough callouses that had developed on her otherwise delicate feet from wandering the forest that surrounded Bastian's house in Haven Falls.

She was admiring the way Tamara's steady hands expertly applied red polish – she'd allowed Sam to pick out the color – to her toenails when the door to the salon opened and alerted her to the fact that another customer had entered the building.

"What do you mean I'll have to wait? I come in here the same time every week. Tamara has never been busy before."

Katherine immediately recognized the voice, but desperately hoping that she was somehow mistaken, she ignored the instinct that screamed she try to hide herself and tentatively peeked at the teenage girl throwing a tantrum at the front of the salon. Her stomach sank. She was right.

It was Mallory Flanders.

"Sam, please tell me my eyes are deceiving me."

"What?" her sister asked, glancing at the small gaggle of teens that had come into the salon. "Do you know those girls?"

She certainly did know Mallory. And Jacqueline. And Heather. And... *Abby?*

True excitement struck her when she recognized her buoyant, redheaded friend. Before she could decide whether she wanted to call out to her or not, however, Mallory's eyes caught hers. They widened in shock as they took her in.

One moment Mallory was behind the desk at the front of the salon and the next she was a mere foot away from her. "What in the hell are *you* doing here?"

The ferocity at which the blonde spit out the words shocked even Katherine. "Nice to see you too," she muttered weakly.

And then Abby was there. "Katherine? Oh my God! Is that really you?" Before she could blink, she had her arms full of a jittery redhead as the girl squeezed her into a tight hug. "I've missed you so much! And I've been so worried! Where have you been?"

"I thought you were dead." Mallory continued, ignoring Abby completely.

"Gee, Mallory, try not to sound too disappointed," Abby snapped in response, releasing Katherine from her embrace.

The blonde girl snorted. "No, I suppose that would have been too much to hope for."

The words were vicious and cutting – too cruel for even Mallory.

"What-" Katherine started, but was cut off before she could get another word in.

"You'll have to forgive me," Mallory hissed. "After all, it's not every day one comes face to face with the person single handedly responsible for destroying her boyfriend's future. He can't even play basketball anymore because of you."

Katherine was bewildered. "What are you talking about?"

"Oh, no one told you?" Mallory seemed truly surprised for a moment before allowing her teeth to show in a truly vicious grin. "Those criminals who burglarized your house and supposedly kidnapped you last October? Well, they broke both of Brad's legs when he refused to tell them where *you* were at. It's a miracle that he can even still stand, let alone walk."

So that's what her mother had meant when she'd solemnly told her that Brad was still alive when she'd asked after his wellbeing.

Guilt threatened to close up her throat entirely, but Katherine forced the words out of her suddenly dry mouth anyway. "I… I'm sorry."

"Not yet you aren't," Mallory spat, not entertaining her apology for a second.

"What's that supposed to mean?"

"Well, you've always been a little attention whore, haven't you? I wouldn't be surprised if you somehow concocted up this whole home invasion and disappearing act just to garner some sympathy when you decided to miraculously show up months later."

"Mallory, that makes no sense," Abby pointed out, her tone broadcasting her irritation.

"Shut up, Abby," she snapped before returning her attention to Katherine. "Don't worry, Katherine, I'll make sure you get the attention that you clearly so desperately want." The words sounded suspiciously like a threat. "Come on, girls," she directed her cronies, "let's get out of here."

Jacqueline and Heather immediately followed her out of the building, but Abby stayed behind. She looked incredibly sheepish. "I'm really sorry about her, Katherine. I swear, she's actually mellowed out a lot since you've been gone."

Katherine seriously doubted *that.*

A horn honked outside, immediately catching the girls' attention. "That's Mallory," Abby said, stating the obvious. "I think she's waiting for me. We all rode together."

The redhead looked torn. It took a moment for Katherine to realize that her friend actually *wanted* to go with the vicious blonde. She supposed they'd gotten close since she'd left Middletown. Life, after all, had surely gone on without her.

"Go ahead," she assured Abby, ignoring the hurt that flared within her. "We'll catch up later."

Abby searched Katherine's eyes. "Are you sure?"

She nodded. "Of course."

"Okay," Abby agreed, pulling Katherine into another hug, this one much tamer than the first. "Call me the moment you get the chance!"

Despite having given the redhead permission to leave, Katherine couldn't help but feel somewhat betrayed as she watched her friend turn her back and walk out the salon door.

You thought Melanie had been your friend too, a traitorous voice whispered in the back of her head. Inwardly shushing said voice, she rubbed her suddenly tired eyes with her hands. "Sam, can we go home?"

"Why? Because of that jealous harpy? Don't let her get to you."

Katherine sighed at her sister's interpretation of the situation. "That was not simple jealousy. Mallory *hates* me."

"Don't be dramatic, Katherine. Besides, why should you let her ruin your afternoon? Now hold still and let Tamara finish painting your nails."

Katherine grumbled under her breath at the bossy demand, but obeyed her sister's order anyway. After Tamara had applied a *third* layer of polish, however, she had had enough and insisted upon leaving.

It wasn't even a half an hour later when they were rounding the corner that led to their street that Mallory's threat came to fruition. The meaning behind her words – *"I'll make sure you get the attention that you clearly so desperately want."* – become all too clear to Katherine as she spied the long line of news trucks lining the curb outside their parents' house.

Mallory's mother, Katherine vaguely recalled, worked for Middletown's local newspaper.

"Shit," Sam muttered, letting out an uncharacteristic expletive as she eyed the chaotic scene.

Katherine didn't blame her.

In addition the seven or eight vehicles clogging up the street, *dozens* of people with microphones and cameras were loitering on the fringes of her parents' lawn. Her father was on the front steps, waving threateningly at a man attempting to set up his equipment on their driveway.

It was an absolute circus.

And she had no doubt who they intended to make the star attraction – the freak, so to speak.

Much like her stomach sinking to the bottom of her gut, Katherine sank into the pliable leather of her seat, wishing somehow that she could disappear into it.

CHAPTER EIGHT

Because reporters had blocked the driveway and clogged the stretch of street directly in front of their parents' house, Samantha was forced to park on the opposite side of the road, a good fifty feet from where their father continued to scold the ballsy cameramen surrounding his property.

Thankfully, Benjamin spotted them. He made a beeline towards the sparkling sedan, rapping on the driver's side window and indicating he wanted Sam to crack it open. She did so. "What's going on?" her sister hissed, glancing at Katherine out of the corner of her eye.

She continued to wilt into her seat, attempting to make herself as small as possible.

"Someone alerted the local newspaper that Katherine had been found. Social media is blowing the story up, and different television stations are clamoring to cover it. Apparently, it's a human interest piece special enough to catch the attention of national broadcasters." He glared behind him. "They're all foaming at the mouth to be the one to interview you, Katherine." He shook his head in obvious anger. "Haven't they ever heard of privacy? I told them all to take a hike, but they aren't budging."

"What should we do?" Katherine asked softly. Behind her father she could see reporters watching them, interest gleaming in their eyes as they tried to spot who was in the sedan.

Her father's eyes flickered to meet her sister's frank stare. "Sam, I want you to get out of the car and walk as briskly as possible towards the house." He met his youngest daughter's worried gaze. "Katherine, honey, while they're distracted by Sam, I want you to get out of the car. I'll wrap an arm around you and you are to hide your face as best as you can in my shoulder. I'll walk you into the house."

The girls nodded their understanding.

"Both of you ignore any questions shouted at you. Eventually we'll have to make a statement, I'm sure, but for now just keep quiet, okay?"

Swallowing down the nervousness rising in her gut, Katherine nodded. "Alright."

Samantha, too, agreed. And then the blonde was stepping out of the vehicle, projecting confidence as she started towards the house, ignoring the gaggle of people with microphones who shouted and followed after her.

Then it was Katherine's turn. She hopped out of the sedan, immediately burying her face into her dad's shoulder as instructed. Ears buzzing with the excited chatter of news reporters, she risked a peek.

And immediately realized that her dad's plan hadn't worked.

They were swarmed by reporters within seconds. Cameras flashed. Questions were hurled at her from all directions, some of which caused more than just a spark of her temper to flare. She grit her teeth as her father lugged her towards the house.

"Katherine, where have you been the last seven months?"

"Have you been held against your will?"

"Is it true that your disappearance was, in fact, a ploy for attention?"

"How did you escape your kidnappers?"

"Were you an associate of the two men who invaded your home in October?"

"How does it feel to be reunited with your family after all this time?"

Somehow she managed to keep her mouth shut, but even as she stepped into the entryway of the house and her father slammed and locked the door behind them, her shoulders couldn't relax. Tension radiated off of her small form in waves.

Her mother immediately wrapped her into a hug. "Are you okay?"

Katherine nodded stiffly.

"Do you know how this could have happened?"

Yes. And she went by the name of Mallory Flanders. But it hardly mattered. What was done was done, and nothing was going to change the fact that a dozen and a half reporters were loitering outside her parents' modest two-story anxiously waiting to get their hands on her.

She shrugged. "Does it matter?"

Samantha raised an eyebrow at the ambiguous answer, obviously suspecting that Mallory was behind the incident herself, but followed Katherine's lead and didn't offer up that bit of information to their parents.

Her dad sighed. "Not really, no," he admitted, running an agitated hand through his salt and pepper hair. "What's important is what we do next. I'll call the police to keep the rowdier reporters off our property, but there's no law that prevents them from waiting on the very public street for you to leave the house." He sent her a sympathetic look. "We'll have to schedule a press conference."

Katherine paled, a protest on the tip of her tongue, but her dad held a hand up to silence her. "I know you don't want the attention, Kit, but it may be the only way to get *them*," he gestured vaguely at the closed door, "to leave you alone. You can tell your story and answer any questions that they may have for you on your own terms. It's better than being ambushed, at any rate."

Realizing he wasn't going to give her a choice in the manner, Katherine tuned out her father as he continued on, mumbling something about calling one of his buddies from college for advice. Apparently, his friend – Mike something or another – had majored in radio broadcasting and interviewed music celebrities on a regular basis.

Katherine was far from a celebrity, but her father hardly cared as he hurried into the kitchen to grab the phone and dial the man's number.

Physically and mentally drained, Katherine followed her dad into the room and plopped down in one of the chairs there. She buried her head into her heads. Vaguely, she wondered what Bastian would think of this mess.

* * *

Three weeks and one grueling interview later, it appeared that the press had *finally* grown bored of her. She didn't spotted a single reporter that morning as she stealthily peeked out of her bedroom window that overlooked the front lawn.

Frankly, it was about time.

Surely, she thought tiredly, there were more newsworthy stories than the tale of a little nobody teenager *re*appearing in the same town she'd mysteriously *dis*appeared from seven months before.

Katherine grabbed a fresh outfit and slipped into her bathroom. For the first time in too long, she actually allowed her muscles to relax under the warm, heavy spray of the shower.

The press conference her father had called had been beyond awful. He'd scheduled it at the police station in Hayfield a mere day after the mass of reporters had shown up outside their house. Crammed between her stoic father and a rather gruff-looking Sheriff Sanders, she'd endured all sorts of questions thrown at her as she stumbled through her cover story, telling the reporters the same information she'd blabbed to her parents and the sheriff – although she'd refrained from mentioning Bastian's name to the press.

She'd clung to her story about amnesia like a life line and flat out refused to respond to questions that painted her as a liar or made it seem that she was the one responsible for her own disappearance.

Immediately after arriving home from the trying interview, Katherine had locked herself in her bedroom, unwilling to speak to anyone. In fact, she'd denied her mom's request to come out for dinner and had stayed holed up until the next morning when Elaine had knocked smartly at her door, relaying to her that she had a visitor. An unexpected – though not *entirely* unwelcome – one at that.

Brad Thompson.

When Katherine spotted him, she took a private moment to gape. She hadn't known who it was that her mother had insisted she get up and see – she thought maybe Abby had finally decided to stop by, seeing as she had never gotten around to calling the hyperactive redhead – but she certainly hadn't expected Brad to be sitting in the living room, her mother doting on him and offering to make him a snack.

"We have chips in the cupboard. It'll only take a few minutes to whip up some spinach dip."

"If you're sure it's not too much trouble," Brad hesitantly agreed.

"Of course not," Elaine assured him before looking up and seeing her daughter standing at the bottom of the stairs, silently taking in the scene. "Katherine!" she exclaimed.

Brad nearly jumped out of his seat at the overly enthusiastic greeting, and his head whipped around in search of her. Their eyes connected immediately.

Katherine wasn't sure what to expect after her disastrous meeting with Mallory a few days ago and braced herself for the worst. She thought her jaw might go slack when the blond boy actually smiled at her. The expression looked sincere.

Using the arm of the couch he was sitting on, he pulled himself up. "Hey, Katherine."

She took him in. He looked much the same as she remembered. Stylish blond hair gelled to look deceptively messy. Blue eyes peering out at her from a classically handsome face.

She took a deep breath. "Hi."

Her mother cleared her throat. "I'll let you two to catch up. I'll be back in a minute with those chips, Brad, dear."

Elaine left and Katherine watched her ex-classmate fidget nervously as an awkward silence descended upon them. He sat back down on the couch. "Do you want to sit?" he asked before shaking himself, just the slightest hint of red creeping up his neck. "I mean – this is your house. You'll sit if you want to sit. I don't know why I asked that. Sorry."

Katherine saved both of them from any further embarrassment by silently taking a seat on the couch cushion not already occupied by Brad. She licked her lips nervously, still waiting for an explosion similar to the one she'd witnessed from Mallory only a few short days ago. "Is that why you came here?" she asked softly. "For an apology? Because believe me, I know I owe you a huge one."

Brad seemed genuinely surprised. "An apology? For what? I just wanted to come see for myself that you were really okay. I've been," he scratched his neck in a seemingly nervous gesture as he hesitated, "very worried about you," he finally finished. "The whole town has been."

"Thanks," Katherine muttered, looking down at her hands. She sighed before forcing them to look back up into Brad's baby blues. "But that doesn't change the fact that you were injured because of me. I asked you over here last October and you end up in a hospital bed. I'm truly very sorry. Mallory said you were really hurt."

Brad did a double take. "Mallory talked to you?"

"Yes," Katherine confirmed. "She told me that it's a miracle that you can even still walk. That you can't even play sports anymore because of me..." her voice slowly trailed off into a whisper.

"Hey," Brad protested, "what those sick assholes did wasn't your fault. And yeah, I'll miss playing sports, especially basketball, but I was hardly good enough to go on to play after high school anyway."

Katherine was positive he was downplaying his disappointment for her sake. "How bad was it?" she asked after a moment.

Brad shrugged. "My right femur was broken in a few places and my left ankle was fractured."

The way he said it made it clear that he was making light of the injuries, and though Katherine appreciated the sentiment, it didn't stop the guilt from flooding her, nearly overwhelming her senses for a moment. "I'm so sorry," she repeated her earlier apology, knowing it could never be enough.

"Like I said, it wasn't your fault." Brad shook his head. "And despite anything Mallory may have said, I, for one, am very glad that you've made it back home safe and sound."

Katherine returned to her previous activity of staring at her hands. "That's really sweet," she said quietly, mostly to fill the silence threatening to descend on them again.

Brad hesitated. "But if you really want to make it up to me, there is one thing you could do."

Katherine frowned. "What?"

"You can say no," Brad continued nervously.

"You haven't even told me what it is," Katherine reminded him gently, fighting to keep the amused exasperation out of her voice.

The blond boy waited until Katherine's eyes were connected with his before blurting it out. "A kiss," he said hurriedly, sheepishly rubbing the back of his neck when he took in her resulting flabbergasted expression. "Believe me, I know it sounds weird, but I guess I've always wondered..." he trailed off. "Will you humor me here? Please? Just one little kiss."

In her shock, Katherine didn't say no.

Brad took it as affirmation. He leaned forward, his eyes intent upon her lips.

And Katherine almost let it happen.

The guilt she was practically saturated in demanded that she did allow him to kiss her, in fact. But she couldn't go through with it. It wasn't that Brad was ugly – he was certainly good looking enough in an ordinary sort of way – or that he was a bad person, because Katherine knew that he wasn't. It wasn't even the fact that she knew he had a girlfriend – a girlfriend named Mallory Flanders – that stopped Katherine.

It was Brad's eyes. They were blue like Bastian's and yet nothing like the other man's at all. They were too light. Too soft. Too easy to read.

At the last possible second, Katherine jerked away from Brad and his lips landed on her cheek instead of on her mouth.

Brad pulled away, looking incredibly embarrassed.

"Sorry," Katherine whispered softly, hating that she had to keep repeating the word to the boy she owed so much too. He really had been a good friend to her.

He sighed sadly, but offered her a halfhearted smile. "It's okay. I sort of figured." He pushed himself up out of his seat. "I should go."

Probably.

"You don't have to," she denied, standing as well.

He peered into her eyes. "Yeah, I do."

Right then, Katherine's mother strolled back into the room with an unopened bag of tortilla chips in one hand and a piping hot bowl of spinach dip in the other. She frowned at the both of them before turning her attention solely on Brad, who looked more than mildly disappointed. "Where are you going, dear? I hope Katherine isn't chasing you out of here." She gave her daughter the side eye.

Bless his heart, Brad shook his head. "No, no, nothing like that. I've just got to get home, Mrs. Mayes. Thanks anyways," he said, nodding at the chips. He looked at Katherine one last time before turning to take his leave. "Bye," he whispered.

It sounded final.

Katherine bit her bottom lip. "Bye," she answered softly in turn, but he didn't look back.

"Katherine Elizabeth Mayes," Elaine demanded as soon as the front door closed shut, "what did you do?"

Katherine didn't answer. She was too focused on the flip flopping of her stomach. She wasn't sure what had caused the nauseating feeling. The awful stench radiating off of the homemade spinach dip in waves? Or the guilt that threatened to swallow her whole as she'd finally taken note of Brad's limp when he had he walked away from her.

Katherine scrubbed roughly at her arms with the loofa she was holding, still mad at herself over how her meeting with Brad had ended. She should have been more... she didn't know, considerate of his feelings? Appreciative of what he'd done for her? Instead, she'd denied him the simplest of requests and couldn't even bring herself to sit still and let the poor guy kiss her.

And it was all because of that jackass. *Bastian.*

Even the act of saying his name in her mind made her want to cry. Stubborn as she was, however, Katherine didn't allow the tears to fall. She *still* couldn't believe that he'd lied to her.

She wasn't a fool. She knew that people lied to each other about little things – nonsensical things – all the time. Every day, even. But this was different. This wasn't a tiny white lie. Bastian had told her that her parents – her very much *alive* parents – were dead. And he'd let her believe it for months.

It made her question everything he'd ever said to her, especially what he'd been so prone to saying before she'd taken off – "I love you."

Yeah, right!

Katherine threw the loofa across the shower, and it hit the white, tiled wall with a satisfying, wet *smack.*

Traitorous tears gathered in her eyes. He hadn't even come to see her since she'd run away from Haven Falls. Hell, the only reason she knew that he'd even come after her at all was because of the second visitor she'd received nearly two weeks after Brad had shown up at her house. If her ex-classmate had not been entirely unwelcome, this visitor had been completely so. And while Brad had entered through the front door, *he* had climbed in through her bedroom window.

Markus.

Katherine just barely managed to reel in a startled scream when she exited her bathroom after a quick shower to see a large, muscular man standing near her bed, examining the framed photograph of her family she kept on her nightstand.

Luckily, she would recognize Markus's wide shoulders and scruffy beard anywhere. The jerk had the nerve to leer at her.

She clutched the small towel she had wrapped around her torso – at least she'd covered herself with something before leaving the bathroom – tighter in one hand and placed the other over her fluttering heart. She willed the initial fear she'd felt at spotting the man to fade and turn into something more productive. Like anger.

It worked.

"What do you want?" she hissed, attempting to keep quiet and avoid alerting her parents of the fact that there was a man in her room, while simultaneously making it clear just how pissed off she was.

She was supremely annoyed at the small part of herself that was maybe just a tiny bit happy to see Markus – the part that actually had the gall to miss Bastian, Markus, and the rest of her pack.

Markus's eyes narrowed. "Well," he said far too casually, "what I want to do is drag your skinny ass out through the window I just climbed in and hand you back over to my alpha – your alpha – to do with as he pleases." He must have seen the spark of fear in her expression that his words had caused because he rolled her eyes. "But don't worry, princess, I think I can manage to restrain myself."

Katherine, still holding onto the towel, crossed her arms in front of her chest. "See that you do," she bit back at him.

Markus crossed his arms himself. "What the hell were you thinking?" he demanded after a moment of tense silence. "The last time I saw you, I thought I'd told you to stay put."

Katherine scoffed. "What makes you think that I would listen to a liar?"

"Hey, I never lied to you." Markus pointed out, seemingly genuinely offended.

"Maybe not directly, but certainly by omission!"

Markus threw his hands up in the air. "You didn't even give us – give Bastian – a chance to explain!"

"He didn't deserve a chance to explain! He still doesn't!" Katherine didn't even realize they'd escalated from talking to yelling until there was a loud knock on her door.

"Katherine, are you okay in there?"

Katherine paled, leaping over a hamper of dirty laundry to turn over the lock on the door. "I'm fine. Everything's fine!" she said through the crack. "I just... um, I stubbed my toe."

She winced at the lame excuse, but her father seemed to buy it. "Okay, if you're sure."

She waited until the sound of his footsteps disappeared before turning around to face Markus – a smug grin suddenly pulling at the corners of his mouth. "Who's the liar now?"

She was tempted to slap it from his face. "Turn around," she demanded. "I'm not having this conversation with you while I'm half naked."

"Why ever not?" he asked faux innocently, but he did as she in-

structed. With his eyes fixed firmly on the opposite wall, Katherine felt safe enough to quickly slip out of her towel and into a thin tank top and pair of plaid pajama bottoms.

"Alright, I'm decent," she said, giving him permission to turn back around.

He did so, giving her choice of pajamas a critical glance over before his eyes met hers again. He looked into them for a while, and Katherine shifted uncomfortably, wondering exactly what it was he was searching for. With a sigh, he finally released her from his rather rude stare. "I wasn't always a nice guy, you know," he said, plopping himself down uninvited onto her bed.

Unimpressed, Katherine raise an eyebrow. "Oh, really? I can't imagine," she deadpanned.

The obvious sarcasm had the corners of his lips pulling back up into a grin again. "Yeah, I know. It's hard to believe, but I was a real asshole before I joined the Prince pack."

Katherine snorted, hesitantly taking a seat to his right on her bed. "And what, pray tell, do you consider yourself now?"

"An upstanding citizen of Haven Falls," he answered immediately, grin still glued to his face. "Badass beta to the scariest alpha on the entire goddamn continent. And, of course, the reluctant keeper of his disobedient mate."

Katherine rolled her eyes, not exactly pleased with the way he made her out to sound like some misbehaving toddler, but she didn't interrupt him to argue.

"I really was an ass, though," he reminded her – as if she needed reminding. "I was one of Rogue's best friends in school. A hard core believer in his rather distinct philosophy. I actually thought Bastian and his parents were a bunch of pansies."

Ignoring the way her temper automatically spiked in defense of Bastian, Katherine swallowed her surprise. "Rogue's philosophy?" she questioned.

"Rogue thought – still thinks, no doubt – that asserting one's dominance over others is the most crucial aspect to upholding the

werewolf hierarchy. And I suppose it is in a way. But not in the manner he thinks. He's convinced that physically stronger werewolves, the alphas and betas of our world, are better than their weaker counterparts. In school he let them know constantly that they were beneath us. That they were born to serve us."

Katherine eyed Markus warily. "You don't still think that?"

"Of course not," he assured. "I realize now how wrong he was – how wrong he still is. Alphas and betas are actually the ones made to serve everyone else – to direct and protect them. Especially little girls who aren't particularly good at listening."

Katherine ignored the dig. "So what happened?" she asked.

"What do you mean?"

"What made you have this epiphany that you were wrong? That Rogue was wrong?" she specified.

Markus seemed reluctant to share that part of the story with her, but he did so anyway. "There was this human girl at school – her father had been bitten and turned some years before, I guess – that Rogue was keen on. He fixated on her, really." He glanced at Katherine. "She looked a bit like you actually, but a little taller and with freckles." He continued before she could dwell too long on that tidbit of information. "He picked on her at school, cornered her a few times, but nothing really serious. Not until he bit her anyway."

Katherine startled. "What?"

"He bit her on the day of a full moon. I was there when it happened, laughing at the stupid crap he was spewing at her. Didn't even see it coming until she was screaming her head off. He just kept biting her over and over again once he started. I ended up pulling him off of her, but the poor girl didn't even make it through more than a handful of nights before she died."

Katherine vaguely realized she was trembling.

"Anyway," Markus continued, "Bastian believed me when I said that I tried to stop Rogue. He gave me a second chance when no one else would. Not even my fuck of a father. Before I was a Prince, I was a Briggs, you know."

Katherine cringed at that revelation. "Is Rip your-"

"My brother?" Markus interrupted. "By blood, yes. And Julius Briggs is my father. But I don't claim them as family. Not anymore."

Katherine ran a shaky hand through her damp locks. "I'm sorry."

He shrugged. "You don't need to apologize to me."

She saw red at what she was sure was a hidden implication. "I don't need to apologize to him either!"

"Hey," he raised his hands in surrender, "I never said that you did."

She frowned. "Then why did you tell me all this?"

"Because making a mistake doesn't make someone a bad person. At least I hope not or I'm screwed. Bastian knows what he did was wrong and believe me, he's feeling pretty damn sorry right about now. He gave me a second chance. I think you should give him one too."

Katherine crossed her arms, refusing the respond to the shockingly sensible argument.

"Besides, what the hell are you going to do, huh? You're a werewolf. That comes with a bit of a furry problem. What happens when the full moon rises a little over a week from now? You can't stay here forever, princess. "

Katherine glared, any sympathy she felt for the man gone as he reminded her of something she was desperately trying to forget. "Watch me."

Markus glowered in turn. "Fine," he snatched a crumpled piece of paper from his pocket. "Here, call this when your common sense returns to you. It's the phone number of the hotel we're staying at in Hayfield."

Katherine licked her lips. "We?"

"We're all here," he confirmed her unasked question.

At her speculative look, he added. "Or, you know, you could just call out Bastian's name. The overbearing prick hasn't let you out of his sight since we managed to track you down. It was a goddamn miracle I was able to convince him to take a break from his protective guard to sleep. But I needed to talk to you, didn't I?"

She didn't process anything past the fact that Bastian was here and had apparently not been far from her at all. She despised the wave of comfort it caused to roll over her. "He's here? He's been watching me?"

"What do you think?"

Katherine squared he shoulders. "Tell him to stop."

Tell him to talk to me, was what she really meant.

Markus snorted. "Tell him yourself."

Katherine turned away from his challenging stare.

She was beside herself when after a beat of silence, Markus added, "I miss you. We all miss you. You don't have to talk to him right now, but come back. Come home."

It was on the tip of her tongue to fire back that she was home, but she knew the words would be dishonest – a pure lie, really. So she just shook her head back and forth like a broken marionette instead. "I can't."

Markus didn't bother asking for an excuse. Snorting in unconcealed disappointment, he leapt out of the same window he'd come in and disappeared into the night without another word.

Katherine shut off the shower by turning the ancient faucet with admittedly quite a bit more strength than necessary. As the last of the water trickled down the drain, she roughly dried herself with a towel before using it to wipe away the condensation that had formed on the mirror from the steam that had escaped her shower.

Sweeping the wet hair that insisted upon clinging to her face behind her ears, Katherine assessed herself frankly. She examined her pink lips that were turned down in an unhappy frown, her cheeks that were still flushed from her shower, and her green, green eyes made even brighter by the dark shadows underneath them. They were practically luminous, peering out at her from her skull – shiny irises nearly as bright as the moon itself.

The moon that Katherine knew was just a sliver away from being full. It was tomorrow night that it *would* be, in fact. And looking into her reflection, Katherine asked herself the same question that Markus had beseeched her a week before.

What in the hell are you going to do?

CHAPTER NINE

There was only one logical solution to Katherine's dilemma. No matter how juvenile she knew her actions to be as she peeked into her parents' bedroom to make sure they were sound asleep and no matter how ridiculous she felt stuffing her pillows under the bed covers and shaping them into something that looked vaguely humanoid, she was going to go through with it.

She was sneaking out.

Katherine slipped on the darkest hooded sweatshirt she could find hanging in her closet – not for the warmth it offered her slender frame, but rather for the assistance it'd provide in hiding her from any prying eyes she may encounter on her way to her destination – and peered out her window.

It was the same one that Markus had climbed in and abruptly leapt out a week ago. It was at least a twelve foot drop, but Katherine figured that if Markus could safely jump to the ground from such a height then so could she.

It was better than risking sneaking down the creaky stairs and attempting to escape through one of the heavy wooden doors on the first floor at any rate.

Grabbing the small backpack she'd stuffed with nothing more than a change of clothes and a flashlight, she pulled herself up on the window's ledge. Not quite daring enough to straight up throw herself from the window as she'd seen Markus do, she maneuvered her body so that she was sitting on the wide ledge, her legs dangling out of the frame.

After taking a deep breath, she used her hands to firmly push herself off the windowsill.

And promptly plummeted to the ground below.

Katherine had heard once that when falling from a great height, one shouldn't try to land on their feet – that the force of landing on them could cause skeletal fractures as far up as the spine – so she tried to land in a roll.

Tried being the key word.

She fell down hard on her left hip for her efforts. Cursing under her breath, Katherine forced herself to her feet and pulled down the waistband of her pants to examine the damage. A dark bruise was already blossoming. "Shit," she muttered, swearing again as she touched the discolored mass. It hurt like nobody's business, but it was hardly the worse pain she'd even been in. Allowing the waist of her jeans to snap back into place, she quickly dismissed the injury.

Nevertheless, she was irritated by a jolt of pain that encompassed her entire left hip every time she dared to put weight on the same side foot. It made for a long and distinctly unpleasant walk to her destination.

She forgot all about it, however, when she'd finally arrived.

She was there. Miller Road.

Katherine peered speculatively at the house at the end of it. It was where she'd been bitten by Bastian all those months ago and where she was going to seek refuge tonight. This time around, however, *she* would be the deadly creature hiding in the foliage that surrounded the house.

She remembered how foreboding the house had seemed that fateful night in September, but she wondered now if it was truly the house that had caused such trepidation to rise within her or if her body had somehow known before she had that *he* was there. Bastian.

She wondered if he was there now.

After what Markus had told her – that Bastian had been watching over her since he'd caught up with her in Middletown, probably only a day or two after she'd initially arrived – she didn't doubt that he was around somewhere, keeping an eye on her from the shadows.

The urge to call out to him and confirm her suspicions was a powerful one, but somehow Katherine managed to swallow her tongue. Bastian could watch over her all he wanted. That didn't mean she had to acknowledge him.

She moved towards the house, gravel crunching under her shoes. The moon, not quite at its peak in the sky, allowed her to see where she was going without having to use the flashlight. Before she knew it, she'd navigated the thick shrubbery around the house and was at its door. Or the half-eroded piece of wood that she suspected used to be its door anyway. Ignoring how unsafe she knew it was to enter a building with a half-collapsed roof, Katherine pushed it open and went in.

The house wasn't quite as decayed on the inside as it was on the outside. It was, however, quite disgusting. A thick layer of dirt clung to every inch of the walls, and the rays of moonlight that managed to shine through the large, gaping holes in the roof revealed an alarming number of dust particles floating in the air. Worst of all, however, were the cobwebs that seemed to cover absolutely everything.

She didn't care if she was a big, bad wolf, spiders were terrifying. And she didn't think she could be coerced into touching one unless her life was in imminent danger. Even then, it was only a maybe.

Luckily for Katherine, her life was *not* in immediate peril, and despite reaching into her backpack, grabbing, and turning on her flashlight, any spiders that may have occupied the house remained out of her sight.

After quickly surveying her options, Katherine decided that the northwest corner of the house was the least objectionable place to sit and wait for the full moon to reach its peak in the sky. Using a booted foot, she cleared the spot on the floor of cobwebs, set down her backpack, and did just that.

She didn't have to wait for long.

She was shining her flashlight through the glassless window she remembered spying through all those months ago, wondering if *he* was out there just as she'd been, when the power of the full moon took hold of her, and she changed. Katherine inhaled sharply as her bones broke and reformed, her skin stretching over them and growing hair. Her clothes, of course, were completely destroyed in the process.

Dazed after the transformation, it took her a moment to open her eyes. Scenting the air, she wasn't surprised by the faint smell of fresh rain and pine that her nose immediately recognized.

Bastian.

She was, however, taken off guard by the intense – almost feral – urge she felt to run *towards* the scent instead of away from it.

Her wolf had missed him.

Her human self was too hurt and prideful to ever admit the same, though, so she did the only thing she thought appropriate under the circumstances and ran. Sprinting in the opposite direction of the tantalizing scent, Katherine left the run down house behind her as she dashed through the foliage surrounding it and into the small stretch of dense forestry that lay directly behind the overgrown shrubbery.

Katherine knew that no one – no humans anyway – resided in the three mile stretch of wilderness. She allowed her inhibitions to drop, distracting herself from the glimpses of fur she spotted here and there in her peripheral vision by chasing down a large rabbit and feasting on its raw flesh.

She was tearing some meat from the dead animal's bones when she caught a flash of fur so white to her immediate right that it could only belong to Sophie. It confirmed what Markus had told her a week ago – the whole pack had followed her to Middletown.

She didn't have much time to dwell on that fact when she caught a hint of *his* unique smell in the air again and was forced to take off.

What happened next was the most intense game of hide and seek that Katherine had ever participated in. There were not many places to hide in such a small forest, however, and as she bolted yet again from the scent that was relentlessly pursuing her, she felt an unexpected ping of sympathy for the rabbit she'd managed to hunt down.

Was this how the poor creature had felt? A toxic combination of adrenaline and fear pumping fire through its veins? Panic taking over its thoughts as an inescapable predator grew nearer and nearer?

Katherine evaded Bastian for as long as she could. It wasn't long, however, before she was cornered, Bastian's earthy scent as thick and heady in the air as ever. She ran. But as fast as she was, when she came upon a small clearing, the large, intimidating form of wolf Bastian leapt in front of her, cutting her off completely.

She almost couldn't halt her momentum in time and nearly ran into Bastian. She managed it, though – barely – and immediately sprung back from him, a low pitched growl already escaping her throat as she glared at him.

Ignoring the way that a small part of her rejoiced at finally setting her eyes on him after *weeks* of being unable to do so, Katherine crouched down into a defensive position, her ears flattening against her skull as she snarled at him.

For a long moment, Bastian just stared, his wolfish eyes a searing blue as they swept over her form, taking her in from head to toe.

Then he did something Katherine would have never expected. Unreadable azure eyes locked onto her furious green ones, he slowly lowered himself to the ground until his furry belly was pressed against the forest floor.

He was prostrating himself before her. *Asking for forgiveness*, she realized dazedly.

Katherine didn't have a clue how to respond.

Her anger towards him didn't fade, exactly, but her wolf and human selves were both so confused and *pleased* by the sight of Bastian essentially bowing before them, that she allowed her defenses to drop for just a moment and hesitantly approached him.

It was a mistake.

As soon as Katherine had padded close enough, Bastian shot up from his position of false submission and sprung at her.

While Katherine hadn't seen the move coming, she still reacted quickly enough to avoid a collision with the massive wolf. Bastian's side brushed against hers as she leapt out of the way. It shouldn't have been sensual, but undeniably *was*, she'd been denied his touch for so long. She was able to avoid two more attempted tackles before he finally managed to pounce on her.

She snarled at him, snapping her teeth threateningly as she landed on her back. He towered over her, the light that radiated from the full moon behind him outlining his sleek form.

Katherine knew he hadn't used his full strength to knock her over – she hadn't even been winded by her abrupt meeting with the ground – but that knowledge didn't subdue her anger in the slightest. And that anger was fanned into a flame of fury when Bastian had the nerve to settle himself over her and nuzzle his long snout into the crook of her exposed neck. He panted as he unabashedly took in as much of her scent as he possibly could, his body molding itself to hers to prevent her from escaping.

Part of Katherine – the part still enamored with Bastian – was shamelessly pleased, perfectly content to lay under the dominating wolf and let him shower her with affection.

Mostly, though, Katherine was just pissed.

Incensed and desperate to be released from the unwanted embrace, she twisted and turned, contorting her body in ways that shouldn't have been possible in her attempts to break free from him. She growled and nipped at him in a decidedly unfriendly fashion.

He ignored her actions completely.

She fruitlessly struggled for what had to have been close to an hour before she finally accepted the fact that Bastian was not going to move. She was stuck there – underneath him – indefinitely.

As much as that realization sparked her anger, it also caused a wave of calm to wash over her. And so she permitted herself to do what she'd been attempting to avoid the entire night and looked into Bastian's eyes. They were as gentle as she could ever recall them being and were staring at her with such adoration that she felt just the tiniest bit of the hurt he'd knowingly caused her fall away and disintegrate. His chest began to reverberate as he not quite growled, but not quite purred at her either – hum, maybe, was the correct term for the noise he was making.

The soothing, gentle vibrations caused her eyelids to suddenly feel absurdly heavy. She valiantly fought the urge to close them. But surrounded by Bastian's overwhelming warmth, she felt the safest she had in a long time, and they slowly slipped closed without her permission. Moments later, a mercifully dreamless sleep overtook her.

What seemed like days – but was actually only hours – later, she struggled to open her eyes as consciousness beckoned. It took a moment for her green orbs to focus, but when they did, they immediately latched on to the same blue eyes that she'd fallen asleep looking into. Now, though, they were set in an indisputably handsome and undeniably *human* face.

"Good morning."

CHAPTER TEN

Katherine blinked. It took a moment for her to regain her bearings and realize just exactly where she was and just exactly *who* she was pinned underneath. When she did, a fury so strong she thought her heart might burst enveloped her.

"I don't see what's so good about it," she spat, splaying her hands over his bare chest and shoving at him with all her might. "Get off me!"

The fact that they were both naked did little to calm her palpitating heart.

Bastian, blue eyes trained on her face, refused to move an inch. "Why? So you can run away from me again?" he asked in a gravelly voice. "I don't think so."

The man's blatant dismissal of her wishes just stoked the fire raging within her. A strangled scream threatened to bubble up her throat, but she swallowed it down, and instead lifted her hands from his chest just to bring them back down as hard as she could at taut flesh.

She slapped at his chest once. He grunted. Twice. He winced. What he didn't do, however, was budge.

"If you don't get off of me right now," she finally threatened, "I'll never talk to you again."

He must have sensed the truth in the statement because he searched her eyes for a moment before shifting and removing some of his weight from her. He still had her pinned to the ground, however, when he made a demand of his own. "No running."

Katherine struggled not to squirm under his intense stare. "Fine," she forced out between gritted teeth.

"Fine *what*?" he goaded.

Katherine's glare sharpened. "Fine, I won't run."

Those seemed to be the magic words, and the man pushed himself off of her, rising slowly to his knees.

Once freed, Katherine immediately sat up, curling her own knees to her chest and wrapping her arms around them in an attempt to preserve her modesty.

Bastian made no such attempt to hide his own nudity, and Katherine fought to keep her eyes focused on the expanse of skin above his waist and not on what she knew was dangling below it.

For a long moment the two stared silently at each other.

The longer the silence stretched on, however, the more uncomfortable Katherine became. Eventually, muscles tense with nerves, she could take it no more. "You lied to me." The words were accusatory and positively drenched in anger and hurt – *so much hurt.*

Bastian physically grimaced at them, running a distressed hand through his dark, unruly hair. "You didn't give me a chance to explain," he countered.

"Explain what?" Katherine exploded, infuriated that his immediate response to the accusation hadn't been to acknowledge his wrong doing and apologize. "You told me that my parents were *dead,*" her voice broke on the last word and traitorous tears wet her eyes. "And worse, you know what that's like! You know firsthand what it feels like when the fingers of grief grab viciously at your heart and *squeeze.* And yet still you told me this heinous lie. *Why?* What could have possibly possessed you to do that?"

Tears had escaped and her chest was heaving by the time she'd finished her rant. She desperately tried to gain control of her breathing, noisily gasping in oxygen while wiping furiously at her wet cheeks at the same time.

Bastian's features were pinched in concern, but when he reached forward to comfort her, she glared so fiercely at his hand that he reluctantly let it drop back down by his side. Katherine managed to suck in a few lungfuls of air. Sniffling pathetically, she added, "For the longest time, I blamed myself for their deaths, you know."

Bastian seemed physically pained by the words she shot at him like arrows. "You're breaking my heart," he admittedly softly.

"I'm breaking *your* heart?" Katherine demanded incredulously. "This is all your fault!" she practically shrieked.

"I know!" Bastian shouted back, pulling hard now at his hair. "Don't you think I know that? It killed me to tell you that your parents were dead and to watch your face crumble in devastation. To hear your goddamn cries for them as you mourned! But you know what? If given a choice, I would do it all over again!"

Katherine was stunned by his horrifying confession.

"Do you want to know why?" he asked, plowing on before she could answer. "Because as screwed up as it was, I did it for you. I did it because I was scared to goddamn death that if you thought your parents were still alive, that if you worried over them and longed to be with them, you'd never accept the wolf that had become an integral part of your soul the moment I bit you. That you wouldn't have had a chance in hell of surviving your first change."

Katherine trembled at the despair that Bastian seemed to have somehow injected into the words.

"But do you know what?" he continued. "You lived. You're alive. And no matter how angry you are at me, I could *never* be sorry for that."

Katherine took in the explanation, twisting the man's logic over in her mind and trying to apply it to his actions. But something didn't quite fit.

"And afterwards?" she demanded shakily, still reeling. "After I had survived the first change? Why didn't you tell me then that my parents were alive?"

Bastian eyed her warily. "I was afraid," he admitted, each word sounding forced, like she'd pulled them one by one from his mouth with a pliers.

Katherine frowned in disbelief. "Afraid? *You?* Of what?"

Bastian lowered his gaze to the ground, his hands positioned on either side of him, digging into the earth. Long fingers clutched at grass and dirt. "I was afraid that if I told you the truth – that I had lied about your parents being dead – you'd hate me. I feared you would reject me as your alpha and as your mate. I thought that you'd leave the pack – that you'd leave *me* – as soon as the opportunity presented itself." Katherine nearly jumped out of her skin when Bastian raised his fists and pounded them into the ground with supernatural strength. Loose dirt flew into the air. "But that's no excuse," he murmured so softly that she almost didn't hear him. "I knew the distress that my lie was causing you, and yet like a coward, I couldn't bring myself to own up to it. I've wronged you and for that, I am immeasurably sorry." His torso slumped forward unexpectedly, and his head hung dejectedly from it as he humbled himself before her.

The words were so painstakingly honest – the apology so obviously sincere – that try as Katherine might to hold on to her righteous anger, it began to slip through her fingers like quicksand. The hurt, though, that his lie had caused was still there, throbbing in time with the beat of her heart.

"Sit up," she finally muttered. "You look ridiculous." The words themselves were harsh, but the bite they had previously contained was suspiciously absent.

Bastian glanced up at her through the fringe of his wild hair, slowly pushing himself back up onto his knees. "Does that mean you forgive me?"

The question was spoken quietly and with genuine surprise so Katherine didn't immediately scoff. "I don't know," she admitted honestly instead, rubbing her shins with her hands as she pulled her legs impossibly closer to her chest. "But... I think I understand at least why you did what you did."

"Thank you," he said, resting his own hands on his bulging thigh muscles. "Though I'm not sure I deserve your understanding," he added hesitantly.

She wasn't sure that he did either, but Katherine kept that thought to herself.

"I missed you," Bastian spoke again, trying to make eye contact and engage the brunette, but Katherine's gaze had fallen to her knees.

Despite everything, she'd missed him too. But her turbulent

emotions wouldn't let her say it back even if she wanted to. And she wasn't even sure if she *did* want to.

Bastian tried again. "We found the SUV broken down on the side of the highway just south of the Canadian border. I was so damn worried about you. What happened? How'd you make it to Middletown from there?"

She could tell that they were questions that had been plaguing him since he'd found the vehicle so she had mercy on the man and answered him. "I was in such a hurry to leave Haven Falls that I forgot to take any money with me and the SUV ran out of gas," she blushed a bit in embarrassment at the confession. "When it did, I hitchhiked the rest of the way here."

Bastian's jaw clenched tightly in an obvious attempt to censor his furious reaction to that, but ultimately the man couldn't help himself. "Do you have any idea how dangerous that is?" he demanded. "You could have been hurt, or worse-"

Katherine shot him a glare so venomous that he closed his mouth with an audible *snap. Certainly he knew better than to lecture her about a situation that he'd had a direct hand in causing?*

Bastian rubbed roughly at his stubbled chin. "Sorry," he muttered quietly.

Katherine rolled her eyes at the rather lack luster apology, but nodded her head in acceptance of it anyway. "It's alright."

"Can I hold you?" Bastian asked softly, taking her off guard.

Katherine tensed at the question, refusing to meet the man's blatant stare and digging her fingernails so hard into her legs that she was sure they'd leave marks.

"Please?" he added when she didn't respond.

Katherine hadn't been prepared for him to beg and shifted her gaze to eye him in consideration. "We're naked," she finally objected half-heartedly.

Bastian snorted incredulously, his lips twitching as he fought back what she knew to be a disbelieving smile. "I don't care."

Katherine was about to retort that she *did* care, but before she could get the words out, Bastian had sprung to his feet and in two quick strides, he had her incased in his steel-like arms. Air escaped her lungs in a *whoosh* as he wrapped the appendages around her and pulled her to him.

She stiffened – her senses suddenly overwhelmed by the heady smell of him. She was struck by the crazy urge to bathe in the overpowering scent. When the shock of her intense reaction began to loll, though, Katherine managed to pull her arms out from where he'd trapped them between their bodies. Instead of pushing him away as a part of her longed to do, however, she relaxed into his arms and drew him even closer. Grasping the back of his shoulders with both hands, she squeezed him to her as tightly as she could and buried her face into the hard, flat plane of his chest.

With one hand still wrapped firmly around her waist, Bastian allowed his other to creep up her back before coming to rest on the nape of her neck, his fingers threading themselves into the tiny hairs he found there.

"No more lies," she murmured, lips brushing against heated skin as she spoke. "Promise me that there are no more lies between us and that there won't ever be any again."

For a second, Katherine feared that the words had been too muffled for Bastian to hear, but after a moment of tense silence, he responded to her plea, strong arms tightening around her as he answered. "If that's what you want then there's something else you should know."

Katherine stiffened at the admission, disbelief coloring her voice as she dumbly repeated the words. "Something else?"

Her attempt at wrenching herself away from the man was thwarted by his sturdy embrace. "Just listen," Bastian begged.

"Why should I?" Katherine snapped, unbelievably irritated that he had the nerve to trap her with his body *again.*

"It's about the present I gave you for your birthday," he hastily explained himself. "When you opened it, I told you that the ring inside didn't have to mean anything if you didn't want it to. But I lied. It did mean something – more than just something, even; *everything.*"

He must have sensed that she no longer had the urge to flee because when she jerked back this time, he released her. Heart fluttering like a hummingbird against her ribcage, she dared to meet his brazen stare. "What is *that* supposed to mean?"

It couldn't possibly mean what she thought it did... could it?

Bastian kept his blue eyes trained on hers, carefully watching her reaction. "It means that I want to claim you as my mate. I want to mark you so that everyone can see that you are mine and that I am yours. I don't want anyone to *ever* question it. Not even you. *Especially* not you."

Katherine willed her facial expression to remain blank, but nothing could stop the telling blush from staining her cheeks all the way up to the tips of her ears. "Claim? Mark?" she forced past her inexplicably dry lips. "Like... *marriage?*"

Bastian gently grasped either side of her heated face, his calloused thumbs resting on the apples of her cheeks. "It is similar to marriage, yes, but more definite than even that. Didn't you learn about claiming ceremonies in school?"

Katherine could vaguely recall something about them, but that particular lesson had been taught during the fortnight of classes she'd missed while recovering from Cain's attack and the resulting pneumonia. She slowly shook her head in response to Bastian's question. "Not really, no."

The man sighed in frustration, allowing his hands to drop to her shoulders and then to the small of her back, where he wrapped them around her once again, beckoning her closer. He couldn't seem to get enough of touching her, and truthfully, Katherine was enjoying the tactile show of affection, which was the only reason she allow it.

"Claiming ceremonies are similar to wedding ceremonies, I suppose," Bastian explained, idly running his fingers up and down her spine. As embarrassing as it was, Katherine almost let out an honest to God *purr* at the sensation. "They take place after a mated pair have claimed each other. They're presented as a couple in front of their pack – or the entire community in our case since I'm the head alpha –

and there's a celebration."

Feeling courageous, Katherine allowed her hands to do a little exploring of their own, tracing the dips she found in Bastian's muscle bound back with her fingers as she took in his words. "But exactly how is it that wolves claim their mates? You said something about," she hesitated for a moment, "marking me?"

"Yes," he murmured, a huskiness in his voice that Katherine was sure hadn't been there a moment ago. "When we make love for the first time, I'll want to mark you." She watched in fascination as Bastian's Adam's apple bobbed. She was so was entranced by the action, in fact, that she somehow managed to stave off a blush as the words "make love" registered in her ears. "I'll bite you where everyone will be able to see the marks my teeth make as they sink into your supple flesh." His knuckle brushed along the sensitive line of her neck. "Right here. Then they'll all know that you're *mine*." The last word came out in a nearly indiscernible growl.

It took every last bit of Katherine's will power to lean *away* from Bastian's touch instead of *into* it. "But I thought," she began, gasping when the man actually placed a chaste kiss where his knuckle had just been. Goosebumps erupted over her skin, and she fought to keep her wits about her. She took a deep breath, trying again. "I thought that you had already marked me before I started school. Or do you not remember peeing on me?" She tried to force irritation into her words as she brought up what she mentally referred to as "the fire hydrant incident", but she was so distracted by his sensual touching that she suspected she largely failed at it.

Especially when he had the audacity to grin at her. "Yes," he confirmed, "I remember. But that was only to claim you as a member of the pack and to aid in warding off recruiters. *This* is entirely different. This will proclaim to all of Haven Falls and to any werewolf who ever crosses paths with you that you're completely *mine* – in every sense of the word."

Katherine's tongue darted out to lick her bottom lip. "And you'll be mine?"

"Of course. I've always been yours." His lips pressed sweetly against her forehead. "Your sire, your alpha, your mate. Claiming each other will ensure that no one will ever doubt that."

"So if we do this, we'll be together... forever?" she asked clumsily.

Bastian nodded solemnly, his eyes not straying from hers for a moment. "I would never let you go."

As enamored as Katherine was with Bastian, all this talk of *ever*, *never*, and *forever* was starting to make her nervous. Even under the spell that Bastian somehow seemed to be putting her under with his pretty words and soft touches, she could feel her belly twist with anxiety. After all, she was only seventeen – not yet considered an adult in many cultures.

"I'm only seventeen!" Katherine blurted the realization as soon as it came to her. Even if most of the time she felt much older.

"So?" Bastian murmured, peppering light kisses on the shell of her ear.

Katherine batted him away. "*So?* So I don't think it's even legal for me to get married."

That seemed to finally get Bastian's attention. He snorted in amusement. "Good thing I didn't ask for your hand in marriage then."

Katherine huffed in frustration. "Okay, fine. I don't think I'm old enough to be claimed – or claim anyone – as a mate," she allowed. "Am I – are *we* – even old enough to pledge ourselves to each other this way?" After all, Bastian himself had only turned nineteen in March.

"Seventeen is the age of majority for werewolves," he reminded her gently, tucking a loose strand of hair behind her ear, "so yes, we are old enough. Some mated pairs even choose to claim each other at a younger age with permission from the alpha of their pack."

Katherine was caught off guard by that tidbit of information. "*Really?* I wonder what their parents think of that."

What would *her* parents think?

The singular thought sent a river of ice water rushing through her veins. The fog that had descended upon her as she stood passively in Bastian's arms, shrouded in his comforting scent and allowing him to touch her as if she was his lover, abruptly lifted.

She pried possessive hands off of her, taking a step back and crossing her arms in front of her bare chest in an admittedly half-hearted attempt to hide her body from Bastian's gaze.

He had the nerve to look hurt by her actions.

But Katherine could hardly concern herself with that. She was too preoccupied worrying over her very sanity.

What in the hell was wrong with her? Was she really considering Bastian's proposal? Pledging herself to a man who'd not only boldly lied to her, but had then preceded to allow the farce to go on for months?

It was born out of the desire to protect her, she now knew, but that didn't make it okay.

And how could she even for a second think about allowing herself to be claimed by him when it would undoubtedly call for her to leave Middletown for Haven Falls? Leave her parents for Bastian?

She wasn't a fool. She knew that was what it would come down to. Bastian would insist that she go home with him. Perhaps he wouldn't press the issue now, but it was only a matter a time. Sometime before the next full moon, she was sure.

What was she supposed to say to her parents? "Sorry, Mom, Dad, I know you just got me back after months of fruitless searching, but I'm leaving. You remember that Bastian character I told you about? Well, he showed up and proclaimed his undying love for me, so we're getting hitched and I'm moving back to Canada. Oh, and by the way, I probably should have mentioned this before, but Bastian and I are werewolves so it probably wouldn't be a good idea for you to visit. Like, ever. Thanks for understanding!"

They'd have her locked in a padded cell before she'd even be able to finish talking.

But Katherine would never dream of doing the alternative and just leave without an explanation. She couldn't just disappear into the night and cause them even more pain and heartache than she already had. It was unfathomable.

But so is living without Bastian, a voice whispered in the back of her mind. *So is living without the rest of your pack.*

Her head began to pound as the warring thoughts battled each other. Before the sudden headache could escalate, however, she forced herself to concentrate on a more pressing matter.

The early morning sun was beginning to creep up into the sky, spectacular hues of yellows and oranges shining through thick branches and highlighting the dewy grass. The presence of the sun meant her parents would soon be up, and they'd undoubtedly worry if they found her missing from her bed.

"I have to go," Katherine muttered, taking another step away from the man still watching her intently. "I don't want my parents to find me gone and assume the worse."

Apparently not quite ready to let her go, Bastian reached forward and gently grasped her wrist, his long fingers overlapping as they easily wrapped around the entire thing. "You never said if you would let me claim you as my mate."

Katherine couldn't quite meet his eyes, settling on a simple, but telling, "I know."

He sighed in obvious disappointment, but freed her wrist. "Can you at least put the ring I gave you back on where it belongs around your neck?"

The part of her still hurting from the lie he'd told her desired to deny him the request out of spite, but an even larger part of her longed to do exactly as he asked. "Okay," she agreed.

He nodded, at least temporarily mollified. "Stay here," he ordered her. "I'll go get your clothes. They're in the bag you left in that rickety house, right?"

She'd long ago figured out that he'd been watching her and so wasn't surprised that he knew where she'd left her clothes. "Yeah," she confirmed, and before she could blink, Bastian had transformed into his wolf form and was bounding away.

It only took a few minutes for him to return with her backpack as well as a pair of pants and shirt he'd apparently brought for himself. She didn't know where he'd grabbed them from and didn't bother to ask either. They both dressed in silence.

She was rising from lacing up her shoes when Bastian grabbed her from behind, startling her as he swiftly wrapped his arm around her waist and pulled her to him so tightly that her back was molded to his front. "You have no idea how difficult this is for me," he admitted softly, burying his face into her hair. "Every cell in my body is screaming at me to take you and run. But I know that's not what you want. I know I have to let you go, at least for now, and it's killing me."

She didn't want to have to leave him either, not really, and the words were out of her mouth before she knew she even intended to speak them. "Come see me tonight in my room. You can sneak in through the window."

She could physically feel his coiled muscles relax against her back at her suggestion. "Thank you," he murmured, placing one last kiss in her hair before releasing her. "I love you."

Katherine froze. "I..." she tried weakly, but the words wouldn't come. "I *really* have to go." She grabbed her backpack from where it sat on the grassy ground and slung it over her shoulder before risking a peek at the man.

A dissatisfied frown was pulling at Bastian's lips, but he nodded. "Until tonight," he bid her farewell.

"Until tonight," Katherine agreed.

It took every ounce of her fortitude to walk away from him. She looked back only once – when a soulful, yearning howl pierced the air – but she could see nothing but trees. He was already gone.

CHAPTER ELEVEN

"Tonight" had come before Katherine knew it.

After she'd left Bastian in the woods, she had high-tailed it back to her parents' house, managing to somehow scale the metal gutters and haul herself back in through the same window she'd recklessly leapt from hours earlier. She'd taken a moment to examine her room and make sure it hadn't been disturbed and another to dig the ring Bastian had given her out of her nightstand drawer and slip the chain it was attached to over her head. Then she'd collapsed onto her bed – physically exhausted from her transformation into a wolf and mentally drained from Bastian's revelations.

No sooner had her head hit the pillow than she was drifting off into a deep, invigorating sleep that her body and mind both desperately needed.

Katherine was so profoundly under the Sandman's spell, in fact, that she slept right through breakfast and lunch, having dazedly shushed and shooed her father away when he'd attempted to wake her for said meals. Elaine had outright refused to allow her daughter to doze through supper, however, and had practically dragged Katherine down the stairs and into the dining room to make sure she ate something that day.

Katherine was able to shake off the last remnants of sleep when the divine smell of braised pork hit her nose, and she quickly devoured three helpings of the succulent meat. While eating certainly wasn't a chore, fielding her parents' concerned questions as she stuffed herself was another matter entirely.

"Are you feeling okay, Katherine?"

"Did you have trouble sleeping last night? You've been out of it all day."

"Has your head been hurting you at all?"

There were only so many times Katherine could assure them that she was fine before annoyance began to tickle the back of her mind and she got prickly.

"I still think you should consider seeing a doctor, honey."

Katherine tensed at her mother's suggestion, a forkful of pork halfway to her mouth. By "doctor", of course, she meant a psychiatrist. A shrink. She'd been pestering her to see one ever since the lab work had come back from the hospital. The blood results had returned with an unusually high white blood cell count, which Dr. Morgan had attributed to the so called fever she'd been running at the time – she had no idea that it was Katherine's normal temperature, of course. The MRI scan they'd performed on her head, however, had revealed that her brain appeared perfectly normal.

It'd been a relief for Katherine, who'd been worried that being part wolf would have somehow changed the chemistry of her brain in a way that was detectable by the scanner.

Unfortunately, the news *didn't* relieve her parents. In fact, it only seemed to cause them more concern. Mostly because Dr. Morgan had suggested over the phone that the memory loss Katherine was experiencing was likely psychological in nature, a "defense mechanism" of the brain, as she'd described it to them.

Of course, what the doctor didn't know was that, in reality, there was no memory loss. Her mother didn't know this either.

She just thought Katherine was traumatized.

"I don't need to see a shrink, Mom," she objected tersely. Logically, she knew her parents' concern was justified, brought on by a lie she'd told them straight to their faces, but unfortunately, that didn't make her irritation with them any less real. Said irritation was compounded by the absurd fear that if she *was* forced to see a psychiatrist, he or she would somehow immediately sniff out the fact that she was full of crap.

"There's no shame in seeing a psychiatrist, Katherine. I know you don't want to, but I think it's a good idea. You never know, he may even be able to help you recover some of your lost memories."

Katherine's fork clattered loudly as it hit her empty plate. "*He?*" she demanded. Her mother had never assigned a gender to the psychiatrist she insisted she see before now.

Elaine sighed, clearly recognizing that she'd been caught. "Yes, he. As in Dr. Fitzgerald. He's highly respected in his field and has an office in Des Moines. He was recommended to me by Dr. Morgan. I've scheduled an appointment for you next week."

Katherine stared. "So what? That's it? It doesn't matter what I want?" When her mother didn't respond, she turned to her father. "Dad?"

He shrugged helplessly. "I think your mother's right, Kit. This will be good for you."

Katherine ran her suddenly shaking hands through her hair. Although in Haven Falls she was considered an adult, in Middletown her parents were her guardians and could essentially force her to do as they pleased. An anger that she knew to be irrational began to build in her belly, and she furiously tried to stomp it down.

"We need to talk about school, too, Katherine. You missed an entire year of it. Unless you want to repeat your junior year, we're going to have to enroll you in summer school."

But she'd just finished school!

"I'm not going to summer school," Katherine argued, not an ounce of compliance in her voice. "And I'd like to see you try to make me see this shrink in Des Moines."

"Katherine!" her mother exclaimed, clearly shocked at the brazen show of rebellion. She recovered quickly, however. "I've had enough of your attitude, young lady. I can understand the fact that you've gotten used to doing whatever you want whenever you want while living with this Bastian person, but you're back home now. Your father and I are your parents and we are in charge here, *not* you. You listen to us, not the other way around."

A fierce tremor swept through her and before she could stop herself, Katherine had sprung up and flung out her right arm, swiftly sweeping ceramic plates and glassware violently off of the wooden surface. They crashed to the floor in a flurry of noise, and both her parents jumped up in surprise. "I don't have to listen to anyone!" she rebuffed her mother harshly. "Not to anyone but B-," she almost named her alpha, but was able to stop herself in time. "Not to anyone but myself!" she finished instead.

But the sound of Bastian's name resounding in her head – the fact that she'd almost said it out loud and had named him as her preferred caretaker over her parents – was enough to bring her senses trickling back to her. She took in the mess she'd made – the broken plates and shattered glass littering the floor – and embarrassed remorse flooded her.

She forced herself to look up into her parents' shocked faces. Her mother's eyes were bright with unshed tears. Her father, on the other hand, looked furious – a red, splotchy blush slowly making its way up his face. His hands came at her – not to hit, but to restrain. The feel of them firmly grabbing her shoulders, however, was enough to spark her fading anger. Because as gentle as his fingers were around her clavicles, she did *not* want to be touched.

For a horrifying second Katherine thought she'd lash out at him with her fists. She managed to control herself, however, and instead jerked violently away from his restraining hands. They dropped uselessly to his sides. "Don't touch me," she snapped at him.

"Calm down, Katherine, right now," he ordered.

But Katherine wasn't calm – her heart was practically pulsating out of her chest – and it was all she could do not to *growl* at her own parents. Part of her wanted to apologize to them for her outburst and clean up the mess she'd made. But the part in control at the moment – it felt suspiciously like the wolf – only managed to bite out a quick "Leave me alone!" before she bolted from the room and rushed up the stairs, taking the carpeted steps two at a time until she reached her bedroom door. She locked it behind her, bringing her still trembling hands up to her chest.

What in the hell was wrong with her?

Katherine contemplated the question as her heartbeat gradually slowed to its normal pace.

One second she was somewhat irritated with her parents and the next she was shouting and shucking dishes off the table in a fit of rage. Both emotions she knew were only cheap disguises for another buried underneath the both of them – guilt. Guilt for having lied to them weeks ago when she'd returned. For continuing to lie to them every day. She didn't have amnesia. *She was a frickin' werewolf!*

But Katherine couldn't possibly tell them that.

If she did, they'd really think she was crazy, and instead of making her see a shrink, they'd be sending her off to some nuthouse. Sure, they'd call it a "hospital" or "institution", but the padded white walls would be a dead giveaway to what it really was.

Even if she transformed into a wolf in front of them and *made* them believe her, she'd be forcing them to uproot their lives and live indefinitely in Haven Falls. Just like all the other family members who knew that their parent, child, or sibling was a werewolf.

Katherine couldn't do that to them.

She stayed locked in her room for well over an hour, sorting through the twisted knot of emotions that sat where her stomach was supposed to be. As she worried herself to near tears, the sky outside of her window darkened from a pleasant light blue to a near black. Her father knocked on her door and attempted to engage her in conversation a few times, but Katherine ignored him, not quite ready to face the consequences of her emotional outburst.

Especially when despite it all, a small piece of her – the wolf, she knew – was still infuriated that they'd had the gall to try to control her. The wolf didn't care that they were her parents and were perfectly within their rights to do just that – it still wanted to snarl and snap its sharp teeth at their attempt.

She ran agitated hands through her hair, stopping in surprise when one of them brushed over something with a rough, flakey texture. She pulled it out of the tangled mess on her head. A leaf. She checked her scalp over carefully with her fingers and pulled out two more of the half-decayed things.

She was astonished her parents hadn't noticed them at the disastrous supper they'd shared, but she was also immensely grateful. The foliage certainly would have been difficult to explain away.

Finding the leaves had reminded Katherine that she was in desperate need of a shower. Gallivanting around a forest all night wasn't exactly ideal for one's hygiene, after all. Deciding she had enough time to nab one before Bastian arrived, she quickly shucked off her clothes and entered her bathroom. She cranked on the shower's faucet and waited for the water that erupted from the nozzle to warm. Right before she stepped into the spray, however, she remembered that she'd used up the last of her shampoo the morning before and had forgotten to replace it.

Cursing, Katherine twisted the faucet and shut off the water. She grabbed a towel and wrapped it securely around her torso. Clutching the overlapping edges to her chest, she walked briskly to her sister's old room – the one she was once again occupying – and knocked on the door. She wasn't about to ask her mother if she could use *her* shampoo after nearly bringing the woman to tears not two hours earlier, after all.

When Sam didn't answer the door, Katherine risked peeking inside. It was dark, quiet, and most importantly, empty. She took the opportunity to quickly duck into the small bathroom connected to her sister's room and snatch one of the many bottles of hair product decorating the shower's built-in shelves.

She glanced at the bottle's label. She didn't know how the thick, purple concoction was going to go about making her hair smell like a sundrenched vineyard, but it was shampoo, which made it good enough for her.

Katherine just about jumped out of her skin when she turned around and nearly bumped into Chad, her brother-in-law, who was suddenly looming in the bathroom's doorway.

"Jesus, you scared me," she scolded, clutching the towel she was holding more tightly in her fist. "What are you doing in here?"

She'd hardly seen the man at all since she'd returned to Middletown nearly a month ago. He was away from the house more often than not, and Sam had confided in her that while he liked to give her vague excuses about work, she knew that he spent most of his time frequenting the bars in town. He returned from "work" completely sloshed more often than not.

Katherine felt awful for her sister, but couldn't say that she'd missed Chad's presence at the house all that much. The man was an expert at making her uncomfortable.

"I think the question is what are *you* doing in here?" he countered, plucking the bottle of shampoo from her hand.

There was no way Katherine could miss the stench of whiskey as he leaned in close to her, and she wrinkled her nose in disgust. "And what are you doing with this, hmm?" Chad continued, seemingly oblivious to her revulsion. "I don't think Sam would appreciate her little sister stealing her shampoo. It's very expensive. I should know, the bitch spends half of my pay check on this stupid shit."

Katherine bristled. She could feel her face heating in anger. "Don't call my sister a bitch," she spat. "And I was only borrowing it. I doubt Sam would have noticed it was missing, let alone have actually cared that it was gone."

Chad snorted. "I call 'em like I see 'em," he retorted. "And did you ever think that maybe *I* care? After all, it was my hard earned money that paid for this shit. Technically, it's *mine*."

Katherine rolled her eyes. She wasn't about to bother arguing with the drunken asshat. "Whatever," she muttered, pushing past him. She'd just have to suck it up and ask her mom to lend her some of her shampoo.

Chad, however, wasn't quite ready to let her leave. This was made apparent when he sidestepped to block the only exit from the bathroom with his body. "Hey, I never said you couldn't have it," he protested. "Just do me a quick favor and it's all yours."

Katherine eyed the man suspiciously. "What favor?" she asked.

She knew that she shouldn't have taken the bait when he offered her a crude grin. "Just let me take a peek at what's under that towel."

The tiny spike of fear that Katherine felt at his words was almost completely smothered by the white hot anger that they had also caused. If her cheeks had been warm before, they had to have been on fire now. She could feel the heat as it climbed all the way up to the tips of her ears.

Then Chad's laughter registered.

"You should see the look on your face," he hooted, slapping his hand on the side of his thigh as he expressed his mirth. The smell of alcohol once again hit her nose, and Katherine lost it. Using her free hand, she unceremoniously shoved the man out of her way. He obviously hadn't been expecting the push and stumbled backwards. She attempted to make her getaway then, but Chad made the mistake of reaching for her arm and wrapping his fingers in an unyielding grip around her elbow. "Hey, don't be like that, sweetheart."

But Katherine was no "sweetheart" and didn't hesitate a second before pulling back her fist and slamming it unapologetically into Chad's impertinent mouth. He immediately released her elbow.

"You bitch!" he hollered at her, and she could see the crimson blood already gathering in the cracks between his teeth before he hid his mouth from her view, holding it tenderly with his hand.

Satisfied that he was aptly distracted, Katherine wasted no time in fleeing the room. For the second time in as many hours, Katherine ran to her bedroom and slammed the door shut behind her.

She didn't even realize that she was trembling until it took her three tries to successfully turn the door's lock.

She took a minute to gather herself. *Why did crap like this always have to happen to her?* She silently prayed that Sam would tell their parents that she and Chad intended to divorce soon and then determinedly put the incident out of her mind. She highly doubted that Chad would be stupid enough to try to corner her again. If he did, she didn't think she could be held responsible for her actions.

Accepting the fact that she'd have to forego shampooing her hair – the jerk had still been holding the bottle of hair product when she'd bolted from the room – Katherine hurried to the bathroom and slipped into the shower anyway. She made an attempt to wash her long tresses with soap and then lingered under the warm spray, trying for once to just *not* think.

When the water began to run cold, she finally cranked off the faucet. She patted her body dry before once again wrapping it snuggly in a towel. Then she wrung her hair of excess water before drying the unruly strands with another towel.

She hadn't realized just how much time had passed until she stepped out of her bathroom and was standing in front of a man wearing nothing but a towel for the second time that day. This time, though, the man was Bastian.

Katherine froze.

The warmth that settled in her belly as Bastian's heated gaze took her in was entirely different from the embarrassment that had flooded her when Chad had seen her in such a vulnerable state. Still, she forced herself to move. "Sorry," she mumbled, incredibly flustered as she blindly reached for her dresser and yanked open a random drawer. She grabbed the first piece of clothing her fingers touched and swiveled back into the bathroom. "Just give me a minute."

Katherine took a deep breath, attempting to compose herself. She looked down at the clothes she'd inadvertently snatched, however, and her attempt was thoroughly thwarted. Although she'd managed to grab some underwear, the pajama shirt she'd seized was probably the most beloved one she owned. It was a simple, oversized night shirt that fell down to mid-thigh. That was all fine and dandy except for the fact that she'd worn the shirt to bed so many times that the gray material it was made of was practically see through.

But she wasn't about to go out there in nothing but a towel *again* and practically admit how nervous he'd made her by digging through her dresser for something else to wear. So she sucked it up and slipped the shirt on. She also took a comb from the countertop under the mirror and ran its teeth through her damp hair a couple of times in an attempt to tame it. She must have been in there for too long, however, because just as she was finishing up, she heard a hesitant knock on the door. "Are you okay?"

Bastian's timbre caused another flash of warmth to shoot through her, brightening her pale cheeks. "I'm fine," Katherine forced out and was proud that the words didn't sound the least bit strangled.

Running the comb through her hair one last time, she gathered up every last bit of her courage and opened the door. Strategically crossing her arms over her chest, Katherine hurried over to the bed, where she sat and immediately covered her bare legs with a blanket.

Bastian's eyes shone with poorly concealed amusement, and Katherine fought the urge to blush. "It's ridiculous how endearingly cute you are," he commented idly.

Katherine scowled, smoothing the blanket over her lap. "I'm not *cute*, I'm fierce," she protested.

Bastian nodded amiably. "That too," he agreed, the barest hint of a smile on his lips. They fell back into a solemn, straight line, however, when he caught sight of the golden ring glinting from where it hung around her neck. He took two long strides forward and fell to his knees before her. The disparity between their heights was so great that even then, she still had to look up slightly to meet his eyes. He reached forward, gently clasping the piece of jewelry between his fingers. "You're wearing my ring."

"I said that I would," she reminded him gently.

"I know, but I wasn't sure..." he trailed off. "Thank you," he finally said in a gruff voice, releasing the bejeweled ring, but not moving from where he continued to kneel before her, seemingly perfectly content to gaze into Katherine's eyes until kingdom come.

She could only take the intensity of his stare for so long, however, before she looked away. "I almost chucked it into a corn field," she admitted, the words tumbling from her mouth before she could think better of them. "I was so mad at you. I'm *still* so mad at you."

Bastian stiffened slightly at the confession. "I know," he acknowledged softly. He tucked a piece of wayward hair behind her ear with gentle fingers. "Even if I apologized to you every day for the rest of my life, it still wouldn't be enough to express the magnitude of my regret."

To Katherine's horror, she recognized the slight sting in her eyes as tears threatening to escape. *Hadn't she cried enough in front of this man last night?* She furiously batted them back. "It hurt so much," she croaked out. "When you told me that my parents were dead, I couldn't even bare to think of them for months afterwards. I was so afraid that I would break down. The realization that you'd lied… that you had been purposefully deceiving me since the moment we met, leaving me to grieve over people who were actually alive… well, that almost hurt more than when I thought that my parents *were* dead."

The words came out disjointed and choppy, and Katherine failed to keep the traitorous tears at bay. Bastian hastily brushed them away with calloused thumbs. "I'm so sorry," he murmured softly, his eyes imploring her to believe him. "Please don't cry. Tell me what I can do to make you feel better. I'd do anything to take your hurt away."

Katherine didn't know how to tell him that the only thing that seemed to ease her heartache was *him*. Despite the fact that he'd been the one to inflict the emotional wound, he was the only one who could mend it. His very presence soothed her more than anyone else's ever could.

The only way Katherine knew how to express this was by pulling the man into a tight embrace, so that was exactly what she did. She wrapped her arms around the back of his neck and pulled him forward, burrowing her head under his chin as she sought the comfort only he could give.

Bastian appeased her immediately, one arm wrapping itself securely around her waist and the other burying itself in her hair. He held her close as she cried. "I'm sorry," he repeated, pressing his lips to the crown of her head as tears poured forth from her eyes. "I'd do anything for you, Katherine, just tell me what you want." He hesitated briefly before adding, "We can even stay here in Middletown. No one can know what we are, but I'll find a way to make it work if that's what you really want."

That caught Katherine's attention and she pulled away from the man just enough so that she could look into his eyes and gauge the truth. "Really?" she sniffled pitifully.

He nodded solemnly.

"What about the pack?" she asked, her voice still slightly wobbly. "I seriously doubt that they want to live here."

"They love you," Bastian contested. "And they're loyal enough to me to stay if I asked them."

Katherine wiped the tears still clinging stubbornly to her eyes away with the palms of her hands. "But what about your duties as head alpha?"

"I left Luther in charge of the council before I left. I'm sure he can manage the job just fine if I choose not to return. *Nothing* is as important to me as you are."

The fact that he was willing to sacrifice everything he'd ever known just because he thought that it was what she wanted awed Katherine to the point that tears were once again threatening to spill down her cheeks. This time, though, she managed to contain them.

"I could never ask you to do that," she said, shaking her head. "You wouldn't be happy here. The pack wouldn't be happy here."

"Of course, I'd be happy here," Bastian immediately protested. "*You* make me happy. If that's what you truly want – to stay here in Middletown – then nothing could ever keep me away."

No matter what he said, Katherine knew that it would be incredibly selfish to ask that of him. And besides… "I don't know what I want," she confessed in a whisper so soft that even her ears almost couldn't pick up the words.

Bastian's expression remained carefully neutral, but there was no way she could miss the hopeful glint that suddenly shone in his eyes. "You want to go back to Haven Falls?" His tone was only cautiously optimistic, but Katherine could practically see the cogs of his brain turning as he undoubtedly thought of the many ways he could snatch her from her bedroom and spirit her away that very instant.

"I don't know," Katherine repeated, hoping to stop such thoughts in their tracks. She wasn't going anywhere yet. "I love my family, but… I don't know if I belong here anymore. Since returning, my life has just evolved into one convoluted lie. I couldn't exactly tell my parents that I was a werewolf when I showed up on their doorstep so I made up some elaborate story about having amnesia. It was all over the news," she added blandly, still having trouble believing that *that* had happened. "Now they want me to see a psychiatrist. And apparently go to summer school even though I've already graduated from the only school that matters. Everything is just a big mess," she admitted, shoulders drooping dejectedly.

"Katherine-"

"Worse than all of that, though," Katherine interrupted the man before she lost her nerve, "is that I'm afraid I'll wind up hurting them. My family. I almost *did* tonight."

Bastian frowned. "What do you mean?" he asked, gently rubbing the small of her back.

"At supper tonight, my mom was talking about the psychiatrist she wants me to see and she brought up summer school. I was irritated with her. But then she said something about her being in charge of me, and I was more than just mad… I lost it. I yelled at her and shoved the dishes off the table. I… I almost lashed out at my dad when he tried to touch me. I just barely managed to stop myself from hitting him. I don't know what's wrong with me," she confessed in a rush of shame-filled words.

"Hey," Bastian soothed, his hand now patting her hair as she once again hid her face in his shirt, this time though, in embarrassment instead of a quest for comfort. "That's not your fault," he assured her softly. "You know that the moon's cycle affects our moods, and that we can be especially emotional and even volatile both before and after the full moon. You can't beat yourself up about something that's entirely natural."

It was true. Passionate outbursts and acts of violence were completely normal and even expected of the werewolves who resided in Haven Falls.

"I know," she admitted, gently disentangling herself from the man's embrace. "But that means that it'll happen again… and that I probably *will* end up hurting them eventually."

"Maybe," Bastian cautiously agreed. "But if you truly want to stay here, we'll figure something out. And if you *do* decide you want to go back to Haven Falls, well, we'll find a way for you to stay in contact with your family. I can't let you own a cell phone – it's too much of a security breach – but maybe I could drive you out to Fort Saskatchewan or another nearby city once every few weeks so that you could call them from a payphone there. And we could visit whenever you want."

Katherine was impressed with how much thought the man had put into the idea. But…"How can I even consider leaving my family after all I've put them through? I'm an awful person." She covered her face with her hands.

"Hush," Bastian scolded. "You are anything but awful. You're beautiful, both inside and out."

Katherine peeked out at the man between her fingers and offered him a watery smile.

He smiled in return, the adorable dimple on his right cheek making an appearance, but his face was soon marred by a concerned frown. He gently traced the knuckles of her right hand. "What happened here?"

Katherine pulled her hands away from her face and immediately realized what had caused the man's mouth to dip into a frown. The knuckles of her right hand were red and slightly swollen. She hadn't even noticed it before, but she couldn't say that she was very surprised that Bastian *had*.

He seemed to notice everything when it came to her.

"I punched my brother-in-law in the mouth," Katherine admitted matter-of-factly.

Bastian tensed in front of her, his body suddenly disturbingly rigid. "Why?" he demanded, grasping either side of her face. "Did he do something to you? Did he hurt you?"

Katherine carefully peeled his fingers from her cheekbones. "Nothing like that," she assured him. "He… he just called my sister a name and it sparked my temper."

She wasn't exactly lying and so didn't feel too bad about the part of the story she'd chosen to omit. After all, Katherine knew if she told Bastian what else he'd said to her and described how he'd grabbed her, Bastian would have Chad in a chokehold in less than a minute. Not exactly the best way for her family to meet her alpha… *her mate.*

Bastian didn't look entirely convinced, however. "Are you sure?"

Katherine nodded and quickly sought to change the subject. "But just so you know, even if I do decide to go back to Haven Falls with you, that doesn't mean that I'm agreeing to let you… *claim* me or whatever."

Bastian grinned, seemingly as willing to banish Chad from his mind as she was from her own. "I know," he acknowledged, "but I'm hoping you'll give me plenty of opportunities to convince you."

Katherine narrowed her eyes at the mischievous smile playing on his lips. "And how exactly are you going to do that?"

Bastian propped himself forward so that their noses were a mere inch from touching. Katherine couldn't help but lean into his touch as he cupped the sides of her face. "Like this," he answered softly, his voice a near whisper, before connecting his lips to hers.

What started off as a soft, sensual kiss – barely more than Bastian's lips lingering tenderly over hers– quickly escalated into a frenzied battle of the mouths. Their teeth clashed, and Bastian's tongue forced itself between her lips, dominating the inside of her mouth as he probed and licked at it. Katherine's breath hitched when he sucked hard at her bottom lip. Trembling with a feeling almost completely foreign to her, she pulled him impossibly closer.

It was like Bastian could read her mind and knew exactly what she wanted because in the next instant, he was on top of her, pushing her back into the mattress as he covered her body with his own solid mass. His hands gripped her waist possessively. The bruise she'd acquired jumping out of her window the night before, however, hadn't quite healed, and she couldn't suppress a pained flinch, immediately bringing attention to the minor injury.

Bastian froze on top of her.

Before she even had time to be embarrassed about it, Bastian was yanking her night shirt up above her waist, his eyes searching for whatever had caused her to recoil from him. When he spotted the patch of discolored skin, his fingers ghosted over the purple bruise that had blossomed over her hip bone the night before. "What happened?" he asked, his voice like gravel.

"It was my own fault," she hurriedly assured him. "It happened when I jumped out of my window last night."

Bastian's brow furrowed in consternation. "Yes, I saw you," he said, reconfirming what Katherine already knew to be true – that he'd been watching her last night. "May I ask what possessed you to do that?"

Katherine scowled at the admonishment in his tone. "Well, I had to sneak out of the house somehow," she pointed out. "When I saw Markus jump from it a week ago, it looked easy enough."

Bastian frowned. "Markus was here?" His tone was unreadable, but something resembling anger lurked in the man's eyes.

Katherine had forgotten that he hadn't known about Markus's impromptu visit.

"Yes," Katherine admitted, "but can we please not talk about *Markus* of all people right now?" She gestured vaguely at the rather intimate position they were in.

Bastian's eyes immediately softened. "Of course," he acquiesced, gently fingering the bruise once more. "Does it hurt much?"

"Hardly at all," she assured him.

Bastian seemed satisfied with that answer and took Katherine by surprise by pressing a soft kiss to the blemished skin. She gasped, goosebumps erupting over her flesh. Her stomach quivered as he placed another airy kiss– a mere brush of the lips – on her belly button. His dark eyes peered up at her. "Is this okay?"

Katherine didn't think she could force her voice to work just that second so she nodded her consent instead. Bastian lips pressed against the pale, unmarked skin of her other hipbone before slowly trailing up her belly, caressing the smooth flesh of her stomach with lips and tongue. His eyes didn't leave hers once.

His hands followed his mouth, coming to rest on the frayed ends of her night shirt, which had been pushed up to just below her breasts. After searching her eyes for a moment, he must have found what he was looking for– some sort of permission – because in the next second he was lifting it further up her body. Katherine allowed it – helped him even, to pull the worn shirt off over her head.

She wasn't wearing a bra.

Nearly overcome with the urge to cover herself – she knew logically that Bastian had seen her naked before, but never under such intimate circumstances – she attempted to cross her arms over her bare breasts. Bastian, though, easily read her intentions and carefully caught her arms. "Don't," he whispered, staring reverently at her body. "Just, please don't do that… you're so goddamn beautiful."

His eyes flickered up to meet hers. "Can I touch you?"

This time Katherine forced herself to speak, releasing her abused bottom lip from where she'd been nervously chewing on it. "Yes."

Bastian's hands were firm, but also incredibly gentle, as they explored her skin. A calloused thumb brushed against one nipple, and she sucked in a mouthful of air as the pink peak pebbled under his touch. She forced herself to shakily exhale, but could hardly concentrate on something as mundane as breathing when he captured the other pink bud between two fingers and gently tugged at it.

Bastian's pupils were blown wide as he watched her body react to his ministrations, and before Katherine knew he'd intended to do it, his mouth was on her, worshipping one nipple with his tongue as he continued to pull at the other. Katherine whimpered, helplessly arching into his touch as she became enraptured by the wonderful sensation his mouth and hands were causing to build in her lower belly. Teeth scraped against her, and a spark of desire so strong shot through her that for a second, Katherine was convinced she was on fire.

"You taste so goddamn good," the man muttered against her skin.

"Bastian," she cried feebly in response.

He shuddered and groaned against her, his warm breath heating her already flushed skin. "Say that again," he demanded.

"Bastian," she acquiesced immediately, the sound of his name coming out of her mouth once again, causing the man to moan.

It suddenly struck Katherine as unfair that she was the only one without a shirt on.

Hastily attempting to remedy the situation, she tugged at the hem of Bastian's shirt. Realizing what she was trying to do, the man sat up and pulled the offending piece of clothing off for her.

Then it was Katherine's turn to explore bare skin, relishing in the way Bastian trembled as her small fingers roamed his chest, dipping into the natural grooves his muscles made as they bulged under his flesh. All too soon, however, he captured her hands, pressing them gently into the mattress so that he could admire her again. He nuzzled his face into her chest, the short stubble that covered his cheeks and chin burning her slightly as the tiny, coarse hairs brushed over her sensitive skin.

After he'd once again lavished her chest with open mouthed kisses, he moved on to her neck, sucking on whatever piece of flesh he could manage to find. The skin on the slender column of her neck ached in the best way as his tongue and teeth fixated on it.

Katherine was consumed by the husky, earthly aroma that radiated off of Bastian in waves as he attempted to devour her, and her eyes glazed over in desire as he nipped at the delicate skin of her ear. Lost in a lustful haze, she didn't recognize the breathy moans escaping her mouth as her own and arched into the man, attempting to get as close to him as possible. She raised her hips wantonly, pressing the most intimate part of her body against him.

He immediately released her hands and grasped her hips instead, wrapping his fingers around them possessively. But instead of pulling her closer to him, he pressed her into the mattress – as far away from him as possible.

Katherine mewed in displeasure. "Bastian," she pleaded pathetically, desperate to be touched.

"Don't," he managed to choke out.

"Please," she begged, arching up again. His grip turned just the slightest bit painful as he determinedly held her down. Unbelievably frustrated, Katherine used one of her newly freed hands to rub daringly against the rather obvious bulge in his pants.

Bastian practically leapt off the bed – *off of her* – and the rush of cool air hitting her naked skin immediately brought Katherine back to her senses. A mortified blush exploded across her face, and she quickly pulled the covers that were pooled at bottom of the bed up to her neck, refusing to look the man who she had *thought* had actually wanted her. Embarrassed tears threatened to well in her eyes. "Maybe you should go," she suggested as blandly as possible, refusing to look at him.

"Katherine, please. You don't understand."

Bastian's voice was so earnest that she allowed herself to glance up at him. The man was shaking so violently that his body practically vibrated, and Katherine immediately jumped up in concern. "What's wrong?" she demanded, touching his arm as she attempted to sooth him.

Bastian clamped his teeth together at the innocent touch, and Katherine immediately dropped her hand, plopping herself back on the bed.

"What's wrong is that I want you too much," he grit out between clenched teeth, "and you don't think I want you enough."

Katherine stiffened at the proclamation. "What's that supposed to mean?"

Bastian shook his head in apparent disbelief over her naiveté. "Can't you feel how much I want you?" he answered her question with one of his own.

Katherine knew he wasn't talking about the obvious way his body physically responded to hers, but rather the crackling attraction that always seemed to seamlessly flow between them.

"Yes," Katherine admitted. "Of course I feel it. But if you feel it too, then why did you stop?"

"Because I'm terrified that I'll claim you, you foolish girl," Bastian exclaimed. He pulled uselessly at his disheveled hair. "I don't think I can bed you and *not* claim you," he admitted. "Even now, every instinct I have is telling me to force myself between your legs and sink my teeth into your neck, but I *know* you don't want that. To be claimed as my mate. Not yet anyway."

Suddenly Bastian's behavior made sense. Katherine was surprisingly grateful. And maybe just the tiniest bit disappointed as well. Because Bastian had basically just told her that sex was off the table until she was ready for him to claim her.

She just wished the stubborn man had told her the reason for his reluctance to be intimate with her earlier. "Is that why you were so distant before I left Haven Falls? Why you refused to do much more than kiss me?" she asked, seeking to confirm her theory.

"That was part of the reason, yes," he readily disclosed. "I was also terrified that you'd hate me when you found out that I'd lied to you about your parents – I was always planning on telling you the truth about them eventually – and that you'd regret allowing me to touch you."

Katherine was silent as she processed that. She was moved he'd so thoroughly considered her feelings.

"Please tell me you understand," Bastian continued when she'd been quiet for too long. "You have to believe me when I say that it is physically *painful* how much I want you."

"I understand," Katherine hastily replied, praying that her face wasn't as absurdly red as she thought it was at his blunt confession. She bit her lip. "We can still cuddle, though, right? The urge to… *claim* me won't be too strong? We've done it before," she pointed out.

An amused smile played at the corners of Bastian's lips. "I think I can control myself," he confirmed.

"Will you stay with me then?" Katherine asked. "Tonight, I mean. I don't want you to leave."

The admission must have calmed the wolf considerably because what remained of Bastian's tremors almost immediately vanished. "Of course I'll stay," he agreed, eyes incredibly tender. "For as long as you want me."

Katherine thought it'd be a bit *too* cheesy to admit that she'd want him forever. So instead, she quickly grabbed her discarded night-shirt off the floor, shoved it over her head, and scooted over to make room for Bastian on the bed.

He clambered onto the mattress, immediately pulling her to his side. She hesitantly pecked a kiss to his cheek before curling up next to the man and laying her head on his bare chest. She fell asleep the most content she'd been in a long time, listening to the lull of his heartbeat as it beat rhythmically under her ear.

CHAPTER TWELVE

Katherine woke wrapped in a cocoon of heavy blankets, the faint impression of a kiss still lingering on her forehead.

Which was why she was so bewildered – *dismayed* – when she turned around to find the other half of the bed empty.

She disentangled herself from the mass of blankets, kicking them to the floor as she peered around her bedroom. With the exception of herself, however, that was also empty. Disappointment swirled in her belly.

Bastian had promised to stay.

She absentmindedly fingered the sheets upon which the man had slept the night before, her forehead crinkling in confusion when they were still warm to the touch. Before she could ponder the mystery for long, however, the sound of her shower bursting to life in the adjoining bathroom had a shock of surprise shooting down her spine. As the surprise ebbed, so too did the disappointment, and Katherine allowed a pleased smile to form on her lips.

So Bastian had kept his promise after all.

Ignoring how ridiculously giddy that thought made her feel, Katherine took advantage of the privacy the man had unknowingly granted her and quickly threw on some black leggings, pairing them with a navy blue tank top she managed to find shoved in the back of one of her dresser drawers. She also gathered her wayward hair into a sloppy ponytail atop her head.

Satisfied that she was at least somewhat presentable, Kathrine eyed the bathroom door once more, the din of running water splattering against tile still sounding from behind of it.

She tried not to think about the fact that Bastian was naked behind the door. Shirtless. Pantless. Underwearless. *Was that even a word?*

She knew firsthand, though, that there was nothing *less* about him.

The sound of her stomach growling irritably distracted her from her inappropriate reverie, and despite no one having been around to hear the rumbling, Katherine's cheeks colored a light pink. Which was ridiculous because of course she was hungry. She *had* missed two meals yesterday.

It occurred to her that perhaps Bastian was hungry as well.

That thought sparked an idea in her head, and before Katherine could question the rather domestic urge that had taken hold of her, she was bounding down the stairs, intent on making a hardy breakfast for the man using her shower.

She'd completely forgotten the fact that she was still avoiding her parents until she'd already reached the bottom of the staircase. Her body tensed when the realization struck her, and she peeked cautiously into the living room and then dining room before hesitantly venturing into the kitchen. Relief washed over her, relaxing her stiff muscles, when that room, too, was proven to be vacant. Her parents must not have been home.

A quick detour into the garage confirmed this theory – one of the two cars that her mom and dad shared was gone. It begged the question of where they were. It was Sunday so Katherine knew they couldn't have been at work. Church maybe?

Her parents hadn't been avid churchgoers before she'd disappeared months ago, but maybe that had changed. *Or maybe they'd gone to pray for their demon-possessed daughter*, a snide voice quipped in the back of her head.

Katherine resolutely ignored the jab, choosing instead to merely be grateful for their absence, whatever the reason, and started preparing the breakfast she had in mind, raiding the refrigerator for what she'd need. She pulled out milk, butter, a block of cheddar cheese, eggs, and a package of pre-sliced ham.

She dug around the cabinets until she found two frying pans, settling them onto separate burners before turning on said burners to a low heat. She threw a spoonful of butter onto each pan and got busy grating the cheese as it melted. Once she had an ample amount of shredded cheese, she loaded one of the pans with ham, backing up a bit as the thick slices immediately began to sizzle.

Katherine's mouth salivated as the smell of buttery meat began to fill the kitchen.

As the ham warmed, she cracked open a half dozen eggs, whipping them together with some milk before adding half of the yellow mixture to the second pan. Once it had cooked a bit, she added most of the cooked ham and a handful of cheese before folding the hardened mixture in half with a spatula. After a minute, she flipped the homemade omelet over and added just a sprinkle more of cheese and a dash of pepper to the top of it. She then transferred the omelet to one of two plates she had readied while waiting for it to finish cooking.

As she examined the perfectly shaped morsel of eggs, ham, and cheese, Katherine found herself feeling absurdly proud of the creation. She may not have been as talented in the kitchen as Caleb – or even her mother – but she could make a mean omelet when she set her mind to it.

Katherine took a moment to put away the butter, milk, and what remained of the block of cheese before quickly starting on the second omelet, pouring what was left of the egg mixture into the newly empty pan.

Unfortunately, the loud crackle of the ham still sputtering away in the other pan disguised the sound of approaching footsteps.

"Making breakfast for me, Katherine?"

The sound of Chad's voice suddenly materializing from directly behind her had Katherine's heart nearly leaping out of her chest. She hoped it wasn't dreadfully obvious that the organ was beating harshly against her ribs when she turned to scowl at the man. Her eyes immediately caught sight of the split, swollen lip he was sporting, and she couldn't quite suppress a satisfied smile.

"And here I thought you weren't as sweet as you looked after the way you treated me last night."

The smile immediately fell from her face, and she glared in disbelief. "The way *I* treated *you*?" she demanded.

Chad outright ignored her hostility. Instead, he had the audacity to reach for the plate that had *Bastian's* omelet on it. Katherine smacked his hand away with the spatula she was still holding. "That's not for you," she reprimanded harshly.

Her brother-in-law narrowed his eyes at her as he took in the half-cooked omelet and pile of ham she still had heating up in their individual pans. "Oh, really? Then who is all of this for?"

Chad had inched his way close enough to her that Katherine could smell the stale liquor still present on his breath from the night before. She moved as far away from him as the stove allowed.

Katherine eyed the enormous omelet she'd already made and the equally large one she still had cooking on the stove. "It's for me," she finally said, hoping he'd buy the lie and leave her alone.

Chad snorted incredulously. "A tiny thing like you? Eat all of this? *Please.*"

"It's true," Katherine protested heatedly, wishing that the man would just leave her alone already.

"Oh? So none of this food is for that little boyfriend of yours you have hiding upstairs?"

Katherine stiffened in shock.

How...?

Chad took in her panicked expression and grinned. "It was hard not to notice when he had you moaning like a whore all of last night. The walls *are* rather thin."

Katherine stared in disbelief – her mind refusing to acknowledge the fact that it was her *sister's husband* who'd just said something like that to her. But then Chad made another grab for the plate that held Bastian's breakfast and Katherine saw red. She jumped into action, grabbing the edges of the dish and attempting to yank it from his hands. "I said that this isn't for you!" she spat at him, refusing to let go of the plate even as he tried to rip it away from her in turn.

What ensued was a no holds barred tug of war over an omelet.

Neither of them won.

Instead, they both lost their grip on the ceramic plate and could do little but watch helplessly as it clattered to the floor. The plate cracked in half – *Fantastic, she'd broken yet another one of her parents' dishes.* – and Chad ended up with a cheesy, eggy mess splattered across his shoes.

They both stared at the destroyed omelet.

"You stupid bitch."

Chad's foul words had Katherine bristling in anger. "How dare you!"

She hadn't seen the backhand coming. Regardless, the knuckles of his hand connected brutally to the side of her face, and blood spurt from her nose at the force of the unexpected attack. For a second, Katherine saw stars.

She quickly recovered, however, blindly groping at her nose. "What's wrong with you?" she yelled at him.

The pain hadn't quite registered yet for Katherine – she was too frickin' pissed.

"What's *wrong*," Chad stressed the word, "is that you just ruined my only pair of black Oxfords. They probably cost more money than your entire outdated wardrobe. Now apologize."

The delusional asshole had just slapped her across the face *and* insulted her fashion sense, yet *he* was demanding an apology from *her*? Katherine gaped at the man.

Chad had the gall to sneer at her stunned nonresponse. "Fine, I have a better idea on how you can make it up to me anyway."

Sensing danger, Katherine grabbed the handle of one of the frying pans when Chad approached and instinctively swung it at him. She had the pleasure of seeing shock widen his eyes before he managed to jump out of the way. She'd just barely missed connecting the pan with his head.

She attempted to hit him again, but he lunged at her, grabbing the wrist of the hand that welded the make-shift weapon and twisting it painfully behind her back until she was forced to drop it.

Immediately after, he slapped a hand over her mouth and forced her to the floor. She made the action as difficult as possible for him, throwing her head back in multiple attempts to nail the bastard in the nose. Unfortunately, she didn't succeed.

It occurred to Katherine that she could break Chad's merciless grip on her wrist by transforming into a wolf. As tempted as she was to try it, however, she didn't want to *kill* anyone. Especially not in her parents' kitchen. Even her sister's asshole of a husband.

Unfortunately, in her human form Katherine was no match for a fully grown man. He pressed her face into the tiled floor before roughly flipping her around and sitting atop her chest. He used his knees to effectively pin down her arms. Almost immediately, they began to numb under his not insignificant weight. But Katherine could hardly allow herself to focus on *that* when she was choking on her own blood. Chad's hand had yet to remove itself from her mouth, and blood from her injured nose was steadily dripping into the back of her throat.

He must have sensed her struggle because he rolled his eyes before removing his hand from her mouth. "Oh, what the hell?" he muttered. "Go ahead and scream. There's no one here to hear you anyway. I saw that boyfriend of your scale down the gutter outside of your room ten minutes ago."

Katherine immediately hacked up blood when he released her mouth, disproportionately satisfied when a few of the crimson droplets wound up on his shirt. She continued to glare up at him despite the way his words had made her heart drop into her stomach.

Bastian had left?

"Why are you doing this? Get the hell off of me!"

Chad's lips transformed into a sneer. "Blame Samantha. The bitch hasn't let me touch her in months." He eyed Katherine speculatively. "Oh well, you're the hotter sister anyway. Even with all the blood."

Katherine stomach lurched at his disgusting words, and she thought she might be sick when he started tugging at his belt. "Stop!" she desperately implored him.

Chad didn't acknowledge her plea and yanked down his zipper.

He pulled the fleshy evidence of his perverse arousal out of his pants, and Katherine fought not to gag as he brought it within inches of her face – her mouth. "Alright, sweetheart," he mocked, "unless you want this shoved somewhere else, I wouldn't even *think* of biting me."

Katherine's heart beat wildly in her chest as Chad attempted to force himself between her lips. Her neck strained as she leaned as far away from the revolting man as possible. In the very back of her mind she was aware of the fact that her entire body was trembling and terribly flushed. Her instincts screamed that she transform and dispose of the imminent danger.

Katherine didn't know what to do – she wasn't even sure if she *could* successfully transform under such stressful circumstances. The only thing that she *did* know was that she was positively petrified… and then, abruptly, Chad was ripped off of her.

And in place of him was Bastian, his broad chest heaving as his eyes, darkened to a near black in his senseless rage, refused to leave Chad's suddenly feeble looking form.

Katherine didn't think the man had ever resembled a predator as much as he did in that very instant.

"What the hell?" Chad spat, picking himself up off the floor onto which Bastian had just viciously thrown him. The fall must have addled his brain because he actually had the nerve to smirk when he spied Bastian glaring at him. "Oh," he mocked, "this must be the boyfriend. Don't worry, dude, I was just going to use her mouth; you still own the rights to her precious p-"

Katherine didn't know if Chad was actively suicidal or just prepensely dumb, but before he even had the chance to finish his sentence, Bastian was upon him, plummeting him with his fists. A brutal blow to the abdomen sent Chad once again sprawling to the floor.

Bastian didn't give him a chance to get up. He sent a ruthless kick at the man's ribcage, and Katherine heard a loud *crack* right before Chad curled up around his belly and howled in pain.

Katherine didn't think that the loud wail even registered in Bastian's ears as he continued to reign merciless blow upon blow down on him. Chad was quickly reduced to little more than a limp punching bag.

In that moment, Katherine truly feared that Bastian would beat the man to death. She almost didn't recognize him, so wrapped up was he in his homicidal rage.

Katherine knew she had to stop him.

As much as Chad deserved what was being dished out to him, she wasn't about to let Bastian murder her sister's soon to be ex-husband in the middle of her parents' kitchen. The potential consequences were too dire for her to bear.

"Bastian!" she yelled, hoping somehow that the sound of her voice would bring the man back from the brink of his ferocious rage.

But not a spark of recognition lit his eyes, and Katherine cringed when he delivered a particularly vicious blow to Chad's mouth, reopening the split lip she'd bestowed upon him the night before.

"Bastian, please stop!" she tried once more.

Again, he failed to acknowledge her.

Katherine saw no other option than to try to physically stop him, so swiftly approaching the man, she wrapped both her hands around an impressive bicep before pulling fruitlessly at his arm. Bastian merely shook her loose and punched Chad *again*.

Katherine grit her teeth before latching on once more. This time, though, she refused to let go. At least she'd refused to let go until a particularly violent jolt sent her careening to the floor. She smacked her head on the corner of the kitchen island on her way down and felt just the slightest trickle of blood dribble down her face to join the crusty crimson pool forming around her nose and mouth.

Bastian's entire being froze, and for the first time since entering the kitchen, his eyes cleared enough so that Katherine could finally see blue. His colored irises swirled with concern and remorse as he took in her prone, bloodied form.

He looked incredibly distraught.

Of course, it was at this precise moment that Katherine's parents chose to come waltzing in through the door.

CHAPTER THIRTEEN

For a second, time stood ominously still.

Her mother and father gawked in the kitchen entryway. Katherine had the perfect view of them from where she lay on the cold, hard tile. Both pairs of eyes took in her crimson-stained face with horrified alarm.

And then chaos erupted.

She heard her mother shriek at the same time that her vision of her parents was blocked by Bastian's powerful form. He scooped her up carefully in his arms, and Katherine tried not to fret over the fact that he was shaking – violent tremors wracking his body every other second.

The man sat her gingerly on the countertop, tucking wayward strands of hair that had fallen out of her ponytail in her tussle with Chad behind her ears as he perused her wounds. He was seemingly ignorant of the other people that occupied the room as he tenderly inspected the small gash on her temple.

Katherine knew it was a farce, though. Especially when Bastian tensed at her father's frantic approach. "Who are you?" Benjamin demanded while her mother continued to screech on the other side of the room.

"Get away from my daughter!" the hysterical woman hollered.

Bastian reluctantly turned to face them – it was obvious to Katherine that he didn't want to take his eyes off of her for even the second it would take for him to acknowledge them. His subtle movement, however, once again gave her an ample view of the kitchen.

And it was just in time to see Sam emerge from where she'd apparently been hidden behind her parents. Her sister's already pale completion whitened further upon taking in the scene. Katherine's heart lurched when she immediately rushed to her prone husband. "Oh my God, Chad! What happened? Someone call an ambulance!"

Chad groaned pitifully from his place on the floor, and Katherine's eyes widened in disbelief when he started talking. She didn't know how the severely beaten man was conscious, let alone in control of his motor functions. What he said, however, was even more outrageous than the fact that he could still somehow form words with his gory mouth.

"Call the police too," he begged his wife, crimson blood dribbling from his lips. "That guy," he gestured vaguely at Bastian, "assaulted me!"

Katherine's own blood rushed to her face as fury enveloped her.

"What?" she cried, speaking for the first time since her parents had entered the room, and taking everyone off guard by the unmistakably panicked tinge her voice contained if their concerned expressions were anything to go by. "You're the one who attacked me," she immediately refuted him. "He was only protecting me!" Her small hands wrapped themselves around one of Bastian's impressive biceps in a death grip.

Sam's mouth dipped into a skeptical frown. "*This* is the result of that man *protecting* you?" she demanded. "Chad can barely move."

Sam's defense of her husband – a man who Katherine knew her sister barely even tolerated anymore – hurt more than words could ever say. Probably about as much as Katherine's next words were going to hurt her.

"Sam, Chad *slapped* me. He forced me to the ground, sat on my chest, and tried to… he tried to…" Katherine faltered in telling the last part of the story, not quite able to make the awful words come out of her mouth, but it was obvious enough to everyone what she was implying.

Bastian's arm was trembling where she had latched onto it, his skin practically vibrating as the soft sound of an unmistakably threatening growl emerged from his throat. Katherine prayed she was the only one who could hear it.

Luckily, the commotion that her accusation had caused sufficiently disguised the noise. "Is that true?" her father thundered at Chad. Her mother's watery eyes demanded an answer to the same question as she stared reproachfully at him.

When the man was quiet for a second too long, Samantha took a faltering step away from him. "How could you?"

"How could I *what*?" Chad asked, his mouth finally functioning again – *unfortunately*. "You're actually going to believe her? Babe, come on, you know that your sister has always had a bit of a crush on me."

Katherine just barely managed to keep the shock-induced laughter – tainted with more than just a hint of hysteria, she was sure – from bubbling up her throat. *Really?*

"*She* came on to *me*!" Chad continued. "I was trying to let her down gently when she went in for a kiss. That's when her little boyfriend walked in and jumped to conclusions."

Katherine was dumbfounded at the pure absurdity of Chad's bold-faced lie. *That* was the best he could come up with? Surely her sister could see through the pile of garbage that'd he'd just spewed at her. At least, Katherine assumed she could. She knew that despite the trouble the couple had been having and the divorce that her sister insisted was imminent, Sam immensely enjoyed the expensive lifestyle that her marriage to Chad afforded her.

Still, she couldn't possibly believe him… *right?*

"Sam, you know I would never do that," Katherine asserted quietly.

Her sister's troubled gaze met hers. Whatever she saw in Katherine's green orbs made her gray eyes softened marginally. "Of course not," she agreed, shoulders slumping for just a second before they hunched up again, tense as can be as she turned to face her lying scoundrel of a husband. "You're disgusting," she spat at his pathetic form. "I want you out of my parents' house immediately. You'll be served with divorce papers first thing in the morning."

"What?" Chad exclaimed, truly flabbergasted. "Come on, Sam. Babe… I… I was drunk!" he shouted in a last ditch effort to worm his way out of the predicament he'd found himself in.

"You heard her," Katherine's father boomed, hastily taking two steps towards the man still slumped pitifully on his kitchen floor. "Get the hell out of my house!"

Chad stared incredulously. "But I need an ambulance!" he whined.

Her dad's neck turned so red it bordered on purple as his temper exploded. "Like hell you do! You put your filthy hands on one of my daughters and in doing so, hurt both of them. You got what you deserved as far as I'm concerned. Now pick your pathetic self up and *get*. If I have to do it for you, you better believe you'll be leaving this house in a body bag and *not* a goddamn ambulance."

Chad must have believed him because he grimaced at the threat and started moving. His face turned as white as a sheet as he slowly used the edge of the countertop to pull himself up to his feet. Even standing, however, he remained hunched over, arms clutching his abused stomach. Katherine couldn't find it in herself to feel sympathy for the man, though, especially when he scowled darkly in her direction from where she still sat, half hidden behind Bastian.

"Unbelievable," he muttered under his breath. Bastian stiffened beside her, his whole body thrumming with tension. For a second, Katherine thought Chad would be dumb enough to say something more, and Bastian would explode into a wolf before her very eyes and tear the man to pieces. But a single glance at the glaring alpha was enough to make Chad hold his tongue and he cowered – or limped, rather – his way to the door.

A heavy silence descended upon the room as soon as the door slammed shut behind him.

"I think I need to lie down for a while," Samantha said after a tense moment, shooting Katherine an indecipherable look before hastily fleeing the room.

Apparently, that was all that was needed to shock her mother out of her stunned stupor, but Katherine could tell the woman was still inwardly reeling from the grisly scene she'd walked into not ten minutes before. "Who are you?" she asked Bastian bluntly.

Before he could open his mouth, Katherine forced the answer past her own suddenly clumsy tongue for him. "Mom, Dad, this is… Bastian."

Her mother stared as her, comprehension slowly dawning on her face. "*Bastian?*" she choked. "The man who you stayed with while you were in Canada? *That* Bastian?"

She turned to face "the man" in question before Katherine could even begin to think of an explanation for his presence. "How did you get here?" she demanded, walking up to Bastian and actually having the audacity to jab a finger into his chest.

Thankfully, her father chose that moment to intervene.

"Elaine, I don't care how he got here," her father sternly admonished her, taking his wife off guard. "He saved our daughter. Why don't you make yourself useful and go check on Sam?" Though it was worded as a suggestion, his tone left no room for argument. Elaine huffed indignantly, but reluctantly retreated from the kitchen.

Katherine didn't know if she'd ever loved her father more than in that exact moment.

"Step aside."

And then he had to go and give an alpha wolf a direct order. Katherine knew the man didn't know that Bastian was what was supposed to be a mythical creature, one that could tear out his throat in a heartbeat if he wanted to, but *still*.

Predictably, Bastian didn't budge from where he'd positioned himself in front of her and actually stepped further into her father's way when he made a move towards her. Katherine didn't know what was going on in her dad's head as he warily scrutinized the man, but she was pleasantly surprised that when he spoke again, he didn't *sound* upset. "I volunteer as a paramedic on weekends," he explained to Bastian. "I'm just going to patch her up."

Katherine could tell that Bastian still didn't want to let the other man – even if it was her father – anywhere near her. But when she gently squeezed the arm she still hadn't let go of before finally releasing it, he took the hint and moved out of the way.

"Do you feel well enough to walk to the couch?" her dad asked after quickly taking stock of her injuries. "You'll probably be more comfortable there while I fix you up."

No sooner had the suggestion left his mouth than Bastian quickly murmured, "I'll carry her," and preceded to do just that. He sat her down carefully on one of the living room couch's soft cushions. Katherine quickly latched onto his hand before he could straighten up, tugging on it and indicating that she'd like him to sit next to her.

He acquiesced immediately.

Her father's face transformed into a pinched frown as he began mopping up the blood that had started to congeal around Katherine's mouth and nose with a damp washcloth.

"It's just a bloody nose," she said, both to assure the men who were staring at her with such concern and to fill the uneasy silence that had befallen the room. "I'm fine."

"You're bleeding all over the place, Kit," her dad scolded gently, tenderly dabbing beneath her nostrils.

He finished cleaning her face in silence, tossing the blood-stained washcloth he'd been using to wipe her up with in the trash can before starting to inspect her nose. He pinched it lighting between his thumb and forefinger, and Katherine winced at the sting. If possible, Bastian tensed up further beside her.

"Well, it's not broken," her dad said after a minute more of examining her nose. "It looks worse than it actually is because of the swelling, but it should heal just fine on its own."

Katherine had to sit still as her father applied an antibiotic cream to a small scratch on her cheek that she hadn't even realized she'd acquired and put one tiny – and probably completely unnecessary – suture in the gash on her temple.

"How'd this happen?" he questioned softly as he made the quick stitch.

Katherine blanked for a moment, but forced her lips and tongue to work together when her father raised an eyebrow at her lack of response.

"I hit my head when Chad pushed me down." The lie that flew from her mouth was the only one she could think of in that moment, but it *was* the perfect explanation.

Her father's eyes narrowed and he exhaled harshly from his nose in an attempt to calm his obvious anger. Bastian, on the other hand, clenched the fists in his lap together so tightly that his knuckles turned bone white.

Katherine hoped the man knew that she didn't hold him responsible for the infinitesimal cut. He'd been so lost in his fury that he'd had very little control over his actions when she'd been pulling at his arm, and she knew he hadn't meant to swat her away like a pesky fly.

"Does it hurt anywhere else?" her dad asked when he finished with the suture.

"No," Katherine hastily assured him. "Like I said, I'm fine."

Both men frowned, but neither pressed her.

"Should I call the police?" her father asked instead. "Do you want to press charges?"

Katherine paled. "No!" she immediately denied. She'd dealt with enough questions from Sheriff Sanders after she'd returned from her seven month absence. Besides, she didn't want him to get wind of the fact that Bastian was in town. Then he'd have to deal with the police too. "Can you make sure Mom knows that too, please?"

She hoped her mother hadn't called them already. She wouldn't put it past her.

Benjamin sighed, but nodded. "Speaking of your mother, the woman could do with better timing, but she made a good point when she asked you how… Bastian," he said slowly, testing the name out on his tongue as he glanced at the man, "got here."

Katherine bit her lip.

"She called me," Bastian spoke up gruffly from where he still sat beside her.

Her dad eyed the man before turning back to face his daughter. "I thought you said he didn't have a cell phone," he reminded her gently.

Katherine nervously played with her fingers. "I lied."

About so many things.

She was even lying about having lied, for God's sake. Bastian, in fact, didn't have a cell phone.

"Is there anything else you feel the need to fess up to?" Her dad pinned her into place with an analytical stare.

So much.

But she had a feeling she knew what her dad was not so subtly referring to. "Bastian is… more than a friend to me."

"More than a friend" was a colossal understatement and didn't come close to defining their relationship, but she couldn't exactly tell her father that they were destined mates, now could she?

Katherine knew that her dad was going easy on her due to the ordeal she'd just been through when instead of prying for more information at her confession, he merely ran an agitated hand through his graying hair. She didn't know if she'd ever seen him look so lost.

After a moment, he angled his body towards Bastian, not quite looking at him as he directed his next words in his general vicinity. "Thank you for saving my daughter. I am grateful beyond words, but I think it's best if you leave now."

Bastian's eyes noticeably darkened, and Katherine sensed immediately that he was *not* going to oblige, so thinking quickly, she hastily threw her arms around his neck and whispered surreptitiously in his ear. "Climb in through my bedroom window. I'll be up there as soon as I can."

When she reluctantly pulled away, his irises were a tad lighter, but his posture was still incredibly stiff as he reluctantly stood up to leave.

"Go ahead. I'll talk to you later," she said aloud for her father's benefit. He didn't need to know that "later" meant as soon as she could escape to her bedroom.

Bastian nodded jerkily, his feet literally dragging across the floor as Benjamin led him to the door. Katherine heard it close behind him with a quiet *click.*

Her father reappeared in the living room. "I'm going to go make sure your sister's okay," he informed her. "Stay here. We still need to talk."

He returned a few minutes later with her mother in tow. If Katherine had known that by "talk", he'd really meant she'd have to brave a teary interrogation, Katherine might have tried to make a break for it.

"Oh honey!" he mother exclaimed, sitting in the same space that Bastian had just occupied and squeezing her hand in what Katherine knew was supposed to be an attempt at solace. It was hard to feel comforted, though, when the tears swimming in her mother's eyes looked like they might overflow at any moment. "Are you alright?"

"I'm fine," Katherine assured her quietly, but the words tasted suspiciously like a lie. While it was true that she was physically okay, now that the shock over the events of the last hour was beginning to wear off, she found that her insides felt a bit like they were trembling.

Her mother nodded doubtfully. "Has Chad ever touched you before?"

Katherine's breath caught in her throat. *Not unless one counted harassing her at his wedding reception or making a grab at her last night in the bathroom.* She exhaled shakily. "No, never." *Another lie.*

She must have been convincing enough, though – or her mother *wanted* to be convinced, at any rate – because her mother's shoulders slumped in relief and she pulled Katherine into a one sided hug. "Oh, thank God," she muttered. "I was so worried that he'd done something like this before and you just hadn't said anything. Your sister felt so awful that maybe she hadn't noticed. *I* felt so awful."

Katherine stiffened and retreated from her mother's embrace, but the woman didn't seem to notice her tense posture. *Her mother felt awful? Her sister felt awful?* Had it occurred to either one of them that maybe *she* felt beyond awful at what had just almost happened?

She had been the one pinned forcefully to the floor, after all.

"Now, honey," Elaine started, seemingly willing to let the subject of Chad drop for now. Katherine was relieved until the woman revealed who she *did* want to talk about. "Your father told me that you and this Bastian character, well, that you're… more than friends."

Katherine pursed her lips at the way her mother said "this Bastian character", but nodded anyway. "Yes," she answered matter-of-factly, "we are."

"And you felt the need to hide this from us? You denied it when we asked you if you were romantically involved with him. Why would you do that?"

"Because you already thought that he was some demented rapist, Mom!" Katherine exploded before she could get a handle on her temper. "But you don't have to worry; he's not anything like your precious Chad!"

Her mother flinched at the words, and the guilt they'd inflicted upon her made the woman's gaze drop to her lap. "I'm so sorry that Chad hurt you, honey. I truly thought that he was an exceptional young man, but you're right. As your mother I should have seen the signs of something like this coming."

Katherine sighed, her anger disappearing as quickly as it'd come. "It's not your fault, Mom."

She thought that was the line that *they* were supposed to be feeding *her* after nearly having been forced to… been forced to…

Katherine couldn't even think it.

And she suddenly felt very tired. It was almost like she could physically feel the last remnants of adrenaline leave her system, and in its place, exhaustion settled in her bones.

It wasn't even noon.

She abruptly realized that her father was talking and forced herself to focus on the sound of his voice. "Look, Kit, your mother and I aren't mad at you, but we need to know if there's anything else that you've refrained from telling us about – if there's anything else that we need to know."

Only that she'd been changed into what was supposed to be a mythical creature. And nothing as flashy or flamboyant as a unicorn or sparkly vampire either.

Katherine curled into herself. "No," she muttered.

Her parents sent each other what Katherine suspected were supposed to be furtive glances. "Nothing at all?" her father hedged.

She felt like she may as well have had the word "liar" branded onto her forehead with capital letters by then, but she forced herself to shake her head in the negative anyway.

Her father sighed, but accepted her answer. "Alright. I know you said that you didn't want to press charges against *Chad*," he spat the man's name from his mouth, "but I encourage you to rethink that decision."

Katherine wouldn't change her mind, but she knew her father meant well so she nodded jerkily. "Okay."

After she had agreed to think about it, her father surprised her by enclosing her stiff form in a tender embrace. He pressed his face into her hair. "Just say the word, and I'll make sure his worthless ass is thrown in a jail cell, okay?"

Her dad didn't wait for a reply, pulling away after scrutinizing her facial injuries one last time.

Her mom offered Katherine a hug of her own. "I'm going to clean up the kitchen," she said after releasing her. Katherine tried very hard not to think of the splattered egg and smeared blood currently decorating the room in question's floor. "Did you want me to make you something to eat when I'm done?"

She shook her head, her appetite having disintegrated into nothing long ago. "That's okay. I think I'm just going to go upstairs and rest."

She needed Bastian.

Her mother and father both agreed that lying down for a while was probably ideal, and Katherine took her leave.

As soon as she stepped into her bedroom, her entire being was smothered by warmth. Bastian's body folded itself around hers, his strong, protective arms encircling her small form and easily carrying her to the bed centered in the room. His hands were everywhere as he checked her over for nonexistent injuries. "Why didn't you tell me?" he demanded gruffly.

And Katherine lost it.

Whatever it was that had been holding her together in the immediate aftermath of the assault buckled under the perceived blame in his voice, and Katherine collapsed into the man's arms. "I'm sorry," she choked out as tears began overflowing from her eyes.

The true horror of what she'd been through was quickly catching up to her.

Bastian recognized his mistake immediately. "Hey, no," he cooed, patting her hair as she buried her face into the crook of his neck. "You have nothing to be sorry for. *I'm* the one who's sorry." He peppered a dozen chaste kisses to the small gash on her forehead as if to prove his point. "I saw Sophie loitering near the house after my shower this morning and knew that the pack was probably concerned that I hadn't return the night before so I went out to assure her that everything was fine." So *that* was why Chad had seen him climbing out of her bedroom window. "When I got back, I heard you yelling downstairs. I rushed down, but I… I failed to protect you."

Katherine could hear in his words how terribly ashamed Bastian was of this, but she was sobbing so hard that instead of telling him that he *had* protected her, all she could manage to do was clutch him to her more tightly.

"I swear on my life, Katherine, I will never allow anything like that to happen again," he vowed, whispering the words into her hair as he held her and allowed her to cry.

Eventually she was all out of tears. She refused to move from her spot on Bastian's lap, however, even as her breathing calmed and the soothing hand rubbing her back became still. Swollen, aching eyes still buried into Bastian's neck, she finally forced herself to speak. "I want to go home," she muttered against him. "I just want to go home."

Bastian's solid arms held her all the more securely.

* * *

"I'm glad to see you eating something."

Katherine had heard the approaching footsteps as she idly waited for the leftover beef stew to reheat in the microwave and kept her red-rimmed eyes averted as she half-heartedly acknowledged her father. "Yeah."

It'd been nearly midnight by the time Katherine had finally decided to leave the bedroom she'd barricaded herself in with Bastian and hadn't anticipated meeting up with her father in the kitchen. She'd locked herself up in her room in the first place because she didn't want her parents or sister to see the shiny, swollen skin around her eyes, clear evidence of the repeated crying fits she'd suffered.

But her stomach's angry growling could only be ignored for so long after skipping as many meals as she had. Bastian had to have been hungry as well, and she would have offered to bring him up something to fill his belly with, but he was fast asleep when she'd managed to somehow pry his heavy limbs off of her and sneak downstairs.

All her hiding had apparently been for naught, though, because there her father was, taking in her pink, puffy eyes with a frown. He refrained from commenting on her haggard appearance, however, and Katherine was grateful. She was grateful for *all* her father had done for her that day.

"Thanks for patching me up this morning." Her words escaped in a rush before Katherine could second guess them. "And for containing Mom for a while too. I… I really appreciate it."

Her father's frown transformed into a gentle smile. "You're welcome, Kit. I'm your dad. I'd do anything for you."

The platitude, as commonplace as it was, rang true.

It gave Katherine pause. "…Anything?" she asked softly.

"Of course."

The microwave beeped obnoxiously, indicating that the beef stew inside had sufficiently warmed, but Katherine ignored it, playing nervously with her fingers instead. She'd been worrying herself all day about how she could possibly leave Middletown – leave her parents. Ever since she'd come to the conclusion that not only did she *have* to leave for the good of everyone, but that she *wanted* to leave, it was all she could think about. She dearly missed her pack and running wild with them through the towering evergreens of Haven Falls.

Katherine knew intellectually that running away would be the easiest way to accomplish that. But she couldn't bring herself to just up and leave – disappearing from her parents' lives without a word *again*. It made her sick just thinking about it.

If only she could just…

"Dad, I want to go back to Canada with Bastian," she forced the words out of her mouth before she lost her sudden nerve. She stared at where her fingers gripped the countertop, bracing herself for his response.

Silence, though, was all that met her bold declaration.

She braved a glance at the man, who, despite his suddenly stiff posture, was gazing unseeingly past her.

"Dad," she hesitated, "did you hear me?"

His eyes focused on her face at the question. "Honestly, I'm pretending not to have," he disclosed, his mouth settling in a hard, straight line. "Are you out of your mind?"

"Maybe," she admitted quietly.

"Why would you even *think* I'd allow you to do something like that? Are… are you pregnant?" he demanded.

Katherine's mouth literally dropped open at the question. "What? *No!*" she immediately denied.

"Then what, Katherine? He's not bribing you or… or manipulating you somehow, is he?"

An angry flush licked at her cheeks at the suggestion. It was too close to what her mother had implied earlier. "Dad, Bastian would never do something like that! He loves me! And I… I love him."

Katherine didn't know who was more shocked by the confession, her father or *herself*. She hadn't been able to force the "l-word" past her lips – at least as it pertained to Bastian – since the very first time the man had told her he loved her months ago.

Her father got over his shock quickly. "Love?" he scoffed, disbelief saturating his voice. "Is that what this is about? Katherine, you're seventeen! What do you know about love?"

Katherine bristled at his tone. "What? So just because I'm young I don't know what love is? My heart flutters every time I even *think* about Bastian, Dad! It thumps so hard in my chest that I'm half afraid it's going to burst every time I'm actually with him. I know my own feelings! Don't belittle them *or* me just because of my age."

"I'm sorry, Kit." He didn't *sound* sorry. "You'll have to forgive me, seeing as I'm trying to process the fact that my *seventeen* year old daughter wants to up and leave the country."

"Seventeen is close enough to eighteen," Katherine protested. "What difference does one year make, really?"

Her father continued to stare incredulously at her. "You're talking like someone who's already made up her mind."

Katherine took a deep breath. *In for a penny, in for a pound.* "Well, maybe I have."

Her father threw his hands up in the air in exasperation, his untied robe flapping comically along with them. "Katherine, what you're suggesting is illegal," he exclaimed, clearly trying to appeal to her good sense. "Fact of the matter is that you're *not* eighteen yet and if you really ran away, I'd call the police and have you dragged back here within hours."

Katherine played with the ends of her hair. "Only if they found me," she pointed out quietly, not quite meeting his eyes.

But Katherine didn't have to *see* the man to feel the tension suddenly radiating from him. "They would," he promised, his voice hardening in anger. "And when they did, I assure you that I'd have your Bastian arrested and thrown in jail for unlawfully harboring a minor."

Katherine knew that Bastian would never allow them to be caught by the police if she *did* run away, but the fact that her father was threatening Bastian – even just legally – had her hackles raised. She swallowed down a growl rumbling in her throat with some difficulty and took a deep breath to calm herself. "Well, running away – or moving out as I prefer to call it – *wouldn't* be illegal if at least one of my parents gave me permission to do so," she rationalized.

Her father stiffened further. "Don't ask that of me, Katherine."

"Dad, please!" Katherine begged, throwing all pretenses of being unaffected by his blatant refusal to the wind. "I swear that I'll call and visit all of the time! It won't be like the last time I disappeared. I'll know that you're okay, and you'll know that I'm okay."

Her father crossed his arms over his chest – probably in an attempt to stop himself from literally trying to shake some sense into his daughter. "Katherine, I just got you back. And now you're asking me to give you up? Because you want to be with some guy that I know absolutely nothing about except that he housed a missing teenager for months on end with nary a call to the police?"

Katherine's gaze dropped to the floor. "Well, when you put it like that, it sounds crazy," she admitted softly.

"Yes, it does," he agreed, a touch of hope in his voice. He probably thought that his daughter was finally beginning to see reason.

But Katherine was quick to burst that bubble. "But it's not even half as crazy as the truth."

Peeking up at him to see his reaction to her words, she immediately spotted his frown. "Truth?" her dad demanded sternly. "What are you talking about, Katherine? I thought you said that there wasn't anything else you needed to tell your mom and me?"

"Well, I lied!" Katherine exploded, running both of her agitated hands through her disheveled hair. "I'm been lying to you, Dad, ever since I've gotten back, and you haven't even realized it!"

She was pleasantly surprised when relief filled her after the confession had escaped, rather than the regret she'd been half-expecting to assault her. It felt *good* to finally speak the truth.

"Lying to me about what?" her father demanded.

Katherine eyed her father in contemplation. "If I tell you… the truth… you can't tell anyone. Not ever. Not even Mom."

His brow crinkled in disapproval. "Katherine-"

"No," Katherine snapped. "Those are my terms or you can forget about me telling you anything."

Her father stared into her eyes for a long time. What he was searching for, Katherine couldn't say. He must have found whatever it was, though, because the next time he opened his mouth it wasn't to protest the fact that what she had to say needed to remain a secret. "Tell me," he requested softly. "Please."

Was she really going to do this? It could go so wrong-

"I'm a werewolf."

...Apparently she was.

For a long moment, Katherine's father just stared at her, not so much as blinking at the revelation, and the small brunette couldn't stop herself from nervously filling the awkward silence that hovered threateningly over them. "Dad, please, I know it sounds insane, but do you remember how I was bitten by that animal –that *wolf* – a few weeks before I disappeared? Well, it wasn't just a wolf, it was a *were*-wolf. And those men who broke into our house? Didn't you hear them call me all those strange names? A monster? A creature? Well, they were calling me those names and they were after me in the first place because they were werewolf hunters and I was, well, a werewolf – though, admittedly I didn't know it at the time," Katherine was horrified by her earnest rambling, but couldn't quite seem to stop herself from prattling on. "I want to go back to Canada because there's a whole community of werewolves living there. I'll be safe there, and *you'll* be safe if I'm there. Bastian will take care of me. He... he's a werewolf too."

She didn't mention, of course, that he was the wolf who'd bitten her in the first place.

Her father had remained eerily quiet throughout her winded explanation and apparently still couldn't quite bring himself to speak now that she had finished.

"Please say something," she asked, voice ridiculously small.

"I... I recognized Bastian when I saw him in the kitchen this morning," he finally said, his eyebrows pinching together in a perturbed frown.

"You did?" It was Katherine's turn to be surprised. The confession shone a new light on the way her father had been continuously eyeing the man.

"I wasn't sure at first… but, yes. I've never told anyone, but after telling you to run all those months ago – back in October – I floated in and out of consciousness until the ambulance arrived. I saw him in the house after you'd left – Bastian. He was fighting one of the men who'd broken in, and I watched him," he swallowed loudly, "I watched him turn into a massive wolf and rip the other man to pieces with his teeth." He took a deep breath. "I thought I'd somehow hallucinated the scene, imagined it, even, so I never said anything when I woke up in the hospital days later. And I tried to force it from my mind as I recovered. I was mostly successful because your mother and I were so preoccupied with our search for you, but the image of that man warping into a wolf always lurked in the back of my head."

Katherine was staring wide-eyed at her father by the time he'd finished his story. "You didn't imagine it," she pushed the words past dry lips. "Like I said, Bastian is a werewolf too. He not only saved me from Chad this morning, but from those men who broke into our house in October."

Her father eyed her thoughtfully. "I take it you don't have amnesia then?"

Katherine slowly shook her head. "No. But I really *did* think you and Mom were dead. I came back as soon as I found out that you were actually alive. I… I missed you so much."

"We missed you too," he responded automatically, but Katherine could tell he was still overwhelmed with the information she'd just unloaded onto him. "So… you can turn into a wolf too?" he asked hesitantly.

Katherine dug her teeth into her bottom lip, hoping the man wasn't going to ask her to prove it to him. "Yes," she hedged, "but I still don't have very good control of that… *part* of myself. I might hurt you, or do worse, in that form."

Benjamin nodded in understanding despite the dazed look still present in his eyes. Katherine was quietly shocked that he was believing her so readily. *She* hadn't even believed it when the pack had told her that she was a werewolf. She supposed he had the benefit of seeing Bastian transform once before, but still. It nearly made her regret the fact that she hadn't told her parents – or her dad, at least – what she'd become the moment she'd returned.

"I'm sorry I didn't tell you sooner," Katherine apologized, speaking her thoughts aloud. "I was afraid that if I told you I was a w-werewolf," she stumbled slightly over the word, "that you'd lock me up in some asylum. I wouldn't have blamed you either. I know it sounds crazy."

Her father snorted. "I still have half a mind to procure us *both* a one way ticket to a nearby loony bin."

Katherine ignored that remark. "So do you see why I have to leave Middletown?" she asked earnestly. "It isn't safe for you or Mom or Sam for me to be here. I… I don't belong here anymore."

"Katherine," her father protested, "you're my child. I don't care if you do turn into a monster once a month – most woman do anyway." His half-hearted attempt to lighten the somber mood didn't work in the slightest. He sighed. "I can't just let you go."

"You have to, Dad. And it goes without saying that you can't tell anyone why," she reminded him.

"We can't come with you then?" he asked, the slightest hint of desperation present in his voice.

Technically, she supposed they could. But Katherine knew without a doubt that her mother and Sam, at least, would never be happy at Haven Falls. She couldn't ask that of them. Their lives were here. Hers was not. "No, that's not allowed. I'm sorry."

She really was.

Her father looked incredibly defeated as he groaned, letting his head hang dejectedly from his neck. "Your mother's going to kill me,"

"Does… does that mean I can go?" Katherine asked hesitantly.

Her father lifted his head and squarely met her eyes. "You'll call every day?"

"Every chance I get," she agreed. He didn't seem to catch on to the fact that she hadn't *actually* promised she'd call *every* day. That, unfortunately, was an impossibility.

"And visit all the time."

"Of course."

Her father sighed. "Alright, yes, you… you have my permission to go."

Surprised elation overwhelming her for a second, Katherine nearly knocked her father over as her arms eagerly wrapped themselves around him in a tight hug. "Thank you so much!"

"On one condition."

Her elation shriveled up into a condensed lump of dread, which settled into her stomach like a rock. "What condition?" she asked, imagination running wild.

"I need to talk to Bastian. Alone."

…That wasn't *so* bad. "Okay, tomorrow I'll-"

"No," her father immediately disagreed, putting a hand up in the air to cut her off. "Now. I know he's upstairs. I'm not *entirely* as oblivious as I seem."

Katherine's heart dropped into her stomach alongside the lump.

"Okay," she hesitantly agreed, seeing no point in trying to deny it. "Wait here."

"Don't forget your food," her father gently reminded her, grabbing the bowl of lukewarm stew from the microwave and handing it to her. Fishing a spoon from a drawer, he forked that over as well. "Make sure you eat this upstairs though. Like I said, I want to talk to Bastian *alone*."

Katherine fought the urge to protest, merely nodding instead. She left the room and dashed up the stairs as quickly as she could without the stew's broth spilling over the edges of her bowl. She jostled the knob with her elbow and used her hip to open the door to her room.

Bastian was sitting up in her bed, looking a bit put out that she'd left him there alone. "My dad knows you're here," she blurt out before he had the chance to say anything. "He wants to talk to you."

A single raised eyebrow was the only evidence of the man's surprise. He certainly didn't look as panicked as she felt. "Okay," Bastian agreed, sleep still sticking to his voice, but he got up and pulled on the shirt he'd abandoned in a heap on the floor before he'd fallen asleep.

Just "okay"? She felt a bit let down by the reaction, or lack thereof.

"He's waiting for you in the kitchen," Katherine said when he looked at her for direction.

He nodded, pressed a light kiss to her uninjured temple, and left the room, quietly closing the door behind him.

He didn't return for nearly an hour. Katherine had gobbled up the stew in about five minutes and had spent the remainder of that hour staring at her bedroom door, waiting for Bastian to come back through it.

When he finally did, his shoulders were stiff and he was wearing a displeased frown. After shutting the door behind himself, he turned to face her. Brilliant blue eyes met searching emerald orbs. "You told him," he accused.

Despite having expected that reaction, Katherine winced. "I didn't know what else to do," she half-heartedly defended herself. "I couldn't just leave without telling my parents *something*."

"So you had to tell them the truth?" he demanded, stalking towards her. "That you – that *we* – are werewolves? Do you have any idea how incredibly dangerous that was?"

"He'd already seen you transform back in October," Katherine argued. "I… I just confirmed our existence for him."

Bastian scowled at her. "He never believed what he saw was real until you told him otherwise," he disagreed.

Katherine knew he was right and picked nervously at a loose thread on one of her shirt sleeves. "I'm sorry," she apologized quietly.

Katherine watched as the anger deflated from Bastian's face. She suspected he might have been harder on her if her own face didn't look quite so much like it'd been used as a punching bag at a professional boxer's home gym.

"Come here," he murmured softly, easily pulling her into a hug. "It's okay. I believed him when he told me he wouldn't tell anyone."

Katherine buried her face into the welcoming softness of his shirt. "Thank you," she said just as softly. After a moment, she pulled away just enough so that Bastian's hands could remain wrapped around her waist. "What else did you two talk about?" she asked.

Bastian's mouth inched up into a smirk as he stared down at her. "He just wanted to make sure I'd take proper care of you. And to remind me that if I somehow failed, bullets work just as well on animals as people."

Katherine gasped in horror. "He didn't!"

"He *did*," Bastian confirmed, but didn't seem upset in the least.

"I'm *so* sorry!"

"It's okay," he assured her, "because he also gave me his blessing."

Katherine stiffened. "What?" she deadpanned.

Bastian was sporting a full-fledged grin by then. "To claim you as my mate. Or marry you, as I explained it to him. But only with your consent and in your own time, of course."

Katherine knew her face had turned redder than the fire hydrant on the neighbor's front lawn and once again hid her face in his shirt. "I can't believe you!" she hissed.

He actually had the nerve to laugh at her.

Katherine refused to acknowledge the feeling of a thousand pleased butterflies flapping their wings in her belly.

"He also said that you had his permission to go home with me," Bastian added softly after a moment, and Katherine risked peeking up at him.

"He did?"

"He did."

Katherine beamed, unadulterated joy forcing a smile on her face despite the slight ache it caused her.

"When did you want to go?" she asked.

"Whenever you want," Bastian assured her, taking in her smile with slightly dazed eyes.

"Tomorrow?" Katherine suggested without hesitation.

"Tomorrow," Bastian agreed softly.

And so Katherine spent her last night sleeping under her parents' roof, Bastian's arms wrapped around her in a protective embrace as she eagerly awaited "tomorrow".

CHAPTER FOURTEEN

Saying good-bye to her parents the next morning as they bustled about the kitchen was a surreal experience for Katherine. Because although they undoubtedly assumed their daughter was simply seeing them off to work, she was in actuality bidding them farewell because *she* was the one who was leaving.

She knew her father probably suspected that might be the case when Katherine very uncharacteristically pulled her mother into a tight hug before she could leave for her office job. She inhaled deeply as she dug her nose into her mother's shoulder, attempting to preserve in her memory the flowery scent that was unique to the woman. Elaine was elated by the unexpected embrace and didn't question it, squeezing her daughter back fiercely before she hurriedly took off for work.

Her father, on the other hand, took his time going out the door, purposefully burning his toast twice before deciding on cereal instead. It took him nearly twenty minutes to finish his Cheerios before he began to meticulously rinse the bowl. Katherine wrapped her arms around him in a hug as soon as he was done at the sink. She feared he was going to change his mind – tell her he'd call the police if he came back home after work and she was gone – but he didn't. He merely released a resigned sigh.

She squarely met his eyes after she pulled away from attempting to memorize the scent that clung to him – something akin to worn leather. "I love you, Dad."

He brushed a strand of loose hair out of her face, his fingers lingering on her cheek for just a moment. "I love you too, kiddo." He kissed her forehead. "Be safe."

And then determinedly refusing to look at her, he grabbed his briefcase and left.

Katherine stood in the empty kitchen for only a minute, waiting to hear the tell-tale sound of a car engine starting up and tires peeling out of the driveway before turning and heading for the stairs.

She wished she could say good-bye to her sister as well, but Sam hadn't left her bedroom since the morning before, and the brunette didn't want to disturb her. Besides… part of Katherine couldn't help but think that the blonde somehow blamed her for her impending divorce with Chad, despite the fact that Sam had spoken of it long before her husband had assaulted her.

Pushing the memory of said assault into the deepest recesses of her mind, Katherine skirted past Samantha's bedroom door and quickly entered her own. Once inside, she threw the small backpack she'd stuffed with her favorite sweatshirt – it used to belong to her dad and smelled of him – and a handful of candid family photos over her shoulder and waited.

Bastian had left shortly after dawn to go pick up the SUV, which he'd apparently kept hidden in a small grove a few miles west of Middletown. He also planned to direct the pack – they'd been staying at a hotel in Hayfield all this time, just as Markus had told her – to get their things together because they were heading back to Haven Falls. She'd been told that he'd pick her up immediately after.

It was half past seven when she finally caught a glimpse of the hulking vehicle. Wasting no time, Katherine rushed down the stairs, stopping only to fish out the note she'd pre-written from the pocket of her shorts, unfold it, and stick it on the refrigerator door where it could easily be found.

She'd written it after Bastian had left that morning. She had stared at the plain sheet of notebook paper for a long time, trying to think of what she could possibly say to her parents – her mother, at least – to explain her absence. In the end, she'd merely addressed her parents, scribbled that she loved them and told them that they shouldn't worry about her. She also assured them that she would call as soon as the opportunity presented itself.

After tacking the note to the fridge, she swiftly slipped on her shoes and headed out the front door, opening and closing it soundlessly as she left. Katherine glanced back at the house that had served as her childhood home only once before hurrying to Bastian's SUV, wrenching open the passenger door, and sliding inside.

As somber an occasion as leaving her family behind was, Katherine couldn't help but flash Bastian a jubilant smile as she pulled her seatbelt across her lap. Because as much as she'd tried to keep them banished from her thoughts, she'd missed her pack mates tremendously and couldn't wait to be reunited with them all. Even Markus.

It hadn't even occurred to Katherine to be nervous for the reunion until Bastian was parking his massive vehicle in the tar lot of the hotel they'd been staying at in Hayfield.

Suddenly apprehensive, she glanced sideways at Bastian, who'd just pulled the keys from the ignition. "Are they mad at me?" she asked.

She'd run away, after all, and had disrupted their lives for what seemed like the hundredth time since she'd been made a member of their pack all those months ago.

Bastian's crinkled brow spoke of true bafflement. "Why would they be mad at you?"

"Because I ran away," Katherine said, as if the answer should have been obvious to him, "and they were forced to follow me. Because for weeks, they've had to stay holed up here," she gestured vaguely at the hotel with a hand, "in a cramped room instead of running freely through the forests of Haven Falls."

When Katherine bit nervously into her plump bottom lip with her teeth, Bastian reached forward and gently released it with a calloused thumb. "Look at me," he ordered.

Who was she to defy him?

"First of all," the man began, "nobody made anyone do anything. I didn't force the pack to come with me when I followed you; they *wanted* to. They care about you, and staying in a crummy hotel for a couple of weeks is only scratching the surface of what they would be willing to do for you. Understand?"

Katherine nodded dumbly, a warm blush blooming across her

cheeks at his proclamation.

"Secondly, not one of them fault you for running away. They wish you hadn't, no doubt – *I* wish you hadn't – but they understand that it was a consequence of *my* decision to keep the truth from you. I should have told you a long time ago that your parents were alive. This whole mess was *my* fault, not yours, and believe me, they've let me know it."

Bastian's words had their intended effect and Katherine's nerves were reduced to nearly nothing. "Okay," she said, unbuckling herself, "let's go."

They exited the vehicle, and Bastian led her to the hotel room they'd been staying at for nearly an entire month. Katherine waited impatiently for him to unlock and open the door before she unceremoniously entered with him.

Her eyes searched the plainly decorated room until they located each member of her pack. Markus was lounging on one of two beds, idly flipping through the channels of a flat screen that hung on the wall opposite him, Zane was sitting on the other bed reading a book, and Sophie and Caleb were playing a game of cards on a small, collapsible table. It was a terribly domestic scene. And just… *wrong*, on so many levels.

One by one, they noticed her, and it was more than a little amusing watching them instantly jump up and abandon their banal tasks. What wasn't amusing was the way all of their faces were creased in concern.

It took Katherine a moment to work out why. She'd nearly forgotten about her bruised nose and cut up forehead.

Markus's voice was the loudest as they swarmed her. "What happened to your face?" he demanded, tactful as ever as he pushed himself up from the bed and strode towards her.

Katherine hadn't noticed Bastian's possessive arm around her waist until the man was pulling her behind him at his beta's fast approach, growling lowly at Markus in warning.

Katherine shot Bastian a confused frown, but he wasn't looking at her, so she coughed and attempted to clear the somewhat awkward air that had befallen the room. “My brother-in-law thought it’d be prudent to introduce me to the back of his hand,” she said as casually as she could manage, giving the pack the short version of the story. They didn’t need to know what else Chad had done as far as she was concerned.

She ignored Sophie’s outraged gasp and the way Zane and Caleb’s faces darkened at her words, choosing instead to concentrate on Markus and the way his pupils narrowed into slits. He wasn’t looking at her anymore, though. His entire focus was on Bastian. “Well, I hope you *introduced*,” he mocked the word Katherine had chosen to use, “the asshole to your fists.”

Katherine snorted, hoping to lighten the mood a bit. “More than just that,” she confirmed in Bastian’s stead. “I think Chad is better acquainted than anyone would ever want to be with Bastian’s boots.”

That pulled an amused grunt from both men. Katherine rolled her eyes, but was inwardly relieved, when they bumped shoulders good-naturedly. She didn’t know why they were acting so odd around each other in the first place.

Sophie snuck around behind Bastian and pulled Katherine into an exuberant hug when the men were sufficiently distracted. “I missed you so much,” she exclaimed. “I can’t even begin to tell you how positively boring it was without you around.”

“Yeah,” Zane agreed sarcastically, popping up beside her. “I don’t know how we managed to go about living our lives without you stumbling into trouble every other second.”

Sophie smacked the man’s broad shoulder. “Seriously, I can’t handle these jerks all by myself. Don’t ever leave me again.”

Katherine nearly squeaked when instead of responding to the blonde, Zane surprised her by pulling her into a one-armed embrace. “I missed you, trouble and all.”

Before Katherine could tell them that she’d missed them too, Caleb was in front of her, hands clasped together in front of him and brown eyes incredibly wide as he stared at her. “I’m *so* sorry,” he said, his soft tone catching the attention of the entire room. "We all are."

Katherine could have heard a pin drop, it had grown so quiet. "For what?" she asked.

"For lying to you all this time. For pretending that your parents were dead when they weren't. For making you feel like you had to run from us. All of it."

Katherine batted back the tears that threatened to well in her eyes. "I…" she hesitated. "It's… okay. I know Bastian ordered you not to tell me." Direct orders from alphas weren't binding exactly, but breaking them was means for punishment or even expulsion from one's pack. "I even understand why he ordered it of you. I still wish that you hadn't listened to him, of course, but I get why you did and I… I forgive you."

Markus broke the subdued silence that followed by reaching forward and roughly ruffling her hair. "Hey!" Katherine squawked at him, stepping backwards and patting her head in a desperate attempt to get the disgruntled bird's nest to lay flat again.

Markus just grinned. "Welcome back, princess," he quipped. "I almost hate to say it, but you were sorely missed. The pack just isn't complete without you."

The spike of annoyance the man's actions had caused all but disappeared at his words, a pleased warmth taking its place in her belly. She wasn't complete without them either – the space they took up in her heart was just too great. "I missed you all too," she admitted quietly.

Surrounded by her smiling pack mates, and with Bastian's warm arm still wrapped securely around her waist, Katherine abruptly realized she hadn't left her *only* family behind in Middletown. *This* was her family too. And regardless of the fact that she had yet to step foot back into Haven Falls, she was home.

* * *

Home, sweet home, unfortunately, wasn't quite an accurate depiction of the shenanigans that followed the week of the pack's return to Haven Falls.

Apparently, Bastian had never told Luther exactly why it was that he had left Haven Falls. And while Katherine had had no idea, it was customary for wolves who intended to claim one another as mates to disappear together anywhere from a couple of days to an entire week to ensure that they were truly a good match before they announced their intentions to their pack.

Never mind the fact that Bastian and Katherine had been gone for nearly a month or that their entire pack had disappeared along with them. The alpha council had concluded that Bastian was on the cusp of claiming Katherine as his mate.

And the jerk didn't deny it either.

Yeah.

She found out the entire community was eagerly awaiting for Bastian to claim her – have sex with her, basically – when her school friends had stopped by two days after she'd arrived back into town.

Knock. Knock.

"Want to play some football?"

Katherine was pleasantly surprised to find her friends – Mack, Agnes, Jon, Leander, Nathaniel, and even Penelope – on the porch when she answered the front door. She'd missed them nearly as much as her pack in the months she'd been gone.

"That sounds great," she immediately acquiesced, calling over her shoulder to let Sophie know she was going outside – Bastian, Markus, and Zane were all off running various errands – before slipping on her shoes and joining her friends on the porch.

They all agreed it'd be easiest to just play in Katherine's backyard.

Katherine thought it a bit odd that not a single one of them said anything about her month long absence, but she certainly wasn't going to be the one to bring it up and merely nodded her head when she was assigned to be a team with Jon and Agnes.

They were beating Mack, Leander, and Nathaniel by no less than three touchdowns – Penelope had insisted on sitting out and acting as a referee, which made sense considering the ridiculous heels she was wearing – when the sky unexpectedly opened up on them and they were forced to sprint inside to avoid the sudden downpour.

After offering everyone a towel to dry off with, Caleb was kind enough to whip up the hungry group of teenagers a couple dozen BLT sandwiches. Katherine was popping the last piece of her heavenly sandwich into her mouth when she realized how incredibly thirsty she was.

"Anyone want something to drink?" she asked, springing up to forage the fridge for something that would quench her thirst.

A resounding "yes" was her answer.

After she'd passed out the various sodas that had been requested, she plopped back down on the couch cushion she'd been sharing with Mack. Apparently she'd miscalculated the trajectory of her behind, however, because a second later she was halfway on her friend's lap.

Mack shot up out of his seat at the unexpected contact before Katherine had a chance to reposition herself, and as a result, she almost crashed face first onto the floor.

"Sorry." The apology burst from Mack's mouth as he settled himself in a new spot on the floor. "I'll just sit here."

Katherine stared at him, completely incredulous.

Mack had done the exact same thing – practically run away from her – when she'd tackled him while playing outside.

In fact, she'd noticed during their impromptu football game that not a single one of the boys had even attempted to tackle her when she was thrown the ball. It'd made for an easy victory for her team, but it'd certainly struck her as strange.

"Do I smell or something?" Katherine demanded abruptly and all heads swiveled in her direction.

Mack frowned, just a hint of color tainting his cheeks. "No, of course not," he immediately denied.

"Then what's your problem?" She ignored the feeling of every-

one's eyes on her. She didn't care what they thought about her outburst. Of all of her school friends, she considered Mack to be her closest, and he'd hurt her feelings.

"Katherine..." he said, obviously at a loss. "I just don't want to cause any trouble."

"Trouble? What are you talking about?"

Mack sighed, glancing at Sophie and Caleb who'd huddled themselves into the living room with the group of teenagers, before running a hand through his hair. "I don't fancy being beat to a pulp by the head alpha, that's all," he admitted, sounding vaguely sheepish.

That cleared up absolutely nothing. "Why would Bastian beat you up?"

"For daring to touch his intended, of course." This came from Penelope, from whom the words practically surged out of. "Why didn't you tell us that you and Bastian were so close? I can hardly believe that he means to really claim you for his mate." Katherine could tell by the rushed way the words escaped that the girl had been holding that in for a while.

She ignored the thinly veiled insult, focusing instead on the fact that they all knew Bastian wanted to claim her as his. How utterly mortifying.

She wondered how they could have possibly known, her face turning an impressive shade of red as she struggled to find something to say.

"What?"

Apparently that was all she could force to come out of her uncooperative mouth.

Penelope rolled her eyes. "Don't play dumb. The whole town knows about it. It's why you've both been AWOL the past few weeks. He's been romanticizing you."

Is that what they thought?

Katherine didn't know whether to laugh or cry about how utterly wrong that assumption was. Due to their silence on the matter, she hadn't even known for sure if her friends had realized she'd been gone, let alone that they'd thought they knew the reason behind it.

That apparently the whole town thought they knew the reason behind it. The reason being that the man wanted to claim her – have sex with her, basically.

Katherine was honestly concerned that her face might start on fire.

Penelope took her distraught silence as confirmation, of course.

"Eek, I knew it! Tell me all about how dreamy he is."

Katherine looked to Sophie and Caleb, hoping that they would help her out of the embarrassing situation she'd found herself in, but Sophie was smirking idly behind her soda and Caleb's eyes were laughing at her.

Jerks.

Not knowing what to say, Katherine floundered. "Uh... well, he's... nice."

Sometimes.

Usually only to her.

Dear God, she was bad at this.

Luckily, judging by their loud protests, the boys didn't seem to want to hear anymore. "Katherine, believe me, we don't need to know about how... nice... Bastian is you," Jon assured her, speaking for all of them.

Katherine was shocked when Agnes, who was usually somewhat reserved when it came to the topic of boys, nudged her knee. "Ignore them. Personally, I just want to know if the man's as good looking up close as he is far away."

Katherine glared at Sophie when the blonde snickered at the question. "He's very... handsome," Katherine admitted.

Gorgeous, striking, and dazzling were all apt descriptions as well.

"Is he a good kisser?" Penelope asked eagerly. "He looks like he would be someone who knows how to use just the right amount of tongue."

Sophie finally came to Katherine rescue with an overdramatic shudder. "You guys do know that you're talking about my brother, right?" she demanded. Katherine thanked the Lord – or whoever it was who was looking down on them from up above – that Sophie had, because she hadn't taken too kindly to the fact that the girl was thinking about Bastian's tongue in such a way. Or at all, really.

Penelope had the decency to apologize at least. "Sorry! I'm just a little excited. Bastian could literally have anyone he wants. Katherine, you are so lucky. If it was me he wanted-"

The small brunette frowned.

"He doesn't. He wants Katherine," Caleb said bluntly, interrupting Penelope and taking Katherine off guard. Caleb was usually so sweet and quiet. She appreciated him sticking up for her.

Penelope, however, pouted at the interruption. "Of course. Anyway, I like being single. You'll probably miss it too, Katherine." Suddenly, it was like a light bulb went off in the girl's head. "Hey, we should throw you a bachelorette party!"

Sophie's ears perked up at the word "party". "Bachelorette party?" she demanded.

Apparently, it wasn't a werewolf tradition.

"You know," Penelope explained, "It's when a bunch of girls get together to celebrate the marriage, or claiming in this case, I suppose, of one of their friends. It'd be so fun! We could go to Fort Saskatchewan and have a night out, just us girls!"

Sophie's eyes were bright when she turned to meet Katherine's gaze. "That sounds great! What do you think?"

Katherine wasn't all that surprised that Sophie was enamored with the idea of a girls' night out. She was always complaining about how she and Katherine were surrounded by a horde of hotheaded males. She was surprised, however, that the blonde thought that she would agree to it. Why would she want a party to celebrate a supposedly impending claiming that she hadn't even agreed to go through with?

And yet... the temptation was there. Katherine knew, after all, that it'd annoy Bastian. She wasn't overly pleased with the fact that he'd let the whole town believe that he intended to claim her, true or not. Why shouldn't she go along with that premise too? Besides, it might just be fun.

"Let's do it."

Convincing Bastian that it'd be "fun" to let her go to Fort Saskatchewan with a gaggle of other girls and no one else – namely him – was another matter entirely.

If Bastian had been overprotective before Katherine had run away from Haven Falls – from *him* – then he'd been a downright overbearing, territorial jackass since she'd returned. As much as his concern warmed her heart, the way he expressed it was becoming more and more exasperating.

Katherine had noticed it before they'd even left the hotel in Hayfield. *How could she not have?* While she'd been helping Caleb collect the last of his meager belongings, Bastian had pulled Markus aside and confronted him over the fact that he'd not only snuck into Katherine's bedroom without his permission, but had given her the genius idea of leaping from her window when he'd performed said feat in front of her.

And what Katherine meant when she said Bastian "confronted" Markus over these things, was that he punched him. He hit him so hard in the jaw that an audible *crack* had shot through the room.

The "confrontation" had certainly explained Bastian's sour attitude towards Markus when they'd first entered the room.

In response to what Bastian had done, Katherine retaliated with what she'd thought was the logical solution at the time. She punched the man back, smacking her tiny fist into his chest as she explained to him that *she* was the person who gave people permission to enter *her* room, not him, and that blaming Markus for a tiny bruise she'd acquired when *she* had decided to jump from her window was absurd.

Unfortunately, the only thing punching and yelling that at the man had accomplished was causing her knuckles to swell in irritation. And making Markus laugh himself silly as he preened that she was his hero for defending his honor.

Ungrateful prick.

Bastian wasn't exactly delighted over her defense of Markus and had spent the first half of their journey home to Haven Falls brooding behind the SUV's steering wheel, barely talking to her – or anyone else crammed in the vehicle for that matter.

He'd gotten over the spat shortly after, but his temper had continued to erupt throughout the week. When she'd nicked her finger as Markus was teaching her how to use the blade he'd given her for her birthday, for example, he'd once again clocked the man after fretfully bandaging the miniscule cut. He'd taken the knife away from her too, only giving it back when Katherine had pleaded with him.

For God's sake, Bastian had even exploded at sweet Caleb just a day ago, snarling at him when he'd found out that he had accidentally walked in on Katherine changing her shirt. As embarrassing as the incident was, it wasn't as if the entire pack hadn't seen each other naked before. They were werewolves. It kind of came with the territory.

Bastian had completely overreacted when he'd heard Caleb apologizing about it afterwards and had grabbed the brown-eyed man by the collar of his shirt and thrown him into the nearest wall. He'd snarled that that if Caleb ever dared to peep on her again, he'd be sorry.

Yes, he'd literally said that the man had "peeped" on her. It'd have been funny if Caleb hadn't looked so ashamed of himself. Katherine had glared at Bastian fiercely as she'd help Caleb up from where he'd sunk to the floor in humiliation.

Bastian had apologized to them both nearly immediately after, but Katherine couldn't help but suspect that it was only a matter of time until the violent mix of protectiveness and possessiveness reared its ugly head again.

Katherine was honestly worried about Bastian. She had no idea what had gotten into him. Zane, however, apparently *did* have an idea and had cornered her the day after he'd thrown Caleb into a wall to tell her what he thought was the solution.

"You have to let Bastian claim you as his mate."

Katherine nearly jumped out of her skin at the sound of Zane's voice. She'd been absorbed in one of the mystery novels he'd bought her and had become oblivious to her surroundings somewhere around chapter three. She hadn't thought she'd be bothered by the large evergreen tree she'd planted herself underneath of to read.

"Sorry, what?" she asked, having only registered the man's voice and not the actual words he was saying.

"You have to let Bastian claim you as his mate," Zane repeated seriously.

Katherine blinked, taken aback by the man's bluntness about something that, as far as she was concerned, was none of his business.

"The sooner, the better," Zane continued, ignoring her wide eyed stare. "Until he claims you, he's going to take every person he sees you with as a threat to your wellbeing or as competition to the bond forming between you two."

Katherine frowned, suddenly deeming the book she'd been reading as unimportant and laying it carefully down on the grass. "Is that why you think he's been acting the way he has? Hitting Markus all the time and threatening Caleb yesterday? You think he views them as 'threats to my wellbeing'?" she quoted.

"Or as competition for your affection, yes."

Katherine's brow wrinkled in confused disbelief. It was bizarre to think that someone as seemingly confident and physically... well, perfect, really, as Bastian was could feel insecure.

"How do you know?" Katherine demanded. "He's never acted like this before," she protested.

Zane scoffed. "Sure," he agreed, his voice saturated in sarcasm. "He's always been so understanding when other men touch you or you inevitably end up hurt somehow."

Katherine glowered. "He's always been protective," she admitted, "but he's never been so domineering about it before. And about such stupid stuff."

Frankly, she was a little concerned that he would start freaking out about the inevitable physical contact that happened naturally between the Prince pack members. Werewolves were very tactile creatures, after all, with less respect for personal boundaries than the average person. It'd taken Katherine a while to get used to the constant touching, whether it be a shoulder brushing against hers in the hallway or someone hip checking her to get her to move out of the way in the kitchen. Or even condescending hands patting her on the head, which had become one of Markus's favorite ways to annoy her lately.

Bastian had just about bitten the man's limb off when he'd attempted it earlier that day.

"Exactly!" Zane agreed. "His natural urge to protect you and his desire to mate with you are swelling out of control. The longer that this bond between you two remains incomplete, the more his hormones are demanding that he do something about it. That means impressing you by driving off danger and other males, basically."

"So, what?" Katherine demanded. "Are you saying that having... sex... with him is the only solution to ending his newfound violent tendencies?" She ignored the heat rapidly spreading over her cheeks.

Zane rubbed the back of his neck uncomfortably. "Claiming isn't only about sex," he mumbled, "but yes," he added more clearly, "I suspect that is the case. He'll still be protective of you, no doubt, that's just a natural part of who he is, but that part won't be as dominating as it is now. The insatiable urge to make sure everyone knows that you're his will ease, too, once he knows that you actually are."

Katherine frowned. "How do you know all of this?"

Zane huffed, tossing her the book she hadn't even noticed he'd been holding. "Not everyone reads drivel for pleasure." He eyed the novel she'd been engrossed in before he'd approached. Katherine read the title of the book he'd handed her – The Physiology of Mating by Daniel Wyatt.

Zane had basically given her a sex education book.

Cue the blush she was already sporting extending to the tips of her ears.

"Look on page 74."

Katherine pursed her lips at the order, but did as she was told.

Thankfully, there were no embarrassing diagrams on the page in question. She did, however, immediately notice the bullet point list under the subtitle Potential Effects of a Prolonged Courtship, where she spotted "violent behavior towards those who are perceived as threats to the developing bond."

Katherine stared. Zane was right.

"I can't let Bastian claim me as his mate just because I'm afraid he'll hurt someone if I don't!" she protested.

Zane frowned, his brow wrinkling in confusion. "Don't you love him?" he asked. "Do it because of that."

He said it like it was the simplest thing in the world. "You can borrow the book," he offered before taking a step backwards. They both noticed Bastian stalking towards them from the other side of the yard at the same time. "Think about it," he reminded her before quickly taking his leave.

Didn't Zane know that she already had been thinking about it? She wasn't ignorant enough to deny her love for Bastian anymore – at least not to herself. She'd even told her father about her feelings. Somehow, though, she just couldn't quite wrangle up the courage to say the words "I love you" to the man himself.

Luckily, for now, all Katherine had to do was wrangle up the courage to leave the bathroom. It was already the night of her pseudo bachelorette party, and she'd just finished getting ready to go out – or letting her friends get her ready to go out anyway – and was eyeing her reflection critically.

She'd made the mistake of letting Penelope do her make-up. She hadn't worn the stuff in months and the goop felt heavy on her face. Sticky mascara clumped her eyelashes together and she wanted nothing more than to wipe off the cherry red lipstick coating her lips. The eyeliner, she could admit, made her green eyes pop, and she liked how Agnes had twisted up her hair into a slick, braided knot atop her head – only a few stubborn strands insisted on working themselves loose and framing her face – but overall she couldn't help but think it was just too much.

Her outfit was much too much too. The dress clinging to her slender framed was a gift from Sophie and was the same color red as her lipstick. It was a strapless number with a sweetheart neckline and a flirty skit that swished around her knees. The only jewelry she wore with it was Bastian's ring, which hung on its modest golden chain around her neck.

Staring at herself in the mirror, Katherine couldn't help but think she looked quite a bit older than seventeen. She didn't think she'd need an ID to get into the concert that she and the girls had decided to go to for her little "au revoir to singlehood party" as Penelope had taken to calling it. She'd never heard of the band who'd be playing, but as a fan of all music genres, Katherine was looking far more forward to going to a concert than a bar or strip club as Agnes had "jokingly" suggested.

First, though, she had to convince Bastian to let her out of the house in the get-up she was wearing. It'd already taken both Katherine and Sophie tag-teaming the man to persuade him into letting her go to the concert in the first place. When he'd finally agreed, he'd attempted to give them a curfew – "Be back by midnight." – but Sophie had merely rolled her eyes at her brother and assured him that they'd be back in Haven Falls by sunrise, but to not expect them a minute earlier than that. The man had huffed, but agreed.

Katherine creaked open the bathroom door and peeked out into the bedroom she shared with Bastian. It was where she and the other girls had been getting ready to go out.

Sophie spotted her immediately. "It's safe!" she assured her. "I think Bastian finally got the hint that this party is for girls only."

The tension causing her shoulders to hunch together fizzled away. "Thank God," she muttered, stepping all the way out of the bathroom.

Sophie, Agnes, and even Penelope ogled her.

"Wow, you look awesome!" Agnes complimented.

Hoping that her blush at least matched her dress, Katherine shifted nervously as they stared. "Thanks, you all look great too."

She wasn't just saying so either. Agnes was wearing the tightest pair of pants Katherine had ever seen, paired with a stylishly frayed tank top. Penelope was wrapped in a skin tight black dress with chunky jewelry hanging from her ears and around her neck. And Sophie wore a practically see through white blouse and a short denim shirt.

Even in her flashy red dress, Katherine felt a bit out of place amongst them. They all exuded such confidence – confidence she could only dream of, at least in her current get-up.

"Well, don't just stand there, sweetie. Grab your bag and let's get going," Sophie ordered.

Katherine, still half worried that Bastian would barge in and have a coronary at the sight of her, immediately obliged.

Sophie had volunteered to drive the group of girls to the concert in Fort Saskatchewan so they all quickly loaded into Bastian's SUV and took off. Three hours of Penelope's incessant chatter later, they arrived. The sky was already changing from the light blue of the afternoon to the burnt orange and pale pink of the evening as they bought their tickets.

The concert was outdoors and the sky continued to darken as they found their seats. Soon enough, the opening act for the main attraction began to play. Then the band everyone had come to see – Tattered Dignity – ran onto the stage.

Katherine was reluctantly impressed as they started their first song. She and the rest of her friends were out of their seats, dancing and attempting to sing along to lyrics they'd never heard before by their second song. Sophie, the only one in their group old enough to buy alcohol, purchased Katherine a fruity cocktail and shoved it into her unsuspecting hand sometime during the third song. After a bit of needling, the small brunette caved and took a sip, pleasantly surprised by the sweet taste. She savored the cold drink as the band played two more songs.

She was feeling more relaxed than she had in a long time by the time the band began playing their sixth song of the night. It was a sappy one about love. Bastian's face immediately popped into her head, and Katherine had to admit that despite the fun time she was having, a small part of her wished that he could have come with as well.

As the band left the stage to take a ten minute break, Katherine's attention drifted towards her friends, and she fought an amused smile as she watched Penelope attempt to flirt with the trio of college boys who were in the seats directly behind them. Unfortunately for her, they seemed more interested in catching Sophie's attention. The blonde was laughing at a lame pick-up line – "I thought angels had wings." – when Katherine's bladder suddenly felt a mere minute away from bursting.

"I have to use the bathroom!" Katherine whisper-yelled into Sophie's ear.

"Want me to come with you?" Sophie asked above the loud bass of the band. They'd finished their break and were beginning to play another song.

She waved the blonde off and grabbed her bag. "I'll be fine."

She'd scoped out the bathrooms as she and her friends had made their way to their seats earlier and hurried in the direction she remembered them being in. Quickly striding past the stand where a heavily tattooed man was serving alcohol, she ducked inside the door with a faded picture of a stick woman on it. Ignoring the distinct smell of mildew that soaked the air in the small space and the suspicious looking grime that clung to the walls, Katherine was pleased to note that only one stall was occupied and rushed into one of the many that remained available. She swiftly went about her business.

She'd finished and was washing her hands in the lukewarm water spurting from one of the sinks when the single occupied stall opened. Katherine tensed and nearly groaned aloud when she recognized the girl who exited it.

Priscilla Wright.

What were the odds?

"What are you doing here?" Katherine demanded before she could think better of it.

Priscilla, whose mouth had pursed in displeasure upon recognizing Katherine, crossed her arms defensively over her chest. "What?

You think you're the only one allowed to go out and do things? I heard that loudmouthed redheaded girl who follows you and Agnes around talking about how you were going to a concert to celebrate your impending claiming. Maybe I thought that I'd like to go out with my friends too. The world doesn't revolve around you, *Katie.*"

Katherine was well aware that the world didn't revolve around her, and was objective enough to admit that to Priscilla, it may seem as if she *did* think just that. But the blonde had demolished any urge Katherine may have felt to apologize about questioning her motives when she purposefully got her name wrong for what had to have been the hundredth time since she'd met the girl.

So instead of apologizing, Katherine rolled her eyes as obnoxiously as possible. "Whatever, *Paisley.*"

Priscilla grit her teeth in obvious annoyance. "You're not the only special one you know! I've found *my* mate too – someone who will take care of me and provide for me! Rip-"

Katherine bristled at the name. "You can't be serious," she deadpanned, not caring how rude she was being to the other girl. No one – not even Priscilla – deserved to be stuck with that asshole for the rest of her life.

The blonde stiffened at Katherine's comment. "Of course, I'm serious. In fact, it's already happened. Rip claimed me and made it official a few days after the Recruiting Rites. Shortly after your brute of an alpha threatened his life for some perceived offense he made against you." *He'd frickin' licked her during the Rites! Priscilla had seen it with her own two eyes for God's sake.* "He may not be as important to the community as your Bastian," the girl continued, "but he's still an impressive catch. He's strong, smart, charismatic-"

"He's an asshole!"

Priscilla's already pale face blanched in what had to have been a cross of embarrassment and anger. "Do you think I'm naïve?" she hissed. "I very well know that Rip is chauvinistic to his core and has a penchant for sleeping with whatever breathes. What red blooded male doesn't? You think that your Bastian is so perfect? You just wait and see. *You're* the naïve one. When you catch him pounding into some girl in the woods behind your house or maybe even in your own bed – and believe me, you *will* – then maybe you'll see that I'm right."

Once upon a time, Priscilla's spiteful words would have sent Katherine into a tailspin. Insecurity would have swelled within her and she may have even fought the urge to cry. But she wasn't that girl anymore, and all Priscilla's speech had done was make her feel sorry for her. She recognized, too, that the blonde was trying to warn her in her own erroneous way.

"I'm sorry."

Priscilla's hard blue eyes softened momentarily at Katherine's quiet apology. "Yeah, well, just don't be surprised when Bastian disappoints you, is all I'm saying. Men aren't capable of loyalty or love like their female counterparts are, but they're still useful in their own way."

Rip had clearly tarnished Priscilla's view of men as a whole, but Katherine knew for a fact that they were capable of love – that Bastian specifically was capable of it. He loved her. He'd told her so over and over again. And she loved him too.

Suddenly, spending the rest of her night listening to Tattered Dignity, as good as they were, seemed silly when she could be spending it with Bastian.

"Anyway, I better get back to my friends. See you around, Katherine."

So Priscilla *did* know her name after all.

"You too, Priscilla," Katherine replied distractedly. She wondered if her friends would be willing to cut the night short and head home early.

After watching Priscilla saunter out of the room, she dried her hands with a couple of stiff, brown paper towels she'd grabbed from a metal dispenser attached to the wall. She was so distracted by thoughts of Bastian that her ears almost didn't register the sound of the bathroom door opening and slamming shut in quick succession.

But they definitely *did* pick up the quiet *click* of a lock slipping into place. And then an appallingly familiar voice.

"Well, well, well. What do we have here?"

CHAPTER FIFTEEN

Katherine recognized the owner of the arrogant drawl before he stepped into her vision, and her eyebrows crinkled together in consternation.

What was *Rogue* doing here?

She glared warily as he took one, two, *three* steps closer to her. "I could hardly believe my ears when I'd heard that Bastian had let his little pet out to play and thought I'd see for myself if it was true. And what do you know? The proof's right here before my eyes."

Katherine grit her teeth at the man's derogatory words, forcing herself to ignore the fact that he'd just called her a "pet". Rogue was clearly made of the same caliber stuff as Rip.

"This is the ladies' bathroom," she pointed out testily instead. "Are you as bad at reading as you are everything else? Or is it that you've got something to tell me?"

Something resembling rage flashed in his dark eyes, and Katherine forced herself to stand her ground as Rogue took *another* step towards her. "Watch your mouth," he snarled at her. He was so close that his spittle landed on her face.

And just like that, she'd had enough of his gaudy show of presumed dominance. "I don't take orders from you," she snapped at him. *Or anyone for that matter.* "Now get out of my way."

She grabbed her bag and attempted to walk past him, but Rogue immediately blocked her exit with his much larger body. When she tried to side step him, he merely moved into her way again. "Try and make me," he taunted her.

Ignoring the feeling of foreboding looming in the bottom of her belly, Katherine shoved him.

She was taken completely off guard when he retaliated by pushing her back so hard that her body was sent flying into the wall behind her, and her head ricocheted off solid concrete. Rogue took advantage of the moment it took for her to regain her bearings by pinning her to the wall with his body and covering her mouth with one of his hands.

Not wanting his disgusting appendage anywhere near her, Katherine bite down hard on the rough skin of his palm, spitting out crimson as Rogue cursed and immediately snatched it back. The coppery taste of his blood in her mouth was downright nauseating, but it was a price she was willing to pay to keep his dirty hands off of her.

Unfortunately, he wasn't overtly fazed by the act of violence. "Feisty," he leered, his face still much too close to hers. "I like it."

"Get off me," she demanded, hating the hint of panic she could easily detect in her voice.

Rogue identified the root of her fear immediately. "Don't worry, Katherine." She cringed at the sound of her name coming out of his smarmy mouth. "I admit that it's crossed my mind to try to steal you away from Bastian more than once. I've fantasized about my mouth on you here," she shuddered in revulsion as he swiped his thumb roughly over her plump bottom lip, "and here," he added provocatively, leaning in so close that she could feel his warm breath against her neck, his mouth a fraction of an inch away from the tender skin of the slender column.

Then the man shocked her by briefly pulling her away from the wall only so he could brutally slam her into it once more. Katherine saw stars as her head smacked into unforgiving concrete yet again. "But that was before I realized that perhaps I detested you even more than I loathed him," Rogue sneered.

Katherine wanted nothing more than to assure the man that he wasn't her favorite person in the world either, but that was made impossible when hands that used to be on her shoulders were suddenly wrapped around her neck, squeezing.

She grabbed the man's wrists with her own hands, frantically trying to pry them off of her. She grew increasingly panicked as his fingers pushed harder and harder into her neck, the pads of them digging viciously into her skin.

Katherine couldn't breathe.

Rogue continued talking to her like he wasn't in the middle of crushing her throat. "Your death will destroy him even more than if I had claimed you as mine. You know, Cain had this theory that you two were destined mates. Who knows? Maybe I'll get lucky and kill two birds – or wolves rather – with one stone." He laughed uproariously at his own joke.

The noise sounded distorted to Katherine's ears and her vision was beginning to darken around the edges. The man's mention of Bastian, however, had her desperately clinging to consciousness. Rogue may not have known it, but Cain was *right* about them being destined mates, and Katherine would never forgive herself if she'd inadvertently cause Bastian's death by dying herself. Because she knew without a single doubt that her death – especially a violent one at the hands of Rogue – would kill him.

Katherine was struggling to fight back against the black rapidly encroaching upon her vision when quite suddenly, she was thrown to the floor.

She stayed down, merely pushing herself up onto her hands and knees as she sucked in precious oxygen and tried to wrap her mind around the fact that she'd almost been choked into unconsciousness. Her harsh gasping was excruciatingly painful as air rushed past the tender insides of her esophagus.

She was painstakingly aware of Rogue watching her with assessing eyes. "But then again," he murmured, "maybe you're not such a lost cause. Perhaps you just need stronger hands than *Bastian's* to mold you into the proper submissive bitch."

Katherine was sickened by the implications behind his words. But she'd make damn sure the man never had a chance to touch her. Rogue had made a mistake by tossing her to the floor. She'd landed right by the bag she'd dropped when he'd pushed her into the wall the first time. Inside was the sparring knife that Markus had gifted her for her birthday – the knife that she was suddenly grateful Bastian had insisted she bring with her to Fort Saskatchewan.

When Rogue took an aggressive stop towards her, she wasted no time in plunging her hand into the bag, pulling the blade out, and quickly unsheathing it.

Keeping the weapon pointed in Rogue's direction, Katherine slowly got to her feet.

She could tell by the way that he abruptly halted his movement that he was taken off guard by the ballsy move. When she met his eyes, though, they were bright with what she was almost sure was amusement.

He actually *smiled* at her, his teeth gleaming in the dim lighting of the dank bathroom. "And just what are you going to do with that, girl?"

His complete dismissal of her as a potential threat, even armed, stung. But if Rogue thought for even a moment that she was going to cower in a corner as he put his filthy hands on her, he was *dead* wrong. She brought the blade forward with a *whoosh.* The motion took Rogue by surprise and he was slow to react, barely able to bring his arm up in time to stop the knife from plunging into chest. Instead, it sliced through the flesh of his lower arm like butter.

It wasn't a fatal wound, but certainly a bloody one as the red substance that gave his body life poured forth from the deep gash.

She didn't know which of the two was more shocked as they stared wide-eyed at the wound.

She'd just *stabbed* him.

But then Rogue was coming at her, so Katherine stopped thinking and swung blindly at him again. This time, though, he was ready for her and easily grabbed the wrist of the hand that wielded the knife. He brutally twisted the limb, and the knife clattered uselessly to the ground. She whimpered as he *kept* twisting her wrist. He had to have been a second away from snapping it completely when he harshly tugged her forward by the appendage.

Rage had turned his eyes into black, soulless orbs. "Have it your way, then. I'll ravage you *and* kill you. Then I'll dump your wrecked body at Bastian's feet and watch him fall apart." Contempt dripped from his voice.

But the man's powerful wrath had distracted him, and Katherine took immediate advantage of that fact by using her free hand to dig her fingers into the seeping wound on his arm. "Screw you, asshole!"

Rogue immediate released her, clutching his arm as he howled in pain. Leaving her bag and knife behind, Katherine bolted, pushing free the flimsy lock on the door before rushing out of the bathroom.

Her red dress masked the blood that had splattered onto her well enough, but it didn't occur to Katherine that her right arm was covered up to nearly the elbow in the red substance until the stranger she bumped into as she flung herself from the bathroom scrunched his brow in concern. "Are you okay?"

Not even close.

Not stopping to answer, Katherine ran, weaving her way through the crowd, ignoring the odd looks she was thrown as she hurried towards where she'd left her friends what had to have been close to thirty minutes ago.

Agnes was the first to spot her. "Katherine, we were starting to get worried-" she gasped, her eyes widening as they took in her bloody arm. "Oh my God!"

"We need to go. Now." Katherine startled at the sound of her voice. Her usually soft tenor had been diminished to a weak, croaky rasp.

"What happened? Where are you bleeding from?" That was Sophie.

"Did you get your period early?" ...And that was Penelope. *What the frickin' hell?*

The girl must have realized how daft the question was as she immediately ducked her head in embarrassment.

Katherine chose to overlook the idiotic comment entirely. "The blood isn't mine. I'll explain on the way home, but come on. We have to hurry." The words felt like knives against the tender walls of her damaged throat as she forced them out of her mouth.

Penelope seemed a bit put out as she'd apparently finally succeeded in garnering the attention of one of the college boys sitting behind them. All three of said boys were looking at Katherine with varying degrees of alarm, but she ignored them completely in favor of snatching Sophie's hand and hurrying her trio of companions along.

They scurried through the throng of Tattered Dignity fans and made it to the parking lot in record time, quickly loading into the gigantic SUV that had brought them there. Sophie gave the keys of the vehicle over to a pouty Penelope so that she could sit next to Katherine on the long drive home.

Once they were on the road, the blonde patiently coaxed the story out of Katherine, grabbing the brunette's hands and interlacing their fingers in an attempt to comfort her when they started to shake.

So much had happened in only half an hour. She and Priscilla had come to a sort of understanding. Rogue had choked her. She'd *stabbed* him. He'd threatened to rape and kill her.

He almost *had.*

The thought that she'd not only nearly died, but would have undoubtedly taken Bastian down with her, was too much for her psyche to handle at the moment, so she stubbornly pushed those facts to the back of her mind.

An almost serene – and entirely fictitious – calm washed over her as she relayed to Sophie and her friends what had happened, using as few words as possible to save her throat the agony of speaking. She told them everything – from the surprise she'd felt at seeing Priscilla at the concert to the fear that had nearly overwhelmed her as Rogue had wrapped his hands around her throat.

Penelope and Agnes were shocked. Sophie, who knew just how vindictive the man could be, was even taken off guard. Not because she didn't think that Rogue was capable of such violence, but because he'd been stupid enough to anger Bastian in such a way.

"He's going to be so furious," she murmured softly. "I'm so sorry, Katherine, I should have never let you go off alone."

Not wanting to continue damaging her throat by talking, Katherine merely shook her head. It wasn't Sophie's fault any more than it was her own that Rogue had attacked her.

The blonde released one of Katherine's hands so that she could examine her neck. Sophie's cerulean eyes swirled in anger as they took in the undoubtedly nasty bruising. "Don't worry," she assured her in a voice brimming with emotion. "Bastian will take care of him. He'll make sure that that *dog* will never hurt you again."

The only thing that was stopping Katherine's heart from pounding with anxious fear was the irrevocable knowledge that what Sophie had said was true.

Bastian would take care of Rogue.

And he'd take care of her too. For once, that was all Katherine wanted – to be taken care of.

They made it back to Haven Falls in record time. Penelope dropped off Agnes and then herself, both of the girls giving Katherine a tight hug before taking their leave.

Sophie hopped behind the wheel to finish driving them home.

"I-," Kathrine winced, each word she forced out causing more pain than the last, "I should clean up before he sees me."

She feared that if Bastian caught sight of her in her current state – namely, covered in blood – that he'd… well, she didn't know what he'd do, but she knew that it'd be bad.

"Okay," Sophie agreed as she parked the SUV. "We obviously still have to tell him what happened," she gave Katherine a pointed look, "but you're right that it's probably not a good idea for him to see you like this."

By "like this", of course, she meant with crusted blood smeared all the up past the elbow of her arm and, though she hadn't noticed until Agnes had pointed it out to her on the drive home, speckled across her right cheek.

Unfortunately, the girls' plan to sneak Katherine into Sophie's shower was a doomed one. The house was dark when they'd arrived – not a hint of artificial light peeking out through the windows – so they'd assumed it'd be safe to quietly creep in through the front door.

They'd assumed wrong.

Apparently the house was only dark because Markus and Zane had heard the girls pulling up in the SUV and thought it'd be fun to scare them. Just as Sophie was closing the door behind them, the two men jumped out at them – Zane yelling "boo" or some such nonsense into Sophie's face and Markus grabbing Katherine's shoulders and giving her a little shake.

Needless to say that after the ordeal she'd been through that evening, Katherine didn't take it very well.

Meaning, of course, that she promptly punched Markus in the face.

It'd been her instinctual reaction – the jolt of fear his actions had sent shooting through her triggering her fight rather than flight reflex.

He'd just been lucky that she wasn't still in possession of the knife she'd stabbed Rogue with as far as Katherine was concerned.

"What the hell, princess?" Markus complained, rubbing his undoubtedly sore nose.

Katherine couldn't speak. She was too busy trying – and mostly failing – to calm her jackhammering heart when suddenly the room was bathed in light.

Caleb, who'd apparently been in on the prank as well, had flipped on the ceiling's light fixture. "I'm sorry. I told them not to-" He stopped mid-sentence, his brown eyes widening to the size of saucers as he took in Katherine's bedraggled, bloody appearance.

Zane's jaw actually dropped, and Markus's entire body tensed.

Their reactions, though, weren't the ones that Katherine was worried about.

Because it was at that precise moment that Bastian chose to make his appearance, stalking down the dimly-lit hallway – probably to investigate what all the racket had been about if the irritated scowl on his face was any indication. "What-"

And then he saw her.

CHAPTER SIXTEEN

Katherine wasn't sure what she expected Bastian to do. Yell? Rage? Break something or maybe even some*one*?

What she *hadn't* expected was for the man to freeze. But that was exactly what he did. His entire body came to an abrupt halt as soon as his eyes caught sight of her disheveled form, all movement immediately ceasing. Katherine didn't even think she could see his chest rising or falling in the tell-tale signs of breathing.

What she *did* see was a tremor so violent pass through him that it literally rippled under his skin.

"It's not mine!" Katherine croaked out desperately as he took in the blood crusted up her arm and splattered against her cheek. But she didn't think the man had heard her.

Because in the next second he was upon her.

Suddenly engulfed in the intense warmth of the man's body heat, Katherine could only stare dumbly at Bastian's shirtless chest as he growled threateningly at the other occupants of the room. He'd wrapped himself around her in such a way that Katherine could scarcely move, and the others could no longer see her.

As much as she appreciated the view of Bastian's glorious, rumbling chest, she didn't want the man taking out his – worry? anger? – whatever it was he was feeling at seeing her in such a state, out on the rest of the pack.

"Bastian, stop," she objected, pressing futilely against his taut muscles with her trapped hands.

He only pulled her more tightly against him.

"Bastian," Sophie tried addressing the man in her stead, but he was incorrigible and snarled in the blonde's direction, baring his teeth at his own sister before she could get more than his name out of her mouth.

And then he was pulling Katherine backwards, her feet a good couple of inches off the ground as he held her firmly to his chest and essentially carried her away. He didn't turn his back to the rest of the pack once as he dragged her in the direction of their bedroom.

No one dared protest.

Bastian didn't let her go even when they'd reached the room. Not after he unceremoniously closed and locked the door. Not when he sat them both down on the bed.

Instead, he held her gently on his lap, keeping her as physically close to him as possible.

Peering into the man's eyes up close, Katherine could see that Bastian's pupils were blown wide, the black almost completely overwhelming the magnetic blue of his irises.

The wolf was *very* close to the surface.

"The blood isn't mine," Katherine attempted to reason with the man again, despite the sharp jolt of pain that each word sent shooting up her tender throat.

She sighed when the man *again* didn't acknowledge her.

She couldn't bring herself to be mad at him, though, not even when his hands began meticulously checking her over for injuries. Or even more strangely, when he began smelling her, pressing his nose to her form here and there as he attempted to sniff out the source of the bleeding.

Except that she *wasn't* bleeding, of course.

Still, she accepted that some part of Bastian – animal or human, she didn't know – needed to do it.

Knock. Knock.

All the same, she was grateful when two firm knocks resounded throughout the room. Bastian's head snapped to the source of the sound, the hands that were wrapped around her waist clutching her impossibly closer to him.

"Katherine, are you okay?"

It was Sophie, and there was more than a hint of concern in her voice.

"Fine," she rasped just loud enough for the girl to hear on the other side of the door.

"Good," Sophie replied, the relief evident in her voice before it hardened into something as strict sounding as her no-nonsense knocks. "Bastian, I know that you're upset, but you need to get ahold of yourself. You're probably scaring Katherine."

The man stiffened at her words, but he showed no other reaction.

"Katherine needs to clean up," Sophie continued bravely from the hallway. "I'm sure it'd make her feel better to take a bath. And while she's in the bathroom, you can take some time to calm yourself down."

It was a brilliant idea, and if Katherine was capable of moving at the moment and Sophie wasn't locked on the other side of the door, she would have kissed her in appreciation. The fact that she still had Rogue's filthy blood plastered to her skin – and possibly more disgusting, stuck under her fingernails – made her itch for a bar of soap. And, of course, Bastian would be much easier to talk to if he could at least *feign* calmness.

Bastian seemed to be mauling over his sister's request. Unfortunately, though, his grip on Katherine wasn't loosening, and the girl was worried that he was still too ensnared in the thralls of his anger to respond rationally.

"Please?" Katherine asked, pitching her voice so that it was as soft and pathetic sounding as she could manage. It wasn't a difficult feat with her throat in the condition that it was.

Bastian's eyes met hers – the black still overshadowing the blue. But the man slowly peeled his fingers and then hands off of her. "Hurry," he managed to choke out, the words the first he'd uttered since her unexpectedly early return from the concert in Fort Saskatchewan.

Katherine could tell he was wrestling with his control and she didn't want to test him, so after jerkily nodding her head and placing what was supposed to be a reassuring kiss on his cheek, she rushed to the bathroom.

Closing the door behind her, Katherine wasted no time in shucking off her shoes and unzipping her stained dress and letting it fall to the floor. Steadfastly refusing to look at herself in the mirror, she started running herself a bath. Not wanting to ruin the clean water as soon as she stepped into the tub, however, she did her best to rinse her arm under the faucet of the sink, watching pink water circle down the drain until it ran clear.

Then she slowly sunk herself into the tub, letting the near scalding water rid her muscles of most of their tension before she grabbed the unscented soap and began scrubbing her skin raw. Once she was satisfied that she was thoroughly clean, she yanked her hair loose of its bun and began lathering the thick tresses in shampoo.

She was about to rinse the mass of suds from her hair when the yelling started.

"Don't tell me that she's going to be fine! I'm going to kill the bastard!"

It was Bastian. Katherine could feel the tension that the warm water had just ebbed from her muscles immediately come rushing back, causing them to stiffen.

"How could you have allowed her to go off by herself?"

Apparently, he'd let Sophie in the room and she'd clearly told him what had happened. Katherine didn't like how Bastian made her out to be some child who needed watching over with his question, but strained to hear Sophie's response to it anyway.

She could only clearly make out the word "restroom" through the heavy wood of the bathroom door.

"I trusted you with her." The statement wasn't a thunderous boom, but accusatory and sharp enough that Katherine's ears could still pick it up. "What if she hadn't thought to pull that knife out on him? Or had tried to swing it at him and missed? God, Sophie, what if she hadn't gotten away from him?"

Bastian's distraught questions had tears pooling in Katherine's eyes, but she stubbornly blinked them back so that she could focus on Sophie's answer. All she could make out, though, was a vague, comforting murmur.

And after that, nothing.

Resigning herself to the fact that Bastian now knew *why* she'd been covered in blood, Katherine quickly finished rinsing her hair. After a few more minutes of soaking – otherwise known as avoiding the agitated man on the other side of the door – Katherine reluctantly pulled the plug and stepped out of the tub.

She grabbed a towel to dry her hair and pat down her body before shoving her arms into the oversized bathrobe that had been hanging on a hook near the bathtub and tying it tightly around her waist.

Then she finally gathered enough courage to look at herself in the mirror.

Katherine winced.

It was worse than she'd thought.

Examining the colorful array of bruises that decorated the entirety of her neck, she could clearly make out where each of Rogue's fingers had squeezed. Most disconcerting was the mass of purple at the very center where his thumbs had brutally dug into her.

Katherine was a werewolf – enhanced healing was a perk of the condition – and the marks would be gone – or at least very faint – in only a week's time, but at the moment, her neck looked like an awful, discolored mess. A nightmarish rainbow of reds, blues, and purples.

She didn't think Bastian had seen the full extent of the bruising earlier because he was so focused on the blood that coated her arm and face, and it crossed Katherine's mind to try to adjust her robe to better cover them. Ultimately, though, she knew she'd never get away with it. Sophie had probably already told Bastian that Rogue had put her in a chokehold, anyway. So wrenching her gaze away from her reflection, Katherine bravely left the relative safety of the bathroom.

Sophie had left the bedroom, but Bastian was standing in the middle of the room, between the bed and bathroom, his head buried in his hands. At the sound of the bathroom door shutting closed behind her, however, he quickly turned to face the nervous brunette.

Katherine saw immediately that his eyes had returned to their normal blue – stormy as the color was at the moment – and an inordinate amount of relief washed over her. Bastian was himself again.

Or at least he was until said blue eyes landed on the purple bruises that adorned her neck like a demented parody of a necklace. In two massive strides, he was mere inches from her. He urged her chin up with gentle fingers so he could take in the entirety of the damage. His hands ghosted over the bruises, not quite touching the discolored skin as he surveyed her neck. His eyes followed the direction of his hands, analyzing each finger shaped bruise, seemingly burning them into his memory.

When he was finished, he took a small, jerky step backwards. Katherine was just thankful that the man had remained cognizant throughout his examination.

"Rogue did this." It wasn't a question, but a statement of fact. Sophie, after all, had already told him what had happened.

Nonetheless, Katherine answered him. "Yes."

Holding her gaze, Bastian gently tucked a wayward strand of damp hair behind her ear. "What else did he do?"

Katherine frowned at the question. "Just this," she assured him quietly, gesturing at her neck in an attempt to refrain from straining her distressed vocal cords. "The blood you saw earlier came from him. I… I stabbed him."

The words felt foreign on her tongue despite the truth in them. What was even stranger was the peculiar sort of pride that enveloped her when the admission caused a ghost of a grin to tug on Bastian's lips. "So I've heard." His smile, however faint, quickly faded. "He… he didn't do anything else to you, did he? Touch you, maybe?"

Katherine flushed, nervously gnawing on the sensitive flesh of her inner cheek as she debated how to answer. When an angry red exploded across Bastian's face, however, she quickly realized that the longer it took her to reply, the more depraved the theories that ran through the man's head became. "No," she choked out immediately, and then more slowly, "he… he just threatened to."

Bastian's entire being tensed with palpable rage at the admission. He snapped his eyes shut, but his fury was plain enough to see. The veins running up his neck were bulging and his jaw was twitching uncontrollably as he ground his teeth together in an attempt to suppress his raging emotions.

After a tense moment wherein Katherine feared the man would once again be lost to his anger, Bastian's eyes snapped back open, immediately meeting hers. "He'll never come near you again, Katherine. *Rogue*," he spat out his name like a curse, "wouldn't dare set foot into Haven Falls after what he's done. And on the off chance that he'd be foolish enough to consider it, I've already sent Markus and Zane to track him down and take care of him."

She didn't know what "taking care" of the man entailed – if Bastian meant for the two to kill Rogue or not – but she didn't *want* to know and so didn't ask. Instead, Katherine focused on the fact that by sending the others, Bastian had chosen to stay with her. She knew unquestionably that the man was aching with the desire to track down the man himself – it was just his way.

She swallowed down the lump of gratitude that suddenly lodged itself in her throat. "Thank you," she said quietly. "For, you know, staying with me," she clarified when his brow crinkled in bemusement.

Bastian's eyes softened immeasurably. "Leaving you never crossed my mind. No matter how much I may want to hunt down Rogue and rip out his…" he trailed off, his eyebrows drawing together in a frown. "I'm sure you don't want to hear about *that*. I… I'm sorry if I scared you earlier."

"It's okay," Katherine hurriedly assured him, "I know you would never hurt me."

Bastian nodded, running a hand through his unruly hair. "I'm glad. I just," he paused, face crumpling as he palmed his chest, directly over where his heart was located. "…it's just so much."

Katherine knew exactly what he meant. She placed her hand over his. "I know," she softly assured him.

Bastian maneuvered his hand so that he could intertwine their fingers. With his other hand he gently cupped the side of her face, his calloused thumb brushing against the apple of her cheek. "Can I kiss you? *Please*?"

Katherine didn't think she could deny the man anything when he asked it in *that particular* tone.

She didn't answer his question with words, but rather with actions, as she closed the remaining gap between them, and standing on the very tips of her toes, she pressed her lips to his.

What started off as an innocent meeting of the lips didn't remain that way for long. Bastian's mouth moved sensually against hers, and Katherine felt the familiar heat that kissing Bastian caused begin pooling in her lower belly. As per usual, it made her love drunk. She boldly caught the man's lower lip between her teeth before sucking it into her mouth.

The only word to describe Bastian's reaction was *primal*. Suddenly the hands that were chastely holding her hand and cupping her face were possessively gripping her waist, tugging her forward so that her miniscule form was flush against his much larger body. And while Bastian had seemed content to let Katherine set the pace of their kiss not a moment before, that was no longer the case. His tongue plunged into her mouth, and he licked the entirety of its cavern, sucking greedily on Katherine's own tongue and nibbling on her lips.

Katherine's body thrummed with pleasure under his ministrations, an unexpected shock of desire shooting through her when his hands grabbed the sensitive area where the back of her thighs met her butt and lifted her into the air, encouraging her to wrap her legs around his waist as he walked them towards the bed.

Not once breaking their kiss, he laid her down gently onto the mattress. He held his body above hers with his arms, his hands gripping the sheets on either side of her head. But while Bastian's hands may have been occupied, Katherine's were not, and she wasted no time in splaying them across his chest, exploring the dips and grooves of defined muscle as they traveled lower and lower. She dared to dip just a fingertip under the elastic waist of his sleep pants when Bastian tore his lips from hers and nipped sharply on her ear in warning. "Don't tease me," he whispered huskily, tenderly kissing the delicate shell and smooth skin behind it, but being careful – *oh so careful* – not to aggravate the bruises on her neck.

"Maybe I'm not teasing," she said, hardly recognizing her own voice, thick with lust as it was.

She was beyond pleased when the man inhaled noisily at her words, and she reached up to place a soft kiss on the hard edge of his jaw. "Katherine…" he warned, his voice so gravelly that it sounded like he'd been gargling rocks.

"Please," Katherine begged. "I want to touch you. Don't you want to touch me?"

Bastian groaned in what she hoped was desire at her attempt at seduction, but he still didn't move to do as she'd invited. "I can't," he choked out, giving her a *very* pointed look.

And Katherine knew exactly why.

"I want you to." She gave him a pointed look of her own.

Katherine had the pleasure of seeing true surprise cross Bastian's face for a moment, but the man *still* didn't touch her. In fact, after he recovered from the slight shock her words had caused, a concerned frown marred his features.

"You don't mean that."

Katherine bristled at the implication that she didn't know her own mind. "Yes, I do. I… I want you to claim me."

There. She'd said it out loud.

But instead of ravishing her, Bastian had the nerve to tenderly brush some wayward bangs from her forehead. "You're just saying that. I know that *Rogue*," his eyes flashed as he forced the name out of his mouth, "frightened you today and that you're feeling vulnerable. But I'm not going to take advantage of that – of *you* – by doing something you don't *really* want me to do."

Katherine wasn't sure whether she wanted to kiss the man because what he'd said was so incredibly sweet… or slap him because what he'd said was so incredibly *wrong*.

"Let me get this straight. You think I just want you to claim me because I'm afraid that someone like *Rogue*," she spat out the name with the same amount of venom as Bastian, "will corner me again? You think I just want to be yours for the protection that it'll afford me?"

Bastian tiredly ran a hand through his hair. "Katherine, what do you expect me to think? You've never even told me that you love me."

The worst part was that the man didn't even sound angry with her about it. He sounded infuriatingly understanding. Like it was perfectly reasonable for her to deny her love for him.

But how could anyone who got to know him *not* love Bastian?

"You're right."

Bastian was visibly startled by Katherine's abrupt confession, but only a moment later, he sighed in resignation. His easy acceptance made her furious. Especially when he shifted his weight like he was about to get off of the bed – get off of *her*.

"I wasn't finished," she snapped, causing the man to freeze. "You're right that I feel safe with you. You're right that you can protect me in ways that, as much as I hate to admit it, I can only dream of. But you're also wrong about something. Awfully, outrageously, infinitesimally *wrong*." It was now or never. Katherine was half expecting her throat to collapse in onto itself before she could get the words out, but it didn't, and miraculously, she didn't stumble over a single one of them. "Because I love you. I love you, Bastian Prince, and I'm so sorry that I didn't tell you sooner."

Katherine's heart was pounding in her ears. But it wasn't because of the usual panic that threatened to envelop her when she tried to say the "l-word" around Bastian. It was because she was so unbelievably proud of herself. She'd finally gathered the courage to announce her feelings, and the resulting rush of endorphins made her positively *giddy*.

And she wasn't the only one pleased to at last hear the words. Bastian attacked her mouth with his in reckless abandonment. Then he peppered kisses to her forehead, cheeks, and even chin as he held her face between his hands.

"Say it again," he demanded, eyes a bright, hypnotic blue as he stared into her green orbs.

Katherine licked her lips, not at all frightened of her own feelings anymore. "I love you."

The breathless declaration had Bastian groaning and bowing his head, dipping his chin to his chest. "God help me, I love you too," he murmured before lifting his head and once again looking straight into her eyes. "Are you sure about this?"

The question sent a yearning so strong through Katherine that she had to take a deep breath to gather herself. She slowly exhaled. "I'm surer about this – about *you* – than I have ever been about anything in my entire life."

Bastian placed a doting kiss on the tip of her nose. "That was exactly what I wanted to hear." But the fond glint in his eyes transformed into something more dangerous – more *carnal* – than mere affection as his gaze lowered to the flimsy, oversized robe that served to hide her body from his view. His Adam's apple bobbed as he eyed the knot that held the robe together. "Can I see you?"

Katherine's breath hitched at the blunt question, but her voice didn't waver once as she answered. "Yes."

Bastian tugged on the knot with uncharacteristically clumsy fingers, and a moment later, the robe fell open, revealing her naked body. Katherine had been in a similar position before – she'd been topless when Bastian had made love to her breasts with his tongue and teeth at her parents' house in Middletown – but she'd had on panties at the time. Now she was completely bare down *there*.

As far as Katherine knew, Bastian had never seen the most intimate part of her body – the center of the wanton ache between her legs. At least, not when he'd been in any position to be aroused by the sight.

She successfully fought off the urge to clench her thighs together and cross her arms over her chest as his eyes roamed reverently over her form, but no amount of nerve could stop the anxious quivering of her belly.

And least not until Bastian laid one of his large, warm hands against the trembling skin, rubbing her nervous stomach soothingly. "You're beautiful," he assured her softly, using his other hand to gently angle her chin so he could press a kiss to her lips.

And for once, Katherine believed it – she *was* beautiful, at least to him, and that was all that mattered.

The tension fled her body, and she relaxed against the mattress as Bastian slowly deepened the kiss. She wound her hands into his wild hair and allowed him to dominate her mouth with his lips, teeth, and tongue. She desperately gasped in oxygen when he abruptly abandoned the task in favor of nipping playfully at her jaw before skipping over her injured neck entirely and…

Katherine moaned when his hot mouth covered one of her nipples, devouring it whole.

Fingers began tugging playfully at her other pink peak and the sensitive flesh pebbled under Bastian's touch. Katherine suspected she would have been embarrassed by the crude noises coming out of her mouth if she wasn't so consumed by the heady desire swiftly overtaking her ability to think at all.

As one of Bastian's hands continued to worship Katherine's nipple, the other ran comfortingly up and down her side, from just under her armpit all the way down to the beginning of her thigh. Katherine tensed when the hand veered off course, some sense – and anxiety – returning to her when his fingers tucked themselves between her legs, rubbing her inner thighs as he gently nudged them apart.

The urge to clamp them together was fierce, but not once did Katherine truly consider pushing away Bastian's hand. She wanted this… she want *him* more than she'd ever wanted anything in her life… and she wasn't going to let a little shyness stop her.

All the same, Bastian must have detected her hesitation because his mouth released her nipple with a wet *pop* and his eyes met hers. She could easily read the question in them. *Are you okay?*

Katherine took a deep breath before allowing her knees to separate and her legs to fall open in answer. *Yes.*

A wild blush blossomed across her cheeks when Bastian pressed a chaste kiss to her belly button before he was suddenly right *there*, pressing his face into the junction of her inner thigh and the focus of all the lovely feelings rushing through her. He inhaled deeply through his nose. "God, you smell so good."

Katherine's blush somehow deepened.

She forgot all about being embarrassed, however, when Bastian pulled himself to his knees and his fingers carefully began exploring her slick, heated skin. A *throb* so intense it was nearly painful pulsated through her when he gently circled the little bundle of nerves about her opening with his thumb.

Katherine whimpered at the sensation, wantonly pushing herself against the man's hand.

"Fuck."

It was Bastian groaning out the curse word as he watched, completely entranced, as she responded to his touch.

She inhaled shakily when a finger was suddenly pressed up against her entrance. Bastian pushed only the tip forward, watching her reaction carefully as his first knuckle was engulfed by her tight heat. Katherine forced her body to remain relaxed as the second knuckle disappeared into her and then the entirety of his finger.

"Okay?" he asked breathlessly, his eyes shining with an intensity she'd never seen before.

The sensation was bizarre, but not uncomfortable, and Katherine's affirming nod was honest. "Yeah."

Sensing that she was telling the truth, Bastian carefully began nudging a second finger in. Unlike one, however, two fingers *were* painful and Katherine stiffened beneath him.

Bastian immediately halted all movement, his form trembling with restraint. "Should… should I stop?"

"No!" Even Katherine was shocked by her visceral reaction to the question. "Keep going," she urged him more calmly.

Bastian obliged and soon two fingers were inside of her, sending sharp sparks of pain down her spine as the man moved them inside of her, trying to prepare her for what was to come.

Desperate to distract both herself and Bastian from the obvious discomfort she was in, and not thinking her actions through at all, Katherine shoved her hand into the man's sleep pants and wrapped her hand around him – well, as much of him as she could, anyway – Bastian's girth was such that her fingers didn't quite meet.

Ignoring his shocked inhale and the stream of curse words that catapulted out of his mouth – and her own surprise at the fact that the tip of his erection was already dripping – Katherine stroked him once, twice-

Bastian grasped her wrist in an iron tight grip before she could do it a third time. Despite the pulse that Katherine could see beating rapidly in the bulging veins of his neck, when he laid her hand down on the mattress, it was with careful, gentle fingers.

Then, in one swift motion, Bastian had his pants pulled down around his knees, ankles, and was throwing them haphazardly onto the floor.

Katherine watched with fascinated eyes as the man's suddenly freed erection bobbed attractively before returning to its proud, standing position, nestled against Bastian's taut stomach.

Katherine had seen Bastian naked before, of course, but she'd never seen him so… well, so *hard.*

She was so small and he was decidedly *not.*

"It's not going to fit."

Katherine's eyes widened when she realized she'd voiced her thoughts aloud, a blush so hot exploding across her cheeks that she was half convinced her face had spontaneously burst into flames.

Bastian had the nerve to smile at her. "Trust me, it will." But his amusement was short-lived, his smile fading into a serious, straight line. "You have to promise me something," he said, gauging her reaction. "If you change your mind, it hurts too much, or for whatever you just want me to stop, you have to tell me, okay?"

Katherine licked her suddenly dry lips, nodding jerkily. "Okay."

He must have judged her affirmation to be sincere because in the next moment, Bastian was kissing her again – his lips and tongue teasing her mouth and stoking the quiet fire simmering low in her belly until it once again grew into a raging inferno of pure *want*.

One of Bastian's hands stroked her thigh reassuringly as the other lined up his erection where his fingers had been not more than a few minutes before. Katherine felt the very tip of him against her and then slowly, agonizing, he pushed himself in.

She'd known it was going to hurt. It was common sense. He was so big and she just *wasn't*. What she hadn't anticipated, however, was how overwhelming *full* she'd feel – how complete.

As Katherine's body slowly adjusted to the feeling of Bastian inside of her, she began to relax. Bastian, on the other hand, was trembling. He was vibrating so violently, in fact, that soon *Katherine* began shaking as a result.

"Bastian?"

No sooner had she said his name than he forced a surprised squeal out of her by grabbing her hips and rolling them over so that *she* was on top of *him*. His trembling, however, didn't ease in the slightest.

"You're so tight," he grit out between clenched teeth. "I'm afraid I'll hurt you."

She supposed she should have been concerned over the fact that Bastian clearly didn't trust himself not to be so rough that he'd somehow break her – but she wasn't. Instead of filling her with worry, the confession shot a thrill of excitement rushing through her.

"Tell me what to do."

Bastian groaned. "Anything," he assured her. "Whatever feels good for you."

Katherine bit her lip. "What about you? I want you to feel good too."

Bastian's answering grin was positively sardonic. "Trust me, you don't have to worry about *that*."

Katherine's response was a fierce blush, but his words had given her the confidence to at least *try* moving, and so she experimentally rocked her hips against him.

The result was an unexpected shock of pleasure shooting down her spine and Bastian cussing under his breath, his grip on her hips somehow – *impossibly* – tightening.

Encouraged by his reaction, Katherine pressed her hands against the man's chest and carefully lifted herself up just enough so that only the very tip of him remained inside of her, before taking a deep breath and abruptly slamming herself back down.

A surprise gasp left her lips at the same time a desperate half-growl, half-roar left Bastian's. Impaling herself on the man had hurt, that much was true. It'd burned even – but it was a *good* burn. And before Katherine could second guess herself, she slammed herself down on him again. This time, though, Bastian couldn't help himself and met her half-way, thrusting up into her at the same time she was coming down.

"Bastian," Katherine keened as an intense flash of pure pleasure swept over her, making her legs suddenly as wobbly as Jell-O.

He moaned in response. "I've got you, sweet girl," he assured her, the hands on her waist helping Katherine keep upright. Once she'd gotten some semblance of control over herself, she once again lifted herself up off of him, only so she could crash down onto him for a third time and a fourth, recreating the wonderful sensation that had taken hold of her over and over again. Working together, they set a swift pace.

"You're doing great," Bastian groaned. He croaked other compliments into her ear too, but only a few – "beautiful", "incredible", "perfect" – filtered through her subconscious. She was too incoherent to register anything else he may have said, all of her attention focused on the lovely, tortuous pressure building up inside of her.

And then suddenly his thumb was right *there* again, pressing hard against the sensitive bud above where he stretched and filled her. And just like that, she was gone. An obscene cry burst from her lips as she fell apart on the inside, an intense flash of heat shooting straight through her core, forcing her muscles to clench involuntarily around him. Katherine wasn't ashamed to admit that she saw stars.

She was so lost to the novel sensation that she was hardly even cognizant of the fact that Bastian had abruptly flipped them around so that it was she who was once again being pushed into the mattress. He sunk her teeth into her neck – the pain didn't even register – and thrust into her once, twice before his entire body spasmed, and Bastian, too, was taken over the edge of pleasure.

It didn't occur to Katherine that she'd *actually* blacked out until she recognized Bastian's concerned voice in her ear what only seemed like a moment later. "Katherine?"

When had she closed her eyes?

"Katherine, are you okay?"

The man sounded panicked, but he was still inside of her so she knew she must have only been out for mere minutes – if that.

She fought the sudden, inappropriate urge to laugh. *Had the man been scared he'd sexed her into oblivion?*

Instead of releasing the giggle – which could have easily been misconstrued – Katherine opened her eyes, peering directly into Bastian's blue, blue gaze and smiling. "I'm better than okay," she assured him.

She was unbelievably sore, and there was a sharp, stinging pain originating from where he'd bitten her, but she'd never felt better in her life.

Because they'd done it – they'd claimed each other as mates. He'd marked her as his. And she knew unquestionably that he was hers. It'd been that way since the very moment that they'd met and it would *always* be that way.

And now, finally, everyone would know it.

CHAPTER SEVENTEEN

Before claiming his mate, it is customary for the dominant wolf of a pairing to present his intended with a gift. If the submissive wolf accepts the gift – usually a family heirloom of sorts – it indicates an acceptance, too, of the dominant's plan to claim her as his mate. In addition to serving as a promise of his intentions, the gift often has an additional purpose of warding off other prospective mates of the submissive partner until the actual claiming occurs.

To claim his mate, a dominant wolf must bite his intended at the juncture between her neck and right shoulder hard enough to draw blood and leave a mark. This most commonly occurs in conjunction with sexual intercourse. While it is the responsibility of the dominant wolf to create the mark, it is the responsibility of the submissive wolf to wear it.

Once the submissive partner has been marked, a claiming ceremony occurs shortly thereafter wherein the couple presents themselves as a mated pair to their pack. The submissive wolf must reveal the mark for all to see in addition to performing an elaborate dance as a gift to her dominant mate and to broadcast to the rest of the pack her pleasure at being claimed by him.

No matter how much Katherine stared – glared, really – at the last sentence of the last paragraph on page 96, the words did not change. She would have to… *dance*?

Katherine wasn't naïve. As tough as she liked to pretend she was, she knew very well who the submissive partner was in her relationship with Bastian. It was her. And she had the mark to prove it.

Which brought her back to the fact that she was apparently expected to *dance*.

Not just in front of Bastian. Not just in front of the pack. But because Bastian was the head alpha of Haven Falls, she was expected to get down in front of the *entire* town.

What kind of sadist had made up such a rule?

Katherine knew there was absolutely no getting out of it either. She doubted Bastian could excuse her from the bizarre ritual without ruffling the feathers – or fur, rather – of the council members who preferred to strictly adhere to tradition. So, like, nearly *all* of them basically.

Besides, she didn't want to hurt Bastian's feelings by asking him if she could skip out on the dancing part of the ceremony. Somehow, despite the man's generally stoic nature, she knew that asking him such a question would do exactly that: hurt his feelings. Even if he sometimes pretended not to have them.

Part of her, though, couldn't help but feel that Bastian had it coming. It didn't escape her notice, after all, what the book had said about gift giving. Bastian certainly hadn't explained to her the significance of accepting the Prince ring when he'd given it to her for her birthday over a month ago. He'd hinted at it in Middletown when he insisted she start wearing it again, but even then, he'd only likened the piece of jewelry to an engagement ring.

Apparently, it'd actually been a gift to mark his intention to claim her and was meant to keep any other wolves who may have mistakenly thought that she was unattached at bay.

It explained why he was so adamant that she wear the ring at all times at any rate.

Sneaky bastard.

Luckily for Bastian, Katherine was too preoccupied with the apparent "elaborate" dance she'd have to perform to bring herself to be properly mad at him.

She wondered if a quick shimmy of the hips counted as "elaborate"?

Besides, she figured the man had already gotten enough of an earful from their pack mates for claiming her last night in the first place.

Katherine awoke swathed in a mass of heavy blankets, half convinced she was in the midst of a heat stroke. She struggled to shove the oppressive blankets off while at the same time attempting to clear her hazy head. It felt as if her brain had somehow leaked out of her ears the night before, only to be replaced with a lump of scratchy cotton – a common side effect of Not-A-Morning-Personitis, which she suffered from regularly.

Having successfully kicked the blankets to the bottom of the bed, Katherine was picking off the damp hair stuck to her sweaty forehead when she abruptly realized something important.

She was naked. Naked as in nude. Completely in the buff.

But she always slept in some sort of pajamas – even if it was just a ratty, too long t-shirt.

And just like that, the events of last night came rushing back to her. The concert. Rogue's attack. Bastian's reaction. And after all that... she'd asked Bastian to claim her.

Her memory was suddenly very, very clear.

They'd had sex. And Bastian had bitten her.

Katherine's green eyes widened, and she slapped a hand over the barely noticeable ache on the juncture of her neck and shoulder, tracing with her fingers the indentations that had been impressed into her skin by Bastian's teeth.

The small wound was throbbing in time with the beat of her heart, but the pain hardly registered. After all, her entire neck was still incredibly tender from Rogue's assault the night before.

Glancing at the bright light pouring in through the gaps of the blinds on the windows – Bastian had replaced the one she'd broken when she'd run away over a month ago immediately upon returning – Katherine estimated that it was already late morning, maybe even early afternoon. Which meant she'd overslept, even by her terms.

She pulled herself up and made a move to get off of the bed. As soon as she attempted to put weight on her feet, however, a fierce ache shot up her legs and straight through her core. She was startled to realize that she was very sore between her thighs. She braved a glance down there and eyed puffy, pink skin, but was relieved to see that at least there wasn't any blood streaked between her legs.

All the same, it served as more physical evidence to what she and Bastian had gotten up to last night. They'd really done it. They'd claimed each other as mates.

Katherine gauged her feelings with as much honesty as she dared, praying that regret didn't rear its ugly head.

She could honestly say that she didn't feel one ounce of it. A small grin broke free across her face. She was actually really, really happy – the happiest she'd felt in a long time, maybe even ever.

Except... where was Bastian?

The grin faded as insecurity welled in her throat.

Determined to find the answer to that question, Katherine forced herself to stand on wobbly legs, this time prepared for the pain that immediate sparked between them. Steadfastly ignoring the discomfort it caused her, Katherine clumsily pulled on the robe that had been discarded on the floor the night before and peeked into the bathroom to make sure the man wasn't hiding in there before heading for the hallway. Softly shutting the bedroom door behind her, she made her way towards the sound of voices that seemed to be coming from the direction of the dining room.

"...Katherine."

When she heard her name spoken in the deep tenor of Bastian's timbre, instinct had her immediately halting. Creeping forward just slightly, Katherine kept herself hidden behind the corner of where the hallway ended and the dining room began and unashamedly eaves-dropped.

"Oh, Bastian, how could you?" It was Sophie who'd responded to whatever it was that Bastian had announced, and Katherine didn't know if she'd ever heard the blonde sound so disappointed before.

"I'm... I mean... I don't know if I entirely approve either." Caleb was apparently in on the conversation as well.

"Making good on the first opportunity that presents itself, huh?" And there was Markus, adding his two cents as usual, except that he

sounded unduly... angry?

What was it that Bastian had said?

The clamor of a scuffle breaking out had Katherine straightening, and she was about to reveal herself when a noise that sounded suspiciously like a head cracking against the wall echoed in her ears. Bastian's authoritative voice boomed from the other side of the wall. "How dare you suggest I would take advantage of Katherine? She asked me to claim her. Who would I be to deny her such a request when I've long for it so long myself?"

So that's what it was that Bastian had proclaimed – he'd told them that he'd claimed her. But why did they all sound so distraught? She thought they all liked – even loved – each other in their own way. For a moment, she allowed insecurity to reign.

Zane speaking over Bastian's loud growling confirmed her suspicions that, indeed, the entire pack was discussing her love life – without her even present to object – in the frickin' dining room of all places. "Markus didn't mean anything by it," Zane attempted to mediate. "He just... we all just..." he trailed off.

Sophie took over for him. "What Zane – what we all – are trying to say is that Katherine was really upset last night. Who wouldn't be after being ambushed the way she was? She was probably feeling extremely vulnerable when she asked you to claim her. You know that we all want you and Katherine to get together already. We're just saying that last night might not have been the best time to actually do it."

The blonde's spiel reminded Katherine eerily of the concerns that Bastian had aired the night before – the man had been worried that she didn't really want him to claim her and that it was just the trauma Rogue had enforced on her talking.

She could practically feel Bastian beginning to doubt himself – beginning to doubt their bond. It incensed Katherine.

"Does she even know what being claimed as the mate of the head alpha entails? How she'll be looked to as a leader in her own right? How about the fact that she'll have to complete the final stage of the claiming – the actual ceremony – in front of the entire town?"

"I..." Bastian floundered for a moment, clearly abashed by the chiding questions.

Katherine had had enough.

Stepping out from around the corner she'd been hiding behind and ignoring her pack mates' startled expressions and the fact that Bastian had Markus pinned against the wall, she began to speak. "Bastian didn't do anything wrong," her voice was as sharp as the bruising of her throat allowed as she scolded at them. "He's right – I did ask him to claim me. But certainly not because I was scared or whatever convoluted reason that it is you've all come up with. I do have needs, you know, just like any other person. I've wanted Bastian for a long time, and what we did last night was... well, it was beautiful, amazing, exhilarating – whatever word you want to use. It was just... right. So please don't stand there and tell Bastian otherwise because you are the ones who are so utterly wrong, not him."

The only response to her unexpected rant was dumbstruck silence. Giving her pack a minute to digest her words, Katherine turned to face Bastian, who looked as flummoxed by her sudden appearance as the rest of them. "Can you please put Markus down now?"

The man immediately obliged.

Markus rolled his shoulders and straightened his crumped t-shirt as soon as he was released. "Thanks," he muttered lowly to Katherine. "And I'm sorry," he added somewhat begrudgingly.

Markus's apology seemed to set off a chain reaction and three more apologies echoed throughout the room, Caleb's especially repentant as he popped up in front of Katherine and entreated her forgiveness.

But it wasn't hers to give. She wasn't the one they owed an apology to after all. She immediately told them so.

"It's Bastian you all accused of taking advantage of me. Shouldn't you be apologizing to him?"

"Of course," Zane immediately agreed, standing and bowing before Bastian. "We're sorry for questioning you, alpha."

Sophie stood up as well, fiddling for a moment with the ends of her long hair before sighing and squarely meeting Bastian's eyes. "I should have known better than to ever think that you could hurt Katherine," she admitted. "I see the way you care for her." Her gaze shifted to Katherine. "The way she cares for you. I'm sorry, brother."

Bastian offered a terse nod. "You were out of line," he agreed, "but I suppose I can forgive your misconduct this once." He glanced around the room. "I know you were all just doing your best to look out for Katherine."

Katherine scowled when Markus mused her already tangled hair with a too rough hand. "It's hard not to feel a bit protective of princess here, especially after she came waltzing in all bloodied and bruised last night."

She grumpily batted the man's hand away, but he just laughed at her put out expression.

Rolling her eyes at Markus's antics, she wrapped her hand around as much of one of Bastian's thick wrists as she was able and tugged. "Now that that's all settled, can I talk to you for a minute? Alone?"

"Yeah, she does have needs, you know. And you apparently meet them so beautifully. Or was it amazingly? Exhilaratingly?"

Dear. God.

Her face, she was sure, reddened enough to rival an overripe tomato. Just barely managing to reel in the urge to punch Markus in his smart mouth, she ignored the others' snickering at his obscene comment and dragged an obliging Bastian back to their bedroom.

She'd only just closed the door behind them when she found herself crushed against a hard chest, strong arms encircling her in an unyielding grip. A chaste kiss was pressed to her forehead. "I love you."

Ignoring the way her heart fluttered at the softly spoken confession, Katherine craned her neck up in such a way that she could look into the man's eyes. "You do know that I don't regret last night, right? I meant everything I said. I... I'm happy to officially be yours."

Bastian grinned. "Just happy? Not overjoyed? Elated? Blissful?"

Katherine fought the urge to smile at the light hearted teasing.

"Fine, I'm over the moon to be yours."

Bastian's grin widened, his lone dimple making an appearance at the pun. "I love you."

Katherine couldn't possibly stop the corners of her mouth from rising this time. "You already said that," she pointed out lightly.

"It's no less true now than it was a minute ago."

Katherine bit down on her bottom lip. "So, you're... happy to be mine then, too?"

"Katherine, it's like I've already told you, I've always been yours."

She had reached up on her tippy-toes and pressed her lips to his after that. What had meant to be a chaste peck had quickly progressed into something *more*, but worried that she might still be sore from the night before – which, okay, she *was* – Bastian hadn't let it progress to anything more intense than kissing.

He'd left to gather the alphas of Haven Falls for an impromptu council meeting nearly immediately after. Even knowing that he was calling the meeting in order to inform the other alphas that he'd had sex with her and claimed her as his mate, Katherine wasn't bothered by his rushed departure.

Mostly because as soon as she heard the SUV start up and the gravel begin crunching under its massive tires, she was free to jam her hand between the mattresses of the bed and pull out the book that Zane had loaned her only a few days before – *The Physiology of Mating*.

She'd firmly shoved the questions she'd overheard Sophie demanding of Bastian to the back of her mind at the time in favor of defending the man, but one question in particular – the one about what Katherine would apparently have to do in front of everybody at the claiming ceremony – had a curious mix of curiosity and dread forming in the pit of her stomach.

After reading what she had on page 96, she'd quickly come to the conclusion that she'd had good reason to feel that way. Because Katherine would have to *dance* at the ceremony. By herself. In front of everyone.

She recalled that Bastian had likened a claiming ceremony to a wedding reception when he'd first brought the topic up in Middletown. Katherine supposed that what she was expected to do could be equated to a first dance of sorts – except, of course, that she would be the *only* one dancing while Bastian got to sit there and watch her make a fool of herself in front of the entire town.

Yeah.

At least she didn't need to say any vows – public speaking wasn't exactly her forte. But, then again, neither was letting her body speak for her.

Which was precisely why she was having a bit of a meltdown.

Katherine didn't doubt that the council would demand the ceremony take place as soon as possible. That probably gave her a couple of days then – *if she was lucky* – to come up with some sort of "elaborate" dance.

Sighing at the predicament she found herself in, Katherine took the only action she could think of and reluctantly trudged out of her bedroom and peeked her head into the dining room. Sophie, Caleb, Markus, and Zane were all still there and accounted for.

"Um, guys? I need your help."

* * *

After an embarrassing brainstorming session with her pack mates – *"For the last time, I'm not going to give Bastian a lap dance, Markus!* – Katherine had thought that she'd come up with an idea that was… well, actually pretty good, to be honest.

The only problem, of course, was that she doubted she'd be able to perform the dance as flawlessly as she'd conjured it in her mind. While her natural grace and flexibility had improved drastically upon becoming a werewolf, cheerleading practice was the closest thing to a dance lesson she'd ever had in her life. And the dance she had planned didn't exactly involve any "rah-rahing" or waving around a pair of pom-poms.

Fortunately, upon hearing of the circumstances that had prompted Bastian to claim Katherine – namely that Rogue had attacked the small brunette and choked her brutally enough to leave an array of ugly bruises around her neck as evidence – the council had agreed to delay the claiming ceremony for an entire week so that she may have a chance to recover. Apparently, the revelation of the claiming mark was considered to be the most important part of the ceremony, and the council wanted the crescent shaped punctures that Bastian's teeth had formed on the juncture of her neck and shoulder to be visible, not hidden amongst an array of discolored bruises.

Katherine hardly cared why they'd chosen to delay the ceremony. She was just glad that they had. She *needed* the extra time to practice.

*Un*fortunately, every time Katherine attempted to sneak away to do said practicing, some well-meaning visitor would drop by the house to offer his or her congratulations to the newly formed couple.

It didn't take long for news of their mating to make it around the town – approximately two hours after the meeting Bastian had called if Katherine were to hazard a guess. It was when the first visitor had stopped by, after all.

Visitors of the female persuasion came baring gifts.

Women and girls she didn't know the names of brought her all sorts of trinkets. They ranged from homemade soaps and body salts to books of recipes and hand forged jewelry. Priscilla had even stopped by to fork over a generously sized tub of body oil that she'd apparently made herself. Agnes, too, who had been sporting an enormous grin on her face at the time, had gifted her a bottle of wine.

Her befuddlement must have shown clearly enough on her face when the first female visitor to drop by had handed her a stack of hand sewn dish towels because once she had left, Bastian explained that it was customary for women of their society to honor the newly claimed mate of an alpha in this way. And she wasn't mated to just any alpha either, but to the *head* alpha of their little society. It was the highest position of power that any werewolf in their town could ever hope to reach.

Katherine felt uncomfortable accepting all of the gifts, but recognized it was an important tradition to the women and girls who offered them to her and so tried to express genuine gratitude as she was handed present after present. She just hoped her smiles didn't look as forced as they felt.

Mostly, though, the visitors just bothered her because it meant she had hardly any time to practice the dance that she'd prepared in her head.

In fact, the only thing about the constant stream of females stopping by the house that irked her more was that nearly all of them asked to see the mark that Bastian had left on her neck. Some were just curious, she was sure, but Katherine recognized the odd mix of lust and jealousy glinting in the majority of their eyes, and it had her feeling strangely possessive of what was basically a blemish on her neck. So possessive, in fact, that she'd taken to wearing her hair down to cover the bite mark from unwelcome, prying gazes.

The days passed like this, one after the other, with Katherine getting next to no time to practice her dance and even less time to spend privately with Bastian. And then, before she knew it, the day of the claiming ceremony had arrived.

Katherine watched with sleepy eyes as Bastian pulled himself out of bed – the faint pinks and oranges peeking in through the window blinds confirming that it was very, *very* early in the morning. After throwing on a clean shirt, the man brushed a stray strand of hair from her forehead before pressing a soft kiss there. "I need to set up the clearing in the woods for the claiming ceremony tonight. I've made sure Markus knows to watch over you until it's due to start this evening. *Please* try not to wander away from the house. "

Katherine huffed tiredly at the man's overprotective request, but nodded her agreement anyway. She understood well enough why he was concerned. After all, Markus and Zane had never caught Rogue when he'd sent the pair of them after him the night of his assault on her. Apparently, despite the tangy smell of fresh blood that had undoubtedly clung to him, his scent had become too convoluted to track in the large crowd at the concert in Fort Saskatchewan.

Needless to say, Bastian had been less than pleased at the news – *understatement of the century* – and understandably paranoid that Rogue would attempt another attack on her. As a result, the man had hardly let Katherine out of his sight all week. The few times that he'd been duty bound to leave the house, he had ensured that his second in command knew to mind her in his stead.

As it were, custom dictated that she and Bastian were not to see each other before the ceremony. Truthfully, they shouldn't have even slept in the same bed the night before, but really… *who would dare question the actions of the head alpha?*

Bastian ran his calloused hand through her soft hair before standing. "I love you." The words, though said plainly enough, caused a warm blush to blossom across Katherine cheeks.

The proclamation no longer caused her heart to beat in anxiety, but in pleasure.

"I love you too."

Bastian offered her an absurdly pleased grin before heading towards the door. "I'll see you tonight," he assured her before ducking into the hallway and pulling the heavy door closed behind him.

Listening carefully, Katherine's keen ears could make out the sounds of more doors opening and closing throughout the house. She heard Zane's grumbling protests, too, as Bastian forced him out of bed. He needed the man's help to clear the area that they were using for the ceremony – the same space that was routinely used for moon gatherings – of debris. Bastian had explained to Katherine the day before that the two men would also need to gather enough wood to continuously feed the large fire that was to be kept roaring throughout the ceremony, as well as haul a dozen or so massive drums over to the clearing.

Caleb, she knew, was staying behind to clean and prepare the large animal carcasses that would be stuck and roasted over additional fire pits in a celebratory meal after the dance she was to perform. She'd been informed that Sophie was going to stay at the house, too, apparently in order to help dress her properly for the ceremony.

After Katherine was certain that Bastian and Zane were nowhere near the house, she pushed herself out of bed and grabbed a random sweatshirt from her closet, quickly pulling it over her head. It was an unseasonably chilly morning for mid-spring.

She ventured out into the living room.

"Markus?"

The man in question was sleepily stuffing his face with gravy-doused biscuits on the couch. He eyed her in acknowledgement.

"Is it alright if I practice my dance in the yard?" she asked him, feeling entirely too much like a little girl begging her babysitter to go play outside.

The man snorted at her question, but nodded. "Just make sure I can see you from the windows," he ordered around a mouthful of biscuit.

She quickly agreed.

And so Katherine practiced. She spun and she jumped. She leapt and she twirled. And most of all, she tried to project confidence. As far as she was concerned, no one had to know what a clumsy fool she felt like if she could mask it with a composed and confident façade.

By the time the sun had reached its highest point in the sky – Katherine had long ago shrugged off her sweatshirt – she was fairly certain that she was as good as she was ever going to get at dancing of any sort.

"Katherine!"

Thus, when an increasingly frazzled looking Sophie attempted to call her in for the umpteenth time, Katherine finally decided to oblige.

Sophie practically hauled her in through the front door when she reached it.

"It's nearly noon already!" the blonde scolded, finger waving and all. "I was about to go out there and drag you in myself."

Katherine didn't see what the big deal was. She knew the other girl was eager to start dressing her for the claiming ceremony, but it was only noon, and the celebration wasn't due to start until seven.

Surely it wouldn't take *that* long to get her ready.

"Here, eat this," Sophie ordered, grabbing a loaded turkey sandwich off the kitchen counter and shoving it into Katherine's hands. She knew the tasty morsel had undoubtedly been prepared by Caleb and she flashed a thankful smile at the man where he stood near the sink, washing an impressive pile of dishes. He grinned back, looking entertained as Sophie dragged her straight past the kitchen – dining room and living room too – and all but shoved her into the bedroom she shared with Bastian. She was fairly certain she heard Markus's amused guffaw from where he sat watching the scene on the couch before the door shut firmly behind them.

Largely ignoring the blonde girl buzzing around room, Katherine plopped herself down on the edge of the bed and dug into her sandwich. She hadn't even properly swallowed the last bite when Sophie was pulling her back up and ushering her to the bathroom. "I'm not going to be able to do anything with you until you take a bath – not offense, but you stink."

Katherine frowned at the blunt words, but couldn't deny that it was true. She was positively dripping with sweat. As soon as Sophie closed the door to give her some privacy, she peeled off the clothes sticking to her like a second skin and started the bath. Before getting in the tub, she decided to sprinkle some of the bath salts she'd been gifted with in the hot water.

After soaking in the steaming water for a good ten minutes, Katherine quickly washed her hair. Satisfied that she was thoroughly clean, she stepped out and dried herself off with a towel she'd set out for herself before stepping into the tub.

She was wrapping said towel around her sopping hair when she spied the satiny slip that Sophie had apparently left hanging on one of the hooks near the bathtub. She couldn't control an embarrassed blush from heating her face as her eyes took in the small, flesh-toned scrap of fabric that would serve as the only piece of clothing she'd be donning under the layers of animal fur that custom dictated she would wear to the ceremony. The furs were the coats of Bastian's most impressive hunts.

Wanting to get it over with as quickly as possible, Katherine shoved the thing over her head, smoothing it out with her hands afterwards and trying to ignore the way that the nearly see through fabric brushed against the most sensitive spots of her body.

Knock. Knock.

Katherine nearly jumped out of her skin at the sudden noise.

"You almost done?" Sophie demanded from the other side of the door.

Rolling her eyes fondly, Katherine cracked it open. "Do I really have to wear *this*?" she asked through the small gap.

Sophie raised a singular eyebrow at the question. "It's only underwear, honey. A bra and panties would be even more uncomfortable under the furs we'll be putting you in. Now, come on, let me see."

Conceding to the blonde's logic, Katherine sighed and opening the door the rest of the way, quickly stepped out of the bathroom.

The edges of Sophie's mouth crept up into a positively devious smirk as her eyes took her in. "Bastian owes me big time."

An undignified snort of mortified laughter managed to escape before Sophie grabbed her hand and led her to the bed. "Sit," she said, gesturing to the floor. "I need to blow dry this thick head of hair before anything else."

Katherine obeyed and let Sophie simultaneously dry and preen over her hair – going on about how soft and pretty its natural waves were – the next half hour or so. Katherine considered it to be more of a disobedient mane than anything else, but knew better than to argue with the older girl.

Once her hair was dry enough, Sophie let her stretch before forcing her to sit again so she could begin arranging it in whatever way she had planned. Katherine had given her free reign to do her hair however she pleased and was curious as to what the blonde had planned for her wild locks.

Katherine was forced to sit still for well over an hour as Sophie pulled her hair this way and that.

"Are you nearly done?" Katherine asked after a particularly hard yank had her wincing.

"Just one more minute," the blonde assured her.

True to form, she let her stand a minute later. Sophie's smile was radiant as she examined her work. "Perfect."

She swatted Katherine's hand away when she brought it up in an attempt to feel out her hair. "You'll see it soon enough. I still have to paint your face."

Katherine frowned. "Paint my face?" *Did she mean make-up?* Because the brunette wasn't planning on wearing any. She preferred that her face be bare – honest – for the ceremony. Sophie *knew* that.

Katherine grew even more confused when instead of pulling her array of make-up products out of the sack she'd packed her blow dryer in, Sophie merely grabbed a clay bowl that she hadn't noticed sitting on the nightstand and gestured for Katherine to take a seat on the mattress with her.

"What's that?"

Sophie smiled. "It's paint, silly. At a claiming ceremony, it's customary for the submissive mate of a pair to paint her-"

"Or his!" Katherine interjected. Although uncommon, there were *some* cases of male partners being submissive to their female counterparts.

"Or *his*," Sophie allowed, "face with a color picked out by her *or his* dominant partner."

Katherine furrowed her brow. *Bastian hadn't said anything about paint.* He'd just asked that she wear the furs he picked out for her to the claiming ceremony.

It was like Sophie could read her mind. "Bastian probably didn't tell you because the color that a dominant partner chooses for his mate is supposed to remain a secret until it's already been painted on her *or his* face."

Oh. "Oh."

"The color they choose is supposed to be representative of their partners. Yellow, for is example, is typically chosen to symbolize someone whose dominant trait is loyalty. Blue is often used to represent those who are wise, and green is representative of a youthful, fun-loving soul. I watched Bastian hand mix this paint himself after you went to bed last night. Personally, I think he got the hue just right. Now, close your eyes. And no peeking!"

Burning curiosity practically demanded that Katherine open her eyes, but somehow she managed to keep her green orbs clenched tightly shut as Sophie rubbed cold goop into her skin. Using the tip of her finger, Sophie painted what felt like intricate swirls on her forehead, cheeks, and chin.

"Alright, I'm done."

Katherine opened her eyes, but to her disappointment, Sophie had already hidden the clay bowl. "Can I see?" she asked, gesturing at her face.

Sophie laughed. "Soon," she promised. "I want to dress you in these furs first," she said, pointing at the large, dark brown pelts that she'd laid out on the other side of the bed. "I want to make sure you get the entire effect when you first see yourself."

Katherine was pleased to discover that putting on the heavy layers of fur was not as difficult as she'd feared. Apparently, Caleb had helped Sophie stitch the pelts into a basic wrap dress that came down to a little below her knees. The dress was loose enough to dance in and was held up by two thick straps that looped over her shoulders. They'd also sewn together a hooded cape that Sophie clasped over the dress. The hood, Katherine knew, was to conceal her face – and the mark that claimed her as Bastian's mate – until she'd completed her dance tonight.

She was also happy to note that the fur was a lot softer than it looked, feeling distinctly luxurious against her skin.

"*Now* can I see?" Katherine knew the question came out sounding like a whine, but she couldn't bring herself to care. Her curiosity could only remain unsatisfied for so long.

"Alright, alright," Sophie conceded with a laugh before leading her into the bathroom and in front of the large mirror there, where she carefully lowered the fur hood still covering Katherine's face.

For a long moment, Katherine could do little but stare at the girl standing where her reflection was supposed to be. Because she looked nothing like little Katherine Mayes from small town Iowa.

She looked like a warrior princess.

The dark fur of her dress and cape contrasted beautifully against her pale skin. Half of her hair had been tied into dozens of intricate braids and wrapped around her head in a sort of crown, the other half flowing freely over her shoulders. And her face... beautiful patterns of swirls and lines and dots were painted over her brow, across the apples of her cheeks, and on her chin. The paint used to create the designs was a striking red.

Katherine couldn't take her eyes off the brazen color. "What does red mean?" she asked quietly.

Sophie smiled. "Red represents passion – desire. It also denotes danger. When chosen by a dominant wolf to represent his partner, the color choice indicates that, above all else, he thinks his mate is fierce."

Katherine licked her suddenly dry lips. "He thinks all that? About me?"

"He *knows* all that," Sophie corrected. "We *all* do."

A pleased warmth filled Katherine's belly at the girl's words, and she couldn't have stopped the blush from heating her cheeks if she'd tried.

"I... thank you, Sophie."

Katherine surprised the blonde by wrapping her arms around her in a tight embrace.

She squeezed Katherine back just as tightly. "Of course. Bastian's not the only one who loves you, you know."

After taking a moment to grin at each other in sisterly affection, both girls withdrew from the impromptu hug.

Katherine didn't embarrass Sophie by pointing out what appeared to be tears swimming in her eyes.

"Alright," the blonde announced, "I better go help Caleb lug the food out to the clearing. We'll finish helping Bastian and Zane set up the space while we're there. You'll be okay with just Markus here, right?"

"I'll be fine," Katherine assured her.

Sophie nodded. "Okay, we'll be back in an hour or so to escort you to the ceremony. See you soon. And don't mess up the paint! Or your hair, for that matter!"

With that, Sophie took her leave.

Katherine watched from her bedroom window as Sophie and Caleb loaded up the feast of seasoned meats the latter had prepared onto two large, make-shift toboggans in the yard and began their trek to the clearing.

They hadn't been gone for more than five minutes when the paint on her face began to itch.

Frickin' fantastic.

She was terrified to scratch it and ruin Sophie's hard work and so she began scrunching and unscrunching her nose in quick session – she desperately hoped that Markus wouldn't walk in on the odd scene – in an attempt to sooth the irksome itch.

Katherine was on the verge of throwing in the towel and just scratching the thing, consequences be damned, when she heard the front door ricochet so loudly against the wall that the resounding *bang* traveled all the way to her bedroom.

Had Caleb or Sophie forgotten something?

Katherine tensed when she heard Markus begin to shout. She shot up from where she'd been sitting on the bed and pressed her ear to the door. She couldn't make out any words, but he sounded very, *very* angry.

And then the sound of a gunshot echoed throughout the house.

For a terrifying second, Katherine's heart stopped – and then it started up again, beating at least twice as fast as it should have been where it had fallen into her stomach.

The only thing that her racing mind could think of was that Rogue had come back for her.

Katherine knew what the smart response would be in such a scenario. If she had any sense, she would rebreak the same window she'd broken over a month ago – albeit for very different reasons – and *run.* She would sprint into the forest – in the direction that Sophie and Caleb had taken off in – and continue to run until she met up with either them or Bastian and Zane.

But Markus was out there. And a gun had gone off. Markus may have been an asshole, but he was *her* asshole – her brother. And though her racing mind demanded she run, her heart would never allow her to actually do it.

Instead, Katherine twisted open her bedroom door and hurried to where she'd last seen Markus – the living room.

The wall was cracked where the door had brutally collided with it, and the couch was overturned. But that was nothing to be concerned with compared to the scene playing out in the middle of the room. Markus was on his hands and knees, blood oozing from a circular gash in his upper arm – *a gunshot wound,* her mind supplied numbly – trying to get to his feet even as the man holding the gun that had undoubtedly caused the injury threatened to bludgeon him over the head with it.

"Markus!" she cried in alarm.

Disbelieving hazel eyes met hers. For the entire time she'd known the man, she didn't think she'd ever seen Markus look so *utterly* furious. "What in the hell is wrong with you, girlie? Run! Get out of here!"

But she couldn't. Because Katherine had turned to look at Markus's assailant and shock had rendered her immobile.

It wasn't Rogue.

CHAPTER EIGHTEEN

Katherine wouldn't have recognized him if it wasn't for the eyes. Black, beady, little things peering out at her from a pale, sunken face. The last time she'd seen those eyes the man they belonged to had been wearing a ski mask. He had claimed to have killed her parents and was threatening to do the same to her.

He smirked at her, the false smile pulling at his lips completely mocking. "Well, what do you know? Looks like I don't need you to tell me where she is after all. How've you been, little beastie?"

His condescending, oily voice confirmed that he was exactly who she thought he was, and her blood ran cold, turning to ice water in her veins. She stared at the gun the man had aimed steadfastly at Markus's crumpled form on the living room floor.

Katherine urged her mouth to open and work together with her tongue to say something – *anything* – to get the man to point the weapon elsewhere, but her heart had climbed up from her stomach and lodged itself in her throat, beating there frighteningly fast and making speech an impossible task.

"What's wrong? Wolf got your tongue?"

The man – *the hunter* – chortled at his own joke, the demented laughter causing a shiver of apprehension to rush through Katherine's small form.

"Well, don't just stand there. Come say hello to an old friend."

The man's words registered in Katherine's ears, but she was still frozen in an unpleasant mix of fear and shock, and she could say and do nothing, let alone follow his order.

Katherine's entire being tensed as he cocked the gun, still pointed unwaveringly at the incapacitated Markus. "Unless you want me this shoot this animal, you better get your ass over here. Now."

Katherine forced herself to move. As soon as she took a jerky step forward, however, Markus was snarling furiously at her, impossibly livid. "Run, princess! That gun is loaded with *silver* bullets!"

"Shut the hell up!" the man hollered, bringing the weapon down in an unexpectedly swift motion and hitting Markus across the face with the blunt metal.

"Stop!" Katherine shouted, uncaring of the terror that could be heard clear as day in her voice as Markus collapsed to the floor, alternately groaning and spitting blood out of his mouth.

Silver bullets. As if getting shot with a *regular* bullet wasn't bad enough. The silver in the round lodged in Markus's arm prevented him from being able to transform into his wolf form.

It was one of the many quirks Katherine had learned about werewolves since becoming one. If in contact with even the slightest bit of silver, a werewolf could not transform out of whatever form he or she had happened to be in when contact with the silver was made. In human form, the silver wasn't actually harmful and merely meant one couldn't transform into his or her wolf form until contact with the silver was severed. But silver was like poison to a werewolf's animal side. If the hunter had shot Markus in wolf form… he could very well have died.

"Get over here," the man barked at her, immediately snapping her out of her panicky thoughts. This time Katherine didn't waste a single second in obeying, scurrying over to him from across the room. She cringed when he grabbed her and roughly forced her to turn around so that he could lock a pair of *silver* handcuffs he fished off his utility belt around her wrists, successfully securing her hands behind her back.

"I'll do whatever you want, just please don't kill him," she spoke softly, staring at Markus and hoping his sharp ears didn't pick up on her pleading. Somehow she knew the man would be furious that she was begging the hunter to have mercy on him instead of worrying about herself. "*Please.*"

As much as Markus liked to pick on her, she knew he'd lay down his life for hers in a second – and not just because Bastian would certainly order it of him. He'd do it for any of his pack mates.

And so would she.

The hunter had the nerve to laugh at her plea. "Oh, don't worry," he breathed in her ear. She cringed at the feel of it hitting her skin. "I won't. Not yet at least. After all, *someone* needs to deliver my message."

Without warning, he grabbed the chain interlocking the cuffs around her wrists and yanked her backwards, nearly causing her to lose her balance. Dragging her over to Markus's form, he kicked her pack mate hard enough in the ribs so that he was forced to roll painfully from his stomach to his back.

"Hey!" Katherine protested as he proceeded stomp his booted foot on Markus's chest and loom over the injured man.

The hunter paid her no mind.

"Tell that alpha dog of yours that I've got his precious bitch, and if he doesn't find her by nightfall… well, all he ever *will* be finding of her is a corpse. I don't think I need to tell you what will happen if he doesn't come alone."

Without further ado, the hunter jerked her towards the front door. This time, though, the unexpected yank *did* cause her to lose her balance, and tripping over her own feet, Katherine landed on the floor with an *oomph*, banging her elbow rather badly on the way down.

The man sneered in disgust at her fallen form, muttering something that sounded vaguely like the word "pathetic" before grabbing her by the scruff of her fur cape and pulling her to her feet. He pointed his gun directly at her head.

"Walk," he ordered.

Swallowing around what *had* to have been her heart still stuck in her throat, Katherine nodded. In no time at all, he'd forced her out of the house, across the yard, and into the section of woods that was in the opposite direction of the large clearing where the claiming ceremony was supposed to take place in less than an hour.

He didn't care one lick that she didn't have on any shoes, not allowing her pace to slow even as the sharp rocks and sticks hidden in the tall grass of the forest floor dug into the sensitive skin of her bare feet.

"Stop."

Katherine tensed, but obeyed, when they weren't more than fifty or so feet into the woods and the order escaped the man's mouth.

"Takes off your clothes."

As the demand registered in her ears, an emotion other than terror finally managed to rear its head – anger. The volatile mix of the two combating emotions – cold fear and hot fury – threatened, for a moment, to make her sick.

When the man dared to touch her – he made an impatient grab for the fur cape hanging from her shoulders when she didn't immediately comply – Katherine did the only thing she could think of and head butted him as hard as she could in the face.

The man jerked backwards and cussed as blood poured from his nose. He wasn't completely incapacitated, however, and quickly grabbed her around the middle before she could run. She tried to kick him as he hauled her up into the air – her heels connecting a few times with his shins – but she was slammed brutally to the ground before she could inflict any real damage.

"Stop your nonsense," the man groused. "I'm not interested in *that*. I'd never lower myself to lusting after a dirty animal like you." He offered her a smarmy smirk. "No matter how sweet you look like you'd taste."

"Disgusting prick," Katherine muttered under her breath, but otherwise managed to bite her tongue as he preceded to haul her back to her feet, and skipping the niceties altogether, pulled a sharp looking pocket knife out of somewhere – his *pocket*, she imagined – and simply cut the fur cape and dress off her stiff form.

When he had finished, the only fabric left on her was the tiny slip that Sophie had picked out for her earlier. He sneered at her nearly naked form. "The reason I wanted this," he held up the ruined fur, "off of you was to ensure that lover boy can pick up your scent. Now go rub yourself against that tree there."

He gestured at a large evergreen.

Feeling the barrel of the gun dig into the small of her back when she hesitated, Katherine reluctantly obliged. Ignoring how the rough bark scratched her skin, she rubbed her bare arm and hip against the trunk of the tree as instructed.

Satisfied, the man once again began to pull her along.

The sky got progressively darker as they continued to walk and he occasionally ordered her to rub herself up against random shrubbery as they traveled further and further into the forest. She thought about trying to make a run for it a few times, but the gun that was more often than not trained on her form kept her from making an attempt. Still, her mind raced as she desperately tried to think of a way out of the deadly situation she'd found herself in.

It continuously came up blank.

They had to have covered at least three miles – her feet were cut up badly, but the quickly cooling air numbed most of the pain – when they came upon a small clearing. Katherine instantly recognized it as the place she'd experienced her first transformation under the light of the full moon.

But tonight wasn't the night of the full moon, and she certainly wasn't there with Bastian and her pack. Instead, she had a vengeful hunter for company.

She flinched when he roughly shoved her back against a small tree, letting one of her hands free of the silver handcuffs only so he could force her arms around the trunk of the tree and quickly recuff said hand.

She wasn't in the awkward pose he'd forced her into for more than a few minutes before her shoulders began to strain. To take her mind off of the discomfort, Katherine finally dared to speak.

"How did you find me?"

The man smirked from where he leaned against a tree opposite her. "Well, now that's an interesting story," he admitted, twirling his gun in a seemingly nonchalant manner and talking to her as if she were an old friend and not someone he'd just kidnapped. The sarcasm that saturated his voice, however, gave him away. For whatever reason, the man *loathed* her. "I was tracking down a lead on a possible werewolf sighting in South Dakota, lounging around my motel room and minding my own business, when a news story on the television caught my attention. You see, a teenage girl had made her way back home to Iowa after having mysteriously disappeared from there seven months before."

Katherine's stomach churned as realization dawned.

"Imagine my surprise when the news reporter said *your* name and a picture of *your* sweet little face filled my screen. Katherine Mayes, the itty bitty girl who'd gotten the best of me all those months ago. I was tempted to hunt you down right then and there, but I finished the job I was on before seeking you out. Of course, by the time I got to Middletown, you were already gone. Fortunately, I remembered that the reporter covering your story had mentioned something about Fort Saskatchewan. I knew that it must have been close to where the beast who'd killed my partner took you all those months ago and where you'd undoubtedly returned. I've been searching the area for weeks. Lady Luck must have truly been smiling down upon me last night when I stumbled upon a piece of werewolf trash drinking himself into oblivion at a seedy little bar just outside of the city. And even luckier, he recognized your name. Had a rather violent reaction to it, in fact, and threw his mug across the room in a fit of animalistic rage. Got the both of us kicked out of the bar."

Katherine's eyes widened in disbelief. *Could it be?* "Rogue?" she croaked.

"Ah, yes. That's what he called himself – horribly uncivilized name, really. It wasn't hard to wheedle the location of your colony out of him, and it was even easier to get him to tell me *exactly* where to find you and your little pack. You know, I don't think he likes you very much."

For a long moment, Katherine was too furious to speak. She knew that Rogue hated Bastian – and by association, her – but to put the entire town at risk by revealing its location to a hunter? It was an unthinkable betrayal.

The hunter was amused by her speechless anger if his subsequent grin was anything to go by. "Don't worry your little head about him, beastie. He wasn't much use to me after I picked his head clean of information. After all, he *was* a werewolf. It would have been remiss of me to let him live."

Katherine blanched at the revelation, but her fury at Rogue didn't entirely evaporate upon learning of his fate. After all, because of him, she might soon share that same fate – death. Unless… it was a long shot, but maybe she could convince the hunter she was more than just some deranged animal that deserved death – that she was human too. It was unlikely, she knew, but she didn't have anything to lose by trying.

"Why are you doing this?" she asked quietly, studying him closely for his reaction. "Is… is it because Bastian killed your partner in Middletown? Were you two close?"

The man snorted derisively. "Hardly. He's not the first partner I've lost in the business of killing monsters."

Katherine swallowed. "Then why? Why go through all of this trouble to find me?"

He eyed her incredulously. "I'm sorry, I thought I had made my intentions clear." He pushed himself off the tree he was lounging on and approached her, leaning in close until their noses were nearly touching. "I am going to kill you."

Ignoring the way her stomach quivered in fright at the bold declaration, Katherine resolutely pushed forward. *It wasn't like she didn't already know what he had planned for her, after all.* "But why kill any of us? Werewolves, I mean?" she asked, grateful that her voice didn't give away her fear. "What happened to you to make you hate us so much?"

She hoped that if she could at least understand the reason behind his abhorrence of her kind that she could find a way to elicit some sort of empathy – some sort of *compassion* – from the man.

He snarled at her question. "That's none of your business."

Katherine licked her lips. "If I'm going to die anyway, you might as well tell me."

The man was quiet for a beat too long, and Katherine was almost certain that he wasn't going to respond when he surprised her by opening his mouth.

"Stubborn little thing, aren't you?" he muttered lowly before squarely meeting her eyes. "If you must know, my father was bitten by a werewolf some twenty odd years ago. He didn't know it, of course – I would like to think he would have killed himself before he had the chance to hurt any of us if he had – but like I said, he didn't know. How could he have? How could *any* of us have? Anyway, a month later he… changed. I watched him morph into a heinous monster with no conscience to speak of. He ripped apart my mother without batting an eye. My sister too. He would have killed me as well if I hadn't managed to break his hunting rifle out of his gun safe and shoot him. I had to unload a half dozen rounds into him until he stopped moving completely – stopped trying to come at me and tear me to shreds too. I was twelve."

The man had kidnapped her at gun point and had cuffed her to a tree, and yet upon hearing his story, Katherine still hurt for him. She hated that she felt sympathy for the man – a killer who was responsible for numerous deaths, including those of Bastian's parents, and yet… there it was, all the same.

"I'm so sorry that happened to you." It wasn't a lie – the sympathy lacing her voice was entirely genuine.

The hunter, however, didn't think so. "*Please*, you're one of them."

"Yes," Katherine hesitantly agreed, "I am. But that doesn't render me incapable of experiencing emotion. I may turn into a wolf once a month, but I'm still human. I still feel. In fact, I think I feel even more now that I've been changed. What happened to you and your family was a horrible accident."

The man stiffened and Katherine knew immediately that she must have said something wrong. "*Accident?* What happened to my family wasn't some *accident*!" he spat. "My father was turned into a monster

– a monster that killed his own wife and child without a second goddamn thought! And I'm sure you can imagine where I ended up when I told the police what had happened. Apparently, claiming that your father had turned into a wolf and slaughtered your mother and sister is enough to earn you a one way ticket to a padded, white room."

"I'm sorry," Katherine tried again after giving the man a moment to calm himself. "You're right. Accident was the wrong word to use. It's terrible that a werewolf bit your father. It's even worse that he abandoned him and allowed your father to transform with other people – you and your mother and sister – nearby. But don't judge all werewolves on the actions – horrible as they were – of one. Bastian didn't abandon me and leave me to fend for myself when he bit me, did he? He made sure that I was safe. He made sure that those around me were safe. We don't want to hurt anyone. Why else would we live here, so far removed from society?"

Unfortunately, the hunter wanted no part of the truth she was dishing out. "Shut up," he snapped at her.

But Katherine wasn't so easily deterred. "Please. I'm *so* sorry about what happened to you. If you just let me go-"

"I said to shut the hell up!" The man backhanded her across the face with his free hand. Her cheek throbbed from the harsh hit and blood flooded her mouth. "Don't bother trying that voodoo shit on me, you rotten creature. I can see straight through your lies."

Katherine was done playing nice. She spat out a glob of blood tinted saliva directly at his face, watching with satisfaction as it hit its mark and dribbled down the man's jaw. "Bastian is going to kill you."

The man sneered, coolly wiping the spit off his face. "Not if I pump him full of bullets first. The silver will *burn* his flesh. I think I'm going to enjoy listening to his begs for mercy as I watch his organs and muscles disintegrate from the inside out."

Katherine jerked fruitlessly at the cuffs shackling her to the tree, paying no mind to the sharp bite of the metal as it dug into the skin of her wrists. "Screw you! I wish it was *you* your father had killed!"

The gun came down at her before Katherine could even think

of trying to dodge it, slamming into her temple with enough force to temporarily disorient her. An odd sort of ringing echoed in her ears, and her vision blackened around the edges for just a moment. Slick blood trickled down from where the gun had connected with her head.

She'd just been pistol whipped.

Katherine hadn't quite recovered from the hit when the man who'd struck her abruptly turned around, aiming his gun at a bit of undergrowth on the other side of the small clearing – a bit of undergrowth from which vicious growling had just erupted.

No.

Terror for Bastian enveloped Katherine as he emerged from the overgrown shrubbery in his wolf form. A fierce snarl was on his lips, his ears lying flat against his head as he fearlessly bared his sharp incisors at the man who had a gun pointed directly between his eyes.

"You must be Bastian," the man greeted him with a pleased grin, unduly arrogant as he faced down a wolf easily twice his size. Twice his size *and* snapping at him like he wanted nothing more than to clamp his sharp teeth around his neck and severe his head from his body. "And here I was starting to think you wouldn't show. I'm so glad you made it. After all, killing this little beastie here wouldn't be nearly as satisfying without crushing her spirit first. And this, I know, will *destroy* her."

The hunter cocked his gun.

Katherine, whose heart was beating wildly in her chest as she took in the man's horrid words, blindly reacted. Vehemently hoping that he was standing close enough to her for her haphazard plan to work, she used the tree at her back as leverage and desperately attempted to kick the hunter. Miraculously, her foot connected with the back of his right knee and it buckled under his weight, throwing him off balance for just a moment.

But that moment of distraction was all that Bastian needed and he sprung himself at the hunter. A shot rang out from the man's gun at the same time Bastian's body collided with his. Bastian snapped his jaws around the wrist connected to the hand holding the gun, and with a ruthless jerk, he forced the hunter to drop the weapon.

"Bastian!" Katherine yelled as she tugged at the handcuffs still effectively chaining her to the tree, desperate to somehow help him even as she felt the blood dripping down her mangled wrists for her efforts.

She needn't have bothered.

The second the hunter was unarmed, he was dead. She didn't think his gun had even hit the ground before Bastian was digging his teeth into the man's unprotected neck. Katherine heard a sickening *crack,* and then Bastian was carelessly tossing his body to the ground. It was a gruesome sight, the hunter's head only half attached to his body, and bone peeking out through the torn flesh of his neck.

The pity Katherine had felt for the man only minutes earlier had fled when he'd first threatened Bastian, and she couldn't bring herself to dredge up that sympathy even now that he was dead. Before she could wonder too much if that made her a bad person, though, her eyes caught sight of Bastian. The breath was stolen from her lungs as she took in his slumped form. He, too, lay bleeding out on the forest floor.

CHAPTER NINETEEN

The continuous rise and fall of Bastian's chest, tightly wrapped in white gauze, was the only thing keeping Katherine anchored to her sanity. Her eyes drank in the sight of it. The tell-tale sign of breathing was the only hint of life the man had displayed since being laid in his bed to recover. Otherwise, he hadn't so much as twitched.

It was a surreal experience for Katherine to be the one steadfastly watching over her injured mate instead of the other way around. *She* was usually the one lying incapacitated in bed.

She *hated* the role reversal.

Absolutely hated it.

Staring at Bastian's pale, silent form, she didn't think she'd ever felt so helpless in her life.

Except perhaps when she'd been chained to that damnable tree in the forest three nights ago – *how could it have only been three nights ago?* – and for several terrifying seconds, she'd been convinced that Bastian was dead.

Blood roared in Katherine's ears as she took in Bastian's crumpled form. "B-Bastian?" she called, her voice quivering slightly in shock. And then more firmly. "Bastian!"

Dazed blue eyes cracked open as she yelled his name, and she watched helplessly as the wolf attempted to get to his feet, only to crumble back to the ground the moment he put even the slightest hint of pressure on his legs.

Katherine's bottom lip wobbled as Bastian whimpered – the most pathetic noise she'd ever heard escape his mouth – and attempted to shuffle towards her on his belly before slowly coming to a halt about five feet away.

After that, his eyes fluttered shut and he didn't move again.

"Bastian!" Katherine yelled, unashamed of the panic that satu-

rated her voice.

Up close, she could see that blood coated the thick fur of his chest, damp and shiny in the light of the crescent shaped moon shining down on them.

Cold, hard fear churned in her gut as she realized that he must have been shot when he'd leapt at the hunter – shot with a silver bullet.

"Bastian!" she managed to choke out as she began to tug wildly at the cuffs that still shackled her to the tree.

But no matter how hard she pulled, the metal cuffs were just too tight around her wrists to slip free.

And no matter how desperately she called his name, Bastian did not get up. As far as Katherine could tell, he wasn't moving at all. He was entirely too still, in fact, and vomit threatened to burn up her throat when she realized that she couldn't tell if he was breathing.

No.

No. No. No. No. No.

Katherine's heart beat so hard against her ribs that she was half convinced it'd burst free of her chest. "Please, please..." she whispered, as she tugged harder still at the cuffs around her wrists, paying no mind to the pain that assaulted her as metal dug into her skin and more and more blood began dripping from her abused wrists.

She was so close to escaping, but her hands just weren't quite small enough so slip through...

Until miraculously they were.

Katherine stared in shock at the blood covered hands that were suddenly in front of her, when after a vicious yank she was able to pull them free with a sick sounding sqlurch.

Blood, she realized numbly, made an excellent lubricant.

"Damn it!" she swore, dropping her hands to her sides when the muscles of her shoulders suddenly seized and the horrid sensation of pins and needles engulfed the entirety of her arms. Katherine couldn't afford to concentrate on her own discomfort, however, when Bastian was laying prone at her feet, and she immediately fell to her knees beside him.

Relief flooded her body when she saw that he was, in fact, breathing, but dread shot through her nearly immediately after when it became clear to her that his body was trembling with the effort it took to do so.

Katherine carefully ran her fingers through the area of Bastian's fur that was matted with blood, searching for the source of the bleeding. Nearly immediately, they ran over a circular gap in his flesh that was slightly raised around the edges. Bastian jerked and an unconscious whimper was forced from him when she made contact with it.

Katherine swallowed thickly at the sound, batting back tears as he ran her free hand soothingly over the soft, downy fur of massive wolf's snout. "It's okay. You're okay."

But it wasn't. And he wasn't. Because the silver bullet had clearly lodged itself into his chest and rendered Bastian incapable of shifting back into his human form, and worse, the silver the bullet was incased with was slowly killing him from the inside out.

Katherine's hand hovered uncertainly over the injury, but she already knew what she had to do.

"I'm so sorry," she whispered hoarsely, pressing her face into Bastian's fur before pulling back and taking a deep breath. Then she dug her fingers into the dripping wound. Bastian spasmed violently at the undoubtedly painful sensation, and Katherine immediately withdrew her fingers.

For a moment, her confidence that she could do what needed to be done waivered.

But if she didn't do it, Bastian will die.

Hardening her resolve, Katherine pressed her fingers into the wound again, this time more firmly. She dug them further into flesh and muscle when Bastian subconsciously tried to shake her off.

After what was only a few seconds – but had felt like a few lifetimes to Katherine – she finally felt the something hard. Squeezing it between her thumb and forefinger she swiftly tore it free from his body.

She flung the bullet away from her. And then she turned her head to the side and wretched. Bile splattered on the forest floor.

After attempting to spit the bitter taste of vomit out of her mouth and carelessly wiping it with a blood stained hand, Katherine stared at Bastian's prone form. For a long moment, nothing happened, and fear had her very insides quivering.

But then Bastian was changing – morphing back into his human form before her eyes.

Where an injured wolf once lay, a human now did – naked and bleeding helplessly into the grass.

"Bastian?" she whispered softly – hopefully, even. But the man didn't respond. He was still unconscious.

But his breathing didn't look quite as labored. At least, Katherine didn't think it did. Praying that it wasn't just her imagination, Katherine forced herself up on shaky legs.

Regardless of whether or not his breathing was more or less labored than before, she still needed to get him help, and with no other option obvious to her, Katherine used the meager strength she still had left in her body to maneuver Bastian into her arms. The best she could manage to do was hold him up by the armpits, so trying to avoid the rocks and branches littering the ground, she began dragging him in what she was fairly certain was the direction of the house.

She struggled, accidentally dropping him twice as her exhausted limbs fought to bare his significant weight. Nonetheless, she continued to pull him along until she knew the only reason she could possibly still be standing was through sheer will power alone.

Her legs were on the cusp of giving out on her when help finally arrived. Zane and Sophie, their faces streaked in panic, burst through the thick of trees in front of her. Both of their eyes widened in shock as they took in Katherine and the man in her arms, but at that point she hardly cared how close to death the pair of them almost certainly looked.

"Help me," she managed to bark hoarsely.

They immediately moved to comply. Sophie gently pulled Bastian from her arms, her eyes shining with worry as they took in her incapacitated brother. Zane made a move to pick Katherine up, but he hadn't even been able to properly wrap his arms around her when her eyes closed against her will, and she promptly passed out.

Katherine had awakened before they'd even made it back to the house – her body too aware of the danger her mate was in to truly rest despite how desperately she needed it.

Bastian, however, had yet to open his eyes.

She'd been forced to watch as Gabriela Atkins, the town healer who'd been fetched by Caleb, had quietly examined him and wrapped his wound. "You did well," the redhead had attempted to assure her. "It'll take a while for his body to recover from the gunshot wound, seeing as it's been complicated with silver poisoning, but I'm confident that in a few days' time, he'll be back on his feet. He's too stubborn not to be."

Even if he wasn't, Katherine was determined to be stubborn enough for the both of them.

Which was precisely why, in the span of three days, she'd only left his bedside for bathroom breaks and to have her own injuries tended to by Gabriela. And the latter she'd only agreed to because Zane had blatantly guilted her into it.

"How do you think Bastian would feel right now if he knew you weren't taking care of yourself?"

That question alone had been enough to convince her to let the healer tend to the scrapes on her feet and wrap the ugly gashes on her wrists in the same white gauze that she'd wound around Bastian's chest.

Her pack had yet, however, to persuade her to eat. Katherine was convinced that her stomach was twisted in way too many knots to even attempt it.

But that didn't stop them from trying.

The distinct smell of beef stew in the air and the sound of footsteps approaching the bedroom door alerted her to the fact that yet another attempt was in progress.

When her door opened, however, it wasn't Caleb peeking into the room with a sweet plea on his lips for Katherine to eat, but Markus storming right in, a scowl set firmly on his face and a tray full of food balancing precariously on his good hand.

Katherine cringed. Her pack must have been desperate if they were sending in *Markus*. She'd only seen the man once since she'd return from her misadventure in the woods and it had been to make sure he was okay. After all, Bastian wasn't the only one who'd been shot by the hunter who was after *her* blood.

Truthfully, she'd been a little concerned that Markus might be avoiding her – that maybe he'd even thought *she* was at fault the injury his right bicep had suffered.

Guilt caused her stomach to churn as she spotted the basic white sling that kept his injured arm secure against his chest, and Katherine quickly looked away.

She wasn't sure she'd blame him if he did think that.

"Here," Markus barked, swiftly approaching and shoving the tray at her. Worried that he'd spill the bowl of hot stew all over himself if she didn't take it, Katherine reluctantly accepted the tray into her hands before setting it carefully on the night stand beside Bastian's bed.

"I'm not hungry," she muttered lowly when he openly glared at her actions. Katherine ignored the glower he directed at her, choosing instead to refocus on Bastian's steady breathing.

"What the hell, princess?" Markus demanded.

Katherine swallowed dryly, still not looking at him. "What?"

Out of the corner of her eye, she saw the man's complexion darken in an obvious sign of frustration. "Don't you think that I – that the entire pack – have enough to worry about right now without adding you starving yourself to death in the mix?" he demanded. "What do you think Bastian would think if he could see you right now, ignoring your basic needs in favor of wallowing stubbornly by his bedside?"

Shame heated her face despite the fact that she knew Markus was only spewing the words out to get a rise out of her – to get her to eat. He – none of them, really – understood that her stomach was too cramped with worry to properly digest anything. "Sorry."

Perhaps she should have been, but Katherine wasn't prepared for the resulting temper tantrum. "You should be sorry, damn it!" he barked, and she flinched. "What in the hell were you thinking, going with that hunter? Letting him put his grubby hands on you? Did you think he was taking you out for a scenic walk through the woods or something? Christ, I told you to fucking run! I practically begged you to! Don't you know what you mean to all of us? To me? I care too much about you to… to…" he trailed off, as if realizing what he'd just said.

Katherine's blinked owlishly, her brain whirling at what Markus had just revealed. She'd always known he cared – well, maybe not *always*, but for a while now, at least – but she was shocked that he'd actually said it. He seemed surprised himself, glaring at the floor with his patent scowl.

Taking a deep breath, Katherine wrapped her hand around the man's good wrist, beseeching that he look at her. "I didn't run – I *couldn't* run – because *I* care about *you*, Markus. You're my brother. I... I couldn't just let that hunter hurt you like that. He would have killed you if I hadn't gone with him."

Markus's shoulders relaxed slightly at her confession and Katherine could almost see angry tension draining from his body.

"Look at me," he demanded shortly.

Because he asked so nicely – for Markus, at least – she graced him with her gaze.

She stiffened when he grabbed either side of her face with surprisingly gentle hands, his hazel eyes serious as they drilled into her green orbs. "Listen closely because I'm only going to say this once. And if you tell anyone about the cheesy crap that's about to come out of my mouth, I will rigorously deny it. Got it?"

Beyond curious, Katherine nodded. "Got it."

"Okay," he muttered, but didn't remove his hands from her cheeks. "As much as I hate to admit it, you probably did save my life from that hunter. I know damn well that you saved Bastian's. That cannot be denied. But the thing of it is…" Markus looked physically pained, almost like she was pulling the words out of his mouth with a seventeenth century pliers instead of him offering them freely to her. "I would have *never* forgiven myself if something had happened to you."

Despite the seriousness of his words, Katherine couldn't help a tiny smirk from lifting the corners of her mouth. "I always knew you liked me."

Markus rolled his eyes at her assertion, releasing her face. "Whatever. Anyway, Bastian would have slaughtered me if you'd been hurt trying to save my neck. The point *is* can you just let us do the protecting from now on? *Please?*"

Katherine couldn't bring herself to lie. "I could never promise that. Besides, I think I prefer playing the knight in shining armor over the damsel in distress."

Markus snorted. "Whatever, *princess*. If you're not even going to agree to that, the least you can do is eat your damn beef stew. There's still a chance Bastian might kill me after all. Consider it the last request of a dying man."

"He would never blame you, Markus," she immediately denied. "It wasn't your fault."

The hunter had been after *her*.

Nonetheless, she eyed the steaming bowl of beef stew she'd set on the night stand. It *did* smell delicious. And he *had* said please. That was as rare as a raindrop in the Sahara when it came to Markus. "Fine," Katherine muttered, "but don't think I don't know what you just did there."

Markus didn't deny the rather obvious manipulation and merely grinned as she dutifully scooped a spoonful of stew into her mouth. "Happy?" she asked around a mouthful of tender meat and potato.

"I will be if you finish that. I want to rub the empty bowl in the others' faces. They tried to bar me from seeing you. Something about how my special brand of honesty would somehow damage your already 'fragile psyche'. But I told them you just needed a little tough love."

Katherine huffed, the words "pompous jerk" coming to mind, but she didn't say them aloud and couldn't deny being secretly relieved that the man *hadn't* been avoiding her like she thought he might have been – that he apparently didn't blame her from his injured arm.

Katherine had the portion of stew Markus had given her tucked away in less than five minutes, a little embarrassed of how fast she'd scarfed it down as she stared at her suddenly empty bowl. It'd been as scrumptious as it had smelled, and she glowered at the barren dish, wishing that it would somehow magically refill itself.

Markus had the nerve to laugh at her. "You want seconds?" he offered in a rare show of gallantry.

But Katherine didn't get a chance to reply.

Because it was at that exact moment that she was almost certain she saw the tiniest bit of movement out of the corner of her eye. Her gaze swiveled to Bastian.

She could have sworn she'd just seen his hand twitch.

And there it went again.

The chair she'd been sitting on toppled over when she shot out of her seat and grasped desperately at the hand she was sure now she'd seen move, squeezing it in a death grip with her fingers.

"Bastian?" she called hesitantly, badly wanting to hope that he'd respond, but afraid to let herself at the same time.

She thought her heart might burst from happiness when his hand once again moved, this time in response to her voice – spasming in her unyielding grip before wrapping itself around her hand and returning her violent squeeze.

Then his brow furrowed and he groaned.

"Bastian!" she exclaimed eagerly.

Her excited eyes met Markus's.

"I'll tell the others," he affirmed without her even having to open her mouth, immediately making his way towards the door.

"Wait!"

He jerked to stop, looking over his shoulder in consternation. "What?"

Katherine bit her lip. “Can… Can you give me a minute alone with him first? Before you tell them?” She felt unbelievably selfish for asking – she knew the others were waiting as anxiously as she was for the man to wake up, especially his sister – but she needed to have him to herself before they all barged in the room. Just for a few minutes.

Thankfully, Markus seemed to understand. “Sure,” he agreed easily enough before offering her his patented smirk. “But no funny business, princess; the man *was* just shot a few days ago.”

Katherine sputtered in disbelief, heat exploding across her cheeks at the insinuation, but Markus didn’t even stick around to tease her about it, swiftly leaving the room. And as soon as he closed the door behind him, her entire attention was absorbed by the man slowly waking on the bed, and she had no room to feel embarrassed.

Bastian’s eyes fluttered open, and like he could sense exactly where she was, the intense blue of them immediately met worried green.

“Katherine,” he spoke softly, his voice cracking half way through from lack of use. Her name was said with such relief and devotion that tears immediately sprang into her eyes.

She badly wanted to throw herself at the man, but was mindful of the gruesome wound hidden under the bandages wrapped around his chest and so did nothing more than squeeze the hand in hers even tighter.

Bastian apparently wasn’t nearly as concerned with his injury. Lunging forward, he grabbed Katherine around the waist, and before she could protest, he pulled her into bed with him, curling his body around hers and digging his face into the crook of her neck. He pressed his nose into the sensitive skin of her claiming mark, inhaling her scent like it was a drug before pulling away just enough to be able to look into her eyes. “Thank God you’re okay.”

Katherine’s eyes widened in disbelief. “*I’m* okay?” she demanded, the slightest hint of anger, irrational though she knew it to be, leaking into her voice. “You… you stupid man! *You’re* the one who was shot! *You’re* the one who’s been unconscious for days! Don’t you ever do that to me again!"

Then she shocked the both of them by crashing her mouth onto his. Grasping him by either side of his face with greedy hands, she kissed him for all she was worth. She moved her lips against his and reacquainted herself with the warm cavern of his mouth, having spent the past three days terrified that'd she'd never be given the opportunity to do exactly that ever again.

Then, just as quickly as she'd begun the kiss, she ended it. Jerking away, she ripped her lips from his. Her chest heaved as she struggled to suck in oxygen.

Bastian looked as dazed as she felt.

"If it means getting kissed by you like that, I'd gladly take a bullet to the chest any day of the week."

Katherine knew it was a joke – a throw away comment not meant to be taken seriously – but tears welled in her eyes anyway. "Don't say that," she scolded sharply before her bottom lip began to tremble. "I – I thought I'd lost you."

And then, completely against her will, she burst into tears. Burying her face into the uninjured side of his chest, she bawled inconsolably.

"Hey," Bastian protested gently, his voice raised slightly in alarm. "I didn't mean anything by it, Katherine." One hand began rubbing her back while the other stroked her hair.

Katherine struggled to catch her breath, gulping in air as she tried to get a handle on her wayward emotions.

"Shh, beautiful. It's okay. *I'm* okay. Just breathe."

After a few moments, Katherine was able to calm herself by mirroring Bastian's breathing pattern as he inhaled and exhaled beside her. "I'm sorry," she muttered pathetically.

"Don't be sorry," he objected, one hand tucking a strand of hair behind her ear as the other remained on her back, continuing to rub it in a soothing motion.

"But I am. I'm *so* sorry. If… if it wasn't for me then none of this would have happened!" It felt liberating to say the truth aloud. "He was after me," she continued, forcing herself to choke out the words. "The hunter; he was after me."

She could feel the weight of his stare on her, but at that moment, a lump of guilt the size of Mount Everest had taken up residence at the bottom of her belly and Katherine couldn't bring herself to look at him.

"You can't possibly believe that," Bastian objected. "That man was a hunter. While it was clearly his aim to kill you first – some sick bid of revenge for getting the best of him all those months ago – eventually he'd have tried to off all of us."

"Maybe," Katherine conceded, "but…" she took a deep breath, gathering her courage, "he only knew where to find us because I'd practically given him the directions," she blurt it out so quickly that her words nearly ran together. "In Middletown, when all those news stations were covering my so-called miraculous reappearance, I told them that I'd been staying in Fort Saskatchewan. He saw the broadcast and went there looking for me. At some point, I guess he met up with Rogue," she heard Bastian inhale sharply at that tidbit of information, "and he told him exactly where to find me – where to find all of us."

"What?" Bastian exclaimed furiously, but she ignored him.

"So, you see? He never would been in Fort Saskatchewan, never would have met up with Rogue, and never would have found us if it wasn't for me. This is all my fault. I… I'm so stupid!"

For a long moment, the only sound that could be heard was Katherine's heavy breathing as she waited for Bastian's response.

"Katherine," he said softly, grasping her chin so that she was forced to look into his eyes. She braced herself to see disappointment shining out of them, but to her surprise, all she saw was gentle understanding. "This was *not* your fault. You did nothing to invite that hunter to come after you. And you certainly didn't give him directions to our house. That, apparently, was Rogue." His jaw twitched. "I swear to God, I'm going to track that fool down and-"

"Don't bother," Katherine interrupted softly. "He – he's already dead. After the hunter picked him clean of information, he killed him."

Bastian stiffened as he absorbed yet another truth bomb she'd dropped on him. "Good riddance," he muttered after a moment. "I only wish I had had the pleasure of doing it myself."

Katherine swallowed, forcing herself to return to the subject at hand. "So… so you don't blame me then? For getting you shot? For… for you almost dying?"

His blue eyes softened immeasurably. "Katherine, you haven't done anything to warrant any blame. And I didn't die. I'm right here." He frowned with something resembling consternation. "Thankful as I am for it, I must admit to being curious as to how it's possible. The bullet I was hit with was a silver one."

Katherine winced. "Well, I pulled it out of your chest," she answered honestly, describing the way she'd dug her fingers into his torn, bloody flesh in the least graphic way she could think of.

Bastian stared incredulously. "You… you pulled it out of my chest?"

Biting her lip, Katherine nodded.

"But you were tied to a tree!" Bastian's eyes sparked with anger as his words forced the memory of it to the forefront of his mind. "How could you have-?"

Katherine held her bandaged wrists in front of herself as proof. They'd previously been covered by the sleeves of her shirt, but now the stark whiteness of them was plain to see. She was just glad he couldn't see the gauged skin underneath. "I freed myself," she assured him.

"He did this to you?" he demanded harshly, but his touch was undeniably gentle as he examined her bandaged wrists.

"Well, technically I did it to myself."

Bastian didn't look impressed.

"What? I couldn't just let you die right there in front of me!"

But the wrath that had his blue eyes flashing black wasn't directed at her. It was directed at the hunter who'd cuffed her to the tree in the first place.

"That damnable bastard, I'm going to-"

"He's already dead," Katherine reminded him quietly.

His jaw twitched. "He's lucky that my wolf was so eager to get his teeth and claws into him that he inadvertently granted him a quick death. It was more than he deserved. I don't know what I would have done to him if I'd found you in any worse condition than you were already in."

"How *did* you even find me?" Katherine asked hesitantly, morbidly curious if the scent trail she'd been forced to leave behind had worked.

Bastian frowned at the question. "When you didn't arrive at the claiming ceremony after Sophie, Zane, and Caleb had left to fetch you, I thought perhaps that you'd gotten cold feet – that maybe you'd even run off." Despite the fact that shame filled his voice at the confession, Katherine couldn't help but feel hurt by it. Not that she could really blame the man for thinking she had ditched him. She'd be the first to admit that she had a penchant for running off when she got stressed. "I left to retrieve you myself, but when I got to the house, everyone was in a panic and Markus… Markus was bleeding out, clinging to consciousness on the living room floor. He told me what had happened." Bastian paused. "I don't remember doing much thinking after that. I transformed and took off running before anyone could even think of trying to stop me – not that anyone would dare. Katherine, I… I feel awful for thinking you'd run away."

"It's okay," she assured him softly. *It wasn't, not really, but she understood.*

"Anyway," he continued, "from there it was just a matter of tracking your scent to the clearing he was keeping you at. It killed me to see the way he had you chained to that tree. And you were hardly wearing anything." Katherine could have sworn his hand was trembling as it gently caressed her cheek. "Katherine… he didn't… did he?"

"He didn't…?" she repeated, confused.

Oh… Oh!

"No!" Katherine nearly shouted when she realized what he was asking. "No," she assured him again. "In fact, he said he'd never lower himself to lusting after a dirty animal like me."

Bastian's grip around her tightened as a muted growl escaped his throat. The vibrations caused the chest she was pressed flush up against to shake. "As relieved as I am that he wasn't foolish enough to touch you," he bit out, "you are *not* a dirty animal. He is – *was* – nothing but a soulless tripe. You, on the other hand, are in possession of the most beautiful soul I've ever seen."

The compliment warmed her from the inside out, and she pressed a chaste kiss to his cheek in gratitude. Then she pressed a not so chaste kiss directly to his mouth. Moving her lips sensually over his, she tried to impart the depth of her feelings for him into the kiss.

She loved him so much.

Bang.

Katherine nearly jumped out of her skin when they were rudely interrupted by the bedroom door being thrown opened. Jerking away from Bastian, Katherine rapidly tried to calm her palpitating heart as her pack mates rushed into the room, Markus leading the way. He had the nerve to raise an eyebrow at the intimate position he'd caught them in. "So much for not getting up to any funny business, though I suppose it wasn't *that* part of Bastian that was shot."

Katherine buried her face into her hands in mortification, and Bastian shot her a bewildered look, somehow missing the terribly tacky innuendo.

But as everyone crowded around the bed to verify with their own eyes that Bastian was, indeed, awake and in good spirits, Katherine's embarrassment was quickly forgotten. After all, Bastian was going to be okay, and she was surrounded by people she loved and who loved her in turn. She didn't have room in her heart to feel anything but joy.

CHAPTER TWENTY

Lub dub, lub dub.

The only thing louder than the steady beating of drums filling her ears was the sound of her heart palpitating violently in her chest.

Katherine swore she could feel it straining against her ribs, fighting to burst free as it pulsated within her.

Lub dub, lub dub.

Smoothing down the flawless animal furs she was swathed in, Katherine tried to distract herself from the feeling as her legs carried her closer and closer to the sound of the drums. To the clearing where Bastian – *and the entire town*, her restless mind supplied – was waiting for her to arrive.

Bastian had recovered faster from the gunshot wound than she'd thought possible, and already it was the night of the claiming ceremony, rescheduled a mere week and a half from when it'd originally been planned.

To tonight.

Only a few minutes from now, in fact, and she'd be standing before Bastian.

The realization caused both anxious trepidation and heady excitement to simultaneously swell within her, a volatile mix that made her head swim.

And her heart race, apparently.

A few hundred *lub dubs* later, the clearing was in sight, and although the hood of furs that was pulled over her head prevented anyone from seeing her face, Katherine could still feel hundreds of eyes swivel towards her as she and her pack mates emerged from the woods. She concentrated on keeping her own eyes connected firmly with the ground, intently focused on not tripping over the hard, uneven landscape.

She already had to dance in front of everyone. She didn't want to add to the monumentally embarrassing occasion by tripping as well.

Her pack mates, who'd escorted her to the ceremony, began leading her to the large fire blazing in the center of the clearing. Smoke swirled high into the air, intent, it seemed, on somehow reaching the moon that glowed overhead. The smell of incense hit her nose as she got closer to the fire – the aroma of pigs and deer roasting over a handful of smaller fires on the outskirts of the clearing assaulting her senses as well.

Risking peeking up from the ground, Katherine quickly confirmed that, indeed, the entire town had shown up for the event. It seemed that the delay of the first ceremony had only added to the excitement of this one. People surrounded the massive fire on all sides, some standing while others lounged on the forest floor, but *all* of them were watching her. Their gazes burned hotter than the fire itself, Bastian's intense stare the hottest of them all.

He had essentially refused to let Katherine leave his side since she'd been "stolen from him" a little over a week ago, as he'd so aptly put it, and it'd been a nearly impossible feat to convince him that she wanted to get ready for the claiming ceremony the way that tradition demanded.

Out of his sight, in other words.

Miles away from him.

It was only after she'd agreed that the entire pack – sans him, of course – could stay behind to watch over her that he'd finally allowed it at all.

Sophie had once again helped her get ready for the ceremony – styling her hair, painting her face, and donning her in the hides of Bastian's most impressive kills. Then, after Katherine had taken a moment to compose herself in the bathroom, they'd left the house as a group and her pack had led her here to the clearing where Bastian awaited.

Her stomach tightened uncomfortably as Markus, Sophie, Caleb, and Zane abandoned her near the flames of the fire before striding forward to take their places slightly behind Bastian where he stood staring, his eyes unashamedly roaming over her covered form.

Katherine's hands shook, her heart beating impossibly louder in her ears as the pounding of the drums abruptly came to a halt.

Her heart, however, did not.

Lub dub, lub dub.

Lub dub, lub dub.

For a long moment, the wild thumping of the organ was all she could hear.

Then, after what felt like an eternity – but in reality was probably only a minute or two – had passed, the drums started up again just as suddenly as they had stopped. This time, though, the tempo wasn't fixed. Instead of a steady rhythm, the music they produced was fast and complex, sending shivers down her spine and sparking within her an impulse to move.

To dance.

So that's what she did.

Ignoring the hundreds of pairs of eyes on her with the exception of one –*his* – she began her dance… by collapsing to the ground, clutching her ankle with her hands.

There was a collective gasp among the throng of people watching her, and Katherine quickly sprung herself back to her feet in one graceful movement, stretching her arms far above her head as she reached for the sky – the moon – before anyone could rush forward to aid her.

She wasn't *really* hurt. It was all a part of the dance routine she'd prepared for her mate. It was the story of them – of Bastian and Katherine.

She twirled for her audience, the movements of her limbs incredibly sharp and wild as she tried to portray the way she'd felt when she'd been bitten and her world had spun out of her control. She'd been attacked by a hunter, thought she'd gotten her parents killed, and was thrust into a way of life she knew nothing about all in the span of a few days. She was forced to live with a group of people she was convinced she hated. She hadn't known then how much she'd grow to love them – grow to love *him*. She was just a scared, resentful, utterly *lost* little girl.

And then her feelings began to change.

Katherine's dancing slowed. She exerted more control over her limbs, her movements shifting from wild to something more refined and graceful. Letting the melodious beating of the drums lead her, Katherine's twirling slowly came to a stop. She clutched her hands to her chest, directly above her heart, and hoped that Bastian knew what it meant.

To her, it symbolized when they'd first spoken aloud their feelings for each other – directly after Cain's unprovoked attack. She left her hands there for a long moment, feeling her heart fluttering restlessly beneath them.

And then taking a deep breath, she scrunched up her face, dropped her chin to her chest and fell to her knees with a soft *thud*. She tried to portray how she'd felt when she'd learned that Bastian had lied to her – that despite his insistence that her parents her dead, they were alive – and incredibly worried about her. While mostly healed, her heart hadn't completely forgotten the betrayal, and it was easy to depict the emotions she'd felt – anger, confusion, and so much *hurt* – when she'd discovered the lie.

But Katherine forced herself to her feet. Because Bastian had atoned for his actions. Because she'd forgiven him. Katherine would forgive him anything.

Slowly making her way towards the man watching her with rapt eyes, Katherine twirled this way and that, embodying the fact that the road they'd traveled together hadn't been an easy one. Their journey had been filled with twists and turns, mistakes and bouts of stubbornness, and too many near death experiences to count. But in the end, they'd made it.

They'd fought for each other.

And they always would.

The beating of the drums reached a crescendo as Katherine finally reached Bastian, and not thinking twice about her actions, she came to a stop in front of him – practically *on top* of him, really, as she contorted her body around his, throwing one of her legs over his and circling her hands behind his neck.

The drums came to an abrupt halt just as Katherine threw her head backwards, the hood flying off of it and her hair dancing in the wind as she bared her neck to the side and presented the mark Bastian had left on her skin for everyone – but most importantly of all, for *him* – to see.

Katherine's chest heaved as she remained wrapped around her mate – *her Bastian*. Her ears finally took note of something besides the drums or the *lub dub* of her heart as the appreciative cheers and whistling from the crowd registered. But there was only one person's opinion that she cared about.

When he was finally able to peel his eyes away from the teeth marks he'd left on her neck and immediately captured her mouth with his, she knew without a single doubt that he approved.

* * *

Katherine couldn't help but stare at the way the droplets of water clung to Bastian's body, a few of the larger drops following the indented paths of ridged muscle as they slowly trickled off his back and disappeared into the grass beneath him.

It really wasn't fair how stupidly lickable he looked in a swimsuit. In a swimsuit *and* soaking wet? Well, it was really no wonder why Katherine had lost all sense of self-control and was unabashedly staring at the man sitting beside her like he was a tall glass of water on a hot, hot day. In the middle of the Sahara.

To be fair, it *was* an uncommonly warm spring day – for Canada anyway – which was how she'd managed to convince Bastian to take her swimming in the first place.

It'd been a week since the claiming ceremony, and she and Bastian had hardly left their bedroom in that time – Bastian had been very "hands on" since the ceremony to say the least – and as much as she loved snuggling in their make shift love nest, she'd been starting to go stir crazy.

Swimming had been the perfect excuse to get out of the house for a bit.

The crystal clear water had felt amazing against her flushed skin on such a warm day, and she'd been having a blast until Markus – the entire pack had tagged along, of course – had dared her to jump from the top of the falls. Despite Bastian's protests, Katherine had propelled herself up the wall of rock. Only to completely chicken out when she got to the top and looked down. Or she would have chickened out, anyway, if Markus, who'd followed her up, hadn't taken it upon himself to pick her up and fling her off the ledge.

The embarrassing scream she'd let out as she'd plummeted towards the water mirrored nearly exactly what she imagined a dying cat would sound like.

Bastian, amidst cursing and threats of bodily harm to his beta, had caught her at the bottom. Markus remained cackling at the top of the falls.

Katherine had taken it upon herself to prevent bloodshed – namely Bastian's promise to rip Markus apart with his bare hands (even if the man deserved exactly that) – by telling him she was tired of swimming and asking if he wanted to step out of the water and sunbathe with her for a while.

The chance to ogle him to her heart's content was a side benefit she hadn't anticipated, but was all too happy to take advantage of nonetheless.

At least until his amused blue eyes caught her in the act.

Crap.

A violent blush burst across her face and she quickly averted her eyes. *How transparent could she possibly be?*

"What are you thinking about?" Bastian prompted mischievously from his spot to her left.

Certainly not how much she wanted to lick his damp skin.

Katherine shouldn't have been as affected by his body as she was. She'd seen him in less than a swimsuit, after all. And more than once, too. In the week since the rescheduled ceremony, there had definitely been sex. Lots and lots of glorious sex.

Clothed or unclothed, she didn't think she could ever get sick of looking at Bastian.

Not that she was about to tell Bastian that. There was no way he didn't already know how attractive she thought he was. Instead, Katherine brought up something that had been on her mind for quite a while, but that she hadn't yet had the courage to voice.

"Don't you find it strange that we've only known each other for a handful of months, but that our feelings for each other are so strong? I mean, I know we're true mates and everything that entails, but there's a lot about me that you don't even know. You don't know what kind of music I like or the names of my favorite authors. You don't even know my favorite color!"

Bastian offered her a bemused smile. "I know what's important."

Katherine couldn't help but raise an incredulous eyebrow at that claim. "Oh yeah?"

"Of course," he assured her. "I know that you're the sweetest, most compassionate, courageous person that I've ever-"

Katherine slapped a hand over his mouth, stopping him before more flattering adjectives escaped from the orifice. She doubted she was the most compassionate or courageous person who'd ever walked the earth, and she knew damn well that she wasn't the sweetest, but the fact that he thought it about her, well… it was almost enough to make her believe that maybe one day she could be those things.

But that wasn't what she said. What she said was: "You're full of crap."

Gently prying her hand off his face, he laughed. "Okay, well if it makes you feel any better, I also know that you're such an awful morning person that I'm half convinced you're allergic to the sunrise, that you drool in your sleep, and that you have a foulmouthed predisposition for name-calling when someone flusters you."

Katherine sputtered. "Yeah, well… you're a jackass."

"And you said we don't know each other."

Katherine rolled her eyes, but couldn't stop a treacherous grin from curling up the corners of her lips.

An easy silence overtook them once more.

"So, what *is* your favorite color?"

Katherine furrowed her brow. "What?"

"What's your favorite color?" Bastian repeated. "You seemed to think it was important that I know."

Staring into his eyes, Katherine blurted out the answer – "blue" – without thinking, a fierce blush overtaking her face immediately after.

He smirked. "Oh? And, why's that?"

He knew exactly why.

"Well, because the sky is blue," she blurt out dumbly, refusing to give him what he wanted. "And… blueberries," she added, cringing internally at how vapid she sounded. "I like blueberries."

What?

Bastian laughed – the guffaw that escaped his mouth the loudest she think she'd ever heard come from him. It was music to her ears and made a smile pull unbidden at her lips.

"Yeah, well, what's your favorite color?" she pretended to huff.

His smirk softened into a smile as he tucked a damp strand of hair behind her hair. "Green, of course."

She swallowed around a nonexistent lump in her throat, suddenly feeling emotional. "Because of the grass?" she ventured.

"No." He slowly shook his head in denial.

She glanced at the trees towering above them. "The leaves?"

His eyes crinkled around the edges as his smile widened, seemingly amused by the game she was playing. "Wrong again." He brought his hands up to gently cup her face, rubbing his calloused thumbs over the healthy skin beneath her eyes. "It's because of these that my favorite color is green." He allowed one hand to stroke her flushed cheek. "Though I have to admit that red is a close second."

Katherine reluctantly disentangled her face from his hands. "Yes, well, I maintain that I like the color blue because-"

"Because of blueberries," he finished for her, his tone of voice speaking of endless amusement.

They both knew she was a reprehensible liar.

"Exactly."

"I love learning new things about you," Bastian said after a moment of contented silence. "The best part is I have an entire lifetime to do just that."

"An entire lifetime with you, huh?"

Bastian grinned. "That's what you signed up for. Not regretting it already, are you? I suppose I could hardly blame you if you were. After all, as you so sweetly pointed out, I *am* a jackass."

Katherine laughed before pressing her lips to his in a chaste kiss.

"Regret it?" *Regret Bastian?* "Not even a little."

END

About the Author

Noelle Marie is a full time stay-at-home mom and a part time writer. When not being driven wonderfully mad by her two adorable (read: deranged) toddlers or staring woefully at her keyboard, she can be found curled up in a comfy chair reading a book or attempting to bake in the kitchen. Occasionally she might be pestered into golfing with her husband, but is largely an embarrassment to the sport.

Made in the USA
San Bernardino, CA
11 February 2020

64296607R00168